TODAY'S
SHADOWS

BECKY MELBY

TODAY'S SHADOWS

LOST SANCTUARY

Book Three

BARBOUR
PUBLISHING

Print ISBN 978-1-61626-240-2

eBook Editions:
Adobe Digital Edition (.epub) 978-1-62029-636-3
Kindle and MobiPocket Edition (.prc) 978-1-62029-635-6

For more information about Becky Melby, please access the author's website at the following Internet address: www.beckymelby.com.

Cover credit: Studio Gearbox, www.studiogearbox.com

Published by Barbour Publishing, Inc., P.O. Box 719, Uhrichsville, OH 44683, www.barbourbooks.com

Our mission is to publish and distribute inspirational products offering exceptional value and biblical encouragement to the masses.

 Member of the
Evangelical Christian
Publishers Association

Printed in the United States of America.

Dedication/Acknowledgments

To my boys,
Scott, Jeff, Aaron, and Mark
You guys are the best dads in the world—
you've had a great role model!

And in loving memory of my father,
John Allen Foght
How I wish he could have met the next two generations.

Thank you to:
Rebecca Germany, for the opportunity.
Jamie Chavez, for fabulous editing.
Jan Glas, for her sharp eye.
Cindy, for praying and talking me through the rough times.
Cathy, for faithful prayer and years of being there.
Todd Wallace, for letting me read the Unpublished
Diary of Daisy Winifred Brumsey.
Carol Feest, of Racine United Methodist Church for
information on the church in 1912.

And thank you to Bill for forty years of love and longsuffering.

*A father to the fatherless, a defender of widows,
is God in his holy dwelling.
God sets the lonely in families,
he leads forth the prisoners with singing. . .*
Psalm 68:5–6

PROLOGUE

Christmas Eve 1911
Racine, Wisconsin

*M*agdalena Mouse clutched the handles of the steaming soup tureen.
Her paws grew clammy, but she dare not set it down without a nod from
Mr. Tabbycat.

Maggie Parker wrote the fanciful story in her head as she stood
in the dining room, trying not to twitch or jiggle the stew as she
waited for a nod from the man who was the Mr. Tabbycat of her
story world.

Her employer sat at one end of the damask-covered table
pointing a butter knife at his son. At the other end, Mrs. Hamilton
worried the tatted edge of her napkin and gaped at the both of
them. In the front parlor, the final notes of "Silent Night" drifted
from a wax cylinder on the Edison phonograph.

Ignoring the butter knife aimed at his chest, Richard Hamilton
gazed at Maggie through flickering candlelight. "And why not? Is
she less of a person than you or I?"

"Of course not!" Mr. Hamilton hammered the table with the
hand that held the knife. The impact dislodged an ivory candle from
its sterling holder. Maggie cringed. Richard caught it.

"It's Christmas, Father. We're down to a domestic staff of *one*."
Richard illustrated the number with a finger in the air. "What sense
does it make for her to take her dinner in the kitchen...*alone?*"

Steam rose from the oyster stew, heating the blood rushing to Magdalena Mouse's fuzzy gray cheeks.

As much as Maggie disliked her job, she could not afford to lose it. If Richard persisted she would spend Christmas Eve in the street like the Little Match Girl. Her eyes burned and pleaded for Richard to stop. His eyes were not listening.

He rubbed his clean-shaven chin. "Slavery was abolished half a century ago. Just because she works for us does—"

The butter knife hand slammed again. "In the first place"—flecks of spit shot onto Mr. Hamilton's four-in-hand tie as he yelled—"she does not work for *us*. She works for *me*. In *my* house. If you finish college and *if* the Mitchell-Lewis Motor Company deems you worthy of hire, then you may someday achieve the lifestyle your parents enjoy and you can hire as much domestic help as you wish and play cricket with them for all I care. In my house we will do things the proper way." He rested his knife on the table. A vein pulsed at his temple. He nodded to Maggie.

On legs that quivered like molded aspic, she made her way to the head of the table and set the vessel in front of Mr. Hamilton. "Shall I serve, sir?"

"I will serve." He held out his hand, palm up, and Mrs. Hamilton passed her bowl to Richard, who handed it to his father. "Evangeline, your silence on this issue is discomfiting. Am I to assume from your lack of backing my stance that you are in agreement with our son? Shall we ask the scullery maid to sup with us? Maybe we should invite the Caswells' stable boy as well."

The edging on the linen napkin appeared in danger of unraveling. Mrs. Hamilton turned fast-blinking eyes on her son. "Let's not spoil our Christmas dinner."

"Of course. Let's not spoil it. For us, anyway." Richard nodded then looked up over his right shoulder and smiled.

One more look like that one and Maggie was sure her jelly legs would melt into the rug beneath the table. She shifted her eyes to stare at the piano, imagining playing a tune that would lift her thoughts out of the moment. But only love songs came to mind.

"What in Sam Hill is going on around here? Next you'll be asking to court her."

"And what if I did?"

Maggie's head jerked. Her hands began to tremble and she clasped them over the front of her apron.

"What absurd notions are they teaching you at—"

"She's a beautiful, respectable, intelligent girl and, because it matters to *some* people, she comes from good stock. Why shouldn't I court her?"

Maggie stared at the swinging door that led to the kitchen. She could not leave until she'd been dismissed. *Heavenly Father, please make them stop.*

"Need I remind you where this *respectable* girl's father is at this very—" He waved away his own words. "This is preposterous. This conversation is over." His squared jaw pointed toward the opposite end of the table. "Evangeline." The name was a command.

Mrs. Hamilton dabbed her mouth with her napkin, though the first course had yet to reach her. "This is out of control, Richard. It's not an appropriate time to discuss it. Let's enjoy our dinner and—"

"*Discuss* it?" Mr. Hamilton set his wife's steaming bowl on the table, away from Richard. "I've held my peace about something far too long, Evangeline." He folded his napkin and set it next to his plate. "I happen to know that you attended a meeting last month at which Olympia Brown was the speaker." His eyes smoldered.

Mrs. Hamilton glanced at Maggie. Her chin lifted. "I did."

"And? You are in agreement with her, too?"

"Not on everything. I certainly don't believe women should be ordained ministers of the gospel. I do, however, support her view that women have as much right to an education as men."

A rough, gravelly sigh rumbled from Mr. Hamilton. "And the vote? Do you also believe that a woman who has not the mental nor physical wherewithal to defend her country should cast votes deciding whether or not her country should go to war?"

The chin rose yet higher. Mrs. Hamilton smoothed the pleated front of her dress and patted the plume of hair jutting over her forehead. "Is it proper and moral that a woman who labors to bring a child into this world"—she darted a look at her son—"should not have the right to decide if a cause is worthy enough to chance losing him?"

Mr. Hamilton's hand slipped from the ladle. "This is a nightmare.

Surely I'll awake and find I haven't lost every last smidgen of control over my household."

Richard seized the handle of the china ladle and scooped a generous portion of milk broth dotted with oysters into his bowl. "I doubt you'll be waking soon, Father. The world is changing for the better and I, for one, shall do my part to hasten it." Bowl in hand, he stood. "Merry Christmas, all. I'll be supping in the kitchen. . .with the scullery maid."

"You should not have done that."

Maggie stood with her back to the stove, glaring at the man who sat at the kitchen table slurping oyster stew with a Cheshire cat smirk on his perfect face.

"And why not? I only spoke what she has believed for ages. If it were up to Mother you would have been adopted rather than hired." He wiped his mouth. "Might I say I'm quite relieved you are not my sister?"

Maggie turned her back on him. Richard did not know his mother as well as he might think. The woman who cared about her reputation more than her next breath would no sooner consider adopting Maggie than she would consider fixing her own cup of tea. "I am not an orphan, Richard. I have a father." She rearranged the plate of cookies no one would eat tonight. "It is precisely because of *my* father that your father can barely stand to have me cooking for him, let alone. . .anything else." *So go away and leave me to my business. It is so much easier to pine for you when you are away at school than to long for you when you are five feet from my heart.* She could not look at him as she carried on the silent monologue.

The chair legs scraped the tile floor. "I will fight for the right to court you, Maggie Parker."

Why? Because you have affection for me? Or because you have something to prove? "Don't do that, Richard."

"Why? Why should I not?"

Because your parents would disown you. Because you wouldn't fight as hard as you think you would. Because I would be left alone. Again. She held her tongue and let her stiffened shoulders answer his question.

"My father is wrong to judge you for the sins of your parents. I'll talk to him tonight. I know I can make him see that."

Magdalena Mouse picked up a date-filled cookie and placed it next to a sugared ginger ball as she whispered at Leo Tabbycat.

"I will lose my position, Richard." *And you are not in a position to save me, to take me away from here. Only in my dreams will you rescue me from this, Richard Hamilton.*

"All right. I will stay silent and keep my distance from you until—"

Glass shattered in the next room. Mrs. Hamilton shrieked. Richard darted toward the swinging door. Its tight hinges creaked as it slowly closed behind him.

"If you want the cook to have the same privileges as the mistress of the house then we will see to it that. . ." The door shut on Mr. Hamilton's words.

A little milk broth, without oysters, remained in the pan. Maggie poured it into a bowl and cut a slice of bread. If she was going to be turned out, she would not go hungry. She sank onto a chair, took a bite of bread, and tried to make a plan.

The Caswells would take her in for the night. They were decent churchgoing people. They would allow her to sleep in Hilde's room. And in the morning she would. . .what? No boardinghouse would take a new guest on Christmas Day. Nor could she inquire about a position on a holiday. Where would she—

Charles. A cockeyed grin appeared in her mind's eye. Charles would help. He knew everyone. Before he'd allow her to end up on the street he'd give up his own space in the Caswells' stable. Not that she'd allow that. And oh *my*, how the gossip would fly if she shared a roof—even a barn roof—with the Caswells' "stable boy." In spite of her dire straits, she had to smile at Mr. Hamilton's use of the term for the driver they often borrowed from the Caswells. Charles had, on several occasions, come to fisticuffs over that tag. Now that Mr. Caswell had put him in charge of the roadster as well as the horses, Charles Gallagher would answer to no less lofty title than "mechanic."

With a sigh of momentary relief, she sipped her soup. Voices rose in the dining room, but she could not make out words. It was good she'd be leaving. Many knowing looks had passed between her and

Richard, but no words of love. Even tonight, he had stopped short of saying he cared for her. He was twenty-two, she twenty, though far more than two years separated their experience with the realities of life. Richard fought for causes. But it would take far more than zealous idealism to bridge the gaping chasm between his world and hers.

Maggie's vision blurred. She blinked hard, stood, and took her dishes to the sink. "It is good I'm leav—"

The door banged open. *Mrs. Tabbycat tripped in, dabbing her face with the lace-edged napkin.*

"S—something awful has happened, Maggie."

Maggie clutched her apron and dashed toward Mrs. Hamilton. "What is it, ma'am?"

"That man I married is as unreasonable and bullheaded as a mule." She sat on the stool by the door. Maggie dashed to the sink, brought a glass of water, and kneeled at her feet.

"He has forbidden me to attend meetings. Forbidden. It is nineteen hundred and eleven and my husband is forbidding me as if I were a child." She fingered an embroidered circle on her burgundy skirt.

"I'm sorry, ma'am. You will be missed, but the women know your heart and know you'll be with them in spirit. Look at all you've done for the cause." She took the untouched water glass from a trembling hand and offered a brief smile. "Maybe you need a respite from all of this clandestine—"

"If Richard had not carried things to the extreme, I wouldn't be in this predicament. The boy has not learned moderation. That nonsense about wanting to court you tipped the scales for Mr. Hamilton, even though he knew Richard was merely illustrating his point."

Magdalena rose to her tiny feet and took a step back. The glass wobbled in her paw.

"And now it is my husband who has taken things to the extreme." Mrs. Hamilton's eyes filled with another round of tears. "He is insisting I learn all of your tasks"—she hiccupped—"so I can r—run this house all…by…myself." She burst into sobs. "Insufferable man. I was not b—born to—" Her mouth froze. "Maggie. I didn't—"

With a mute nod, Maggie turned and walked toward the stairs used only by those who were born to serve.

CHAPTER 1

I will not be spineless. I will not be pathetic. I will be confident and courageous."

Mouthing her new battle cry, Heather Conrad flipped her hair over her shoulder and stepped off the Coach USA bus that had brought her from O'Hare International to a truck stop just off Interstate 94 in Racine, Wisconsin—home of Johnson's Wax, Danish *kringle*—an indescribable ring of frosting-topped, heaven-filled pastry—her ex-boss, and her new life. She tipped the bus driver, grabbed the handles of three wheeled suitcases, and scanned the parking lot for a dream car with her name on it.

Muggy air condensed on her air-conditioned skin as July heat rose from the pavement. She felt like an old mercury thermometer—the silver line rising from the bottoms of her sandals, up through ankles, calves, thighs. At the moment it reached her armpits, she spotted it—the ride of her most outrageous car fantasies: a cognac metallic Porsche Panamera Turbo S, the color of a milk chocolate Hershey bar and sporting a license plate that said it all. LUSHUS.

Rattling like a bag lady with a full grocery cart, she sped across the blacktop and punched the key pad with the code numbers Natalie had e-mailed before boarding a plane for a thirty-day East Coast cultural extravaganza with her seven-year-old daughter. The doors unlocked. The keys fell into her open hand when she lowered the visor. Until August 12, the day her ex-boss returned and she turned back into a pumpkin, the car was hers.

"We're not in Kansas anymore," she whispered to the phone peeking out of her purse. She stuffed the trunk and the espresso-colored backseat with her thirty-day-vacay survival gear, got in, and told the GPS to take her to her temporary home away from the place she'd called home until her boyfriend decided he'd rather be her brother-in-law.

Heather pursed her lips, sighed through them, and stretched her face muscles with an exaggerated frown. It felt good. Anything not-smile felt good. She'd actually wondered—after topping weeks of dress shopping and bridal showers with an interminably long ceremony and the maid-of-honor toast to end all m-o-h toasts—if an artificial grin could become so much of a habit it simply couldn't be reversed. *I'm thrilled for you, Jen. Don't be silly. I got over him long ago—though I'm a little perplexed as to why he was still signing his e-mails "Love you forever" three hours before he proposed to you. Old habits die hard, they say.* She hadn't actually verbalized the part about the e-mails, though she'd wondered, right up until she'd caught the bouquet, if she should have.

Thoughts of her clueless sister and the tractor-driving two-timer began to fade when she spotted signs for a Kohl's store and Panera Bread. The thoughts receded further when she passed the gold-painted, spaceship-shaped Golden Rondelle Theater she'd seen on the Visit Racine website then vanished altogether with her first glimpse of Lake Michigan glittering in the afternoon sun. In that instant, life for Heather Conrad became a blank slate. She was twenty-eight, single, and driving a sleek chocolate car. Around the corner and two blocks down waited a massive house filled with new furniture and peace and quiet. She'd have a month to find a job, an apartment, and finish the business plan that would launch her into a confident and courageous future.

The Porsche took the corner like a dream. The GPS informed her she had arrived at her destination. The three-story white Victorian matched the description Natalie had e-mailed.

Except for the moving van in the driveway.

Feeling stiff and plastic like the Barbie she'd once stuffed into a pink-and-teal convertible and pushed off the garage roof, Heather gripped the steering wheel and glared at the semi taking up every inch of the driveway she was supposed to park in. She took a deep breath and rotated her head to the lake view. A man leaned against a skinny tree holding a camera to his face. Tiny whitecaps teetered on miniature waves. Far off, a barge crept along the line separating sea and sky.

She turned back to the house. There was a logical explanation for the truck. There was a logical explanation for everything in life. Except a guy who tosses dice to decide which sister to marry.

As she got out of the car, she glanced back at the lake. The man no longer leaned on the skinny tree. He now stood on the sidewalk. Facing her. She waved and he turned and walked away.

"Whatever." Heather marched, head held high, into a morass of boxes, lamps, mattresses, end tables, and sweaty men in dark green shirts. She walked onto a porch, through propped-open mahogany doors, and stopped at the foot of a wide oak staircase. Her lips parted at the majesty of the carved spindles and newel posts. Her breath caught at the vision silhouetted in multicolored light from a stained glass window at the first landing.

A little girl. Not a statue, but a living, breathing, pouting little girl—who was supposed to have deplaned at LaGuardia over an hour ago.

"Izzy?"

"Heather!" Blond curls shimmied as she flounced down the stairs and wrapped herself around Heather's legs. "Isn't it soooo awful?"

Yes. Whatever "it" was, it was destroying her immediate, work-and-relaxation-filled future. "What happened? Why are you still here?"

"The movers were late and Mom's boss called and said she had to—"

"Heather!" A second vision appeared in the rainbow light, this one far more disturbing. Natalie Brooks, sans makeup, heels, or defrizzing hair product. Her ex-boss sank onto the stairs. "You're

15

here. I was so afraid you'd be mad and just turn around and fly back—"

"Mad?" Her voice squeaked like a pubescent boy's. Only then did she remember the phone in her purse still set on airplane mode. "What happened?"

"The moving van got in an accident so they had to transfer everything into a different truck. I didn't call you because I knew you wouldn't have a problem doing my unpacking and. . ."

Seriously? You knew that? Of course she did. When, in the nine months Heather had worked as Natalie's personal assistant in her swanky Chicago office, had she ever refused to do anything?

". . .called and said I was the only one left who could go to the International Hotel Conference in Venice. . ."

Okay. Good. You're still leaving. So I'm still on for—

". . .taking care of Izzy, but I'll leave you money and—"

"*Who's* taking care of Izzy?"

Natalie's untinted lips stretched in a contortion Heather knew all too well. "You don't mind, do you?"

Wha. . .what. . .whoa. . . Heather stared blankly at the seven-year-old scrunched on the bottom step, chin in hands, bottom lip inverted.

"I'll pay you double, plus expenses, and Izzy won't be here much anyway. I was just looking online for places for her to go during the day. There are swimming lessons and an art day camp and after that a gymnastics camp and—"

A tiny gasp rose from somewhere under a mass of shaking blond curls.

"There's a pamphlet in the kitchen with a Wisconsin events calendar." Natalie nodded in what Heather assumed was the general direction of the kitchen. "On the weekends you could go to the state fair or the Dells or Noah's Ark or the beach—"

"Wh–when are you leaving?"

"At three."

"O'clock? Today? You're leaving in two hours?"

"You're right. Why am I sitting here?" She stood, turned, and walked up two steps. "I have to unpack and repack and cancel our hotels and"—she stopped and turned back—"you can take me to the airport, right? I'm flying out of Milwaukee. I hate to interfere with your first day here, but..." Her voice trailed her up the winding staircase.

Like the time she'd fallen off the hay wagon and had the wind knocked out of her, her chest shuddered but couldn't pull in air. Seconds passed until her lungs filled in a sudden rush and then exhaled on a single word. *"Natalie!"*

⚜

"I'm so glad you're here, Heather." Natalie pulled a peach camisole out of a box. "I wouldn't trust her with just anyone, you know. But you and Isabel have a special connection. She'll be so happy with you. And I know you—you're going to absolutely fall in love with this house. I saw it years ago with a friend and I swore right then and there if it ever came up for sale I'd buy it. It's so unlike me, isn't it? But after the year I've had, the drama, the allegations, I just need something wholesome and solid, you know. It'll be good for me, I think. I need—"

"I had plans, Natalie. I need to work on my business plan." Heather plopped onto the bed between a pair of painfully high heels and a Coach purse.

"Isabel goes to bed at eight and doesn't get up until seven. That'll give you lots of time to work." Natalie peered at her over the top flap of her suitcase. "I'll pay you well. And you know I'm doing this partly for you, right?"

You're going to Venice for me, or leaving me with your daughter for me? Keeping the sarcasm down took every ounce of strength, leaving nothing left for an answer.

"If I make a good impression on Mr. Barker, he's much more likely to listen when I say I need a personal assistant and I have the perfect person in mind." Shaped brows rose.

Perfect because I am—I was—spineless and pathetic. "I'm not really looking for another job...like that."

"I'll be in a position to put in a good word for the kind of job you do want. Just name it."

It was more of a lame and naive-sounding shot in the dark than a confident and courageous career move, but she had nothing to lose. "I want financing for the prototype of my new coffee shop concept."

Natalie blinked. Her lips parted. "That's a bit—" The sound of her swallow filled the bare-walled room, and then a strange transformation took place before Heather's eyes. Her features relaxed. Her eyes sparked. "Why not? You've got a better head for business than a lot of people twice your age. You finish that business plan while I'm gone and e-mail it to me. I'll see it lands on the right desk at the right time."

Say what? A queasy combination of déjà vu and anticipation splashed over her. She knew that look and that tone. It said, "I'm in control here. I hold the power. The man is putty in my hands."

Natalie Brooks was not going on a business trip.

Not solely business anyway.

Heather stood. "Thank you."

"Does that sweeten the deal just a bit?"

Her stomach churned. Her mouth tasted sour. Natalie, who was not a hugger, hugged her. "And you feel free to have some fun while I'm gone. I don't mind you having men here as long as Isabel isn't aware of what's going on."

"I wouldn't do that."

Natalie swept her hand as if whisking away Heather's prudishness. "You'll meet people. Even with Isabel. I know you. You're friendly and outgoing and you'll find ways to get connected." She laughed. "You'll be *confab*ulating in no time."

Rubbing her arms, Heather walked out the door, wondering if there were doctors in Racine, Wisconsin, who did backbone transplants. She needed to put her name on the waiting list.

❦

Dropping onto a polished oak step, Heather pooched her bottom lip like the little girl beside her.

"I won't be a problem. I promise." Izzy mopped crocodile tears with the hem of the striped shirt she wore over purple leggings. "I have lots to do. I have to put my clothes away and I like to draw and read and I can be real quiet. I promise."

Heather blinked. Izzy's words squeezed her heart. She

remembered the feeling. *I'll be good. Just let me go along. Please.* She only had to close her eyes to feel six again—standing on the front step, her hand gripped in her mother's, fighting tears as she watched her sister drive away with the grandmother they didn't share. She put her arm around Izzy's shoulders. "You could never be a problem, Iz. Remember the good times we had when I worked for your mom?"

The dimpled chin stopped quivering. "We made finger hats and we never told Mom I sat in her chair or ate her Twizzlers."

"We had some fun secrets, didn't we?" Heather glanced over her shoulder. "Can you keep another one?"

Izzy nodded. "I *luh-uv* secrets."

Leaning close to her ear, Heather whispered, "I'm not sending you away to any old day camp you don't want to go to." She held out her hand. "Deal?"

The high-five thwack echoed off the empty walls. "Deal." Izzy's shoulders straightened. "Do you want to see my new room?"

"I want to see your room and the whole—"

"Heather, would you do me a huge favor and find a Starbucks and go get me a blended Extra Coffee Caramel Frappuccino? I'm in desperate need of a transfusion and I doubt you'll find the coffeepot in this mess for days."

But you knew I wouldn't have a problem with that, right? Heather pulled Izzy out of the way as a man in a snug-fitting green shirt clunked toward the stairs pushing a handcart teetering with boxes. She dug her phone out of her purse and turned it on. Five missed calls, eight e-mails, and nine texts waited for her. Maybe, just maybe, she'd have a minute at the end of her first relaxing vacation day to look at them. She jabbed at the little stickpin-looking icon labeled "places" then tapped on the coffee cup. As she scrolled through a list of coffee shops, it dawned on her that this was what she'd come here to do. Over coffee on Sunday morning she'd told her mother, "I want adventure. I want to meet people and do things and experience life in a whole new place." No better time than the present to start adventuring. She tugged on a baby-fine curl. "I'll take Izzy."

"Here." Dollar bills cascaded onto the hunky man with the handcart who'd stopped on the landing to tighten a strap.

"I've been waiting my whole life for this stuff to fall from the sky." The man laughed as Izzy scrambled around him, giggling as if she'd just struck the cracking blow on a piñata.

Straightening up, Izzy pulled several bills from the wad in her hand and handed them to the man. "You should have a double coffee caramel thing, too." With that she ran down the steps and around two men pulling a piano on rollers.

Heather caught up to her on the front porch. "Does your mom play the piano?"

"No. I will. I have piano-playing genes from my dad."

"You—?" Heather cut off the question. It was none of her business. As she opened the car door, she looked out toward the lake.

The man with the camera now sat on a park bench.

Pointing his lens at the chocolate Porsche.

♔

Huge oil paintings in gaudy Baroque-looking frames hung at random angles on the old brick walls of Racine Beans. Heather typed her first impressions on her phone.

Izzy slurped her chocolate chip whip. "What are you doing?"

"I want to open my own coffee shop someday, so I write notes on decorating and on how people meet other people in coffee shops."

"Like dating, you mean?"

"Yes, but not just that. Years ago, people used to sit on their porches and talk to their neighbors, but nowadays people have to work harder to make friends."

"Facebook is easy. So is eHarmony."

Heather smiled around the iced cocomocho sliding through her straw. "So tell me what you think of this place."

"Wellll. I think it's quirky. I luh-uv that word, don't you?"

"I do." She pushed half of her half of a chocolate chip cookie over to Izzy. "And I think I'm going to luh-uv spending time with you."

"Me, too. With you." Izzy's eyes darted back and forth. "Can *you* keep a secret?"

"Cross my heart, hope not to die soon." She swiped an X across the left side of her chest. "I always thought 'hope to die' was just dumb."

"Me, too." The giggle combined with a slurp. "The secret is I never wanted to go all those places Mom said we were going to go. Ballets and operas." She opened her mouth wide and stuck her finger on the back on her tongue, producing a real gag reflex. "Only Disney. That's the part I was sad about."

"I'm sorry you're not going to be able to go."

"That's okay." The voice held a maturity far beyond seven. "So what I think about this place besides quirky is fun and colorful. The paintings are silly and the chairs are stripy." She pointed at her shirt. "Stripes are happy, don't you think?"

"I do." Heather raised her cup. "Now tell me what you think of the people. Look at that lady over there."

"The one with the sparkles on her jeans? She's a cougar."

Heather gasped. "Do you even know what that means?"

"Of course. I'm seven. A cougar is an old lady trying to act way young to meet guys who are way, way young. Like that one."

Fighting with the splash of cocomocho that took the wrong pipe, Heather covered her mouth with her napkin and looked at the way, way young man the cougar was scoping.

The lady had impeccable taste. The guy, maybe a year or two older than Heather, wore a uniform. Black pants and a short-sleeved gray shirt with a red emblem on the front pocket. He sat alone at a small table. An unzipped, empty backpack lay at his feet. A coffee cup perched on a stack of books. "I don't think he's her type."

"Nah. I don't either." Izzy's fingers splayed across her face. Her eyes danced. "I think he's *your* type."

"Cute." Heather held her cup in front of her face, making a show out of peering around the cup at the man who was engrossed in highlighting what appeared to be every word in a thick book. His hair was dark and short, sticking up on top like he'd gelled it. A nice square jaw, respectable biceps, strong-looking hands. She faced Izzy, cup still in place. "I think you're right."

Her last word barely emerged as a man walked out of the florist shop across the street. A man with a camera.

Heather shoved her chair back and reached for Izzy's hand. "Let's get your mom's drink and go home."

CHAPTER 2

Stephannie Lansing pulled the phone out of the pale hand camouflaged against hospital sheets and read the text again.

I FOUND YOUR DAUGHTER. SHE LOOKS LIKE YOU.

She scrolled up to the picture. In spite of her second sharp inhale, her father didn't stir.

A woman—Stephannie's age, maybe a year or two older—reaching toward a dark brown car. Svelte, tanned, long dark hair blowing in the wind like a photo shoot pose. Behind her stood a little girl with light blond hair.

She didn't recognize the phone number and there was no history of previous calls or texts from that number.

It had to be a mistake.

The address book in her father's personal phone held six numbers. Hers, her mother's, her grandparents', her father's best friend, and his minister. His business phone was another story. But he never gave out this number.

It had to be a mistake. Or a hoax.

Stephannie paced toward the window. From the eighth floor of Northwestern Memorial Hospital, Lake Michigan appeared gray-green. Chicago rush hour traffic stopped and started on East Superior and East Huron. The only sound in the room was the *blip* of the heart monitor and the hum of oxygen. Too quiet to think.

Her mother would know. A woman would know if her husband had fathered a child before they were married.

But her mother had enough to worry about. An ex-husband to stress over. A corporation to run. A daughter to be ashamed of.

Stephannie pulled her hair off her shoulders and swirled bleached strands into a bun. That was one thing she could do right. She could do hair. Not that she ever would. *Can you believe it? Parker and Dianna's daughter a beautician?*

A year-old headline flashed before her conscience. STEPHANNIE LANSING—CHICAGO'S ANSWER TO PARIS HILTON. She clamped her forearms over her belly and walked to the hospital bed. "I'm sorry, Daddy. For everything." She put her hand in his and he squeezed it.

She was still her father's princess, though she'd done nothing to deserve it. If the unthinkable happened, she'd done nothing to deserve the fortune that would be hers.

If, indeed, she was her daddy's *only* princess.

👑

Heather closed the trunk of the car and turned her back on the good-bye unfolding in front of the curbside check-in station. Skinny arms and legs wrapped around her mother like ivy vines climbing a tree trunk, Izzy clung and sobbed. Heather tried to block out Natalie's unending stream of guilt-relieving promises.

The child didn't want water parks or toys or Six Flags Great America. She wanted to know she was special, that she mattered more than a job. Or a man.

The niggling conviction had intensified when Heather handed over the caramel coffee and shared the flash of genius that had hit her as she'd scanned the traffic in her rearview mirror on the way home from the coffee shop, praying the man with the camera was only a tourist and seeing him across the street was only a coincidence. "We'll join you," she'd suggested. "I'll keep Izzy occupied while you're in meetings and then you two can go and do something fun together every day."

All natural color had leached from Natalie's face. Spots of newly applied blush and shadow stood in sharp relief against a pale canvas. "That would never work. It's not a hotel that caters to kids."

Or a lifestyle that caters to being a parent.

Even a seven-year-old was smart enough to question this trip. Two hours ago Heather watched Izzy pull a red bikini out of her mother's suitcase, throw it on the floor, and stomp out of the bedroom.

Natalie had called after her daughter. "We'll go to Noah's Ark when I get back."

Great parenting, Nat. Water parks make everything better. Heather stood silent as her own memories of make-it-all-better promises echoed across twenty-plus years of trying to let it go. Promises that had flowed every time the Cadillac with the Florida plates drove away with Jen in the backseat as Heather stood in the driveway, waving, smiling on the outside, and feeling like Cinderella missing the ball.

Exactly the way she'd felt two days ago, blowing kisses and bubbles from a tiny plastic bottle, as Jen drove away in a white limo. With the prince.

Natalie grabbed her arm and pulled her into a three-way hug. "Here, take her."

Izzy made the transfer without a word. Soft, hiccupy breaths shook her as she nestled into Heather. Natalie smoothed her champagne-colored blouse, brushing at the tear stains on her shoulder. "I'll call you as soon as I know my itinerary."

"Call when you land." Heather locked eyes with the woman she once took orders from. "We can Skype every night. If you call anytime before three in the morning your time, you can talk to her and show her where you are." *And what she's missing.* She chose a tone that made it not an option.

"Yes. Of course." Natalie pulled Izzy's hair away from her damp cheek and kissed her. "I'll buy you a new dress for the first day of school. What color do you want?"

Izzy let out a cranky whine and buried her head in Heather's neck.

"I'll just surprise you then." Natalie bent and brushed a piece of grass from a French manicured toenail. A gold toe ring peeking out from black heeled sandals caught the sunlight. She looked at Heather. "I'll be logging in to my checking account every day. If I don't see you spending enough money, you'll be hearing from me. Your job description is to have fun. This is your vacation, too."

Heather couldn't even muster a wave as glass doors opened automatically and Izzy's wail covered the clacking of her mother's heels.

♔

"Let's make a plan." Heather glanced at Izzy in the rearview mirror. Her eyes were still red, but the tears had stopped. "I have to go to coffee shops and do some writing every day, so we'll pack a bag with books and things for you to do while I'm working and then we'll plan something fun for the rest of the day. Okay?"

Izzy looked up from her *Monster, Inc.* video and nodded. "In kindergarten I got the Whisper Award one day 'cuz I used my naptime voice the whole day."

"Good for you. Maybe I'll have to come up with awards, too. How about the silliest face award?"

Crossed eyes, an open mouth, and a cockeyed tongue followed.

"You win for today. What should be your prize? Ice cream?"

Blond curls shimmied. "Chocolate chip whip at Racine Beans."

"Was it really that good, or do you just like rhyming words?"

"It was really that good. And I like rhyming words. And I want to see if the cougar lady hooked up with the way young police guy."

Heather cringed. *Does your mama have any idea what you watch on TV? Does she care? And what does "hooked up" mean to a seven-year-old?* "I'm pretty sure the cougar and the police guy went home by now, but let's go get a chocolate chip whip and then we'll go shopping for some healthy food. From now on, I think we'd better stick to one sugary treat a day."

"Pooh." Izzy turned away from the video player attached to the back of the seat in front of her and stared out the window. Heather merged into rush hour traffic heading south on I-94. By the time she dared glance at the backseat, her little charge was asleep.

Naptime brought her the first quiet moment of the day. The sheer number of adjustments she'd had to make in the past six hours was more than she could process. As she passed a billboard sporting a twenty-foot-tall man-of-your-dreams kind of guy, she pressed the

25

heel of her hand against her sternum, confirming two things—her heart still beat, and the emotional bruise from the Zach Merten kick was still there.

She exited via the Highway 20 off-ramp and punched the radio button. The music calmed a vague anxiety that had been growing since they'd left the airport. She was heading home to an empty house. She hadn't even seen all the rooms. The events of the day seemed surreal. Maybe she'd fallen asleep on the plane and any moment she'd wake up to the pilot announcing their descent into Chicago. She'd get on the bus, find the house she was supposed to sit organized and empty.

If things had gone according to plan, empty wouldn't bother her. Factor in a little girl and the coincidence of seeing the guy with the camera across the street from the coffee shop, and empty became ominous. Who was he and what had he been photographing? Historic homes, expensive cars, or. . . ? A shiver skittered along her back. She hadn't mentioned the man to Natalie. As her thoughts had time to sort, all of the strange occurrences of the day converged on one moment—Natalie's face when Heather had offered to go along. *Fear.* Until this moment, she hadn't stopped to label it.

She'd imagined Natalie running to someone. What if she'd been running *away from* someone? Heather knew only too well why Natalie had left her last job, but why had she left Chicago? And if she were running, why didn't she take Izzy?

Unless her daughter was safer without her.

Questions filled the car until she parked on Sixth Street and looked up at the intentionally haphazard letters spelling out RACINE BEANS. Something about the place felt welcoming. "Who wants a chocolate chip whip?"

Izzy yawned. "I do." She stretched one arm over her head while pushing her hair out of her face. With Houdini speed she unfastened her seat belt and opened the back door.

"You're fast."

"That's nothin'. I figured out how to get out of my car seat when I was only three so it would be easier for Mom 'cuz she's always in a hurry."

Well, that would be the important thing. Make life easier for Mom. Too bad every career woman in her midforties didn't have a pint-size time and efficiency expert. Heather bit down on her bottom lip. If she didn't quell the sarcasm, it would snowball. Having spent the past year creating a mental thesaurus of acerbic synonyms for Zach, she knew how easily one thought spawned another.

They walked through the front door. Izzy came to a dead stop directly in front of her. Heather grabbed a newspaper rack to keep from toppling.

"He's here." The conspiratorial whisper was followed by a giggle. "It's a sign."

Heather planted a loud kiss on the top of Izzy's head. "It's a sign they have good coffee here. Or his parents own the place." With a discreet neck stretch, she found the man Izzy was gawking at. The dark hair looked the same, but this guy wore navy pants and a light blue shirt with some kind of embroidered patch on the sleeve. "That's not him." She put her hands on Izzy's shoulders and propelled her forward.

"Yuh-huh, it is."

"The other guy was wearing a gray—"

"May I take your order?"

Heather gave their order and steered Izzy toward the pick-up window. As she waited, she typed a mass text to her parents and the two friends, one in Chicago, the other in Kansas, who had propped her up after Zach put her ring on her sister's finger. I'm here. Trip uneventful. Had a little surprise waiting for me. Natalie left her daughter behind. Explain later tonight. Love you.

She studied chocolate-dipped sugar cookies and cinnamon-drenched snickerdoodles. "Which do you like best?"

Izzy didn't answer. Heather looked down then to her left and right. "Izzy?" Panic coursed along every nerve fiber. *Izzy?*

"Over here."

In a booth-for-two under a Tiffany lamp, Izzy chatted with the man in the blue shirt.

Didn't your mother teach you anything? Heather snatched their drinks as the girl behind the counter turned to grab plastic lids. "Thank you. Gotta run." Dumb thing to say when you're just running to a corner booth. A booth where a man with short dark hair, a nice square jaw, respectable biceps, and strong-looking hands sat drawing on his fingers with colored pens.

27

"See! It *was* him."

Heather nodded. The next ten seconds would tell if Izzy went to bed early for talking to a stranger or walked out with the cookie of her choice. She fixed her eyes on the man. Not a difficult task. "I'm so sorry." An apology was in order even though he didn't appear the least bit bothered by Izzy's presence, if the happy little faces on his fingers were any clue. "We saw you in here earlier and—"

"No prob. I saw you guys here before, so it's kind of like we're old friends." He held out his hand. "Ryan Tobin."

She returned his squeeze. "Heather Conrad."

The man slid out of the bench. "Here. Join us."

By the time the "us" comment clicked, he'd picked up a chair, turned it around, and straddled it, resting his arms on the back. Tan arms, covered with gold-flecked hair. The left arm sat on the right, giving her an unhindered view of a ringless ring finger.

She sat. It seemed the only logical option. She pointed at his wall of books. "You're a policeman?"

"Not yet. I'm on a waiting list. Eventually, I'm hoping to make detective. Hence the books." He nodded at Izzy. "This charming lady tells me you just moved here. Or *she* just moved here, but her mommy is on vacation and you're her nanny for a little while. Did I get that right?"

She nodded.

"So are you a local, or did you move from Chicago with Izzy's family?"

Heather's throat tightened. What were the chances this guy just happened to be here at the same time as they were for the second time today? As coincidental as the man with the camera just happening to be at the florist's shop. Her palms dampened. She slid Izzy's drink across the table. *Pick it up, baby.*

The moment she did, Heather jumped to her feet, stepped around the man who straddled the chair, and grabbed Izzy by the arm. "I just remembered something. We have to go."

"But I need a straw and Ryan made finger puppets and I told—" Chocolate chip whip slopped Izzy's striped shirt as she stumbled to the car.

Hands shaking, Heather buckled her in, darting glances over

her shoulder. Heart hammering her sternum, she slid behind the wheel and slammed the door. As it locked, she remembered the cocomocho on the roof of the car. Ignoring the splat as she peeled from the curb, she looked at the bewildered face in the mirror.

"Didn't your mother ever tell you to never, ever, ever talk to strangers?"

✿

8:02 p.m.

Stephannie glared at the time projected onto her ceiling. Room-darkening shades covered the windows. She hadn't gone to bed this early since she was five years old, but none of the distractions Andrew had suggested sounded better than curling in a ball on a king-size bed in a light-blocked room.

Her phone, muffled by a down pillow, announced an incoming text. Eyes still riveted to giant blue numbers, she slid her hand along the microfiber sheet and pulled out the phone.

How's your head? Need me to massage it?

Stephannie smiled. Andrew Rivera was the one bright spot of hope in a life that had lost much of its luster. Six-foot-three, with eyes the color of the water off Boca Catalina Beach in Aruba and a body that belonged on a magazine cover. And he loved her.

Are you sure?

Her skin turned clammy. Doubts always did that to her.

She hadn't seen Andrew for three weeks, and even though the texts he'd sent since she got back in the country two days ago and his soft-as-microfiber-sheets voice on the phone said he'd forgiven her, it was going to take awhile for her to believe it.

Because Andrew Rivera had a lot to gain from pretending to be in love with her, and a lot to lose from not being who she wanted him to be.

She pushed a button, turning on a soft glow of light around the perimeter of her fourteen-foot ceiling. Her bed, a white upholstered platform, seemed to float in the center of the hand-scraped maple floor. White-framed photographs on white walls achieved the starkness she'd strived for when designing the penthouse.

Tonight it felt cold. And sterile. Too much like the hospital room where her father fought to recover from a blocked coronary artery.

"Daddy." A teardrop landed and spread on the sheet.

Would she have lived the last few years any differently if she'd known her father might die at fifty-two?

It wasn't like she'd planned on partying for the rest of her life. In spite of what her mother thought, she did have a plan, and it only involved two more years of freedom. At seventeen, the year her parents divorced, she'd given herself ten years to make up her mind about life—to travel and experience, to revel in the benefits of being Parker Lansing's daughter and escape the expectations of being brought into this world by his wife.

The plan hadn't involved photographers capturing every indiscretion, every one-drink-too-many karaoke song at a club in Belize, or every Lamborghini or Mercedes she'd left a party in.

It hadn't included running off for three weeks after a fight with Andrew and only coming home when she heard on TV that her father might not make it through the night.

In the forty-eight hours since she'd been home, her life had not flashed, but scrolled before her eyes like a marquee at the bottom of the nightly news. To her surprise, she'd found more good than guilt.

Weeks at a time on the yacht. Ski trips to Lake Louise, Mont Tremblant, and Vail. Weekends in New York. Good times. And running between and around all the big bright memories, like lead in a stained glass window, were quiet moments when her last name didn't matter and she was simply Daddy's little girl—sipping hot chocolate or sitting by the pool or sharing a piano bench.

All that ended one bright sunny day in a courtroom where her parents divided everything right down the middle.

Including her.

She scrolled to the picture she'd sent from her father's phone. Resting her fingers on the brown car, she spread her fingers, enlarging the face of the dark-haired woman who could be her sister. A tinny-sounding laugh bounced off the high ceiling. Maybe life would be simpler with two Lansing girls. One for Mom. One for Dad.

But her mother wouldn't want the brunette. And she already didn't want the one who'd just spent nine hundred and twenty-eight dollars to stay blond.

There couldn't be two Lansing girls. It had to be a mistake.
Or someone was soon going to wish it was.

⁂

Christmas Day 1911

Plum pudding steamed on the back of the stove. Peeled potatoes
boiled on the front. The goose waited in the icebox, wearing a
Christmas cloak of salt pork. Maggie poured coffee in two Haviland
china cups and set them on the breakfast tray. Breakfast for two
this morning. Not the usual one, nor the three she'd expected for
Christmas morning. Richard had stomped out just after dawn, valise
in hand, headed back to school early. "I cannot spend one more day
with this bigotry."

Holding back the rush of tears pressing for release and the
words that accompanied them, she'd packed a lunch for him to
take on the train. *It's Christmas, Richard,* her heart had screamed.
*Your parents may be unreasonable, but they love you. At least you have a
mother whose heart you can break. And what about us? Is this what you
call fighting for me?*

When he'd left, she'd dashed through the backyards to spill her
pent-up words on her best friend.

That had proved to be a mistake. She'd expected understanding
from Hilde. Not envy masquerading as indifference.

Maggie set the tray on the dumbwaiter and pulled the cable
hand over hand until the shelf bearing Christmas cheer disappeared
and the cable stopped moving. She scurried through the door beside
it and wound her way up stairs that for three years now she alone
had used. Though she didn't fully understand such things, not a day
passed that she did not thank almighty God for the near-collapse of
the stock market in 1907. As the ripples that started in New York
City were felt in the center of the country, her employer's company,
Hamilton Lock and Latch, appeared in danger of bankruptcy. In a
panic, he had fired all domestic staff save one. Overnight, Maggie
went from cook's helper to lady's maid, cook, and housekeeper.

And she rejoiced. Not at the work, but at the quiet, and the
garret room that was now hers alone. Where Cook's bed and trunk

once took up half the floor sat the most beautiful desk she had ever seen. Beautiful because it was hers and crammed with books and a sheaf of paper half-filled with essays she would never show anyone—and the Magdalena Mouse stories that danced in her head and kept her sane.

She'd worried, when Hamilton Lock and Latch suddenly seemed to be on an upswing, that Mr. Hamilton might replace the staff he'd fired. All that wasted anxiety. Now, it seemed, he intended to let her go as well. She would have been better off sharing her garret with the ornery snoring woman with whiskers on her chin.

How long could she prolong Mrs. Hamilton's training? She had to make it long enough to find another position.

On the second floor landing, she slipped her fingers into a recess. The Hamilton latch popped open and Hamilton hinges pivoted without a sound. She stepped into the hallway and opened the dumbwaiter door. Lifting the tray, she padded silently along the Persian rug to the door at the end of the hall. Setting the tray on the half-round table, she opened the watch pinned to her uniform. Mama's watch. Her fingertips trailed over the tiny gems encrusting the case. She waited through nineteen clicks until the longest filigree hand rested on twelve. And then she knocked.

"Bring it in, Maggie." Mrs. Hamilton sounded as if her tears had not suspended for the night.

Maggie balanced the tray in one hand and opened the door with the other. "Merry Christmas, ma'am."

A languishing sigh answered her. Mrs. Hamilton sat in bed alone, her hair cascading over her shoulders. She held *Anne of Avonlea* in her hands, but her wire-rimmed reading glasses perched on a lace pillow beside her. "I don't know if anything will be merry about this day."

Magdalena gritted her tiny mouse teeth. "There is the birth of our Savior to rejoice in, ma'am."

"Well, of course, there is that. But without Richard—" She waved away whatever she was about to say. "Are all boys this age so difficult?"

"I'm sure I don't know, ma'am." *I know they are not all so handsome, nor so funny, nor—*

"Maggie? Are you listening?"

"Sorry, ma'am. Just a little Christmas daydreaming."

"You'll have time for that later. You have the evening off, you know."

With no one to spend it with. "Yes. Thank you." *Thank you for the hour that will be left of the day after cleaning up from your dinner.*

"Please take Mr. Hamilton's portion and toss it."

Maggie glanced toward the door leading to his dressing room. "Is he ill, ma'am?"

"Not ill, just ill-tempered. He took the sleigh out this morning."

"This morning? I didn't hear him. I didn't oversleep, ma'am, I promise I—"

"I know. I know." Mrs. Hamilton gestured toward the fireplace. "The room was warm when I awoke. You are fine, Maggie. Mr. Hamilton left in a huff long before dawn after a heated discussion with our son and a sleepless night."

Maggie nodded, eased the tray onto the nightstand, and dished eggs and ham and a slice of *julekage* onto Mrs. Hamilton's plate. She pushed the dish of eggs and the other three slices of Christmas bread aside then set the tray on her mistress's lap. "Enjoy your breakfast, ma'am." She picked up the plate and turned.

"Maggie?"

"Yes, ma'am?"

"I've been thinking." Mrs. Hamilton straightened her silverware. "I'm going to host the Ladies Guild meeting the second week of January as scheduled. Mr. Hamilton will be headed to Boston that day and I'll just make sure the ladies know that we must refer to it as a luncheon. We've met at Mrs. Torson's while her husband was away and he never was the wiser. But for now I will act the part of the submissive wife. However, just because I am *forbidden* to attend meetings does not mean you are."

"Without you? Is that allowed?" *What will the lady cats have to say about a mouse in their midst?*

"Why shouldn't it be? If our goal is to elevate the role and rights of women, how could anyone disparage you because of your position? Think of the awful irony in that scenario."

Thinking of the "awful irony" that had taken place in the kitchen last night, Maggie only nodded.

"So I can tell the ladies you'll be there representing me?"

No, you can tell the ladies I'll be there representing me. *And I will not sit quiet as the mouse you'd like me to be.* "Yes. I'll go. Anything else?" She backed toward the door.

"Actually, there is something else." Her gaze roved to the life-size portrait of Richard across from the foot of the bed. "Do you fancy my son, Maggie?"

As if a downdraft had wafted from the chimney, warmth gusted into the room. At least in the spot where Maggie stood. "Fancy, ma'am?"

"Yes. Do you find him attractive?"

"I s—suppose I do."

"And, other than what you witnessed last night, is his disposition admirable enough?"

Maggie swallowed reflexively. "He has a very agreeable disposition."

"Good. Very good." Mrs. Hamilton took a bite of Christmas bread. "I'm glad to hear that." She sipped her coffee. "Richard will graduate in the spring and, Lord willing, be employed at the Mitchell-Lewis Motor Company."

"Yes, ma'am."

Mrs. Hamilton glanced toward the window. "I don't understand why Maxwell won't even consider the possibility of taking him on. I think Hamilton and Son Latch and Lock has a lovely ring to it and people trust a family-owned company that's been in the same hands for—oh, that's neither here nor there at the moment. I have other things about my son's future to concern me. And that's where you come in."

"Yes, ma'am?" Had the woman had a revelation since last night? A visit from an angel?

"I believe it's time Richard takes a wife. And I know just the girl." Her eyes sparkled over a forkful of ham.

Perspiration beaded on Maggie's lip. "You do?"

"Yes. And I'm going to need you to help persuade her."

CHAPTER 3

Ryan glared at the smiley faces on his fingertips. *Way to blow it, Tobin.*

But what should he have done? Told the little girl to go mind her own business? Called her nanny over and read her the riot act for paying more attention to the bakery case than the kid she was in charge of?

He'd done the right thing. If he hadn't kept her occupied she could have gone to the next table and met up with the wrong person, or she could have run right out the door.

The nanny definitely didn't see things his way. Did he really look all that dangerous? Didn't the security guard uniform count for something? Chicks loved uniforms—and all the better if the badge actually spelled out S-E-C-U-R-I-T-Y. It seemed to have a positive effect on the women behind the counter. Their glances and whispers were getting longer and louder by the day. He might have to find a different place to study.

He closed his laptop and opened a book. Had the nanny even taken the time to read the titles on the fortress surrounding him? *Police Operations: Theory and Practice. . .To Better Serve and Protect. . . Essentials of Investigative Interviewing.* Of course, she might have glanced at the one on top. *Deadly Force Encounters* could have put that strange look on her face. Or the novel. Had *Deception* put her off?

No, there was something else going on. He'd watched her fast getaway when he'd been in here earlier. Just like this time, it was as if something had suddenly spooked her.

Maybe it wasn't that she'd thought he was a shady character, maybe she'd run because *she* was the SP. Now that he thought about it, she'd seemed pretty friendly when she first walked up to the table. More concerned about the little girl bothering him than in analyzing him for creepiness. She'd taken his hand, even squeezed it a bit, and sat at the booth. She'd shot a nervous glance at the window before sitting in a place without a view of the street, but then she'd seemed to relax for a moment—before he slammed her with questions. *Note to self: Never practice interrogation techniques on people you've only known for eight seconds.* But they weren't intimidating questions.

He opened one of his books and found the chapter on how to educate the public to identify SPs.

> *A suspicious person is either one who is exhibiting suspicious behavior, or who is in an area or doing something that is not normal. Suspicious behavior is sometimes difficult to define, but is one of those things that most people "know when they see it." It is something that is out of place, not quite right, or just makes you feel "weird" about it.*

He scanned a list of possible suspicious behaviors. She hadn't been wearing clothes too large or too heavy for the weather. The dark green top with the narrow straps and the lacy semi-see-through flower thing in front seemed totally appropriate. She hadn't made an attempt to turn away by pretending to read a bulletin board or anything like that. In fact, he'd been the one squirming under searching, deep brown eyes. Very deep. Okay, so he hadn't actually squirmed. Hadn't really minded at all.

Four bullet points down he found one that fit. *Being evasive when asked a direct question. Attempts to change the subject.* The second part didn't fit. She hadn't changed the subject. She'd left.

He kept reading. *Giving too many details that are unrelated to the conversation.* She hadn't stuck around long enough for that. *Carrying items that do not fit in with what they are doing (e.g., a student carrying a toolbox into a lecture classroom).* She'd had a cup in each hand when she came to the table. No problem there. He couldn't remember a purse. Have to learn to be more attentive. A few inches later he read just that, under the heading "What to Do If You See a Suspicious Person."

If you see someone who is suspicious, note the following: What he looks like (height, build, hair color, skin complexion, etc.). Check. *What he is wearing.* Check. *The direction he is heading (if he is moving).* Easy one. She'd moved toward him. And then away. Still couldn't get a fix in his mind on a purse, but he'd pretty much memorized the other details. He had a photographic memory in selected areas. Which came in handy for the last one: *Any vehicles he is using (include type, color, and license plate, if possible).*

Check.

Porsche sedan. Chocolate brown. LUSHUS.

⁂

Half an hour earlier than usual, Ryan went into second-shift mode. *Turn off computer. Close books. Stuff backpack. Sling pack over shoulder. Laugh like Santa Claus. Bask in laughter from girls behind counter. Take on-the-house maple latte from girls. Drop generous tip in cup. Wink twice.*

"Thanks, ladies. See you tomorrow."

"Have a good night, Detective Ryan."

Hard as he tried not to show it, he loved the sound of that. The title was just a dream. First he had to get off the waiting list and into the police academy. Then it could be years on the police force before he could test for detective, but this was good practice—giving his ego time to adjust. "You, too."

Halfway through the near empty room, he turned around. He tossed his Spider-Man keychain into the air and caught it again. "Either of you happen to notice the woman and the little girl that came over and talked to me awhile ago?"

"The whip-extra-cream and a cocomocho." Jalissa retied the ends of her scarf at the back of her neck. "That was her second order today. Exactly the same. Very pretty. I didn't get a good look at her little girl." She lifted an eyebrow. "Is she our competition?"

37

"No one could compete with you two. You're the only women in my life. Other than my mom. And sister. And two sisters-in-law. And three grandmothers. Don't get me started on all the women in my life, but the point is, you're the ones I pay to be with." He saluted them with his eyebrows and the latte. "That's why I come here. Silence, and the joy of your company."

Kylee batted bizarrely long lashes. "We voted you our favorite customer."

"I am honored. So, about the woman in the green shirt. Ever see her before?"

"No." Jalissa filled a glass container with straws. "But you're not the only one wanting to know about her. Some guy came in after she was here this morning, asking if she was a regular."

Ryan pulled out his phone and pressed his finger on the MEMO icon. "What did he look like? Do you remember what he was wearing?"

"Yeah. He looked like he just got off a cruise ship. He was wearing a Hawaiian shirt."

"Anything else?"

"Yeah. I saw him across the street when the girl and the kid drove away. He was taking pictures of them."

👑

Izzy folded her arms across her tummy and stuck her tongue out at the back of Heather's hair. *You are not a fun person*, she whispered in her head. Thanks to Heather, she had chocolate splotches all over her favorite shirt.

Heather parked Mom's car in the garage and pushed the button to close the big door. "I'm sorry I rushed you, Iz, but we don't know that man. We can't just sit down and chat with someone we don't know."

Why not? "Why do grown-ups always think that people you don't know are going to hurt you? Why do they think just because you're a kid you can't tell if somebody is good or not? I can tell. Bad guys aren't named Ryan. He looked nice and maybe he has kids. We hafta get some friends."

"We'll go to a park and meet moms and kids. Maybe we'll go to church."

Izzy made her eyes squinty. "I bet bad men sometimes go to churches and parks."

Heather looked like she couldn't think of anything to say about that. "Let's go explore this house."

They went in through the back door. There were two locks on the door and Heather turned them both. Heather was being strange. Did she really think that man was going to follow them here?

With all the lights on, the kitchen made her blink like sunshine on a snowy day. She liked their new kitchen. In their condo in Chicago, everything was black. In this one, everything was white or silver. The cupboards were white and about a hundred feet tall and had windows in them. They looked really old, but the refrigerator was silver and new. And empty. Heather forgot they were supposed to go buy food. The counter was gray and shiny with sparkly pieces in it like the stones in Mom's necklace. There was a thing on the wall that looked like a painted paper plate. She'd asked what it was last night, but as usual Mom was on the phone and she didn't get an answer. "What's that?"

"That's where a stovepipe connected to the wall. They probably had a woodstove when the house was first built."

For a minute she thought Heather meant a stove made out of wood. It made her laugh when she didn't want to. She followed Heather through a swinging door that was white on one side and dark brown on the other. A fancy gold light hung in the middle of the room over Mom's black table. There were boxes everywhere.

"It's not fair we have to put everything away."

Heather walked over to the window where you could see the lake. "We'll make an adventure out of it. And then we'll laugh when your mom comes home and can't find anything."

Maybe Heather was a little fun. "We should hide things. We should put her hair dryer in the microwave and spoons and forks in her nightgown drawer. Stuff like that."

Heather laughed. "That would be—"

Her voice made a scared squeak. Izzy ran to the window. Right before Heather grabbed her arm she saw him.

Maybe bad guys *can be* named Ryan.

⚜

Ryan looked for a security system sign, but couldn't find one. The house was huge. Four thousand square feet at least. Three stories, if you count an attic with dormers. And a basement with wood-casing windows. Easy to break into. A trellis ran up to the flat porch roof below one of the second floor windows. Easy to climb. No curtains on any of the windows. At night, with lights on in the house, the place would be like a theater. And he sat in the front row.

Was it really just the two of them in that big house? What about a dog? What about a gun? Would she know how to use one if she had it? Would she have the guts?

Tall hedges separated the house from its neighbors on all three sides. Very secluded. Lots of places to hide. Across the street, nothing but grass, maybe fifty yards of it before the water's edge. He looked up and down Main. Not a lot of traffic on this end of the street.

He pulled a manual out of his backpack and paged to the "Home Security Self-Assessment."

Turning back to the window, he jumped. The two of them stood at the window. They'd seen him.

Only one thing to do now.

⚜

"What is he doing here? Why is he just sitting in his car like that? Is he going to get us? Is he going to come in the house while we're sleeping?" Izzy's heart pounded inside her like a drum. "What if he comes in and—"

"Izzy! Stop." Heather picked her up, pushed her head down on her shoulder, and walked up the stairs. "It'll be okay."

She was too big to be carried around, but right now she didn't feel all that big. Heather sat down on a box in an empty room. Izzy stared at the pointy heels on the shoes all jumbled in a box. "We could use Mom's shoes for weapons."

"We don't need weapons." Heather's voice shook like when you ride your bike over stones. "I think he liked us and just wanted to see where we live."

Izzy slid off Heather's lap and picked up a shoe. "I think we should call the police."

"We can't call the police just because he's sitting in his car for a few minutes. If he's still there in a little while I'll report it."

"I'm going to find a place to hide."

"Why don't we play hide-and-seek? We can explore the house that way."

If Heather wanted to make a game out of keeping them safe, she could play along. "I'll hide first. Close your eyes." She slipped off her flip-flops and ran down the hall in bare feet, quiet as she could be. She knew exactly where she was going—the short cupboard in the wall at the end of the hallway. She'd almost gotten to explore it once then Mom yelled at her to tell the moving men where she wanted her dresser.

She tiptoed up to the door and turned the handle real quiet. She had to climb up to get in and scrunch her knees up to her chin, but, like in "The Three Bears," it was just her size. A grown-up couldn't fit, but she could. She reached for the door to close it.

The floor jiggled. Then dropped. She screamed. And everything turned black.

CHAPTER 4

Izzy! What happened? Can you hear me?"

Heather gripped the trim of the small door and stared into a two-foot-square dark hole. She hated to imagine how deep. *Dear God, help.* "Izzy!"

"Get me out of here!" Her muffled cry was barely decipherable.

"I will." Heather yelled into the hole. "Are you hurt?"

"No. I'm scared. It's really, really dark. I can't"—pounding echoed up the narrow chute—"I can't get out!"

Heather pulled her phone out and held it over the hole. The light illuminated about three feet down. Izzy hadn't broken through the floor. She'd dropped into some kind of shaft. Thick cables made of twisted wire stretched tight in all four corners. Heather's breath seeped out in relief. "It's okay, Iz. You're in an elevator. I just have to figure out how to use it. Hang on. I'm going to find a flashlight."

Where would she find one in this mess? She ran down the steps. And screamed.

The man they'd met at the coffeehouse stood at the door, peering through the glass sidelight window. Keys—and a flashlight— hung from his belt.

Bad guys aren't named Ryan. He looked nice.

If she opened the door, would she be letting in help or. . . ? She'd prayed for help. Was he her answer? She took a shaky breath and unlocked the door.

"Hey." The guy touched the bill of a dark blue cap with Security embroidered across the front. "I know this looks odd, but I—"

"Can I use your flashlight? Izzy fell into an old dumbwaiter shaft and—"

"Where is she?" His eyes darted toward the stairs as he unclipped his flashlight. "Up there?"

"Yes. No. The opening is up there. I don't know how far down she is." She ran up the stairs with Ryan at her heels. "She says she's not hurt. I don't know if she fell or if it just lowered when she stepped on it. There are cables, but I couldn't see how to work them." She led him to the open door. Soft sobs drifted up.

"Izzy? It's Ryan—the finger puppet guy. We're going to get—"

"No! Go away!" Sobs followed the fear-filled words.

Gray-green eyes flashed at Heather.

"We saw you sitting outside and she got scared." Heather fingered the top button on her blouse. "We both did."

"That's why I came in. I didn't want you to think the wrong thing." He turned back to the elevator. "Izzy? I'm a security guard. Like a policeman. I followed you home just to make sure your new house was all safe." He turned to Heather. "I took down the license plate on the car you're driving. It's not yours."

"It's Izzy's mom's."

He nodded, as if her explanation had passed muster. "I assumed so. It took some doing to track down her new address."

Did he want a pat on the back?

Ryan looked down the hall, then back to the dumbwaiter shaft. "I have reason to believe someone might be following you."

Her stomach tightened. "So do I."

The flashlight didn't help, except to show that the shaft stretched down more than one full story. "I'm coming to get you, Izzy. I'm on my way."

Ryan turned and looked into panic-filled dark eyes. "It's Heather, right?" The woman nodded. "Where are the stairs to the basement?"

"I have no idea. Kitchen, maybe?" She pointed to the back of the house.

"I'll find it. And there must be doors for this thing on each floor." He smiled, hoping to ease the tightness on her face. "Not much point of a dumbwaiter if you can't get things on and off, right?"

"I g–guess."

He squeezed her upper arm. Apparently not the right thing to do. She pulled away, backing into a corner. This wasn't the time to try convincing her he was a good guy, but he prayed there'd be a chance for that later. Like after he'd rescued the girl and looked like a hero in those huge brown eyes. Maybe when he sat down and went through the *Home Security Self-Assessment* with Heather. As he ran down the steps, he wondered how he was going to handle the bullet point that read, "Never open your door to a stranger."

Sometimes you just have to go with your gut was not in the manual.

He ran downstairs and found the kitchen. He stared at the wall in the spot where the dumbwaiter had to pass on its way to the basement or cellar or whatever lay beneath the house. He shoved aside a stack of boxes, but there was no door, no opening. He ran into the dining room, opened a built-in china cabinet, looked behind still more boxes. Nothing.

Was there an outside entrance? He took three fast strides to the back door and grabbed the knob.

"Ryan!" The swinging door to the kitchen crashed open. Heather flew in, eyes wild. "She stopped answering me! I can't hear her crying and she's not talking and—"

"Look for a door to the basement. I didn't find it. I'm going outside to look for an entrance." He tore his eyes away from hers and ran onto a porch, through another door, and out into the yard. He scanned the stone foundation and found what he was looking for. A bulkhead door almost concealed by bushes. He dropped to his knees. Two slanted metal doors met in the center. A padlock linked the handles of both doors.

Pulse accelerating, he jumped to his feet and ran to the nearest basement window. Recessed in a deep window well, only about six inches of mud-spattered glass showed above ground level. Still, if he could jimmy it open, he might be able to see inside. At the very least, he could yell. He yanked and wiggled the handle. It didn't budge. He searched for a rock and found half a brick. Taking his jacket off, he wrapped it around his hand and slammed the brick into the window. It shattered, glass clattering to the floor.

"Izzy! Can you hear me?" He stuck his head into the window well and had to turn almost upside down to peer in. A pale square of light from another window lit a cage-like door in the right place for the dumbwaiter. He couldn't see anything beyond the crisscrossed bars. Was she lying on the floor? "Izzy!"

No answer. He ran back to the bulkhead doors and grabbed the padlock. The door shifted. He yanked. Rusted hinges on the right side disintegrated. *Thank you.* He wedged his fingers under the edge and lifted. The hinges on the opposite side snapped as if made of balsa wood. As he hefted the door Heather ran out of the house.

"I heard glass."

"I broke the window." As he wrestled the door out of the way, he nodded toward the phone in her hands. "You'd better call 911 and—"

She maneuvered around him and darted down four concrete steps. The door landed on the grass at the exact moment Heather screamed his name.

"She's not here! Ryan! She's not here!"

He ran down the steps and aimed his light. The cage at the bottom of the dumbwaiter was empty.

⬦

Izzy rubbed her cold arms, happy to be out of that icky place. The stairs weren't bright like the kitchen, but still she had to squint after being in the dark. She crept up the skinny steps on tippy toes. She'd closed the door at the bottom so carefully even she couldn't hear it. There had to be another door at the top. Heather and the finger puppet guy would be so scared when she jumped out. In her head she practiced yelling "Surprise!" They would scream and she would laugh and say, "I won! You didn't find me!"

Way far away she heard glass breaking and then a loud sound like the time Mom bumped into another car and part of Mom's car broke off. What was happening? Was Ryan hurting Heather? Was he coming after her? All of a sudden it didn't feel like a game anymore.

"Heather!" She ran up. The steps curved around like a Twizzler. She came to a door but there was no handle. She felt like she couldn't breathe. Her heart thumped loud in her ears. She pounded on the door. "Heather! Open the door!"

No one answered so she kept running up and up until she got to another door.

Another door without a handle.

"Heather!"

♔

"I hear her!"

Heather grabbed Ryan's arm. "Listen." A faint scream came from somewhere above them. A sob shuddered in her chest. Relief and fear tangled together. "Izzy!" she screamed into the dumbwaiter shaft. "Where are you?"

"I'm upstairs! I can't open the door!" The voice didn't come from the shaft.

"I hate this house." Heather followed the sweep of Ryan's flashlight. He faced a wall of cupboards and doors. Dark, rough, ugly wood. "Keep yelling, Iz. Sing me a song really loud and I'll find you!"

A tiny far-off voice began, "Twinkle, twinkle, little star. . ."

Heather turned and ran back up the cement steps and into the house.

In the kitchen, the voice was louder, but still seemed to be coming from upstairs. She flew through the swinging doors, ran through the dining room and up the stairs, half expecting to wake any moment from a nightmare. Maybe it wasn't a dream. Maybe Izzy had slipped into the Matrix. An alternate dimension. She felt laughter rising as she tripped onto the second floor—laughter teetering on the brink of hysteria.

". . .like a diamond in the sky. . ."

"I hear you nice and loud, Iz." Heather whirled in the dimly lit hall. Where was the door? "Tell me what you see. What does it look like?" *In your dimension.*

"I'm on the steps. Curvy steps. I found two doors, but there aren't any handles."

Doors. Good. "Are you by one of the doors?"

"Uh-huh." A loud knock reverberated in the wide paneled hallway.

"Keep knocking." Heather ran her hand along the wall to the right of the dumbwaiter. "I feel it!" She knocked.

"I felt that!" Izzy giggled. "Open the door!"

It's not a door, baby. Some past owner had paneled over it. She was suddenly grateful for a stranger in the basement. A stranger who could borrow a power saw from a neighbor. *Call 911.* She'd ignored him. Help could be on the way right now if she'd listened. But they could do this without more men in uniform adding more trauma to the poor girl. "Where's the other door?"

"Down some steps."

"Go to the other door and knock on it, okay?"

"Ok–kay." The little voice shook.

Heather ran back down to the kitchen and again felt the wall. Izzy knocked. Heather pounded the side of her fist against the painted wainscoting. Something clicked. And the wall—the door—swung toward her. As Izzy tumbled into her arms, they heard footsteps racing up the stairs.

"I found it! I found the stairs, Heather! I'm coming, Iz. . .zy."

Ryan gaped at them with an expression that seemed far more disappointed than relieved. But his mouth closed and in seconds he flashed a smile that crinkled the corners of his eyes. He raised his hand and wiggled the faces still inked on his fingertips. "What a cool house, huh, Izzy?" He used a squeaky voice, fit for a cartoon character.

A man who tried this hard to make a little girl smile couldn't be a bad guy, could he? There was something transparent about his expression, something honest. More than just the word on his cap gave an aura of safety. And then there were those eyes.

Izzy nodded. "Cool. But a little scary."

A smiley-faced finger crooked. "Only till you get to know all the secret passages."

Heather stared at the staircase curving up and down from where she stood. An invisible weight pressed on her chest. No more secrets. No more unknowns. The massive house with its alternate dimensions and hidden doors seemed to symbolize the life she was walking away from.

Izzy pulled out of her arms and turned to Ryan. Standing three steps down, he was almost at her eye level. "Wanna explore?"

"I'd love to." He raised his arm and looked at his watch. "First, I'm going to call in to work and tell them I won't be in tonight."

There it was again. That combination of expression and tone—and gorgeous eyes and muscle—that said, "You're safe with me." Or was that just what she wanted to hear? "You don't have to do that. Thank you so much for being here and helping, but you can't get in trouble at work because of us."

"It's not a problem." He glanced at Izzy. "I can't leave. I have a door and a window to fix."

Did she really want to talk him out of staying when there was a wide-open hole leading to the basement and "reason to believe" someone might be watching her? "Can you do that? Just call and tell them you're not coming in?"

The smiley fingers waggled. "My boss loves me."

"Well. Okay then. I guess it's settled." Why was she accepting that for an answer? Had Zach ever slowed her brain function the way this guy did?

"We maybe should get supper somewhere first." His shoulders gave the slightest shrug. One brow rose, like an unspoken *pleeease?* tacked on to his suggestion.

Heather gestured at the patch on his shirt. TKJ SECURITY. "What do the letters stand for?"

One side of his mouth rose in a lopsided grin that made her think, once again, of a cartoon character. "I'm not supposed to divulge that information, but maybe I'll tell you over dinner." Again, the question-asking shrug.

"Okay. Dinner. Yes. Give us just a minute to change into clothes without chocolate stains and we'll be ready."

We will? He's a security guard and he looks nice. *Are you nuts?* Her personality split with a slithering sound like a zipper opening, peeling one side from the other.

"I'll cover up the holes I made while you're changing. Hope you don't mind a stop at Home Depot."

"We don't mind." Said the girl who swore that in her new life she would dive headfirst into an empty swimming pool before going on another hardware store date. *Zip.* How many degrees can a person separate from her true self before being classified as certifiably schizoid?

Izzy in tow, she ran upstairs. Before that man slowed one more thought, she had to do some research. She found the website on her phone and punched in the number.

"TKJ Security. This is Marissa. How can I help you?"

"Hi. I'm wondering if you can verify for me that Ryan Tobin works for your company."

"Yes, ma'am, I can verify that. Anything you'd like to know about him?"

Everything. "Can you tell me a bit about his work history?"

"He's worked for our company for ten years. He's an experienced security guard and installer."

"Installer?"

"Yes, ma'am. May I ask why you're inquiring?"

Nothing came to mind but the truth and that wasn't the right answer.

"Ma'am, have you spoken to Ryan about a job or has someone referred you?"

"No, I haven't spoken to him about a job yet. I just wanted to verify that he worked there. First."

"If I can have your name and address or e-mail I can send you some information. Are you interested in a security system?"

"Yes. Very much so." She walked to the window and stared out at the lake. "My name is Heather Conrad and my—"

"Heather? Excuse me, but is Ryan with you?"

"Y–yes."

A sputtering laugh fizzed in her ear. "Hi, Heather. So you're the tall brunette with amazing eyes he's skipping work for, huh? Let me tell you a thing or two about my big brother. . ."

December 28, 1911

Charles held out his hand to help Maggie into the sleigh next to Hilde, then handed her a fur blanket. "Wind's as sharp as a mother-in-law's tongue."

Maggie gazed at the leaden sky reflected in the rutted surface of the lake and laughed. "And what would a bachelor stable boy know about mothers-in-law?"

A bump formed in Charles's cheek as he aimed a warning glance her way. The only thing it warned of was his intent to get even in their ongoing duel of words. He hopped onto the driver's seat. The springs squeaked. "I hear things."

"If you're lucky"—she nudged Hilde—"you'll marry a woman whose mother lives in Ohio."

Hilde's features resembled the breakers along the shore. "*Maggie.*"

Charles shot a grin over his right shoulder then tapped the reins on the team's backs. "If I'm lucky, I'll marry a woman who doesn't even have. . ." An icy gale off the lake swallowed his words.

Darting a look at Hilde's chiseled profile, Maggie chose not to ask him to repeat the comment. She spread the blanket over her knees, tucking the edges beneath her wool coat on her right and flattened the blanket against the handbreadth space of leather between her and Hilde, sealing all the gaps. The gesture felt symbolic. Since Christmas, her relationship with Hilde had mirrored the diminishing line of mercury on the thermometer outside the kitchen window. Whenever Maggie brought it up, she was answered with a "Nothing's wrong," and a smile as stiff as a celluloid doll's.

Magdalena turned away from the cold, beady eyes of her friend. Jealousy is a hideous creature, she thought. It has the power to turn the warm heart of a passive little mouse to ice.

Maggie looked from the back of Charles's wool cap to the gros-grain bow beneath Hilde's chin. "Where is Mrs. Caswell?"

"Charles took her earlier to help with the lunch." Hilde's tone flattened like waves on a windless day.

"What are the dainty warriors discussing this afternoon?" Bells jingled against harnesses as Charles urged on the team. "How to poison your man's tea without leaving a trace?"

Maggie laughed. Hilde stared straight ahead, her fur muff set just-so on her lap. Folding her gloved hands beneath the fur robe, Maggie seesawed between empathy and irritation at Hilde's plight. Could the girl not see the way to Charles's heart was laughter? If she would simply relax and not put on such affected airs, she'd turn Mr. Caswell's mechanic to mush.

Maybe what Hilde needed was a how-to lesson.

"We have no interest in extinguishing the male population. Today we are discussing potions to render a man temporarily mute." She cupped her hands around her mouth. "So our logical and legitimate demands can be heard."

A barely audible huff wafted from the ice statue sitting beside her. The tiniest of regrets made itself known beneath Maggie's breastbone. More than once, Hilde had accused her of flaunting her knowledge of words.

But this is how it's done, Hilde. A little melodrama, a little faux disdain. . .and watch the boy come alive.

Burnished curls tickled the edge of Charles's collar as his head tipped back. A chortle sparred with the rush of the wind. "*Legitimate? Logical?*" The words roared over the clopping of hooves on hard-packed snow. He eased the reins to the left and the sleigh made a wide arc onto Twelfth Street. "Where on God's green earth would it be logical to give brainless puppets like Mrs. Hamilton and Mrs. Morton the right to decide how the United States government spends money?"

"*Charles.*" Maggie drew her hand out from under the blanket and pressed her fingers to her mouth. "How utterly unchristian of you."

" 'Neither shalt thou bear false witness against thy neighbor.' " He guided the horses onto Wisconsin Avenue. "If I were to make them out to be intellectual wonders, that would be nothing less than a false witness."

Maggie giggled. She didn't chance a direct gaze at Hilde, but gauged her reaction by the stiff set of the arms forming a circle with the fur muff. Compassion took over as, for a moment, she imagined herself in Hilde's skin, feeling the envy prickling as her best friend boasted about the man who had said he would fight to court her.

She had to do something to restore her celluloid friend to life. She leaned forward to be heard over the rattle of harness and jingle of sleigh bells. "So, Mr. Honesty, if we were to ask you to give your true thoughts of the women behind you, what would we hear?"

Again, the fringe of wavy hair skimmed the wool collar. Charles's elbows pulled back. The team slowed. In the shelter of brick homes and arching oak skeletons, the wind lowered to a whisper. Charles turned in the seat and doffed his cap. "You would hear"—he aimed a steady gaze at Hilde—"that one of you is pretty, kind, gracious, and giving."

Maggie stifled the desire to jab Hilde with an elbow, but did not refrain from watching the arms relax and softness return to her friend's face. *See, Hilde, he likes you. Now do something about it.*

Charles swiveled back to the front and around to his right. Laugh lines branched from twinkling eyes. "And you would hear that the other is feisty and strong and courageous, with eyes that dance and a bigger heart than she wants anyone to see." With a wink, he turned back and gave a gentle lash with the reins.

Hoofbeats reverberated against brick. Between houses, the wind's spearheads found them once again. The muff drew in toward Hilde's stomach.

Feisty and strong. Eyes that dance. Maggie fought for words to take the edge out of the air.

A car passed on their left, tires sliding on the slippery road. The horn honked. The horses startled. An ivory face surrounded by fur peered through the back window. A gloved hand rose in a royal wave.

Emma Rose Mitchell. The girl who would be perfect for Richard.

"The minutes stand approved as read."

Mrs. Morton set a silver-rimmed teacup aside and picked up a booklet with a tan cover. "Olympia is out East this week, but she graciously gifted us with a copy of her book, the one we've all been hearing about." She held up a copy of *Acquaintances Old and New, among Reformers*.

"What a heritage we have, ladies, and what a call to action, to not grow weary. I can't urge each of you strongly enough to purchase a copy. It's so easy for us to feel alone, as if our little handful of noble soldiers were climbing this mountain alone, but we are not alone, we are surrounded by a great cloud of women witnesses who. . ."

Maggie longed to nudge Hilde, to share the humor in this woman's melodrama, tangled metaphors, and appalling mix of scripture and suffrage slogans. But Hilde sat across the room next to Liberty, personal maid to Emma Rose Mitchell. The girl who would be perfect for Richard.

Between scribbled notes for her employer, Maggie rehearsed how to carry out her orders in a way that would hurt no one—especially herself. Her last promise as she'd walked out the door, leaving behind a blubbering Mrs. Hamilton, was that she would talk to Liberty and find out if Emma had marriage prospects, and, if so, was that man equal to Richard? Evangeline Hamilton had actually used that word. Equal. As if she had the slightest idea what it meant.

Mrs. Morton flipped to the back of the little book. "And here we have a charge to us, ladies. To *us*." She straightened the black ribbon tie on her white shirtwaist and cleared her throat. " 'Shall our grand Wisconsin be recognized as the honored leader in reform, the first of the states of the Middle West to recognize the rights of its women? Or shall the cause be voted down and discredited, the women of the state disappointed, and our glorious commonwealth disgraced?

" 'The result will depend upon the wise, judicious, persistent efforts of the advocates of the cause.' "

Eighteen pairs of hands clapped. Maggie joined in, but, in truth, she was tired of the topic. Month after month they met to discuss impending legislation, starts and stops in Madison and Washington. But in the end, all they did was talk. To be fair, there were many who had attended their meetings—Olympia Brown, Ada James, and Mrs. Henry Youmans—who put feet to their words. Maggie respected them for their action, even the actions she didn't totally agree with. But she had to concur with Charles. *Where on God's green earth would it be logical to give brainless puppets like Mrs. Hamilton and Mrs. Morton the right to decide how the government spends money?*

She held her peace until Mrs. Morton asked if there was anything else anyone wished to discuss. Like a schoolgirl, Maggie raised her hand, but didn't wait to be called on. "There is something I'd like to talk about. A project we could get involved in right now while we're waiting for things to change on the state or national front."

The collective inhale was visible rather than audible. This was the first time Mrs. Hamilton's housemaid had spoken above a whisper in this gathering.

Mrs. Morton blinked. Once. Then again. "Maggie, isn't it?"

"Yes. Maggie Parker."

"Maggie is the Hamiltons'"—she pressed her lips together—"is in the employ of Maxwell and Evangeline Hamilton, for those who may not know. Go on, Maggie."

"I do believe Racine is way ahead of most cities in workplace reform. I have read glowing things about the Mitchell-Lewis Company"—*things like they may be hiring the most handsome man I know*—"and we should all be proud of the safety innovations and worker benefits they have pioneered. But there are new manufacturing plants springing up all the time that don't share those goals and ideals. The new Industrial Commission has great plans, but I think there are things the citizens of this town can do to help ease the suffering of overburdened women and children." Now who was being melodramatic? "I'm sure none of us can forget the horrifying pictures of the Triangle Shirtwaist Factory fire that killed a hundred and forty-six people in New York nine months ago. That fire could have been prevented."

With a smack of lips, Mrs. Christensen flattened the ribbon woven into her collar and glanced at her watch. "We all remember. It was a great tragedy, but this is not New York. We don't have ten-story buildings without fire escapes."

Cords tightened on the sides of Maggie's neck. *Calm me, Father.* She took a deep breath. "I didn't mean to imply that what happened there could happen here, merely to awaken our concern for the plight of those less fortunate. What we do have in this city are fourteen-year-old children working fifty-five hours a week, more if employers can get away with it. These young people don't have access to an education that could help them better their situations. That's where

54

I believe we can help. We can implore businesses to allow breaks for children under eighteen by explaining how performance declines and accidents increase without periods of rest. And during those breaks we could go in and teach—"

"Where did you receive your education, Miss Parker?"

Maggie couldn't remember the name of the woman in the tailored navy suit with her graying hair done up in a concoction of twists and braids the likes of which Maggie had never seen even in a magazine. Her question, heavy with innuendo, raised chins around the room.

"I am self-taught, ma'am. My father"—a low vibration seemed to hum in the room—"taught me to read and to relish learning. The Hamiltons have made books and papers available to me and I frequent the library." Imagining patronizing smiles, Maggie squared her shoulders and kept her eyes on a mother-of-pearl comb in the mass of braids. "Resources are available. I believe every person who is taught to read and whose natural curiosity is allowed to flourish can teach himself—or *her*self—much, and that is exactly why I want to pursue education opportunities for—"

"The children who are employed by your employer?" The voice came from a mousy-looking woman in a stiff-looking black suit with her hair pulled back in an unfashionable and unbecoming bun so tight it made Maggie's scalp hurt.

"We would, of course, ma'am, but there is no one under seventeen employed at Hamilton Lock and Latch."

The woman raised an eyebrow, stretching already taut skin.

"There are laws already in place, Miss Parker"—said the woman who had asked where she'd received her education—"that allow for all children to attend school." The pearl comb took on a purplish cast as the woman tipped her head to the right. "We do not discriminate by income level or station in life."

We? Who was this woman?

"We all appreciate what you and your family have done for this city, Mrs. Starbuck." Emma Rose Mitchell smiled demurely at the older woman.

Mrs. Starbuck? Maggie had just cheekily addressed the wife of the publisher of the *Racine Daily Journal.* As if that were not humiliation enough, the girl who was perfect for Richard had come to Maggie's defense.

"We are going to miss you dearly when you move to California." Emma's smile cut through the ice that now coated both sides of the windows. "We have a fine school system, but I know you'll agree that even though all children are welcome, not all can avail themselves of the privilege." Her violet eyes turned to Maggie. "And I, for one, think your idea is an excellent one. May I join your endeavor, Miss Parker?"

Under the glare of Hilde's fiery stare and with the background of tittering whispers, Maggie squared her shoulders. With a decisive nod, she joined forces with Emma Rose Mitchell.

The woman she was supposed to convince to marry the man who was supposed to alter the course of Maggie's future.

CHAPTER 5

Andrew Rivera closed the cover of his laptop, snapped off his desk light, and walked toward the wall of windows looking down on Chicago from the thirty-eighth floor of the Lansing Building. The sun hovered just above the horizon, silhouetting brick and concrete monoliths against a canvas of orange. He loved this city, felt the purposeful rush of cars and bodies pulsing through his veins. The knowledge that he played a part in the ever-evolving organism spread out below energized him. He had plans. A vision to implement.

The embolism in Parker Lansing's heart did not fit his plans.

Andrew had just put a period on the final sentence of his proposal when the news came. *"They're rushing Mr. Lansing to the hospital."* He'd stood in this same spot a week ago, watching the lights of the ambulance as it screamed away. It was the kind of moment when a person was supposed to pray.

Instead, he presented himself to Mr. Lansing's secretary. *"I'll handle everything, Lanette."*

That's how he'd found himself spending as much time behind the CEO's desk as his own, and how he came to prefer the odd-looking mesh of an Aeron chair to the Italian leather he'd parked in for two years. Lanette's fidgety interruptions broadcast her fear that he was becoming a bit too comfy in the ergonomic chair.

She didn't need to worry. He didn't want Parker's job. He wanted Parker's ear. He wanted him healthy and back at his desk. Andrew's future depended on the man living, on Lansing Corporation not falling into the hands of its co-owner—the shrew whose office adjoined her ex-husband's.

Dianna Lansing didn't like him. She'd balked at his ideas from the moment he'd moved into the office with the leather chair. Andrew didn't know what he'd done to get on her bad side. Maybe it was just that she didn't have a good one.

He often wondered if the woman had any idea he'd asked her daughter out just to spite her.

Andrew rubbed his hand across his face and contemplated the problem of Stephannie.

👑

Izzy waved from a mesh-sided cockpit at the top of a maze of looping slides and tubes. "Don't fly too far away," Heather yelled.

Seven-year-old giggles reverberated off plastic.

Heather took a sip of strawberry shake. "This is just what she needed."

"Hope she can get some of her wiggles out and sleep for you tonight." Ryan swiveled away from the play area and faced her. "Do you think it'll be hard for her the first night without her mom?"

"To be honest, I doubt it. She's pretty independent."

"How long have you known her mom?"

"I worked for her for nine months. She was a CEO for Coventry Hotels. I was her personal assistant."

"Swank. How does one get a job like that?"

"I got my degree in Hotel Management. My mother was in PR for a hotel chain for years before I came along, so I grew up hearing stories of her travels and all the famous people she met. In spite of all the conniving and nastiness, I loved my job. But then Izzy's mom moved on, leaving me jobless. She felt pity on me and offered me the house-sitting job, which somehow morphed into a month of nannying."

With head bent and lips pursed around his straw, Ryan looked up at her for an unnervingly long moment before releasing the straw. "So it's temporary?"

She nodded.

"What's next?"

"How much time do you have?"

He glanced at his watch. "I have to be at work by eight. Including travel and shower time. . .fourteen hours."

And here she'd thought she'd forgotten how to make a laugh sound that wasn't faked. "I'll try to finish in twelve so you can fit in some sleep."

"Very thoughtful of you."

"I wrote my master's thesis on"—she took a deep breath—" 'The Potential Role of the American Coffee Shop in the Contemporary American Citizen's Quest for Purposeful Community.' "

Ryan flopped back in the booth, head bouncing, mouth ajar. "Say what?"

Heather leaned on her elbows. "In spite of the plethora of social media options available today, many, maybe most, people don't experience true community. If your career takes you away from family, you form relationships in the workplace, but due to the transitory nature of most of us, those connections are often temporary. So you turn to clubbing or social media or online dating, but often the best a person ever experiences in any of those scenarios is pseudo intimacy."

The dazed expression faded. "I have an answer for that."

"You do? I spent two years researching this topic when all I had to do was meet you?"

He nodded. "But you won't like my answer."

"Try me."

His posture straightened. "Generations ago, when people first came to this country, they made shelters for their families and then they joined together to build a church. Not just because they thought it was a holy place or they couldn't worship God in a grove of pine trees, but because they wanted a gathering place. To steal from an old sitcom, they wanted a place where everybody knows your name."

Church. His answer was church? *Insert pretend smile here. Thank you, Zach and Jen, for all that practice.*

"You can tell me to shut up or leave anytime you want and I won't get offended, but you just hit one of my passion nerves."

Passion nerves? "Go on."

"I'm a Jesus freak. There, we got that out on the table." He stared, seemingly daring her to get up and leave.

Part of her wanted to, but she held his gaze. "I have no problem with the Jesus part. It's the freak part that scares me. I'm of the opinion that faith ought to be lived, not shoved."

"I like that."

"Go on. I interrupted you."

He scratched the stubble on his chin. "I'm still part of the church I grew up in. My whole life I've been surrounded by a bunch of broken, imperfect people who most of the time do a pretty fair job of sharing each other's burdens and joys. Because of that, at twenty-six I know who I am. I'm grounded and connected and I don't need to look online to see how many friends I have today. So my answer to the problem of disconnected people is 'Find Jesus and start hanging out with His kids.'" Again, the unblinking stare daring her to shoot him down.

She couldn't find fault with any of it, but was this just the tip of his freaky iceberg?

Out of all the single men in this town with sweet kringle breath, why did she have to meet the Jesus freak with passion nerves? She crumpled her napkin and tossed it on the tray. "Let's go to Home Depot."

Only in an alternate universe would those words have come out of her mouth.

♔

"Why would there be stairs that don't lead anywhere?"

Heather gazed up at the ceiling that met the top step in the stairwell curving up from the second floor.

"Could have just been made for storage." Though he seemed to be a guy who liked to have answers, the furrow between Ryan's eyes said he was as puzzled as she was.

"I suppose."

Izzy sat on a step holding Ryan's flashlight and peeling strips of string cheese with her teeth. "I think it was made for a secret hide-away," she garbled. "So the children who lived here in the old days could play hide-and-seek."

Ryan ruffled her curls. "I think you're right." He walked down several steps. "I'd love to explore with you guys, but I have a window to cover."

"And I have groceries to put away." Heather followed him into the kitchen. "Thank you, by the way, for stopping at the store."

"Hey, you didn't complain once about half an hour at Home Depot. Besides, I'm not one of those guys allergic to shopping. I'd rather hunt, but I don't mind gathering."

She sighed her approval. "A man who shops."

"After I get things squared away outside, I'd like to give you some info on security systems that you can pass along to Izzy's mom."

"Sounds like a good—" Her phone rang. "There she is now. I'll bring the phone out to you if she's interested."

Ryan nodded and waved as she walked toward the door. Happy face fingers did strange things to the rhythm of her pulse. She held the phone to her ear. "Hello."

"Heather. I'm at JFK. How is everything?"

There's a man stalking me, another one broke your basement window, we just found a secret stairway. . . "All in all, things are going well. We just got groceries and Izzy is helping me put them away."

"She's not in bed yet?"

Don't you start on me, lady. "Nope. It's been a busy day."

"How much unpacking did you get done?"

Heather glanced at the little girl sitting on top of a box marked "Kitchen," munching mozzarella. The top of the box sagged under Izzy's bottom. "Izzy's putting quite a dent in it even as we speak."

"I don't want her getting overtired."

Should have thought of that before you put me in charge. "She's fine."

"I guess I should have mentioned it, but Izzy occasionally has night terrors if she's overtired. Or if she eats sugar in the evening. Or dairy."

The last strip of cheese dangled over Izzy's mouth. Fresh splotches of chocolate decorated the shirt she'd donned before going out to dinner. *Yeah, maybe you should have mentioned it.* "I had them when I was a kid."

"See? I knew you could handle this."

"When do you take off again?"

"We—they'll start boarding in about five minutes. I had time to grab dinner and get caught up on e-mail and I wanted to see how things were with you before I board."

Heather bit back a remark about priorities and walked casually into the dining room. "There's something I wanted to talk to you about."

"Talk fast."

"I'm getting some information on security systems. In fact, there's a representative here right now looking at the house. I think—"

"Whoa. Heather. I gave you carte blanche with the debit card, but that was for entertaining Izzy. I don't need a security system. That's why I have you. As long as people see you coming and going and see lights on, everything will be fine. The house is in a great neighborhood and I don't have anything worth stealing."

Heather looked into the front room at a fifty-inch plasma TV flanked by two towers of surround sound speakers. *What about your daughter? Or the person taking care of her? We just might be worth stealing. Or worse.* "I think it would be a good idea to at least—"

"I have to run, Heather. Just keep the doors locked and everything will be fine. Give Izzy a kiss for me."

"Do you want to talk to your—"

The phone went dead.

Ryan closed his toolbox and brushed his knees. He'd nailed a piece of plywood over the window and replaced the hinges on the bulkhead door. Wouldn't hurt to do a quick sweep of the outside to get a rough estimate of what would need to be done to secure all the windows.

To secure Heather.

After only one evening with her, he could imagine nods of approval at Sunday dinner. He'd learned the hard way not to allow feelings for anyone until she'd survived the Tobin family gauntlet. Would this Sunday be too soon to put this particular girl to the test?

His phone rang. Marissa. Reading his thoughts again.

"Hey, Mar."

"Are you still with Heather?"

"Yes. Well, not right with her, but I'm at her house."

"I like her. She said she likes Asian food, so Amanda and I decided we'll do a buffet at her house. I'll make my pad thai and I know Tammy will—"

"Stop." Ryan raised his hand like the cop he hoped to be someday. "Back up. Heather *said*—? When and how did you talk to her?"

"She didn't tell you? She called to verify that you were who you said you were, and I just kind of asked a couple questions. And invited her to dinner on Sunday."

Ryan closed his eyes and his hand. This couldn't be happening. "Tell me you're kidding. Tell me she didn't really call, or if she did you handled it like the consummate professional we're trying to turn you into."

"I was very professional. I told her how long you'd worked for the company and that you came highly recommended and"—she cleared her throat—"a few more things about you and then, being the friendly consumer relations person I am, I asked what her favorite food was. She said anything Asian, so I said I make a mean shrimp pad thai. And said maybe she'd like to try it. Sunday."

The running of the gauntlet was supposed to occur at his suggestion. In person. With a girl of his choosing. "Marissa. . ." His groan echoed against the side of the big white house. "You know she's taking care of—"

"A seven-year-old, I know. I told her you had an eight-year-old niece so that wasn't a problem."

"Way to corner her." He brushed the dirt off his knees. "Take away all her excuses. How am I supposed to—"

"Come on, Spidey. Don't you even want to know what she said?"

"I don't know. Do I?"

"I think you do. She said, 'What can I bring?'"

"Sleep tight."

Heather closed Izzy's door partway and stood in the hallway waiting for an "I'm scared" or "I want my mommy."

Silence.

63

Her bare feet padded on wide, polished oak boards, the soft taps absorbed by a garden of pale blue wallpaper flowers. Sconces of frosted glass in burnished iron holders created pools of pale, diffused light. She glanced into Natalie's room. Shorts, T-shirts, and sandals cluttered the bare mattress. The sleek blond wood of the Scandinavian-design bedroom set seemed at odds with the busy iris-and-cattail print on the walls.

For only the second time since she'd arrived, she walked into the room that would be hers. Her breath hitched as she turned the dimmer switch and amber light from an ornate ceiling fan illuminated walls that could have lined the throne room of a Persian prince. Two-foot-wide borders in intricate Oriental mosaic patterns—burnt orange, rust, and several shades of blue—flowed along the top of the walls. The patterns were repeated on the ceiling. Far East-inspired scalloped edges framed cream-colored walls decorated with rust and blue medallions, stripes, and pendant shapes. All it needed was a Persian rug and a mountain of tasseled pillows. Instead, it held high-gloss white furniture with chrome hardware. The manufacturer's stickers still clung to the mirror above a long, low dresser.

Picking up the smallest of her three suitcases, she plopped it onto the bare mattress next to a pile of sheets and blankets. "This is so not what I signed up for." She opened the case, glanced at her computer, and shut it again. Not tonight. She needed to put sheets on the bed and find a toaster and silverware and cereal bowls. She needed to think. About the time she wouldn't have to work on her business plan. About whether or not she could stand working for Natalie again. About making peace with her sister. About the guy with the camera. And the man with the hazel eyes.

She'd start with finding a coffeepot.

In worn-comfy pajamas, she carried her toiletries bag into the bathroom and claimed three drawers. A cardboard flap on an open box of bath towels wagged in a burst of cool air from a vent—like a giant, mocking tongue. *Na-na-na-na, you're a sucker.*

"I am. I totally am." *I always have been.* She'd spent twenty-three years in Jen's graceful blond shadow. In spite of the pain of coming in second in Zach's hunt for a lifemate, the freedom she'd felt when she left Manhattan, Kansas, after the breakup was indescribable. . .and short-lived. She'd stepped right into the shade created by Natalie's imposing stature. And then there was the Zach cloud, the one she couldn't shake even though she was utterly single, the one she'd once thought sheltered her everywhere she went when for who-knows-how-long it rested over Jen.

She kicked the box flap and jammed a brush into a drawer. "What's wrong with me? Why can't I say no? Why can't I read people?"

The wounded box didn't answer. The air conditioner turned off. Cool silence filled the tiled room. She glanced at the claw-foot tub and considered hiding in a mound of bubbles until her skin wrinkled and she was too tired to care about the shadows lurking over her. . .and possibly outside, across the street, with a camera.

With a shiver, she turned out the light. As she headed for the stairs, a shrill scream shattered the quiet.

Izzy occasionally has night terrors if she's overtired. Or if she eats sugar in the evening. Or dairy.

CHAPTER 6

Heather had just thrown away their paper plates from lunch on Tuesday when she heard a knock on the screen door of the back porch. "Anybody home?"

"Come on in." She brushed potato chip crumbs off her faded T-shirt and redid her ponytail as Ryan stepped into the kitchen. Shaking her head, she smiled at him. "Do you really have a job?"

"Hi, to you, too." He held out a TKJ Security brochure. "I'm working. Wanna buy a security system?"

"As a matter of fact, I do."

His eyes widened. "Any more problems?"

"Nothing from outside. Izzy woke up screaming. It took me awhile to wake her. Scared the stuffing out of me, but she doesn't even remember it. Other than that, everything's fine. I got up twice during the night and checked outside. I think I may have just been spooking myself. The guy was probably a tourist and I was a little jumpy at the thought of spending the night in this place."

"Probably." His tone didn't match his answer. He carried a box of canned goods to an empty space on the counter and started shelving soup cans in an empty cupboard.

Heather stared at his back, at the way his shirt pulled tight each time he reached out with another can. She tried to imagine Farmer Boy in the kitchen, doing anything other than eat. She couldn't.

"Izzy asked if you were coming over today."

He tossed a can of tomato soup in the air with one hand and caught it with the other. His eyes looked more green than brown today and seemed to stare through her. "And what did you tell her?"

"I said I didn't know." She set a box of baking soda next to the cornstarch. "I guess I should let her know you're here." *Now.* She spun on her heel and plowed through the swinging door like a lineman practicing tackles.

This wasn't smart. She wasn't like Natalie. She wasn't the kind of girl who collected guys like shoes. She hadn't dated anyone other than Zach for years, and a girl on the rebound was about as stable as uranium.

Instead of calling up the stairs for Izzy, she took her time walking up, trailing her hand along the banister as she relaxed her shoulders and cleared her brain. Ryan was a nice man. He'd come to her rescue when she needed help. She'd worked with a lot of nice, helpful even-handsomer-than-Ryan-Tobin men over the years, and hadn't fallen for a single one.

But that was then. And this was now. And *now* she didn't know how to think or what to feel because she didn't have the slightest clue how to interact with a guy without the Zach shadow.

👑

Heather took her time following Izzy into the kitchen. Time to bring her pulse and blood pressure back within normal range. When she sauntered back in, casual as a girl who was used to being just friends with guys, Izzy was bouncing up and down like a Super Ball, clapping her hands and squealing. Ryan stood in front of her, laughing and holding an armful of cookbooks. He looked up at her. "So what *are* you going to bring, anyway?"

"Bring where?" Heather opened the refrigerator door and took out a bottle of iced mocha and one of apple juice.

"To my sister-in-law's house on Sunday." He made a slow turn. Gleaming eyes pinned her to the fridge.

She handed the juice to Izzy and held the other bottle against the pulse point of her left wrist. "Pork fried rice. And homemade fortune cookies."

"You make fortune cookies?"

"I do."

"Wow." He leaned against the counter. Folding his arms across his chest accentuated well-defined biceps. "I'm impressed. What kind of messages do you put in them?"

"Depends on the crowd. I have a file of quotes. Things like, 'He who laughs last is laughing at you,' and 'A woman who seeks to be equal with men lacks ambition.'"

"Funny." He shook his head. "That last one will get you an in with the women in my family."

She handed him the iced mocha. "They're liberated women, I take it."

"They'd like to think they are. Amanda, my brother Kurt's wife, is a militant. If this were the sixties she'd be burning things left and right."

"I've thought of burning some stuff lately."

Ryan arched one brow. "Want to explain that or shouldn't I ask?"

"Well. . .three days ago I was maid of honor at my ex-boyfriend's wedding. How's that for sad?"

"Wow." He rubbed his chin. "If you ask me, you got the best end of the deal. The bride got the jerk and you got a new dress. And your freedom."

Her mouth opened as if he'd said something deeply profound. Her abdominal muscles began to vibrate in uncontrollable laughter. "She did. And I did. That's very wise."

Broad shoulders shrugged. "I've spent most of my life listening to relationship drama." He tapped his temple. "I know things. I know things like there are worse things than being unattached."

Heather stared into eyes that seemed to invite questions. "Did you learn that from your sisters or from personal experience?"

He grasped the front of his shirt with both hands. "Want to see my scars?" Tipping his head toward his shoulder, he seemed to study her. Oddly, she didn't feel self-conscious under his gaze. His slight nod gave the impression she'd passed some kind of test. "I'm glad my sister invited you to dinner." Smile lines splayed at the corners of his eyes. "Saves me the trouble of working up the courage to ask you myself."

Adventurous. That's what she'd said she wanted to be. She put a bag of rice on a shelf then allowed a slow smile. "Would you have?"

"Probably not."

"Oh." So much for adventurous. She eyed the vegetable crisper and wondered what it would take to compress herself into it.

"I—"

"*Heather!*" The muffled yell came from somewhere above them. Heather turned and stared at the concave top of the box Izzy had perched on just moments ago.

"Not again." Ryan pushed away from the counter. "You're going to have to put a tracking device on that kid." He walked toward the swinging door.

"Let's try this first." Heather pushed on the wall next to the dumbwaiter. The invisible door popped open.

"I can't imagine they had latches and hinges like this when this house was built."

"Iz, are you on the twisty stairs?" Her voice boomeranged back to her as she climbed the wedge-shaped stairs.

"I'm in a bedroom." Izzy's voice still sounded muted and distant. "I can't open the door."

✦

Izzy sat down on the curlicue wires of the skinny metal bed. There wasn't a mattress on it and it made a squeaky noise. While she waited for Heather to open the door, she looked around. The room was smaller than Mom's closet back home. Back in *Chicago*. This was home now, and she was happy about that, or she would be as soon as she figured out how not to get stuck in all the secret hiding places.

Up next to a wall was a thing with shelves and drawers and a mirror. It would be pretty once she wiped all the dust off it. That's all that was in the room. A bed and the dresser thing. On the wall was a metal plate like the one in the kitchen.

Whose bedroom did it used to be? Maybe a girl like her whose wicked stepmother made her hide away so no one knew the girl was way prettier than her stepsisters. Or maybe a girl whose daddy made the room just for her so she could have a special place to read and

69

draw and tell secrets with her friends.

Far away, Heather called her name, and then Ryan. She kind of wanted to stay quiet and let them hunt for her. She wasn't scared anymore like she was when the door closed and she couldn't find a handle to open it. Now she knew they were looking for her and she would get out. It would be fun to make them guess where she was, but yesterday when she thought they were playing a game, she could tell Heather was scared and she didn't want to scare Heather. She'd promised she wouldn't be a problem and she didn't want to break her promise. "I'm up here!"

Light shined through a window too high to look out of. Tiny pieces of dust floated and danced like fairies in the sunshine. The walls were the greenish blue color of her toothpaste and kind of cracked and dirty. She would get somebody to paint it bright, bright yellow so the whole room glowed. And then she would hang pictures—covers of her favorite books in frames. She would put striped sheets and pillows in every color of the rainbow on the bed and get a stool tall enough so she could climb up and look out the little window. And if she moved the dresser thing with the mirror on it, she could make room for another bed so she could have sleepovers.

The dresser thing didn't look too heavy. She got up and squeezed into the corner and pushed. It rolled away from her. It had wheels. She pushed again and then let out a squeal.

Behind the dresser was another door. And this one had a handle.

⚜

Heather walked into the closet of the bedroom in the northwest corner of the house. She could hear Izzy louder in this spot, but there was no sign of her. "It's empty. This is ridiculous."

She heard a click out in the hallway followed by the banging of a door against the wall. Ryan called for Izzy and the same garbled "I'm up here in a bedroom!" answered him.

"Heather, come here."

Fighting the absurd tingle birthed by her name on his lips, she walked across the empty room and met him in the hallway.

"She's up there." He leaned into another door to the hidden stairway and pointed toward the spot where the stairs ended.

"Izzy?" Heather called up the stairs. "Sing a song again. We know where you are now."

Izzy didn't answer.

"Okay, this is legitimately creepy and very déjà vu-ish. That has to be a door."

"Seems to fit the pattern." From behind the wall came the sound of something heavy rolling across the floor. "Isabel?"

"What?"

Ryan's sigh matched hers. "Are you okay, Izzy?"

"Yep. Fine."

When they reached the top, Ryan reached around Heather with both arms. His hands flattened on the wall. He smelled of something spicy and musky that mingled like an intoxicating potion with the scent of old wood. The door clicked and sprung inward.

Izzy stood with her hands clasped behind her back in the middle of a small room. "I bet this is where the people who lived here in the old days hid from pirates who came in on ships in the middle of the night to steal all their money and their jewels. Or maybe the wicked queen wanted to steal all the girls in the city to sew beautiful dresses for her so the dad hid his little girl away in this secret room and the queen never ever knew where she was and her soldiers could never find her so she lived happily ever after."

Heather narrowed her eyes at Izzy. She was acting beyond strange. "You read too much."

"I'm hungry. Can we make popcorn? Or go buy some ice cream maybe?"

"Slow down." Ryan put a hand on her head. "Give us a few minutes to look around. This is a cool room."

"Yeah, but it's just little. There isn't anything to see."

An old iron bed sat against one wall. To Heather's right stood an antique secretary desk. She walked over to it and opened a glass-front door shielding five shelves. "It's beautiful."

"Wouldn't have been fun hauling it up those stairs."

"That's probably why they left it."

Ryan reached out and pressed on a diamond-shaped piece of loose inlay. A small compartment popped open. He jumped back. At the same moment, the door to the room swung shut. "This whole place is booby-trapped." He pushed on the door the way he'd done on the other side, but nothing happened.

"Look." Heather pointed to an almost concealed groove on the edge of the door.

Ryan tried sticking his fingertips in the indentation, but his fingers were too thick. "You try." He didn't move out of her way. She stretched her arm parallel to his. Her fingertips slid into the crescent dip. The door opened effortlessly when she pulled. "Just needed a woman's touch."

He laughed, his breath feathering wisps that had sprung loose from her hair band. "Most things do."

"So. . ." She couldn't imagine what was supposed to follow that intro word. She stepped back as if allowing herself room to give the desk a critical eye. What she needed was room to breathe. The man in the blue uniform sucked the oxygen out of every room he entered.

But not in a bad way.

Stop. Pretend you have a spine. She couldn't let herself think he was interested in anything more than being a nice, helpful Jesus freak. Hadn't he just admitted he wouldn't have invited her to Sunday dinner?

Ryan opened the first of three drawers. "Nothing here." He pulled open the second. A square photograph flipped down, as if it had been plastered to the side of the drawer. He picked it up. "June 1978. Looks like prom." He handed it to Heather.

The whole photograph had an amber hue. A tall, skinny teen in a white tux with a ruffled shirt stood next to a lime green car. Waves of dark brown hair hung to his shoulders. He wore sideburns to his chin. "He's in the backyard next to the garage."

"Hmm." Ryan looked over her shoulder. "He'd be, like, fifty now."

Heather handed it back to him and kneeled in front of the shelves. She slid her hand along each one. On the third one, she felt something way in back. It moved when she extended her fingers. She grasped it and pulled it out. A black cylinder with a small metal clip. Unscrewing one end revealed a gold nib.

Izzy stood with her chin leaning over Heather's forearm. "What is it?"

"It's a pen. Whoever used this had to fill it with ink to write."

"Cool." Izzy shifted from one foot to the other. Her gaze darted toward the door.

Heather felt along the other shelves then put her hand in the hidden compartment Ryan had found. "What do you think this was for?"

"I don't know. Money maybe. It's a girly desk. What would you keep in it?"

"My cell phone."

"Well, there you have it. The turn-of-the-century version of the cell phone was"—he pointed to the fountain pen—"what you have in your hand."

"Didn't they have big phones back then?" Izzy stood on tiptoes trying to see in the compartment. "Like the kind you couldn't fit in your pocket?"

Ryan crouched down to Izzy's level. "How we got the telephone is really interesting. It was invented in 1876, a hundred years after the signing of the Declaration of Independence, by Alexander Graham Bell, but it didn't look anything like the ones you've seen and the people who built this house probably didn't have one until about nineteen—"

Heather cleared her throat.

"What?"

"She's seven."

"So?" He yanked on one of Izzy's wayward curls. "You're interested in how the telephone got invented, aren't you?"

"Nuh-uh."

"Oh."

" 'Cuz I already read about it. Alexander Graham Bell said 'Mr. Watson, come here' and Mr. Watson heard him so that's how the telephone was made."

Ryan looked up and winked at Heather. "Seven going on forty-eight."

Izzy grabbed his hand. "Let's go downstairs."

"Don't you want to see if we can find anything else in here? Isn't it fun to think of somebody sleeping in this room and writing with this pen a long, long time ago? Before there were cell phones or computers or TVs. Maybe even before there were cars or electric lights."

"It's kinda interesting, but kinda boring, too."

Heather opened a panel that folded out into a desk. Bending down, she peered into the opening.

"Find anything?"

"Nope. No pirate treasure map or summons from the queen."

Ryan pressed on the wood panel on the side of the desk. "Could be more hidden compartments." He checked the other side.

Izzy chewed a fingernail and danced on one foot. Heather leaned toward her. "Do you have to go to the bathroom?"

"No. Um. Yes. But I want you guys to come downstairs with me 'cuz what if I walk in the wrong door and I can't figure out how to open it and I get stuck again and maybe it would be another elevator with a bottom that falls out and this time I'd fall and hit my head and it would bleed and—"

"Okay. I get it. We'll come downstairs with you."

With a sigh and a giggle, Izzy ran ahead of them down the curved stairs to the first floor landing.

Izzy sat on the edge of the bathtub that had four feet that looked like claws wrapped around white balls. She waited and thought and then flushed the toilet in case Heather was listening.

She would tell them what she saw. Just as soon as she had a chance to explore. If she told them now it would spoil the adventure and she hadn't ever had a real adventure. Falling down in an elevator didn't count because it happened way too fast and she got scared and Heather was a little bit mad. A real adventure had to be at night with a flashlight and a friend who could keep secrets good.

How was she going to get a friend? She turned the water on and then off and walked out to the kitchen. Ryan was putting ice in a glass. It was funny how it felt like this was how it was supposed to be. A few days ago she was going on a trip she didn't want to go on and now here she was with Heather, and a man she never knew before was taking ice out of her new freezer just like he'd always lived there. It was funny, but nice funny. Was it wrong that she didn't miss her mother? When Mom called at bedtime tonight she'd pretend she was kind of sad.

She walked up to Ryan and said, "Hey." He jumped and she laughed.

"Hey yourself, pipsqueak."

It was a silly name, but she liked it because maybe Ryan didn't call anyone else pipsqueak. "I have a problem."

He crunched down so she could look right into his eyes.

"I need some friends."

"Hmm." He rubbed his chin. "We'll have to do something about that." He looked up at Heather who was wiping off the counter. "How would you and Heather like to go to the beach on Saturday? I'll bring my niece Skylar and maybe a few other kids."

"The beach? Really?" She made her eyes huge and looked at Heather. "Can we?"

☙

The guy wouldn't have invited her to dinner with his family, but going to the beach was okay? Did she not live up to his family's standards? Was he afraid she'd embarrass him? Heather glanced at Ryan then back at Izzy. "I don't know. We'll see."

Izzy's bottom lip protruded. Ryan stood and ruffled her hair. A lopsided grin spread. "We were interrupted at kind of a crucial point a little while ago. You asked if I would have invited you to dinner with my family."

"And you said, 'Probably not.'" The brittleness in her voice was out of proportion. Rejection did that to a person.

The grin morphed symmetrical. "I did, didn't I? And if I leave it like that it might ruin Izzy's chances of making friends."

"It might." The cracks in her voice had already smoothed, but she wasn't going to let him out of an explanation.

"What I was going to say was 'Maybe not *this* Sunday, but definitely the next one."

"Oh." *Why?*

"I need time to explain about my family." He gestured toward the table and they sat down.

"Your family can't be as dysfunctional as mine." *My sister who isn't really my sister but used to be my best friend is, at this very moment, honeymooning with my ex-boyfriend who is now my brother-in-law.*

75

Can you top this, Mr. Tobin?

Izzy wiped a juice mustache off her mouth. "Are they bad people?"

He laughed. "No. Not at all. Actually, we're probably as *un*dysfunctional as a family can be. We're just weird. If you walk in unarmed, you may not make it out alive."

"Weird as in a hundred cats?"

Ryan leaned against the back of the chair and stretched his legs out, crossing them at the ankles. "Weird as in they will want your résumé and references if you ever hope to see me again." His cheeks turned ruddy. "Not that that's the reason you were invited, but if there were a chance you. . .we. . ." His hand rose to his face and melting hazel eyes peered out between splayed fingers.

"And if there were a chance I wanted to see you again, how would I have to be armed in order to survive your weird family?"

His hand lowered. His shoulders visibly relaxed. "You'd need a nine-millimeter sense of humor and skin as tough as a Kevlar vest."

She laughed. "After what I've been through in the past year, that is no problem. No problem at all."

👑

January 3, 1912

"It's so much bigger up close."

Maggie stared up at a plume of smoke from the tallest smokestack she'd ever seen. Next to it stood a water tower with a cone-shaped top. The complex reminded her too much of the state prison at Waupun. Not something to dwell on today. Across the front seat of the Mitchell Baby Six, she smiled at the girl she was supposed to hate. "The whole place is so much larger than it appears from the street."

Gripping the steering wheel with hands gloved in supple-looking gray leather, Emma Rose Mitchell smiled back. "Seventy-five acres." The whistle and chug of a train coming to a stop less than a block away almost covered her words. "It's hard to explain the pride I feel about this place. Almost like I built it myself." She drove slowly past rows of long brick buildings. "Twenty-five hundred people on the payroll."

76

Positioning her arm over a worn-smooth spot on the pocket of her coat, Maggie shook her head. She couldn't envision that many people all in one place. "How many cars do they. . .*you* produce?"

"Seventy-four cars a day right now, and we ship all over. The cars you'll see being built today could end up on the other side of the world. Cuba, Brazil, Guatemala, Mexico, Chile, Canada, Hawaii, Belgium, Italy, Portugal. . ." Her list dissolved in easy laughter.

"Makes you want to hide in one and make the trip with it." Maggie's face colored. What an unsophisticated thing to say.

"I know! I'd love to see our cars in all those places and meet the people who own them. Have you traveled, Maggie?"

Have you been out of Racine, Maggie? That would be the real question. "No. Not yet, but it is a dream of mine. Every night I sit in my little garret and read of faraway places." Her cheeks suddenly blazed. She had just made herself sound like the poor stepdaughter waiting in the attic for her fairy godmother.

"I do hope you have the opportunity. Don't you love that word—*opportunity?*" Emma tipped her head to one side. "Is your room in the turret?"

"I live between the walls, ma'am," Magdalena answered. *"I tiptoe between the floors and try to make myself very, very invisible."*

Maggie nodded, feeling the gap between their worlds widen. An ocean instead of the front seat of an automobile.

"I remember when the Hamiltons' house was being built. I was probably five or six and I remember dreaming about living in that tower."

Was it well heated in the winter of your dreams? Did the window open to let in cool breezes and the sound of birds in summer? Did you have a rug under your little-girl feet and pictures on the wall? Maggie smiled as genuinely as she could as she fought the discontented voices in her head. She had a bed and clothes and food and she was wrong to complain.

Emma gestured toward a field, barren except for a road that ran in a large circle. "That's the testing track. Uncle Henry let me drive new cars on it a few times. Such fun. As I was saying, don't you love that word—*opportunity?* That's what we're going to open up by what we're doing. I'm so excited I can hardly sleep lately. Ever since I came back from Wellesley I've felt like a racehorse at a starting gate, just waiting for God to give me something to do. The very moment you brought up the idea of visiting factories and offering tutoring it was like the heavens opened up and the angels sang, 'This is your mission, Emma Rose.'" Once again, laughter filled the car. "I suppose that sounds just plain silly."

"No. Not silly at all. I've often felt the very same feeling of waiting for God to tell me what's next." *Ever since my mother died and my father was arrested.* Their starting points were so very different, but their hearts so much alike. It was impossible to dislike this woman even though she'd wanted to, and even though, before the end of the day, she would have to fulfill her promise to inquire of Miss Emma Rose Hamilton whether or not she would be flattered by an invitation to dinner at the Hamilton residence for the sole purpose of becoming more acquainted with their son.

Emma pulled to a stop in front of a three-story brick building. "I hope this doesn't bore you. I just thought we needed something to compare the others to. Oh, that sounds so pompous, doesn't it? But our family and the Lewises have strived so hard to make this company the safest and the best work environment and I'm sure what we'll encounter will be woefully short of the standards used here—except for Hamilton Lock and Latch, of course." She winked. "Anyway, this tour will show you what's possible." One gray-clad fingertip touched her chin. "Of course, there are no women employed here. I once asked my uncle if working conditions would be less. . . agreeable if Mitchell-Lewis employed women instead of men."

"And what was his reply?"

Maggie picked up her reticule. "He didn't answer. He is a good man, and I believe my question deeply offended him."

Over the next two hours they walked through five of the buildings. Maggie's feet screamed for relief. She spent her days on her feet, but not in her Sunday shoes. Her brain overflowed with facts on crankcases, cylinders, piston rings, clutches, and wheels. She'd visited a warehouse that stored half a million tires and she'd seen enough milling, drilling, grinding, boring, and facing off to last a lifetime. She'd commented over and over on the cleanliness of the concrete floors and the safety measures enforced in every department. They had spoken to men in overalls and others in suspenders and bowler hats or wool caps, all remarkably clean considering the work they were doing. Each had explained his job with obvious pride.

Though she wouldn't admit it to Emma, the only part that truly held her interest was the building where the newly painted chassis rolled in and the actual assembly began. The polishing process fascinated her, as did the upholstering. Now they stood on the Chicago, Milwaukee, and St. Paul Railway loading platform. The wind whipped their hats as they watched men in white overalls fill railroad cars with shiny new Mitchell automobiles—some on the first leg of journeys that would lead, as Emma had said, "to the other side of the world."

Emma pressed her hand to the crown of her felt hat as they walked back to the office building where they'd started their tour. "I keep thinking of what you said about hiding in one of the cars. What country would you want to visit first, Maggie?"

"Denmark. My mother was born there. I grew up hearing stories of her hometown. I'm sure life was much harder than she described it, but still it sounds so peaceful."

"Well, my dear, we're just going to have to find you a nice, rich man with a bit of wanderlust."

Maggie swallowed hard. She'd already found all that, but it wasn't hers to keep.

Emma opened a door at the back of the building and let Maggie walk through.

"Thank you." She reminded herself to square her shoulders and to glide with the carriage of a woman who had a right to walk through a door held open by Emma Rose Mitchell.

"Wait." Emma's boots almost skidded on the marble floor. She stopped beneath a light fixture with three milk glass globes suspended from a long cord. "What about Richard Hamilton? He's all of that—wealthy and adventurous—and surely you couldn't have worked for the Hamiltons all this time without a spark of interest." Emma's gloved hands clapped with the muffled sound of rabbit feet on new-fallen snow.

Magdalena suddenly felt as if her fur were much too tight. Her best friend would not listen. Could she trust this new one? Could she talk of

Leo Tabbycat and his promise to fight for her?

Maggie tittered, a hollow-sounding laugh, and shook her head. "Richard needs a woman from a good family. Someone who is respected in the commun—"

"Oh, posh. You don't really believe such an outdated notion, do you? What Richard needs is what every man needs—a woman to love who loves him back. Her background, *and* her parents, are of no consequence. I don't know him well, but I think you would be perfect."

"Emma, Richard's mother asked me—"

"Richard's mother is also of no consequence." She clapped again. "I'm going to have a dinner party, and you are going to be there. And so is he."

"Emma." The temptation to hold her peace was strong, but she could not return home without an answer. "Mrs. Hamilton would like to hold a dinner party and invite *you*—for the same reason you are inviting me. . .to get to know her son."

"Me? And Richard Hamilton?" Emma stopped walking. Her brow furrowed in what seemed to be a combination of surprise and serious consideration of the idea. And then she laughed. "Tell her I am flattered. And honored. And then tell her to open her eyes and see that there is someone just right for her son under her very nose." Her gaze ran quickly along Maggie's coat. "Perfect. My grandmother sent me a dress for Christmas that I absolutely can't breathe in. I think it will fit you perfectly."

But. . . Trailing unspoken objections in her wake, Maggie Parker walked down the marble-tiled hall, chatting with the daughter of a millionaire and envisioning life on the street.

As the Little Match Girl.

CHAPTER 7

*D*addy!"

Stephannie fought the arms muscling her into the corridor. The high-pitched hum of the heart monitor screamed in her ears. "I was just asking him a question and he grabbed his chest and the monitor stopped—"

"We're doing everything we can, Miss Lansing. Have a seat and someone will be out to talk to you as soon as we know." The woman guided her into a chair, turned, and strode away.

As soon as we know. She stood and walked back to the door. Her arms folded across the ache in her belly. *Oh God, please. Please don't let him die. Please give me a chance to show him I can change, to show him he can be proud of me.* She slumped against the wall. Her father had survived beyond the critical forty-eight hours. The doctors had thought he was out of the woods.

Her question had done this. She'd pretended she was just making conversation. *Were you ever serious about anyone before you met Mom?* That was all she'd said. And he'd started to answer. *"There were a couple of—"* And the *bleep-bleep* stopped.

She covered her ears, but the hum of the flatline had imprinted on her brain and she couldn't make it stop.

God, I know You don't know me, but You have to believe me. I can change. I can be the daughter he wants me to be. I can stop— A sob doubled her and she sank to the floor. *He doesn't need to find another daughter. I can still be his princess. I'll show him, I'll show You, if You just let him live. He's the only one who really loves me.*

As she sat, huddled and alone on the stark white floor, she tried to make the words a lie. Her father was not the only one. Andrew loved her. In spite of what she'd done. In spite of who she was.

He did.

☙

Another crisis.

Andrew paced Parker's office, the phone in his hand still hot from pressing it to his ear to hear Stephannie through her sobs.

"Andrew." Dianna Lansing stood in the doorway of her ex-husband's office, her tan suit rumpled. The pallor of her face surprised him. "Did you hear?"

"Yes." Should he say he was sorry? Was *she?*—considering what she stood to gain if Parker did not survive? "He's a fighter."

A short burst of air through her nose followed a ghost of a smile. "He used to be."

Andrew nodded, reading layers in her response. Parker Lansing had changed in the past year. "His edges may have softened, but he hasn't lost his strength."

"I hope you're right." Her voice reflected none of the ever-present tension between them.

"I'm heading to the hospital." *Are you?* Should he offer to give her a ride?

"You don't need to do that. He's in ICU."

"I know." He straightened his shoulders to match hers. "Stephannie asked me to come."

Color returned to her face. "You've talked to her?"

How else would she have asked me? He clasped his hands behind his back, sandwiching his phone between them, and simply stared.

"Andrew. This isn't wise."

For me, or for you? Or could it be she was thinking of her daughter for once? In that case, he'd have to agree with her. "Stephannie needs someone to lean on right now." *Are you offering?*

Dianna tucked straight blond hair behind her ear. A tastefully small pearl caught the light. "She'll only hurt you again, Andrew. She can't seem to help it, can she?" She reached out and patted the door frame twice and turned away.

As her footsteps disappeared, Andrew gaped at the empty doorway.

Was it possible that all this time she'd been trying to protect him? With a glance at the uncluttered surface of his boss's desk, he walked out and down the hall in the opposite direction of the fading footfalls.

⚜

The doctor walked away. Stephannie felt the rush of Andrew's sigh on her arm. "That's good news."

She studied Andrew's hands, enclosing hers. Large, strong, capable. He'd hardly left her side for two days. "But they said that before. They said he was going to be fine and then he almost wasn't. I c—can't. . ."

"Yes, you can. All the strength you need is inside you, Steph." The plastic waiting room chair groaned as he leaned toward her and brushed a kiss across her forehead. "Let's take one day at a time. Can I get you anything?"

"No. I'm fine." She searched his face for any trace of leftover anger. It made no sense that he'd forgiven her so quickly.

A month ago they'd fought over his work schedule and his lack of time for her. That was nothing new. But this time she'd decided to teach him a lesson. So she'd left the country. Because that's what Stephannie Lansing did. She ran when the world ganged up on her.

"You were starting to say something before the doctor came in." He opened the warm cocoon of his hands.

"Let's take a walk. Outside. I don't want anyone to hear."

Andrew smiled as he pulled her to her feet. "Sounds mysterious."

"That's exactly what it is."

They rode the elevator in silence. Stephannie waited until they'd turned the corner before showing him what she'd forwarded from her father's phone.

" 'I found your daughter.' Weird. It has to be somebody trying to scare money out of him. That ploy's as old as the earth. Someone he knew before he met your mom is hard up for cash and plays the paternity card."

Stephannie ran her fingers through her hair. "Why hasn't she asked for money? There was only that one message."

"Your dad didn't answer so she gave up. She—or he—read in the papers that he's hospitalized and that put an end to it."

She slowed her steps, staring up at him. "I've tried telling myself that, but the way it was worded doesn't fit. It sounds like my father was looking for her and this person found her."

He enlarged the face of the dark-haired woman. "Do you think she looks like your dad?"

"I don't know. His hair used to be dark like that." She took a shaky breath. "My dad had girlfriends before my mom. What if he got one of them pregnant and now he wants to see his daughter? Or what if"—in spite of the warmth in the air, she shivered—"what if it was my mom who gave birth to her?" She swallowed hard as bile scalded her throat. "Years ago, I was maybe twelve, I heard my mother talking to a friend. She said she'd gotten pregnant before they were married. 'Parker paid for everything,' she said. I always assumed she meant he paid for an abortion. What if she meant he paid for the birth?"

She pressed her hand to her temple. "It's making me crazy." Her breath shuddered. "I know it sounds like the spoiled rich girl doesn't want to share her daddy's fortune, but that's not it. I just want a chance with him."

"A chance?" Confusion coated Andrew's voice.

"I don't like who I am." A passing car sucked her words under its chrome-centered wheels. "I don't want to be the person everyone expects me to be. Especially my dad. I don't want to let him down anymore."

"He still loves you." Andrew's arm slid around her shoulder.

"I know. I don't know why, but I know he does. But I don't want him to be embarrassed about me anymore. I want my father to be proud of me." She sounded like a five-year-old. Had there always been a whine in her voice? "I want to change."

"And you don't want someone else stealing your place in your father's life."

Her breath caught—an aftershock from days of crying. She nodded against Andrew's chest.

"Then we need to figure it out." Andrew tightened his arm around her. "I'll find out who she is and if she's any threat."

"How?"

He patted her arm. "Just leave it to me."

"You need a break."

Andrew held out his hand to Stephannie and lifted her from the chair next to her father's bed. Seventy-two hours had passed without another cardiac event. All reports were "cautiously optimistic."

The *cautious* part scared Andrew. Sitting here, listening to beeps, watching the numbers morph, he'd had time to envision the worst. He wasn't the kind who could sit back and wait for unknowns. He hadn't gotten where he was by letting chance take its course. "Go down and get something to eat. I'll stay—"

"Steph? Is this a good time?" A man in khaki pants and a light blue shirt walked in. He had a black book tucked in his hand.

Andrew cursed the timing as he stood and held out his hand. "Pastor Dave."

The middle-aged man shook his hand then gave Stephannie a quick hug. "How is he? Any change?"

"The arrhythmia seems to be under control." Stephannie offered a weak smile. "They don't think the damage is as extensive as it looked at first."

"Good. That's so good. And how are you doing?"

"Okay. Scared." She gestured toward the seat Andrew had just occupied.

"Understandable." The man walked to the bedside and slid his hand over Parker's. "Think I'll just stand here for a minute." He closed his eyes.

Andrew sat on the window ledge.

"Hey, friend." The pastor ran fingertips under his eyelashes. "We were supposed to have breakfast together this morning, you know. You left me with a cliff-hanger the last time we talked and I was looking forward to hearing the rest of the story."

Parker's eyelids fluttered then opened. A smile flickered in the gaunt face. "She's got my—" His eyes closed.

Andrew stepped to the end of the bed, ears straining.

Pastor Dave patted the pale hand. "Stephannie and Andrew are here keeping you company. You're surrounded by people who care about you."

A comforting statement? Or a warning? *She's got my. . .* Eyes? Hair color? Andrew touched Parker's ankle. "What's this cliff-hanger all about? Always love a good story." His voice rang as artificial as a car salesman's.

The pastor smiled. "Parker and I are accountability partners." He continued to pat the hand that sported a hospital bracelet. "That allows us some secrets, doesn't it, Parker?"

Secrets. Like the name of the woman Stephannie might have to split her inheritance with. Andrew glanced at the narrow closet. Behind the door was a bag containing the clothes Parker wore when he came into the hospital. Clothes, shoes—and a phone. "Pastor, I was just trying to talk Steph into going down to the cafeteria. Maybe she'll eat something if you go with her."

"I'd love to accompany you, Miss Lansing." He held out his arm.

"But I'm not—"

"Hunger has nothing to do with it. Your body needs sustenance and so does your soul." He shot a smile at Andrew. "A little clerical levity there."

Andrew laughed. "Thank you for taking her."

"My pleasure." Pastor Dave fixed Stephannie's hand to his arm and they walked through the doorway.

Leaving Andrew alone with Parker and his phone.

He opened the closet, reached to the back of the top shelf, and found it. It didn't take long to find the text from a number with a 312 area code. Cook County. Was the sender someone he knew? He copied the number to his own phone.

Andrew stared at the picture, closer than he'd dared with Stephannie on his arm. The woman was gorgeous. Late twenties, maybe. Four or five years older than Stephannie, he'd guess. Was the little girl hers? He looked over at the man in the bed who seemed to have aged at least a decade. It wasn't hard to envision Parker as a gift-bearing overindulgent grandfather. She'd be one lucky little girl.

Cha-ching. The sound of yet more of Stephannie's future disappearing chimed in his ears.

Had Parker had any contact with the person who made the call since this text? He had no way of knowing.

Was it worth the risk?

Yes. He tapped his thumbs to the keys. FEELING STRONGER. DOCTORS ARE OPTIMISTIC. DO YOU HAVE A NAME AND ADDRESS FOR THE GIRL?

He silenced Parker's phone, slipped it in his pocket, and walked to the window. Less than a minute later, the phone vibrated.

THANK GOD FOR GOOD NEWS. ONLY HAVE AN ADDRESS.

Andrew copied the address in the fourteen-hundred block of Main Street in Racine, Wisconsin, and put the phone away.

He had enough information to warrant a trip to Wisconsin. A solo trip.

Hadn't he promised Parker's secretary he'd take care of everything?

CHAPTER 8

I owe you one, Amanda."

Ryan waved at what remained of his sister-in-law as ten busy hands, including his brother's, covered her with sand. In obedience to Amanda's orders to "Chill with the brunette," he kicked off his sandals. With Heather distracted by the burial ritual on the beach, he scrambled to spread out his embarrassing red-and-blue beach towel before she turned around. Or so he'd thought until the grin altered her profile.

"Spider-Man?" Bare feet still planted in the sand, she swiveled at the waist. Her oversize shirt skimmed tanned thighs.

"It was a gift from my family."

Turning her back to the breeze, she flicked her solid school bus-yellow towel. It billowed and landed with barely a ripple in the terry cloth. "Your family who thinks you're a superhero, right?"

Peripheral vision and an awareness heightened by her nearness let him know she'd removed the shirt and was lying down.

He shifted to his side and leaned on his elbow, knowing immediately that move was a mistake. He'd mirrored her posture, landing no more than eighteen inches from deliciously curved, full lips. Tantalizing, but awkward. *Go with it, Tobin. Act natural. Breathe.* Sunglasses could hide a lot, and a humid eighty-five degrees could be blamed for the excess sweat. He cleared his throat. "If I tell you the truth you'll laugh. If I don't, you'll hear it anyway."

"Go on." Gray lenses bracketed by half circles of faux diamonds hid her eyes.

"When I was four I refused to answer to anything other than Spidey." He brushed a smattering of sand from the inside of her elbow. "It stuck."

"It fits. You were Izzy's superhero." She lolled onto her back. "And mine."

The view from here was even more awkward. And off the charts on tantalizing. Her two-piece deep blue suit against the orangey-yellow blanket made him think of a Butterfingers wrapper. Food analogies were not a good idea at a time like this. Again, he copied her pose, finding relief in the blank canvas of a clear sky that gave his retinas a rest from too much, too close tanned skin. A few clouds would have helped—would have prompted his imagination to conjure fluffy animals instead of chocolate-covered flaky-caramel-peanut-butter candy melting in the sun.

"That's about as close as I've ever come to anything genuinely heroic." Not that he hadn't tried. Once. He blinked away the thought, exchanging it for something that didn't come with regret. "Sooner or later my brothers will tell you about a legendary tantrum I had when I was three. I threw up on my red cape and my mother committed the unforgiveable sin of washing it. Supposedly I hammered the washing machine screaming, 'Take it out! I have to save the world!'"

Her laughter mingled with the scent of coconut rising from warming skin. "I bet you still have the cape."

"I wish." He gave an exaggerated sniff. "My mom found it in a box in their basement a few years ago. The mice had gotten ahold of it and..." Another fake sniff. "I can't talk about it. My brothers tried for years to convince me Spider-Man doesn't even have a cape, but I knew the truth." He dabbed at nonexistent tears. Risking blindness, he turned toward her and was rewarded with a deeply sympathetic smile.

"I'm so sorry." She stretched one arm heavenward. Without the shield of her arm, he noticed a mole about two inches north and slightly east of her navel. Now he knew why they called those beauty marks. "Guys need that, don't they?" Her palm turned up as if waiting for the sun to drop into it.

"Need what?" He ripped his thoughts away from the beauty mark. "Red capes?"

"The hero thing. The whole damsel-in-distress concept was kind of lost on me until a week ago."

"Does this have something to do with the wedding you were in?"

"Very perceptive."

His gut told him not to jump in, to wait out her answer. A gull squawked overhead then swooped out of sight. Children's giggles formed a counter rhythm to the lapping waves.

"I was dating—or thought I was dating—the boy next door."

"Where was that?"

"Manhattan."

"You seem too earthy for a New York City girl."

"Manhattan, Kansas."

"Ah."

"Our farms bordered each other. I used to beat him in dirt bike races and then we graduated to Jeeps and I still won." She folded her arms across her middle. "All those years, while Zach and I slid around in the mud, my fake twin sister stood by in little flowered dresses. I should have seen what was happening in sixth grade when Zach splashed mud on her and she cried. He gave up his Chiefs bandanna to help her clean up and picked bachelor's buttons for her." Again, she fell silent. He chanced a look and noticed coconut oiled abs quivering. She was laughing. "That's pitiful, isn't it?" Her sun-cupping hand lowered to cover a grin. "Like you really want to know my whole pathetic life history."

Ryan turned back onto his elbow and fixed his sights on the curve of her chin. "Oh, I do. But you have to clear up something first. What do you mean by *fake* twin? Your sister wanted to be just like you?"

"No. Our mom dressed us alike." She turned her head toward him. "My sister is three months younger than I am."

"Huh? Oh. *Oh.*" He felt his brow furrowing with the effort of finding an explanation. "I'm guessing you had different mothers—not the same mother in labor for ninety days."

She laughed and he managed not to look at her abs. "Different mothers *and* fathers."

"Okay, I give. I confess to cluelessness. Wait. She was adopted."

"*I* was adopted." She turned back to the sky. "When Jen, my sister, was three, my mom found out she couldn't have any more kids. They didn't want her growing up spoiled rotten"—the laugh that followed could only be described as rueful—"so they went in search of a playmate for her. They ended up with me."

"So you weren't a baby when you were adopted?"

"No." Her voice seemed suddenly flat. "I was four."

With her eyes shaded, he remained clueless about her emotions. "Was that hard?"

"Only when every single person I met mentioned how I didn't look anything like my petite, blond sister."

"Why would you want to be petite and blond when you could be. . .you?" He was halfway into the thought before realizing he'd voiced it out loud. "You're a beautiful woman, Heather, and even covered with mud you'd be—"

A shadow stretched across them. Sand skittered onto Ryan's legs. "Excuse me." A lifeguard-looking guy stood over them. Bare-chested, gold chain hanging on a hairy chest, sunglasses he'd probably dropped two hundred dollars for. Teeth that had to have been professionally bleached gleamed at them. He held up a red, white, and blue can as if toasting. "Sorry to bother you. I forgot ice and noticed you had a cooler. I was wondering—"

"Of course." Heather rose like a charmed snake and stretched toward the cooler. She filled a cup with ice and handed it to the man.

"Thank you." He took a long drink and stared out at the lake. "I haven't been to Racine since I was a kid. Beautiful lakefront."

"Where are you from?"

"I hail from Indiana. How about you two? Do you. . ."

Whitened teeth and a perfectly trimmed soul patch blurred as he chattered on in a voice made for radio. Ryan sat up and brushed the sand off his legs. It was then he noticed something strange.

A tag—a manufacturer-applied row of *L*s on a clear, removable strip—on the back of the man's right thigh. He might look like a lifeguard, but it was mid-July and those trunks had never seen water.

Had she asked the guy to sit? She couldn't remember, but she wasn't complaining. A week ago, fighting tears as she flew across Missouri and Illinois, she couldn't have envisioned sitting on a beach flanked by two hunky bookends.

They weren't exactly a matched set. She only had to turn her head to the left to look into Ryan's eyes. If she stood next to the guy on her right it would probably take a couple of minutes to crawl up the crags of a dimpled chin, across a bridge of white framed by manly shaped lips, up a Romanesque nose, sneak behind one-way glasses to what she could only imagine as pools of glacial blue—

Stop! With a mental slap to her cheek, she ripped her focus off the man and onto the shore. Izzy squatted frog-like next to Skylar, Ryan's eight-year-old niece. The two dug and tossed sand like a scoop conveyor.

"Which one is yours?"

She stared at the man. "Mine?"

"Which kid is yours?"

"Oh. None of them. I'm just—"

Ryan's hand on her bare knee stopped her. "They're my brother's kids." The pressure from his fingers increased until it actually hurt. She glared at him. What she saw on his face startled, irritated, and warmed her all at the same time.

The guy was jealous.

Flattering as that was, he had no right to act like he owned her. Or to touch her knee. She straightened her leg and he let go. She smiled at the man in the Oakley shades and held out her hand. "I'm Heather." She nodded toward the tense-as-steel-girders man on her left. "This is Ryan."

"Mike." The man took her hand for only a moment, but somehow managed to relay the impression he'd like to linger. Reaching across her belly, he shook Ryan's hand.

Ryan seemed to have responded without an attempt to crush the guy's knuckles. "So"—Ryan leaned over her, blocking the sun— "what brings you to Racine?"

"It was just a good day for a ride with the top down, you know? Nice to get away from the city and the corporate stress. What about you two? What do you do with the rest of your week?"

"I'm in security systems."

Go, Spider-Man! What was it with guys that they couldn't just come right out and admit what they did? What was wrong with, "I'm a security guard"? She'd seen this phenomenon with Zach way too many times. Never once did he simply say, "I farm." Instead, it was always a long, drawn-out "Got my degree in agribusiness management and then decided to branch out into blah-blah-blah. . ." *Men.*

"And what about you, Heather?" Mike turned a dazzling smile her way and slowly lowered the Oakleys.

Her pulse flip-flopped. A muscle twitched in her cheek. Those eyes. He looked like some actor. Who was it? Someone she'd seen in enough movies to feel like his face was familiar, like someone she'd once met or seen in person. Just as she started closing in on it, he raised his glasses. Like a force field. She lost all context of the gorgeous eyes, except for the lingering sense that she hadn't liked the characters he'd played.

And what about you, Heather? The question still hung, unanswered. *I'm a certified doormat.* "I'm taking a sabbatical at the moment to work on a business plan. I have my master's in—"

"Sand castle building." Ryan jumped up, grabbing her hand on his ascent. "And it appears"—he yanked her arm—"her expertise is needed at the building site."

He shot her a look she couldn't decipher then grabbed their towels and the handle of the cooler with his free hand. "Nice to meet you, Mike. Have a nice drive home."

Not knowing if she should thank him for rescuing her from some unseen danger or slap him and run, she stumbled behind him to the water.

Izzy squinted her eyes so they looked all the way closed but really weren't as Ryan carried her up to her room. She was too old for naps, but if they knew she was awake, they'd stop talking. Again.

Heather and Ryan hadn't talked on the way home until they thought she was asleep. And then she could tell Heather was really mad.

"It is not ridiculous." Ryan laid her down and kissed her forehead. That was weird. But nice. It was like having a dad. Would Ryan get mad if she pretended he was her dad? Maybe she just wouldn't tell him.

Heather pulled the covers up. "It *is* ridiculous." She kissed the top of Izzy's head. "Haven't you ever forgotten to pull a tag off something you just bought?"

"That's not the point. There was a sticker on the bottom of his sandals, too. A *white* sticker."

"So he bought his trunks and sandals at the same time."

"In July? Who buys that stuff in July?"

"Rich people." Heather snapped off the light.

Izzy tried not to squirm while she waited for the door to shut, but it was hard to pretend sleeping when there was sand between your toes and you were waiting to start an adventure.

"Did you see how tan he was? That's a guy who's been in the sun all summer and it doesn't make sense he'd need both things at the same time." Izzy heard someone touching the door handle. She froze like a lying-down statue and waited. "You're absolutely sure he wasn't the guy with the camera?"

"Absolutely sure. Camera guy was old enough to be my father and he was short and bald and round and—"

"I get it. He was everything tall, dark, and cocky wasn't. But they could still be working togeth—"

The door closed. Izzy counted to twenty then jumped out of bed.

Finally. The chance she'd been waiting for. As quietly as she could, she hunted through a box of stuff from her dresser in Chicago until she found her Dora the Explorer flashlight. She'd told Mom to give it to the Goodwill children because she was too old for Dora, but now she was glad she still had it.

'Cuz she just might need it when she went on her adventure.

⚜

He'd come on too strong. Made the boyfriend mad.

Andrew grabbed the blue-and-gold bag and got out of the car.

He hadn't even gotten the new trunks wet. What a waste of time. Sitting outside the house, watching the clock change. Waiting for over an hour until a little brown car backed out of the garage. He'd followed them to the beach, watched them playing in the sand, then sped off to the yacht club gift shop.

The beep of the remote lock echoed off the concrete walls of the parking garage.

The ride home was fast, but without the exhilaration he'd felt on the way north. He hadn't learned a thing. No, that wasn't exactly true. He knew her name was Heather and she had an overprotective boyfriend, but no ring on her finger. And he'd seen something in the girl's eyes that spun thoughts of his next step.

It happened the moment he'd lowered his sunglasses. A split second of heat. Oh, she'd compensated quickly, but like a high-speed lens, he'd captured the change in her, and he sure hadn't missed her irritation when the boyfriend's hand laid claim on her knee. The look she'd thrown over her shoulder as she followed the jealous creep had almost made him want to stay. And wait.

He didn't mind waiting for some things.

⚜

January 10, 1912

In spite of her nervousness, Maggie couldn't help but smile as she walked a step ahead of Emma into the M. M. Secor Trunk Company on Lake Avenue, clutching a stack of books to her chest. She'd just finished reenacting Mrs. Hamilton's shock when Maggie had told her, over breakfast, that the woman who would be perfect for her son had respectfully declined the opportunity to become better acquainted with him.

Emma giggled. "She actually swooned?"

"Very nearly. I had the cupboard open, ready to grab the smelling salts," Maggie whispered.

A gray-haired man approached, putting a damper on their laughter. "Miss Mitchell, how good to see you." He spoke with a strong German accent.

"And you, Mr. Baumann. Let me introduce you to Maggie

Parker. This tutoring opportunity was all her idea."

"Miss Parker." The man extended a hand. "Thank you for your concern for the youth of our fair city. You'll find our work environment quite revolutionary, and if we can offer a few minutes of education to our people, all the better. Four of them should be gathering as we speak." He pulled out his pocket watch. "We'll give you ten minutes with them and then bring in another group."

Ten minutes? Maggie exchanged glances with Emma. What knowledge could they possibly impart in ten minutes? "Thank you, sir."

"Follow me." He led them through a front office, down a hallway lined with more offices, and into a vast open room that smelled of leather and varnish. The sound of saws and hammers bounced off the high ceiling.

Maggie scanned the area, looking, as Emma had instructed her, toward the farthest corners. Emma was right. The floor within forty feet of where they stood appeared well-swept. Toward the corners and far wall, pieces of leather and chunks of wood littered the floor. Still, it appeared relatively clean. They followed Mr. Baumann to a rough-hewn table under a stairway leading to a loft crowded with piles of lumber. Two boys who couldn't possibly be fourteen yet sat on one bench. Across from them sat a girl of no more than twelve and a young woman in her late teens or early twenties. Both wore scarves covering long, single braids. Poorly fitted gray aprons covered skirts and blouses.

Emma nodded to Mr. Baumann. "Thank you for allowing us this time. I'm sure Mr. Secor would have approved."

"Those are kind words, ma'am. It was one year ago on the fifth of January that he passed. We are all keenly aware of his absence."

"You honor him with this opportunity for his employees."

Maggie listened and took notes. So this was how it was done. All this flattery just to be granted the "opportunity" to teach children who ought still be in school.

Mr. Baumann stepped to the table and nodded to his young employees. "Miss Mitchell here, whose family is well known and respected in the community, has graciously volunteered to teach you. She and her assistant, Miss Parker, are giving of their time and I expect nothing short of exemplary conduct from you. Understood?"

Magdalena felt suddenly smaller than small. She'd hoped that out here, away from the big house, she would be seen as something more than just a mouse. Or an assistant.

Four heads nodded.

"Then I'll take my leave. Thank you, again, ladies."

Emma turned to Maggie with one eyebrow raised. Maggie cleared her throat. Jitters tumbled in her stomach like bits of carrot roiling in a stew. As she opened the book on the top of her stack, she noticed the hands of the girl closest to her. Strips of dirty, blood-tinged cloth wrapped several fingers. The sight banished every trace of nervousness. It was as if she suddenly knew this girl. As if she *were* this girl.

"Let's start with you. Tell us your name and how old you are."

"Kiersten, ma'am. I'm f–fourteen."

In quick order, the others followed. Trina said she was eighteen. Holleb and Cerek both claimed to be fifteen.

Believing only one of them, Maggie began. "It's so nice to meet all of you. We're going to start with some very basic things today." She laid a copy of *McGuffey's First Eclectic Reader* in front of each, opened to page eight.

Holleb raised a tentative hand. "I don't mean to seem ungrateful"—his accent thick, he metered out words with precision—"but I lose job at *schlossfabrik* because I have book like this in my coat and I try to teach myself to read. It is against laws of factory and they fire me."

"*What?*" Emma's question shadowed hers.

Maggie hugged an open book against her blouse. "Why would they say such a thing? If you can read you are an asset—a help—to the company."

The boy shook his head. "If I can read I will know they are unfair. When they charge too much or do not pay enough. And then we will cause trouble."

"That's—" Maggie bit back the word. "Where did you say you worked?"

Holleb shrugged. "I work at the lo—" He jerked suddenly then sat up straight. "*Es ist nicht wichtig.*" He sucked his lips in. "It is not important."

Maggie looked down at Cerek's foot, still swinging from its impact with Holleb's shin.

Oh yes, it is important. She had seen the word *schloss* on papers on Mr. Hamilton's desk. She would remember the word *schlossfabrik*. She would ask Mr. Hamilton what it meant. And then *she* would cause trouble for whoever scarred this boy's mind with fear.

⚜

Maggie had thought of every excuse not to attend Epworth League tonight, but had lost the battle to the tug of the Spirit. Now, sitting in the basement of the Methodist church and listening to Reverend Leek read the very words of Jesus, she knew why she was here. " '. . . Inasmuch as ye have done it unto one of the least of these my brethren, ye have done it unto me.' "

I was in prison, and ye came unto me. Like sugar on the glazed walnuts she'd made yesterday, the message clung to her.

Reverend Leek asked what the words meant to them as present-day followers of Jesus. A girl a bit older than Maggie raised her hand. "Well, the missionary society collects clothes to send to missionaries to give to people in poor countries. We should give things we don't wear anymore to them instead of throwing them away."

The chatter that followed was much of the same.

Maggie wrapped her fingers around her pocket watch. "I wonder if, along with the good causes we've mentioned, we aren't all called to reach out to needy people right here in our city."

Reverend Leek nodded. "Well spoken, Miss Parker. It is what we do when we pack boxes of food for the needy every Christmas."

That's merely a token. "I've recently been visiting several factories in the area, offering to tutor the chil—the young men and women in their employ." She went on to explain the vision.

The two girls across from her sat with polite smiles and hands folded on open Bibles like cloth dolls cut from the same pattern. The boy next to Reverend Leek, son of a church trustee, made a sweep with his eyes. "And will you be including Hamilton Lock and Latch in your mission?"

Maggie felt her chin jar back instinctively. "There is no one

98

under seventeen employed at the Hamilton Company."

The boy made another full circuit with his eyes. "Maybe you should—"

"Tell us more about your project," Reverend Leek cut in.

"I've been making these visits with Emma Rose Mitchell. I'm sure most of you know who she is."

The name acted like a magic wand sprinkling wake-up dust on the eyelids of every person in the circle. Even the minister straightened to attention in his straight-backed chair. "This sounds like something the church would very much like to get involved with."

☙❧

Exhaustion threatened to overtake her by the time she finished dishes that night. After packing Mr. Hamilton's valise for his trip to Boston in the morning, Maggie fixed milk toast and ran a bath for Mrs. Hamilton, then made three trips to the wood pile to fill the wood boxes. She piled the last armful extra high, reserving several medium-size logs for herself. It was after ten when she finally pressed sore hands against the door that led to the curving stairs. Logs in one arm, lantern in the other, she almost fell as her foot slipped on an envelope.

Her father answering one of her many letters? A pleasant and rare surprise.

She turned it over. Her pulse skipped at the Western Union symbol.

In her entire life she'd only received two telegrams.

One to inform her that her mother was dead. The other to announce her father had been transferred to the state prison in Waupun.

Her hand shook. She didn't breathe until she saw Richard's name at the bottom. Then she breathed so fast and shallow she had to sit down.

DEAREST MAGGIE. REQUEST YOUR COMPANY AT DINNER PARTY HOSTED BY EMMA MITCHELL FRIDAY NIGHT.

Her heart did a pirouette. *Yes, Richard, I'll go with you!* Her eyes wandered from the page. Staring at the blank wall, she saw herself descending the stairs in the gold gown Emma had given her. She could see the light in Richard's eyes and feel his hands brush her arms as he helped her into her coat.

Again, the light-headed feeling swept over her. *Breathe.* She looked down at the second line.

OUR SECRET. RICHARD.

Her exhale descended the twisted stairs to the basement.

There would be no floating down the stairs in her hand-me-down dress. She would get ready in her tiny room, slip down the back staircase, through the kitchen, and out the back door with her coat already on. Would they even arrive at the party together or would she have to humble herself and ask Charles to drop her off?

And then she rallied. It was for her sake he wouldn't tell his parents. For the sake of her job, not his pride. Concentrating on "Dearest Maggie," she climbed the stairs.

In her room, she stirred the embers of the fire she'd started before running Mrs. Hamilton's bath. Mr. Hamilton forbade her to start a fire before she went to her room for the night. Most nights she obeyed, but with the temperature dropping into the teens, that would mean a night of sleeping in her clothes and still never getting warm.

She added another log. Sparks skittered up the pipe from her little stove. The wool quilts on her bed called to her. Still in coat and gloves, she draped the log cabin quilt over her shoulders, sat at her desk, and turned up the wick on the lamp she'd lit from the kitchen stove.

Magdalena's paws shook like poplar leaves quivering in a stiff wind as she opened the telegram. . .

Recording her thoughts as if her life were being lived by someone—some*thing*—else helped her sort out problems in a detached kind of way.

She'd written two paragraphs when something pinged against her window. A stubborn hickory nut maybe, trying to hold on to its branch through the winter.

And then it happened again. And again. Not a nut. A stone. But who. . . ?

Her heart thudded and she pushed the door open. Richard? Home early to surprise them, but forgot his key? She padded down the stairs, into the kitchen, and flew through the back porch. She couldn't see a thing through the window, but she flung the door open.

Emma, a fur-lined hood almost covering her face, stood on the step.

With her arm around a young girl.

CHAPTER 9

Izzy tiptoed into the hall and waited until she was sure Heather and Ryan were in the kitchen, way on the far side of the house. She walked slow and quiet like a cat walking on carpet. When she got to the invisible door next to the elevator door that still made her shiver, she pushed with both hands. The door made a click. She held her breath and waited. Way down in the kitchen, Heather laughed.

Good. They hadn't heard the door. She pulled it closed behind her. For a second it was hard to breathe. *Don't be a baby*. Ryan had showed her how to open the doors from both sides. And besides, if she really did get trapped, her big strong pretend dad was here to save her again.

She scampered up to the top and pushed her hands flat against the door. *Pop!* She walked into the little room. It was hot and stuffy.

Heather had laughed when she said she wanted this to be her special sleepover room. Ryan had said it was a cool idea. He said if it was okay with her mom, he'd help her paint it and now that she and Skylar were almost best friends, she had someone to sleep over.

It was a cool room. She wished she knew who lived here in the old days. At first she wanted it to be the girl with the wicked stepmother, but the more she thought about it, the more she was sure it was a girl who got kidnapped by pirates and had to live on a ship for a lot of years but one night she stole a sword from the captain who had a hook where his arm used to be and stabbed him—*whop!* Izzy fell against the old bed. "Right in the stomach." And then the handsome good pirate carried the huge treasure chest full of gold and they jumped into a little boat and sailed back to her house and hid the gold in the room next to her bedroom and they were rich forever and had lots of children but then they moved and forgot there was still some gold left in the treasure chest.

And it was still there when a little girl pretended to be asleep and snuck away to the secret stairs to find it.

⚜

The air-conditioning turned up automatically when the condo door closed behind him. Andrew tossed his keys onto the salmon-colored countertop that ran the length of one end of the loft. Most days, the sound of keys hitting marble acted like a conditioned response, bringing on near instant relaxation. Today, the noise jangled already jittery nerves. He pulled a wine bottle out of its coiled steel holder and lifted a glass from the rows of crystal suspended above a stainless steel island.

Glass in hand, he pushed a button, filling the two-story loft with acoustic guitar music. Kicking off his shoes, he settled into black leather and lifted his feet onto the oversize red pillow atop his glass coffee table. He didn't get how Stephannie could exist in her all-white living space.

Then again, maybe he did get it. It fit her. Simple. Empty. Stephannie Lansing cluttered her calendar, but not her mind.

Ripping on Stephannie did nothing to alleviate the despondency hovering like toxic smog. What was it? Could it be he was finally experiencing empathy for the man who'd said he'd seen a spark of creative genius in him and given him a huge break six years ago?

No. The pressing heaviness had nothing to do with Parker.

It had everything to do with Parker's daughter. But not the one who'd be arriving here in minutes. This had to do with the one who probably had no idea her carefree anonymous life could turn upside down with the final blip of a heart monitor.

If Parker found out who she was before his heart gave out. And if he claimed her.

Andrew slouched into the soft leather and closed his eyes. Maybe Parker was only curious. Wouldn't a man on the verge of dying want a glimpse of the daughter he might never have seen?

Curiosity. A glimpse. To see if she had his hair. Or his eyes. Those eyes.

A tingle of energy snaked along his arm from the crystal stem in his hand. He'd made a connection with Heather and it wouldn't be smart to wait too long to reconnect.

The more he could learn about her, and the faster he learned it, the better armed he'd be.

<hr>

Heather slammed an unopened bag of flour on the kitchen table.

Why couldn't Ryan just admit it? He was jealous, plain and simple. That wasn't something to be ashamed of. It was flattering to a girl to know a guy was jealous.

As long as he didn't drag her off by the hair like a brainless barbarian.

She yanked open the fridge, and pulled out eggs. The last thing she wanted to do right now was make food for tomorrow—when she'd spend half the day with the barbarian's family.

She was doing this for Izzy and her new friend.

Separating eggs was tricky with shaking hands that would rather crush whole eggs than cleanly crack them. She slid the yolks into a plastic container she'd found in a box. The translucent plastic looked like it had never touched food. Not surprising. Natalie wasn't the type to bother with leftovers.

Safety seals snapped as she opened vanilla, almond extract, and a bottle of vegetable oil. After emptying every box marked KITCHEN, she hadn't come across a single baking item other than salt. Had Natalie thrown everything out before the move or had she never owned things that required such menial labor?

Get a grip. She measured the extracts and breathed in the hearth-and-homey scents. *Relax. Think of someone you're not mad at.* Jen? No. Zach? No. Grandma Beth? Natalie? Ryan? Mom? Maybe. Dad. Yes.

A surge of homesickness rocked her. In spite of not wanting to be under the same roof as her sister, it had felt so good to wake up in her old room again, to the smell of Dad's home-roasted coffee beans and Mom's fresh-baked orange rolls. Part of her soul had reveled and healed in the from-scratch goodness of home.

Part of her soul.

Setting the measuring spoons on the table, she picked up her phone and dialed Manhattan.

"Conrad residence."

A familiar fist pummeled the imaginary bruise from the Zach kick. "Grandma Beth." *It's Cinderella, remember me?* "It's Heather. I didn't realize you were staying so long."

"I wasn't planning on it, but after seeing Jen and Zach's apartment, I couldn't very well just leave."

"You're. . .staying at their apartment?"

"I'm having it painted. Can't you just imagine Jen's face when she comes back from Texas and finds everything done?"

Everything she wanted to do to make their first home *their* first home? "I can imagine she'll be in shock." *When she comes back from touring the stockyards on her honeymoon.*

A smile cracked her stiff face. For a brief moment, as she pictured her sister on the arm of her cowboy surrounded by lowing cattle, she no longer wanted to crush eggs.

The bride got the jerk and you got a new dress. And your freedom.

"I'm going with all neutral colors. I found her paint chips, but the colors are too loud. She doesn't realize how quickly they'd get tired of that. This way she has a nice canvas and she can change accent colors whenever she wants."

"Sounds very workable." *And I'm fine, Grandma. The house I'm staying in is beautiful, although there is that pesky problem of the man with the camera. And the man with the mirrored sunglasses and sticker on the bottom of his sandal. And the jealous barbarian.*

"She just has to learn to tone things down a bit. Jen always has had a flair for color. She got that from me."

Whereas I, on the other hand, got nothing. She jammed the beaters into the hand mixer. "Is Mom around?"

"She just ran to Walmart."

"Okay, I'll call her cell."

"Good-bye then."

"Bye." *Love you, too. Well, I could have if—*

The whir of the beater smothered the thought that had worn a permanent track in her brain. The mixture in the bowl frothed, matching her rabid mood. She measured out flour, sugar, salt, and cornstarch and topped it with three teaspoons of water. The dribbles rolled off the sides of the cornstarch then sank into the middle. Like she wanted to do. Just sink. Free fall into something white and fluffy and never bother to surface.

She shoved the lever on the mixer handle. White powder plumed from the bowl, coating her hand, her shirt, and her nostrils. She coughed until tears smarted her eyes. And wouldn't stop.

She hadn't touched her business plan, hadn't had a moment of relaxation, and the guy she'd thought was nice, decent, and single-but-not-desperate turned out to be a control freak who ruined her one chance with a guy who just might know how to treat a lady.

Tears streaming down her flour-dusted face, she blended the mess into dough and thought up snarly things to write in fortune cookies.

♛

Izzy turned the door handle so slowly it didn't make a single sound. The door wasn't much taller than she was. She opened it and walked through as quiet as a feather.

She looked around for a place to put the flashlight and found a hook right over her head. Standing on tiptoes, she looped the pink strap and the whole room turned light. It was just a regular closet and there was nothing in it except one thing: a treasure chest so big she could hide in it.

Just like in the movies, the treasure chest was shaped like a loaf of bread. It was mostly black but it had silvery metal on the top and the front and wooden stripes. The metal part had bumpy butterflies all over it. And just like in the movies, it had a big round thing on the front where it opened, but there wasn't a big lock on it. There wasn't a lock at all.

She lifted a piece of metal shaped like a tongue. It whined like she did when Mom woke her up for school.

On her knees, she used both hands to open the top. It was way heavier than she thought it would be and it made a loud creaking noise.

The light hit two big, but skinny books. One black and gold, the other silver and blue. She set the books on the floor, then picked up a green vase, or maybe it was a bottle. A glass straw stuck out of the side. She set it on the books. Next were a bunch of papers. Big letters on a newspaper said KIM JONG IL DEAD. She pushed more papers away and gasped. "Dresses!" A yellow one and a blue one, with lace and ribbons and shiny buttons. So, so carefully, she picked up the blue dress. Ladies in the old days wore dresses like this when they went to balls and danced with soldiers.

Under the blue dress was a red one. Izzy squealed, forgetting she was supposed to be quiet. She put her hand over her mouth. This was her secret and only one other person was going to know about it for a long, long time.

Skylar would be so surprised when Izzy showed her the best dress-up clothes ever.

✦

"What are you making?"

"Fortune cookies to take to Skylar's house." Heather smiled at the tousled hair. "Sleep well?"

Izzy yawned and stretched, then yawned again. "I had a really good nap." She peered into the mixing bowl.

"Your hair is all staticky." She put her hand on Izzy's back and felt her heart beating like a tympani drum. "Did you run down the stairs?"

"Yeah. Can I help?"

Heather dropped a teaspoon of dough onto a cookie sheet and flattened it with the bottom of her spoon. "I'm just going to put the first one in the oven to test it. While it's baking, you can help me think up more fortunes, okay?"

"Like what?"

Like. . . An angry woman will soon walk out of your life. She slid the cookie sheet in the oven and started the timer. "There's a list in my cookbook."

"You brought your own cookbook?"

"Those are recipes I've been collecting for the coffee shop I want to open someday." She slid the book closer to Izzy. "We can use these or we can write our own. Nice things like 'Something good is going to happen to you soon.'"

Izzy's eyes lit. "Like 'You will soon find a secret treasure'?"

"Exactly." She picked up a fine-point marker. "Let's write that one."

"A girl in my old school had a party and we got cookies that said things about God and Jesus. We should maybe write things like that."

Did Ryan put you up to that? "That would be a nice idea, but I don't know where there's a Bible."

"We could just say 'Jesus loves you.'"

"Okay."

Izzy began printing in precise block letters. When she'd added a period, she looked up. "Do you think He does?"

"Who? Do I think Jesus loves you?"

Heather stared at the timer on the stove. Eight minutes left. "I know He loves *you*."

"That's what Martha always said. She lived next to us in Chicago and she read me stories about Jesus. Mom doesn't think God is real, but I know He is 'cuz I talk to Him all the time. He's like my dad, only I can talk to Him and I can't ever talk to my dad." Her head tipped to one side. "Why are you mad at Ryan?"

"Who says I'm mad at him?"

"I'm not a little kid. I can tell, you know. You didn't laugh one time or talk in the car when we came home from the beach."

Seven minutes left. "Sometimes grown-ups are silly, aren't they?"

"Yeah, but I hope you don't stay mad at Ryan 'cuz I'm pretending he's my daddy. Is that okay?"

"I think that's okay. I think that would make Ryan happy." *Not that I care.* "You know, we can write some funny things to put in our cookies, too."

"If you're mad at Ryan, you should write things like 'You smell like a monkey and you look like one, too.'" Izzy picked up a pen. "Y-o-u s-m-e—"

Heather's phone rang.

Izzy pointed. "Look! It's Ryan."

She closed her eyes, took a calming breath, pasted a smile for Izzy's sake, and said hello.

"Hi. Hey, I know I didn't handle that right, but I just have this feeling in my gut about that guy."

"I think your Spidey sense is a little off this time. What if he was just a frazzled businessman who wanted to enjoy the weather in his convertible so he drives to Racine, sees the beach, and decides a swim would be fun so he goes to the store and buys what he needs and then he wants ice so he sees these people he thinks are normal and approachable and—"

"And the girl is gorgeous so he figures he can just move in on—" He blew a loud breath in her ear. "The real reason I called was to ask you to please be careful. If the guy shows up again, you'll know it's not a coincidence. Unless you wrote your phone number in the sand while I wasn't looking."

Why didn't I think of that? "Too many comic books, Spidey." She stood, turning her back on Izzy. "You know, I lived in downtown Chicago all by my lonesome for nine whole months and didn't get murdered or abducted or mugged even once." She pushed through the swinging door and took her shrill voice into the dining room.

"The other thing I called to say was you don't have to come to dinner tomorrow. I'll make excuses for you."

You can't uninvite me, mister. You weren't the one who asked me in the first place. Remember? "I couldn't do that to Izzy and Skylar."

The timer buzzed. She said good-bye, stomped back into the kitchen, and picked up a marker. A verse came to mind.

"Love is patient, love is kind. It does not envy. . ."

CHAPTER 10

Stephannie pulled out of the parking garage and headed north toward the Riverwalk. She turned left on Ontario Street, but when she reached State, her plan changed.

Opening a zippered pocket in her Valentino clutch, she found the keys to the house she'd grown up in. The clock on the dash read 11:23. Andrew had wanted her to spend the night, but she'd turned him down. Without an excuse. Maybe because her dad was in the hospital. Maybe because she'd told God she was going to change.

She passed her turn onto Sheffield Street and drove on to Lincolnshire. Could she let herself in without waking Baxter? Probably not, and the dog would alert Jason, her father's grounds-keeper, who was staying at the house while he was in the hospital. She slowed the Mercedes, but didn't turn around. She needed to silence the nagging question once and for all. If she couldn't find an answer here, she'd find a way to get it from her mother.

The forty-five-minute drive passed in a blur of tangled thoughts. Her head hurt by the time she parked in the circle drive and walked along the lit cobblestones to the massive white door. She turned her key in the lock. Baxter barked. In high school, she'd been able to do this without waking anyone.

Dropping to her knees in the foyer, she wrapped her arms around the wiggling, whimpering animal. "Come with me, baby." She led him into her father's study and shut the door. "Should I start here?" she whispered to the dog slobbering on her hand. Turning on a lamp, she surveyed the dark wood and deep burgundy of the walls that had absorbed so many father-daughter talks. And lectures. And apologies.

"I'm so sorry, Daddy." The phrase came automatically, as if it were the magic word allowing entrance to her father's realm.

Family pictures covered the wall above the fireplace. The mantel was cluttered with frames and mementos. A fat hippo she'd made from clay, a "World's Greatest Dad" medal she'd painted in grade school. A man this sentimental would have kept something to mark an event as significant as fathering a child. Even a child he didn't want to—or couldn't—raise.

If something—a picture or diary—existed, it would probably be in this room. Her mother was not a sentimentalist. She was a practical woman who took what she needed and left what she didn't. Including a daughter.

Stephannie rifled through the drawers of the oak desk. Tape dispenser, ruler, a tangle of wires, and an old answering machine. Useless without a landline. She moved to the built-in file cabinets. Insurance information, computer software, warrantees. Files in the bottom drawer were packed so tightly she could barely separate them enough to read the labels. Receipts, check registers, cancelled checks. Dating back to the eighties.

"Here we go, Baxter. I don't know what I'm looking for, but I bet it's in here." She sorted through the check registers and took seven. The seven years before she was born. The woman in the picture didn't look over thirty. The woman who could be her half sister, her father's love child.

Or the firstborn daughter of Parker and Dianna Lansing.

The true heiress of the Lansing empire.

Her daddy's long-lost princess.

👑

"I found your movies, Iz!"

Heather called up the stairs and Izzy scampered down. "What were you doing up there?"

"Packing my backpack to take to Skylar's house."

"We'll only be there a few hours." *Probably less if Ryan has anything to say about it.*

"I still hafta take things to show her."

The second-grade equivalent to a bottle of wine or bouquet of flowers. Heather gestured toward a box in the living room. "Do you want to watch a movie on my computer while I do some unpacking?"

Izzy nodded and sorted through a Pixar and Disney buffet. *Beauty and the Beast.*

Fitting. She slid it onto the square black tongue protruding from her laptop. Izzy curled into a ball on the leather love seat. Tags still dangled from the back of it. "I'll make popcorn in a minute."

A half moon cast a silver sheen on the rippled surface of the lake. If she were alone she'd run across the street and walk barefoot in the sand in the moonlight. An eerie sadness seeped in with the thin light. She felt stranded. Like a paper boat bouncing on the waves, without the power to move away from shore or the strength to sail back to solid ground. She pulled her phone out of her pocket and called home. Her mother's voice brought the sting of tears.

"Heather! I was just thinking of calling you. Texting just doesn't cut it for me. I need to hear your voice. How are you?"

"I'm good."

"Really?" Her mother's voice hushed.

Heather closed her eyes and mentally followed her mother into the pantry. The door clicked. "Are you in your talking place?"

The laugh echoed. "You know how it is."

"Grandma hasn't left yet."

"Mm-hm. So how are you doing, really?"

"Not so great at the moment. I'm just feeling kind of lost." She smiled and flicked tears with her fingertips. "I need my mama."

"Oh, sweetie." Her mother's voice cracked. "You've had more than your share of unfairness lately. I just keep thinking—"

"Mom. Don't. What could you have done? Told Jen she had to be nice and share Zach the way you made her share the Barbies Grandma gave her?"

A sigh met her ear. A sound, she knew, encompassing twenty-four years of guilt and powerlessness.

"I'm okay, Mom. I really am. I've had a year to get over him. The wedding stirred things again, but it's not losing Zach that's hard. It's losing him to Jen that's the killer."

"I know. For what it's worth, she feels horrible."

Once again, she pictured her dainty sister stomping through the cattle yards. "I'm sure she does."

"I'm praying there'll be a man in your very near future."

Sorry, Mom, they're all in my very near past. Lost one a week ago, another today, and I'm going to figure out a way to lose one tomorrow. She changed the subject to the quarts of tomatoes her mother was canning, then said good-bye and headed to the kitchen to pop corn, steam rice, and forget men.

⚜

Heather lined the DVDs on the bottom shelf of the entertainment center. Was G-rated entertainment allowed in this room, or would the leather, glass, and satiny blond wood be reserved for adults?

Framed pictures filled two boxes. Portraits of Izzy from newborn on. Exquisite photos of a little girl in designer dresses. She carried the boxes to the closet in the foyer. Hanging pictures was a personal thing.

Shoved in a corner of the living room was a box marked PIANO. She pulled the tape off and threw it aside. Sheet music, songbooks that appeared to be from the sixties, and an old brown book with *Crowning Day* printed on the cover. Heather opened it. A hymnal. She turned to the copyright page.

THE RUEBUSH-KIEFFER COMPANY

MARCH 20, 1894

It seemed an unlikely thing for the practical Natalie to keep. It must be a family heirloom.

"The mouse stories were in that book." Izzy pointed to the hymnal.

"This is a songbook."

"I know. It's my dad's." Izzy turned back to the movie.

Heather opened an unmarked box. Files labeled MEDICAL RECORDS. COV. BUS. INSURANCE POLICIES. BIRTH CERTIFICATES.

PASSPORTS—minus the one that flew to Venice. Important papers that should be in a fireproof safe. She tucked it away in the closet on top of the pictures and tackled another box.

More papers, but these were loose, apparently tossed in at random. The top paper was the calendar of events for Prairie School. Beneath it, a paper with the name of Izzy's teacher and a list of school supplies. "Did your mom buy all the things you need for school yet? Paper and pencils and things like that?"

Gaze riveted to the screen, Izzy shook her head. "Just my backpack."

Pressure swelled like an inflating balloon, pushing against Heather's temples. She forced a long, slow exhale. *I can do this. I can do this.* "Guess we'll have to go shopping."

"Can we take Skylar?"

"Maybe."

"And Ryan?"

The pressure intensified. Something popped at the back of her skull. Aneurism? "Men don't usually like shopping."

"But you said Ryan did. You said, 'A man who shops' and you smiled all lovey-dovey."

"Lovey-dovey? Where did you learn that?"

Izzy shrugged. "I just know things."

Heather sat next to Izzy with the box on her lap and nudged Izzy's elbow. "You make me smile, kid."

"You, too. Make me smile." She flashed a wide grin then turned back to the movie.

Sorting through the papers, Heather laid them out in categories across the coffee table. School papers. Invitations. Bills. *Natalie, you best be paying these online. I don't want to flip a switch some night and find out you didn't pay the electric bill.* It was as if Natalie had swept everything off the top of her desk into a box. Two thick envelopes that appeared to be wedding invites hadn't even been opened.

Toward the bottom of the box, her breath caught. She pulled out a stapled sheaf of papers. *Termination Contract.*

None of your business, Heather. But her eyes weren't responding to her brain's commands. Her lips moved as she silently read.

Employer [Coventry International] and Employee [Natalie S. Brooks] hereby agree to this Termination Contract.

Employee hereby agrees and obligates [herself] to the following:

1. *Employee will not engage in any competition with Employer for the period of [one year], which includes employment with another company in the same or similar business as Employer, establishment of a new company in the same or similar business as Employer, or any contractual arrangement under which Employee consults, advises, or assists another company in the same or similar business.*

She forgot, for a moment, how to close her gaping mouth. This was not a non-compete clause saying she couldn't work for another hotel within a certain radius. Even now, in Venice, Italy, Natalie Brooks was in breach of contract. "What were you thinking?"

"Huh?"

"Nothing, sweetie. Just talking to myself." Tossing the paper back in the box, she focused on the movie. On Belle, sitting across the table from the Beast, watching him slop porridge on himself and the table as he tried to use a spoon. The teacup laughed. A look of tenderness crossed Belle's face. She discarded her spoon, picked up her bowl, and slurped directly from it. And then she sang about the something sweet and almost kind she saw in the creature who had been mean and coarse and unrefined.

Heather's thoughts turned to the beast she would dine with tomorrow.

⁂

He had nothing to go on. Not a fingerprint or a license plate. Nothing but a picture in his head.

Ryan circled the grounds of Wingspread, thirty-six acres jutting into Lake Michigan on the Wind Point Peninsula. For an hour now he'd been wandering the walking paths cutting through prairie tall-grass dotted with paper birch, cottonwood, and black willow trees, but his thoughts were not on the security of the conference center.

His thoughts were on his unfounded suspicions of the guy with the brand-new swim trunks.

He jumped when a raccoon lumbered across his path. "Cool it, man."

Walking along one side of the Guest House, he looked through the wall of glass opening onto the terrace. Conferees huddled, drinks in hand, in front of the massive limestone fireplace. "Guest House" was an outrageously inadequate term for a forty-two-room, thirty-eight-thousand-square-foot lodge. Nothing quaint and cozy about this place.

He'd often imagined being on the inside. Especially on winter evenings, he envisioned walking across the rich Brazilian cherry floor to dine at the birch harvest table made from an aged log recovered from the depths of Lake Superior, or looking down the snow-covered bluff at the iced-over pond. He'd be holding a cup of something hot in one hand, and the hand of a gorgeous blond with the other.

Scratch that. Edit the script. Make it a brunette.

Dream on.

He walked on to the building the Johnson Wax family had commissioned Frank Lloyd Wright to design. Wingspread. Fourteen thousand spare feet that "embraced the prairie." He thought of a Wright quote he'd wrestled with since coming to work here: "The building, as architecture, is born out of the heart of man, permanent consort to the ground, comrade to the trees, true reflection of man in the realm of his own spirit."

He wasn't so sure he wanted to think of himself as "consort to the ground" or "comrade to the trees."

With an hour left of his shift, he checked gates and locks and prayed about the girl who wouldn't back out of dinner at his sister's because she wouldn't "do that to Izzy and Skylar." Not because she wanted to see him. Or even give him the benefit of the doubt that maybe, just maybe, a guy who'd spent ten years working in security could recognize an SP when he saw one.

He bent and picked a scrap of paper from the sidewalk. A corner torn from an envelope. He stared at the Wingspread logo. Stylized wings over a blue circle. He turned it upside down. It reminded him of something. Another logo.

An anchor.

He'd seen it just hours ago.

On the white sticker on the bottom of a brand-new sandal.

Sunday morning. Andrew had tried to sleep in, but the questions sparring in his head made too much noise.

I always assumed she meant he paid for an abortion. What if she meant he paid for the birth?

He kicked at the tan sheet and rolled over. *What if?* If Heather was the child Parker and Dianna had given up for adoption, the implications were terrifying.

He hadn't breathed a word to Stephannie about his trip to Racine, and wouldn't until he knew more. What he did know was enough to send chills scrambling up his back. Heather was not only beautiful, she was poised and articulate, had her master's degree in something, and was working on a business plan.

What kind of business? Was she hoping to open a quilt shop or a cupcake bakery. . .or had she gone to school for business management or something else Parker would interpret as potential? Before the girl knew it, she'd be training to follow in the footsteps of the father she never knew she had.

If he lived.

And if he didn't. . . ? A sudden flash of Dianna—face beaming with pride as she embraced her child of promise—forced him out of bed.

The first thing he had to do was hire someone. He knew people who could cut through red tape like butter. He knew attorneys who could find names and bios and most likely skate like pros around obstacles like adoption privacy laws. Scooping his phone off the dresser, he gazed out at morning light gilding his city, coating it in gold and shimmer and promise.

"What in the world do you have in here?"

Izzy grabbed the pink backpack Heather handed her through

117

the open door and snapped her seat belt. "Just stuff."

Heather got in and started the car.

"A couple of books and some clothes in case we want to play dress-up. Eight isn't too big for that, is it? I don't want her to think I'm a little kid."

"You can never be too old to play dress-up. Last Christmas my sister and I held a fancy tea party and everyone wore fancy dresses and hats."

Oh. . . Oh! "We hafta do that." The blue dress would be too small for Heather, but the hats and gloves and. . . Her mind whirled like a cotton candy machine. "Promise we can have a party like that after we meet more people. Okay?"

"Okay. I promise."

As they backed out of the driveway, the smell of fried rice filled the inside of the car. Heather had let her crack the eggs and wash the bean sprouts. "Can I eat just fried rice and fortune cookies?"

"I think you should try everything. Skylar's aunt is making pad thai. It's a yummy dish with noodles and chopped peanuts and shrimp. Do you like shrimp?"

"Yeah. I guess. Are you going to try everything?"

"Yes."

"Are you going to try not being mad at Ryan?"

January 11, 1912

Bathed and wearing Maggie's flannel nightgown, the girl took the cup of cocoa Maggie offered and smiled for the first time.

With the addition of more wood than Maggie was supposed to use in a night, the fire in the little round stove crackled and spit, sending its glow into the dark corners. Angelica sat in the middle of Maggie's bed and Maggie sat on the floor, swaddled in blankets she'd borrowed from Richard's room. Blankets that wafted the heady scent of bay rum cologne whenever she moved.

"Are you warm now?"

"Yes. Warmer than I've been in a long time. Thank you." Angelica looked around the room. Shadows from the stove and the kerosene lamp danced across the slanted walls. "This is your room? All by yourself?"

Maggie nodded, wanting to ask what kind of conditions she was accustomed to if this tiny room caused her eyes to open in awe—as if she'd entered a resplendent castle. "I used to share it with the cook, but she was let go, so now I have to do all the cooking, but it's worth it because I get this room all to myself and I don't have to listen to her snoring like a steam engine."

Angelica laughed. "My little brother snores. Mama said his tonsils are too big."

"Can I ask. . ." Maggie lowered her voice. "Where is your family, Angelica?"

The girl shrugged and stared into her cup. "My pa went back east to find work. Mama works at a tavern. The old owners let my brother and me stay there, but there's new people running it now and they don't want children around, so Mama sent Woody—his real name is Woodrow—to live with my grandma in Green Bay. I stayed here 'cuz of working at the mill."

"The woolen mill?"

"Mm-hm."

"Where have you been staying?"

The girl's eyes shifted right then left. Her lips pressed in a tight line. "I m–made a place behind the stairs at the mill. I only used one blanket—one that didn't pass inspection. They get donated to the orphanage, so I didn't think it would be so wrong to use it." Tears balanced on her bottom lashes. "I cannot lose this job, Miss Maggie. I need to send money to my grandma to feed my brother."

"I understand." Maggie rose and sat next to Angelica. The girl was twelve. Maggie had been only a year older when the minister had found her sleeping under a church pew. "Where did Miss Mitchell find you?"

"I g–got locked out. I usually hide before they lock up at night, but I hadn't eaten all day and I thought I could run out and f–find something to eat and get back before. . ." She wiped her face with the nightgown sleeve. "Miss Mitchell was driving around. She said she was looking for someone just like me. But the lady who usually takes girls like me had too many and Miss Mitchell brought me to her house. There was an awful row with her mother and I c–couldn't stay there."

"I'm glad she brought you here."

"W–will you get in trouble?"

If they find out, yes. Mr. Hamilton was leaving for Boston in the morning. He'd be gone more than a week. How long could she hide a child? How long could she get away with feeding her, washing her clothes, helping her sneak a bath, like tonight, after midnight? But there were places for girls like this, weren't there? She wasn't an orphan. The YWCA was moving to a new location on the other end of Main Street. Would they have more room? Would they take her in? Maggie's pulse sped up. She thought of Emma's words. *I've felt like a racehorse at a starting gate, just waiting for God to give me something to do.* She rearranged the quilt that had slipped off one thin shoulder. *Is this the something You have for me to do, Lord? To help this girl?* At the YWCA Angelica could learn skills, take classes and Bible studies. Come morning, she'd ask. If they said no, she'd start looking for something else. She'd talk to Reverend Leek. She'd find a place. *Heavenly Father, help me do this. Don't let Mr. Hamilton find out. Please.*

Hoping her fear didn't show in her voice, Maggie laughed, "That's one of the special things about having a room way up on the third floor. If we don't make a lot of noise, no one will know you're here. What time do you start work in the morning?"

"S–six."

Maggie's jaw tensed. The girl should still be snug in bed at six in the morning. "I'll wake you up and we can have breakfast together and you can be out the door before anyone else is up."

"That would be nice." Her eyes still glistened, but a sweet smile played on her lips. "I won't be trouble. I promise. And I can help. I'm a really, really hard worker."

"You must be to get up so early to go to work." Maggie took the cup from the girl and set it out of the way under the head of the bed. "Do you like stories?"

"I looove stories. Mama used to read to us every night. Mostly from the Bible, but for Christmas last year a church lady gave me *Little Women* and gave Woody *Treasure Island* and we read them over and over."

Maggie stood. Wrapping the blankets and the scent of Richard close about her shoulders, she walked over to the desk and opened the door. From behind the dictionary the Hamilton's had given her for her birthday, she pulled the brown envelope that cradled the dreams she would never realize and the angst she would never share. Except in story form. "Lie down and I'll read to you."

"You've been so kind." A fresh tear balanced on the girl's lashes. "You didn't have to take me in."

"Can I tell you a secret, Angelica?"

The girl nodded.

"One night, when I was only a little older than you, I woke to a fierce pounding on the door. The police marched in and arrested my parents."

Angelica gasped. "What had they done?"

Her throat tightened and she questioned the wisdom of sharing her heartache with someone so young. "My parents were very well-respected people. They worked at a company that made buttons. My mother got very, very sick and needed an operation, but they didn't have enough money to pay for it. In desperation, my father stole money from the company he worked for."

"Did your mother get the operation?"

"No. My mother died in prison. I will be twenty-five by the time my father is released."

Angelica rested her hand on Maggie's. "I'm so sorry. How did you survive?"

"I ran away. I hid in a church for a while and then I got a job at the hotel." She rubbed her arms. In spite of the spit and crackle of the fire in the stove, she felt as if she sat in a room devoid of heat. She thought back to the backbreaking months she worked at the Hotel Racine. "I worked in the kitchen. From five in the morning to seven at night, six days a week, I peeled potatoes."

"Dreadful."

Maggie smiled. "That's the exact word. *Dreadful.* But then I found another job, working at a factory that made door locks." There were still days she looked at her hands and imagined them stained black from the brass.

"How did you get here?"

"The Hamiltons own that factory and they were my parents' friends. When Mrs. Hamilton found out I was working on the assembly line, they hired me." *If it were up to Mother you would have been adopted rather than hired.* Richard's words rang in her head. But she did not believe them. "Well, we can talk more of our dreadful jobs tomorrow. Now we both need to get some sleep. You have blankets to make tomorrow and I have to serve an old hen to a bunch of old hens." Her hand flew to her mouth.

Angelica laughed until her eyes watered. She gripped her side. "You're funny, Miss Maggie. I like you."

"I like you, too, Angelica. I'm glad you're here. It gets lonely sometimes in this little room."

"I know I can't stay, but—"

"*Shh.* We'll talk about all that tomorrow."

"Where will you sleep? I can't take your bed. I'll sleep—"

"I'll get another mattress tomorrow." Cook's mattress, flat though it must be, was probably rolled up in the attic somewhere. "Right now, I'm going to be snug as a bug with all those blankets." She pointed at the stack on the floor.

"But—"

"*Shh.*" She arranged her quilt over Angelica, pulling it high over the girl's shoulders, then sat as close to the fire as the heat would allow and pulled the lamp closer. Goose bumps skittered on her arms as she opened the packet of papers. She'd never shared her stories or essays with anyone nor even read them aloud. She cleared her throat. " 'In a fanciful land just west of your fondest dreams and due east of the Isle of Imagination—' "

Footsteps pounded on the stairs. "Maggie. Maggie, wake up. Richard is home and I need you"—the door flew open—"to start a fi—" Her mouth gaped. "Who is *that*?"

👑

"I can't deal with this now." Mrs. Hamilton tightened her robe across her chest. "That *thing* is coming today and we have the luncheon to prepare for and now Richard is home and. . ." With her hair in a thick braid over her shoulder and the flicker from Maggie's candle softening her features, she looked like a pouting, petulant child rather than the mistress of the household.

"You needn't worry about any of that. The pastry shells are baked, the chicken is cooked, and I'll make friends with the 'thing' on my own and then I'll show you. As for Richard"—her heart banged her ribs like a newborn colt—"I'm sure he's dead tired and he'll sleep until the ladies have all gone home."

"And the girl? What if she makes a noise? What if Mr. Hamilton hears her or she comes downstairs during the luncheon?"

Angelica would be threading a loom at the time of the luncheon. "Maybe one of the women"—one who has a husband with an ounce of compassion—"would be willing to take her in."

"Oh. I don't think so."

"But there are several who have donated money for books for—"

Mrs. Hamilton shooed her words with a wave of her hand. "I would never ask. That's an imposition beyond. . .well, look at how she's disrupting our household. She has to leave. The church must have—"

"She works at the mill. She'll be out of here at dawn."

"She. . .works?" The pout transformed into a look of genuine surprise. "How old is the child?"

"Twelve."

"But that's. . . ?"

"A fact of life, ma'am." Maggie's tone bordered on disrespect, but it seemed a thing beyond her control. "Her father lost his job and went east to find work. Her mother has lodging where she works, but she was forced to send her little boy to her mother in Green Bay and Angelica has been sleeping under the stairs at the mill. Tonight she got locked out."

"Oh. My. How sad. Well, I suppose she can stay the night."

"I'll find another blanket in the attic and put Richard's back in—"

"No. I'll give Richard the extras from my room. The girl is probably dirty."

"She had a bath."

"Yes. Well. But there are things. . .she may have lice or"—her eyes widened—"if she has bedbugs we'll never get rid of them."

"I took her clothes to the burn barrel while she bathed and I brushed her hair myself. There's no sign of lice."

"It appears you've thought of everything then." She laid a hand on Maggie's arm. "You always seem to. Your father would be so proud of you."

Eyes stinging from the compliment, Maggie slipped into her uniform, piled her hair quickly on top of her head, and set about making a fire and a midnight snack for Richard while a little girl, snug and warm in Maggie's bed, silently disrupted the house.

CHAPTER 11

Ryan strung paper lanterns over the nails he'd just pounded in the pergola over his brother's deck.

"These are Japanese lanterns," he muttered to the females scurrying around the bottom of the ladder.

"And your point is?" Amanda set a glass filled with chopsticks on the picnic table.

"Marissa made pad thai. Thai as in Thai*land*."

"And I made sushi. It's an Asian cuisine party. Hush up and create some atmosphere."

"Oh, there's going to be atmosphere here. We need igloos and mukluks for the atmosphere we're going to have here."

Amanda backed away from the table and looked up at him. Her hands went to her hips. "Do we need to talk, little B-I-L?"

"Maybe." He looped the last lantern onto a nail and straightened the cord. "Plug this in and see if it works."

Soft, diffused light lit the shaded deck. Atmosphere. Romantic atmosphere.

"Well, get down here and talk. She'll be here in a few minutes."

Like an obedient puppy, he climbed down. Straddling a bench, he ran his hand through his hair. "We had a. . .disagreement and I told her she didn't have to feel obligated to show up today, but she didn't want to disappoint the girls, so she's coming."

"Mmm. Icy."

"If Skylar and Izzy are friends, but Heather can't stand my guts, it's going to get complicated."

"Dare I ask what you disagreed about?"

Ryan's sigh bobbed white blossoms stuck in a vase of blue marbles. "You saw the guy who came to talk to us at the beach yesterday."

Amanda nodded. "I'm married, not blind. A friend of Heather's?"

"No. A complete stranger. And there was something strange about him."

"Ah. A strange stranger. The Spidey sense picked up a clue." The gleam in her eyes said she wasn't going to take him any more seriously than Heather had.

He repeated the sigh. "Never mind." He pushed himself off the bench.

As Amanda grabbed his sleeve, Marissa walked out with a basket of silverware rolled in napkins. "This looks serious. Can I join in?"

Ryan rubbed the spot above his right eye that was starting to hurt. "Yes, please, gang up on me." Marissa sat across from him and rested her chin on her knuckles. Not making eye contact with either of them, he told them about the guy with the camera and the tags on the trunks and sandals of a guy he was pretty sure wasn't named Mike. "I did a search. The sandals were from the marina gift shop. I talked to the lady who was working yesterday afternoon. She remembered him because he was clearly in a major hurry to buy those two things and get out." He looked up. Two identical expressions reflected nothing but amusement. "Fine." He got up, marched in the back door of the house and out the front. They could all just entertain Heather without—

A little brown car pulled into the driveway just as he burst onto the step.

Making him look like an overanxious welcoming committee.

⚜

Ryan was right. The Tobins were the most undysfunctional family she'd ever met.

The meal was delicious, and the conversation full of laughter. Heather set the empty fried rice bowl and a bottle of soy sauce next to the sink and picked up the basket of fortune cookies.

Marissa pulled back the cloth napkin folded over the cookies. "You actually made those?"

"Yep. They take time, but they're easy. Izzy helped write the fortunes. She didn't even let me see all of hers."

"That's scary." Marissa laughed and put the coffeepot on a tray of cups. She picked up the tray, then set it down. "Hey. Heather. I just want you to know that even if things don't work out with my brother, I'd still like to be friends."

"Thank you. I would, too." She rearranged the cloth napkin. "Is it that obvious that I'm tense around him?"

"No. But Amanda and I made him talk before you got here. I don't want to sound like I'm trying to talk you into something that might not be right for you, but my brother's really an unbelievable person. He just never got over his little kid imagination."

"I've noticed that." She sighed. "It might just be me. I'm on the rebound, as they say, and a bit hypersensitive."

Marissa grinned. "See? We were meant to be friends. I just went through a yucky break-up. Again." She held a finger gun to her temple. "I'm a control-freak magnet."

Heather laughed. "To be fair, I guess my ex wasn't so much controlling as he was"—she searched for a descriptor that had eluded her for months. . .*years*—"unbendable. He's a nice guy. He never said 'My way or the highway,' he just said, 'My way' and for too long I nodded like a bobblehead doll. He knew what he wanted his life to look like and four years into our relationship it dawned on him that I was the puzzle piece that didn't fit." She smiled, reveling in her newfound ability to find something positive about being unZached. "As it turned out, my sister was just the right shape."

"*What?*"

Marissa's eyeball pop made her laugh.

"He's dating your sister?"

"Worse. As of a week ago, my ex is my brother-in-law."

"Oh, girl, I feeeeel your pain."

"Thank you." Heather glanced out the sliding glass door at the back of Ryan's neck. "But I'm starting to feel less and less sorry for myself with each day that goes by. If I'd really wanted the guy,

I could have pretzeled myself into the woman he wanted."

"And been mi—" Marissa stopped as Kurt, the middle brother, walked up to the sliding glass door and slid it open.

"Keep talking about me, girls"—he walked around them and opened a cupboard next to the sink—"I know I'm amazing. It won't embarrass me at all." He opened a prescription bottle and dropped a pill into the palm of his hand.

Marissa turned to Heather. "Kurt has the cure to what ails us, girlfriend. Anti-rejection meds."

Kurt laughed and held out the bottle to Marissa. "Want some?" He put the cap on and slid it back in the cupboard then directed his gaze at Heather. "I don't think *you* need it." Eyebrows jiggling up and down, he grinned and walked back outside.

Marissa crossed her arms over her middle. "I would have to agree with him on that. If you can get around the Spidey complex."

Gaze fixed on the back of a tanned neck, Heather nodded. "I might have overreacted just a bit to his overreacting."

Marissa laughed and they walked back outside.

👑

" 'Jesus loves you.' "

Skylar's grandma turned the paper around for everyone to see. "Someone with very neat printing wrote this."

Izzy looked down at her plate. "That was me."

They took turns breaking fortune cookies and reading the papers out loud. Izzy's said, "The fortune you seek is in another cookie." Skylar got the one that read, "Don't kiss an elephant on the lips today." When Heather and Ryan weren't looking, Izzy winked at Skylar and at the same time they switched Heather and Ryan's cookies for the special ones Heather had let her make all by herself. Izzy held her breath.

Heather cracked hers open, picked up the paper, opened her mouth, and gave Izzy a mean look.

"Read it!" Skylar's aunt Marissa tried looking at it over Heather's shoulder.

Heather's eyes got all squinty. She shook her head and kept staring. Izzy's heart started pounding, and then all of a sudden Heather shook her head and smiled. Izzy was sure she looked at Ryan for just a second and then looked back at the paper. "This is one Izzy wrote. It says, 'Love is the only medicine for a broken heart.'"

Skylar's grandpa clapped his hands. "Amen to that." He had a loud laugh. "Ryan, you're next."

Ryan broke his then looked at Izzy exactly the way Heather had. "It appears that Izzy wrote this one, too. It says, 'The one you should love is closer than you think.'"

Izzy didn't breathe for a long time and then all of a sudden Ryan jumped up, shook his finger at her, and said, "You'd better run, pip-squeak, 'cuz I'm gonna get you!"

With a squeal, she hopped out of her chair and ran across the yard with Ryan chasing her.

Just like a dad would.

"Smart cookie. The kid, I mean."

Ryan handed her the empty cookie basket.

Heather nodded, set it on the counter, and went out to help clear the table.

The deck was empty. The girls had gone upstairs to play and the entire rest of the family was walking out to Amanda's garden. *This is a conspiracy.*

"Guess they thought we needed some time to talk." Ryan stacked plates and cups then stood and stared at her. "Do we?"

Do we need to talk? No. You just need to apologize. "I suppose."

He sat down. The lantern light shimmered in his eyes. He wore a faded khaki-green shirt with a fingertip-size hole on the seam of the sleeve. Tammy had scolded him about his choice of clothes before dinner. Studying it now, Heather had to disagree with Ryan's sister-in-law. Up to now she'd only seen him in a uniform. Or no shirt at all. The back of her neck warmed. This shirt fit beyond perfect and it brought out the green flecks in his eyes.

She sat across from him, staring out at the group huddled around the garden. Seven of them—Ryan's parents, his two brothers and their wives, and Skylar's little brother, Pax. "You have a wonderful family."

"Thank you. I'm blessed."

"You all get along so well."

"Most of the time."

She watched Amanda rest her head on Kurt's shoulder. His arm slid easily around hers as they walked. "This might not be any of my business, but did Kurt have some kind of a transplant?"

Ryan's eyes closed a fraction of a second longer than a normal blink. When they opened, he stared down at the table then looked toward the group surrounding the garden. Heather watched his Adam's apple lower then return to normal. "He had a kidney transplant seven years ago."

"And he's doing okay?"

"Yeah." Again, the slow-motion blink. "He's doing fine." He picked up a pair of chopsticks, still wrapped in paper, and tapped the table. His next breath seemed to shudder. "While it's quiet, maybe we should clear the air. About us."

"Okay." She tried a light note, one that would show she wouldn't be affected by the outcome of this discussion no matter how it turned out. She doubted it fooled him.

"So what do you think?" he asked. "Where do we go from here?"

The moisture in her mouth evaporated. Her tongue, and her words, stuck to the roof of her mouth. "Isn't that supposed to be the girl's line? We're the ones who ask for the Define the Relationship talks."

"So ask."

That wasn't the response she'd expected. "Okay. Where do you think we should go from here?"

"Well, we could try to talk through what happened yesterday, try to understand each other's point of view, or we could just shake hands and say the ol' 'Let's just be friends.'"

Laughter floated across the yard from the garden. She took a courage-boosting breath. "I've spent most of my life letting other people lead me around. I'm trying to break that, so when you grabbed my hand yesterday, something kind of snapped."

"I'm sorry."

So there it was. He'd said it. She stared into eyes that reminded her of a forest floor camouflaged in soft moss and drifting leaves.

"So am I. I shouldn't have gotten so—"

A yelp of pain stopped her words. It came from directly above them.

"I'm bleeding!" Skylar's voice shrilled. "Help! Izzy! Get this off me quick!"

Ryan jumped up and was already in the kitchen by the time Heather flung her leg over the picnic table bench. "We're coming, Skylar! Hang on!"

⚜

Heather's heart slammed her ribs as she ran up the stairs on Ryan's heels. At a bedroom door, Ryan smacked his hands on the frame and stopped. She plowed into him. He stepped aside, his arm sliding around her and resting on the small of her back.

In the center of the pink-and-green-striped room stood two girls in long sparkling dresses. Skylar held one hand away from her body, supported by her other hand. A thin thread of blood ran down her thumb and onto the tissue Izzy shoved at her. Neither girl's attention was on the blood. Their eyes were focused on the inside-out white glove in Izzy's hand. A long ivory glove with a red splotch on the thumb.

"That's it? We ran up here for *that*?" Once again, Ryan's voice held that hint of disappointment. Once again, his hero skills weren't needed.

"I was trying to open this pin"—Skylar held up a round brooch encrusted with pearls and bright blue stones—"and it poked me through my dress-up glove. Can we wash it?"

Izzy shrugged. "Maybe in hot, hot water."

Heather gasped. Ryan was a hero after all. They'd gotten here in time to save the glove.

She stepped away from the heat she was sure was leaving a permanent imprint of a hand on her back. She took the tissue and wiped Skylar's hand. Ryan shook his head. "I'll go find something to stop the gush."

"These gowns are gorgeous, Skylar." Heather fingered the gold mesh overlaying champagne-colored satin. The empire waist landed at Skylar's hips. The skirt pooled around her feet. Izzy was practically drowning in blue satin and ivory lace. The musty smell of an old attic wafted from the fabric. The pieces looked like they ought to be hanging in a museum. "Your mom lets you play with these?"

Skylar shrugged. "She doesn't know."

"I see." *Not sure I want to be around when she finds out.*

Ryan came back and wrapped a pink plastic bandage around Skylar's thumb. "Nice threads, ladies."

"A bit too nice." Heather rested her hands on her hips. "Are they family heirlooms?"

"I've never seen them before."

"How about if we take off the ball gowns and hang them up, girls? They're a little too delicate to play with. Where do they belong, Skylar?"

Izzy picked up her skirt and walked over to a shelf of chapter books. Skylar bit her lip then pointed to Izzy's backpack.

"You brought them, Iz?"

"Yeah." She spoke to the books.

"Does your mother know you play with them?"

Another shrug, her back still turned. "She's never told me not to."

It should surprise her that Natalie would allow her seven-year-old to play dress-up in a dress probably valued over a thousand dollars. But it didn't. Nothing was too expensive if it kept the little girl happy. And quiet. She gave herself a mental slap as she gently lifted the gold and ivory gown over Skylar's head. The girl looked skinny and tomboyish in shorts and T-shirt. Heather folded the gown as if the gold mesh were made of spun sugar. "Do you wish you could wear all this frippery every day?"

"All this what?"

"Frippery. It's an old-fashioned word for fancy clothes."

"Oh." Skylar looked longingly at Izzy, still draped in satin.

Izzy slipped one shoulder and then the other out of her gown and stepped out of it. Heather cringed as her flip-flop landed on a swath of lace.

"Let's go get another cookie." Izzy didn't look at her once before running out the door.

Ryan snagged the blue dress by the shoulders. "Here. I'm scared to touch it."

Heather spread it out on the bed and folded the sleeves into the center. "Something's up. Coventry hosted a vintage clothing expo last year. Dresses like this went for a couple grand each. Though I wouldn't be shocked to find out Natalie let her play in these, she looked guilty."

"She brought them in this?" Ryan picked up the pink backpack. "There's still stuff in—"

Heather looked up. Ryan held something round and flat and gold, about the size of a silver dollar. She stepped closer. "It's a pocket watch."

Leaves and stems carved into the cover were topped by flowers made of tiny red and green jewels. At the center, six clear stones surrounded a single green gem.

Ryan pushed the stem. The top flipped open. Roman numerals encircled a white face decorated with faint gold filigree. Behind a disk of scratched glass on the opposite side, was a sepia-toned photograph of a fortyish woman with a high lace collar and hair piled on top of her head and a man with hair slicked straight back and a droopy mustache.

"My grandfather had one of these. Not this fancy. It had a dust cover. . ." Ryan pressed the tip of his tongue between his teeth as he slid his fingernail into an almost undetectable recess. The back popped open, revealing the watch mechanism—a maze of tiny gears and screws. There were words stamped in the inside of the cover he'd just pried off.

ECHAPTA CYLINDRE ET HUIT TROUS EN RUBIS

"I took a year of French in high school. It says something about holes in rubies. Eight holes in rubies. Make any sense?"

"No, but this does." He walked over to a desk and flipped on a lamp. "See that?" He pointed to the head of an eagle, about the size of a kernel of popcorn, etched into the metal. "That means it's at least eighteen-karat gold."

"How do you know that?"

"I will only tell you if you pinkie swear not to laugh."

She pressed one hand to her diaphragm, where laugh spasms

were already forming. Holding out the little finger of her other hand, she looked at him with all the solemnity she could muster. "I promise."

He linked his finger with hers, squeezed, then pulled away and turned toward the window. "It was in *Cyboraider and the Jupiter Jungle War.*"

"A comic book."

"Yeah. Cyboraider was transported from Jupiter in 2812 back to nineteenth-century Paris and he found a necklace he thought had once belonged to Cleopatra but the eagle hallmark meant it couldn't have been that old so. . ." He looked back at her with a grin, part little boy, part anything but.

She shook her head, picked up the backpack, and pulled out what appeared to be a passport holder. Inside, she found only a torn scrap of paper. A telegram.

Heather read the first line and gasped.

FEB. 1, 1912 RECEIVED OF R. HAMILTON £594. TWO FIRST CLASS TICKETS R.M.S TITANIC. SAILS APRIL 10. PICK UP TICKETS WHITE STAR OFFICE SOUTHAMPTON.

CHAPTER 12

Stephannie spread the check registers out on her alpaca rug, laid down on her belly, and picked up the oldest one. Her father would have been twenty-four. He would have been out of college, living on his own, and working. . .where? There was so much she didn't know. Because she'd never cared enough to listen.

She lifted the paper cover of the little gray book. Her breath caught at the sight of her father's handwriting. Bold and sure, even back then. Not swirled and wispy and uncertain like hers.

Electric company, gas company, telephone. The basics. At the end of every month he'd written checks for four hundred and fifty dollars. Rent? She looked up at her white suede couch, the flat screen TV on the wall, and the cascade of teardrop-shaped bulbs floating from the chandelier above her. Snatches of her father's college tales surfaced. Pranks and practical jokes and all-night study sessions. Camping, canoeing, backpacking. Living on the typical college fare of pizza and ramen noodles. Her father hadn't been born into money, and now that he had it, he still knew how to enjoy the simple things in life. That fact had always annoyed his wife.

She leafed through that year and the next. In the fourth book she noticed a change. Rent doubled, utilities increased. Next to several deposits he'd written "Bonus." Several months into the increase in his deposits, he quit adding and subtracting. The total column was empty. So unlike her father. Had he reached a point where his cushion was large enough that it didn't matter? Was life too hurried to take the time to reconcile his checkbook? Or did he not want someone to know how much money he had?

An entry from the next book jumped out at her.

New York Jewelers $4378.97

Her mother's engagement ring.

She imagined her father at twenty-seven—the age she'd set for finally growing up. Young, in love, rapidly scaling ladders in the hotel business. Four thousand, three hundred and seventy-eight dollars was an investment in future happiness.

An investment that didn't pay off in the long run.

What had gone wrong? Had it blindsided him, or had he entered into marriage to the daughter of a man who owned one of the largest buildings on Michigan Avenue with a gutful of doubts?

She skimmed the next few pages until another line took her breath. Written with a light hand and a fine-point pen, it was difficult to make out the amount.

PP $34.00

Or was it $340.00? She stood and walked to the window, holding it in direct light. A smudge to the right of the four made it impossible to tell.

PP. Planned Parenthood? Was this a check her father had written to cover a pregnancy test?

Or the end of a life?

⚜

Andrew leaned back in a gold-cushioned chair. Superior Street traffic drifted up to the rooftop lounge from the base of the Peninsula Hotel. He slipped a lychee nut off a toothpick with his teeth, then lifted his glass and stared at the Terrace through the amber fog of his Ning Sling.

Rose-filled vases sat on low black tables. Wrought iron frames towered over couches stacked with pillows that coordinated with the colors of his drink. Below the Shanghai Terrace were rooms that cost more than many people paid for a month's rent or a mortgage payment. Thirteen hundred dollars for a night in the deluxe suite.

He knew that firsthand. He'd plunked down over two grand for a weekend here with Stephannie.

He remembered it as an uneasy two days. Spying on the competition with the boss's daughter had not proved relaxing. She'd wanted to party. He'd wanted to slink around undetected, talking to housekeeping, sweet talking—or paying—his way into staff-only rooms and gold-walled suites with candlelit Jacuzzis overlooking the Magnificent Mile.

Travel + Leisure magazine readers had voted the Peninsula the number-one large city hotel in 2011. It deserved the award.

He raised his glass to the man he'd been waiting for. Jerry Karstetter, as lanky and angular as when they were in college, loped across the terrace and thrust his hand into Andrew's. "How's it going?" He pushed up dark-framed glasses then swept an arc with one long arm. "Is this allowed? Shouldn't we be patronizing the Lansing?" He took the chair across from Andrew.

"Not for this conversation."

A server materialized behind Jerry and set the drink Andrew had ordered for him on the small table between them. Jerry picked up the old-fashioned glass and nodded. "You remembered."

"Hospitality is my game, Jer."

"That it is." Jerry sipped his mai tai. "How's the old man doing?"

"Looks like he'll pull through."

"Good." The horn-rimmed glasses slipped. "Though I imagine you would have benefited. . ."

Andrew cringed inwardly, reminding himself he'd invited the man because of who he knew and what he could do. Not because he liked him. "Not really."

"So what can I do for you? I'm guessing we're not here to catch up on the good old days." Pale blue eyes took on a steely glint.

Leaning forward, Andrew set his drink on the table, rested his elbows on his knees, and tried to assess the trustworthiness of a man who made his living breaking trusts. "This doesn't go beyond this spot, understood?"

"Of course."

"I need some information. I have reason to believe Parker Lansing has another daughter."

"Whoa. Tell me what you know."

"I'll send you the address. She lives in Racine, looks to be a couple of years older than Stephannie. That's it." He picked up his glass. "No, there is one more thing. She has a master's degree and she's working on a business plan."

"For what?"

"That's what you're going to tell me. Among other things."

"This is a pleasant surprise."

Dianna Lansing looked up at the massive baroque mirror angling out from the striped wallpaper at Table Fifty-Two.

It's too far away, Mom. Can't see yourself in it. But you should. Stephannie reached out and smoothed a stray strand of white-blond hair her mother had missed. She'd missed a lot this morning. It was disconcerting to see her mother less than polished. Their server came and took their order. Her mother ordered an egg-white omelet with asparagus, mushrooms, and heirloom tomatoes. Stephannie pointed to the fried chicken and waffles then handed the menu to the server.

"We haven't spent much time together lately." *Or ever.* "I just thought we both needed a change of scenery."

Her mother narrowed her eyes. "You've changed. Something's different about you since you got back."

I was almost fatherless. That's different. She picked up her coffee cup and wrapped her hands around it. *Different is what I want to be, God. Nice different. But I don't know how.* "I've had time to think about what's important, I guess."

"And what is important to you, Steph?" Her mother set her cup down, shifted in her chair to face her more completely, and folded her arms across her pink blouse.

Stephannie's eyes stung. She wanted a picture of this moment, a photograph that would freeze the look of genuine caring on her mother's face forever. "I want. . .to grow up."

"And what would that look like?"

Defensiveness rose like uncorked champagne. She felt her eyes narrow.

Her mother raised a hand. The corners of her mouth tipped. "I didn't mean that like it sounded. I meant, tell me what you want to be. . .who you want to be."

"I don't know yet." She didn't have an answer because she hadn't known it was what she wanted until it popped out of her mouth. "More responsible, I guess. Seeing Dad lying there with all those tubes and wires woke me up. Life is short and it's. . .precious." Had she ever used that word to describe something she couldn't wear?

"What do you want to do? Do you have a first step in mind?"

Always the planner, the practical one. Stephannie sipped her coffee. "I want a job."

The flash of shock on her mother's face made her smile.

"Where?"

She'd planned this part, intended to use it as leverage, but when it came to the moment of putting it into words, she realized she'd actually be okay with things either way they ended. "I'd like to go to cosmetology school."

If the look she'd seen a moment ago was shock, words didn't exist to label this one. Face blanched, eyes wide, hand plastered against her throat, her mother looked about to gasp her last breath. Stephannie hid the sheer ecstasy of the moment and imagined walking into the Northwestern Memorial admitting office. *We'd like a room for two, please.*

"W–why don't we look at some options. You know what we've always said—you can do anything you set your mind to."

If I could set my mind to anything. Her parents had never openly acknowledged the attention deficit diagnosis. Impossible that the combined genes of Parker and Dianna could have resulted in anything less than perfection. But they had.

The second time around anyway.

She set her cup down and poured a swirl of cream into it. "What were you like at my age, Mom? Did you always know what you wanted to do?" *Did something happen to change you?*

"I was more serious than you. Too serious, your father used to say. Obsessed about school, then obsessed about work." She glanced up at the pressed copper ceiling. "I was your age when we got engaged."

Stephannie leaned in, resting her forearms on the table. "Were you madly in love? I've never heard you talk about how he proposed."

"It wasn't"—she tapped her napkin against her lips then refolded it—"like in the movies. Sometimes things happen to change the way two people—"

Their server approached with glasses of orange juice and a coffee carafe. By the time he left, the softness had left her mother's face. The window had closed. Her mother sipped her juice, set it down, and offered up a straight-lined smile. "That was a long time ago and we're here to talk about you. As I was saying, you have so many career options..."

Andrew set the phone down on top of the notebook page where he'd scribbled a name. Natalie Brooks. The house in Racine belonged to her.

So how did Heather fit in? Was her last name Brooks?

His laptop beckoned, but he resisted. He was paying Jerry so he could avoid the work and frustration.

He walked to the refrigerator, opened it, and stood staring at half-empty shelves, wondering why he'd opened it in the first place. He grabbed an apple and a bottle of iced tea and wandered over to the window. He spent a lot of time staring out of windows, gathering different perspectives of the city—from his office, Parker's, a hospital room, and here, the place he called home, but for some reason it hadn't felt like one for weeks.

Resting his forehead against the glass, he looked down at ant people milling on the sidewalk, their Sunday evening pace less frenetic than it would be tomorrow morning. Where were they all going? What did they want?

It was his job to know. Or rather, he wanted it to be. The first line of the proposal he might never get to propose claimed he understood the mind of the average American. Specifically, he understood their vacation needs in a down economy. They wanted a Disney experience on a camping budget, a Vegas getaway close to home. They wanted an economical, all-inclusive, pretend-you're-somewhere-far-away Lansing-Rivera Escape.

Days, weeks, months of visualizing every corner—every lobby, wall mural, light fixture, bedcover, faucet, and coffeepot had resulted in a vision he could walk through in his mind as clearly as if he'd been there. Lansing-Rivera Escape Hotels—a new concept in vacationing. The only hotel chain in the world that reinvented itself with every season.

His phone rang again. He picked it up, smiled at the name on the screen, and answered it. "You're good, Jer."

"You had doubts?"

"Not a one." *Fears, yes. Doubts, no.*

"Think we're going to find some intriguing stuff here. You ready for this?"

Andrew picked up his pen. "Shoot."

"Natalie Brooks lost her job in April."

"Okay." *And I care because...?*

"She worked right here in the Windy City." He paused, clearly intending to ramp the tension. "Natalie Brooks is the ex-CEO of Coventry Midwest Hotels."

Andrew sank into a leather chair. "So she's the one..."

Jerry laughed. "She sure is."

⁂

January 12, 1912

"I think you just have to turn the knob." Bending at the waist, Maggie gripped her skirt and apron with one hand, reached out, and twisted the silver knob on the new electric range with the other. She took a step backward, nearly toppling Mrs. Hamilton, who quickly righted herself and once again took up her place of safety behind Maggie.

Nothing happened. "I'm sorry, ma'am, but it doesn't appear to be—" She echoed Mrs. Hamilton's gasp as the iron coils glowed red.

"Is it supposed to do that?" Maggie inched closer.

"I don't think we should chance making the cream sauce on it."

We? Maggie suppressed a laugh. There would be no "we" today. With more pressing things on her mind—the man who slept directly above the kitchen and the girl she'd told to return here after work—and in no hurry to begin the process of turning the wife into a *house*wife, Maggie popped open the gold watch pinned to her

141

bodice. "You'll want to be dressing, ma'am."

"Yes, you're right." Mrs. Hamilton patted the pouf of hair above her forehead. "Everything is in order?"

Maggie gestured toward the miniature pastries lined up like parade marchers on the enamel-topped table. "You'll be serving crème puffs filled with creamed chicken and garnished with cranberry relish, and I tried a jelly roll recipe I found in the new Fannie Farmer cookbook."

"The one Mr. Hamilton bought for *me*." The woman looked as though she'd just bitten into a cake made with salt instead of sugar—like the one she'd baked for her husband's fiftieth birthday. "Lovely." She straightened the waistband of her skirt. "Maggie, I swear, I don't know if I'm more afraid of Mr. Hamilton finding out about this meeting today, or of learning to run this house. This was not what I signed up for when I married Maxwell Hamilton."

"By the time Mr. Hamilton returns, you will be able to fix mashed potatoes and a fine pot roast."

Mrs. Hamilton fingered the cameo on her ruffled collar. "He will change his mind about all this nonsense, won't he? Once I've convinced him I've set aside my 'silly notions' of women having the same—"

The door to the back porch creaked open and slammed shut. The next sound was unmistakable. The clunk of the two leather satchels Maggie had tucked under the carriage seat just this morning.

Mr. Hamilton strode into the kitchen, took one look at the pastries assembled on the table, and marched into the dining room where the table was laden with gold-rimmed china. "What in thunder is going on here? I've been gone five hours and you've already arranged a party?"

Maggie glanced at the woman whose face matched the tablecloth she'd pressed before dawn and knew if she didn't save the day she would lose her position before she had the opportunity to work her way out of it. "Mrs. Hamilton is hosting the Ladies' Art Guild this afternoon."

"What in tarnation is the Ladies' Art Guild?" He waved away the answer before it had time to form in Maggie's imagination. He walked into the living room and picked up his pipe. "Cancel it, Evangeline. My trip is off and I'm in no mood for a gaggle of women in my house."

Horror masked Mrs. Hamilton's face. Her standing with the women depended on her ability to stand up to this man—if she couldn't deceive him.

Maggie nodded toward the kitchen. The woman who was supposed to be ordering Maggie Parker's days stepped through the doorway on command. The door swung shut behind them.

"Go along with him. Agree to cancel," Maggie whispered. "I have an idea." She untied her apron and pushed the button on her watch. The top sprang open, giving her a glimpse of her parents. Lifeless, in shades of gray. She veered her gaze to the fine gold watch hands. "We have one hour." She untied her apron. "There is coffee made." She slid the apron over her head and threw it on a chair. "Bring him some and soothe his nerves. I'll be back as soon as I can." The last words whipped over her shoulder as she flew out the back door.

She wove between barren rosebushes and navigated around the fountain, whispering as she ran. "Be home, Charles. Be home and make this work."

CHAPTER 13

Izzy fell asleep before eight, but Heather promised to wake her when her mother called.

Propped against pillows on the bed in her Persian throne room, Heather glanced at the clock. Nine thirty-six and still no need to wake Izzy. She sighed and opened her computer. Two new e-mails— one from a friend from Coventry letting her in on all of the latest corporate gossip. The other had an attachment—and a subject line that tightened her throat like a cinching lasso.

We're home!

Like a gaper at the scene of an accident, she gazed down, knowing she might feel sickened at the sight, yet powerless to keep from looking.

We had such a wonderful time. Can't wait to talk to you and tell you everything. I love, love, love being married! Got our pics from the photographer. Here's one. I'll send more later and some honeymoon shots. Hope all is going well with you. Mom told me about getting stuck with the little girl. I know you're making the best of it and turning it into something fun.

Heather waited for the nausea to pass. Her finger hovered over the touch pad. Did she really need the added torture of a wedding picture? Then again, maybe looking at it would show her how far she'd come in a week. She tapped the pad. The picture filled her screen. And pain slammed into her sternum like the hoof of a half-ton steer.

Jen in strapless, sparkling, lacy white. Zach in starched white, black, and a bolero tie. Tall, tanned, crooked smile beaming down at the girl on his arm. Jen stared back with a rapt and wide-eyed Disney princess gaze.

She closed her laptop and her eyes and breathed away the tears the way laboring women staved off pain during contractions. *I'm over him. I'm so over him.*

To stop the pain, she imagined herself in a place where Zach would feel out of place.

CONFAB—COFFEE & CONNECTION.

Just visualizing the pumpkin-colored letters and her mirror-image-coffee-cup logo on the cover of her unfinished business proposal calmed her. She slid off the bed and stretched her arms over her head, then bent and touched her toes. If not for the little girl sleeping down the hall, she'd go for a run to work off the stress damage inflicted by a single photograph. Instead, she stretched out on the floor.

"One." She curled, tightening her abs. Closing her eyes, she pictured warm welcoming colors swirled on the walls, round fireplaces, individual New Orleans-inspired desserts in white oval dishes. Bread pudding with caramel sauce, pecan pie with cinnamon whipped cream, praline cheesecake, lemon icebox pie.

"Two." Soft, pink-tinted lightbulbs in "quirky" free-form glass fixtures. Royal blue, spring green, ruby.

"Three." Leather couches, chairs, and love seats with mandatory footstools and fanciful pillows. Gold, sage, plum, and wine.

"Four." Round black tables. Curvy, contoured counters. Not a straight line in the place. A subliminal message. . .*gather round.*

"Five." *Spice. Five spice.* Anise, cloves, cinnamon, fennel, Sichuan pepper. Exotic spiced coffee scents to lure, calm, and make you want to linger.

"Six." A second room. Rheostats to adjust the lighting to fit the mood and occasion.

She finished the crunches, extended her arms, and reached, elongating her torso.

Her phone rang. She sat up, scrambled to the bed, and grabbed it, baring her teeth at Natalie's name. Natalie, the mother who had not called her daughter for two days. "Hello." *What's your excuse? Better make it good even though I'm not the one who needs to hear it.*

"Heather, listen, we're swamped down here, but I just wanted to let you know I'm okay. I knew you'd be thinking I'd disappeared and left you with Izzy." Her laugh seemed just a tad wobbly.

How does one get "swamped" at a conference? "Izzy's fine. She made a new friend. We had lunch with—"

"Can I give you a call tomorrow? I'm in the middle—"

"One quick question. Do you let Izzy play with your vintage dresses?"

"Vintage dresses?"

"Yeah. There's a gold one and a blue one. Victorian looking. And there was a watch—"

"I let her keep two dress-up dresses—a white one she wears when she plays bride and a seafoam bridesmaid dress I wore in a wedding about ten years ago. That's all."

"You're sure?"

"Of course I'm sure." Familiar irritation coated her voice. "Maybe they came with the house. Anyway, I have to run. I'll call soon."

"Yeah. Sure. I'll tell Izzy you"—the background noise stopped. She stared at the screen—"called."

♔

Ryan trudged up the stairs to his apartment around quarter to ten on Sunday night. He'd watched a movie with Paul and Kurt after Heather and Izzy left. At least he'd tried to watch the movie. The women in his life did everything in their power to make him miss the last half hour. After the kids fell asleep in sleeping bags in the playroom, Tammy, Amanda, and Marissa planted themselves on the floor and began a round-robin inquisition.

"What is she going to do after Izzy's mom gets back?"

"Is she planning on staying in Racine?"

"Should we invite her next Sunday?"

After trying to get by with grunts, shrugs, and nods for about twenty minutes, he'd finally picked up the remote, paused the movie, dodged pillow projectiles from his brothers, and attempted to silence them. "Why didn't you interrogate her when you had the chance? Isn't that why you invited her in the first place?"

Tammy looked at Marissa. Marissa grinned at Amanda. "Duh. We didn't put her on the hot seat because we *like* her."

Ryan smiled to himself now as he punched the key code on the pad next to his door. He loved the sound of the bolt snapping back against the hub. *Smack.* He'd brought up the security system topic with Heather again today—right after they looked up antique gold watches. Some were selling for a gob of money. Who knew what kind of valuables Izzy's mother had sitting around in cardboard boxes?

Maybe the guy with the camera knew.

He deposited containers of fried rice and sushi in the fridge, flopped onto the couch, flipped on the TV, then shut it off again. He picked up his phone. He'd started the day hoping Heather wouldn't show. He'd ended it wishing the day wouldn't end. Watching her with the kids and his sisters—the easy way she pitched in with dishes and the way she bantered with Paul and Kurt. "She fits," his mother had whispered as his parents left.

She fits. In his family, yes. He couldn't help but imagine how she'd fit in his arms. But he wasn't likely to find out soon. They hadn't gotten to finish the talk they'd started before Skylar's scream.

He pushed a button on his phone. Now was as good a time as any.

⚜

One hand holding her phone to her ear, Heather walked through the house, snapping off lights as Ryan rattled on about her need for a security system.

She stopped at the front window. Moonlight dappled the uneven surface of the lake, shining through the slats on the back of the empty park bench. Silhouetted against the silver glow, the lamp-post directly across from the house resembled an arm rising out of the water with a glowing orb in its fist.

"I'll talk to her about it again tomorrow." *If she calls.*

"Thank you."

"Thank me? For the potential sale?"

"No." The single word seemed rough, deeper than his usual voice. "Thank you for agreeing to do something to keep you safe."

Heather swallowed hard and sat down on the window seat. It was her turn to talk, but she didn't know where to take the conversation. "You're welcome" didn't seem like the appropriate response. And then the answer landed on her tongue. "Thank *you*"—her voice hit the same gravely tone his had—"for caring."

She walked over to the couch, sat down, and waited while the time on the DVD player morphed from 9:59 to 10:00. She heard him take a breath.

"That's what that scene at the beach was all about, you know. Me caring about your safety." The clock changed to a symmetrical blue number. 10:01. "Me caring about *you*. I had a bad feeling about the guy. Something just didn't add up. I know I looked like some kind of jealous control freak, but I was only trying to stop you before you said too much. I'd rather err on the side of caution, you know?"

Me caring about you. The words drained the last remnants of her resentment. "I should have seen it like that instead of getting all militant on you."

"If he never shows up again, you are free to call me a nutcase. And if he *does* show up again you are also free to call me."

"And you'll be my real live hero?"

She was sure she heard him swallow. "I'll do everything in my power to be your hero." He laughed. "Sorry. Should have been a 'corny line' alert for that one."

"It wasn't corny. It was nice. Every girl needs a hero."

⚜

Ryan poured a glass of orange juice and held it to his forehead. He walked over to a window and slid it open. It wasn't so much her words as the way she'd said it. *Every girl needs a hero*—hushed and breathy. He could almost feel the words tickling his ear.

Get a grip, Tobin. "Would I sound controlling if I said I wanted to take you somewhere to show you something, but I don't want to tell you what or where?"

She laughed. "Maybe a little."

"Amanda offered to watch Izzy if I could convince you to go out. So can I?"

A short pause, and then a breathy "Yes," that heated the room. "Tomorrow afternoon then." He groped for a neutral topic. "What did you find out from Izzy's mom about the dresses?"

"She didn't know anything about them."

"Weird."

"Very. And Izzy's being so strange about it. She says she found them in a box, but every time I press for details she changes the subject or acts like she can't remember."

"She's too smart for that. She's hiding something."

"You're sure she couldn't have gotten them at Kurt and Amanda's?"

"Absolutely. I told everyone about them after you left. I may not be very good at describing a dress, but somebody would have said something if they had vintage dresses tucked away. The girls were all just intrigued. We got ourselves a mystery, Miss Conrad."

"So use your Spidey sense and let's figure it out."

"It's kind of obvious. If she didn't get it at Kurt's and her mother doesn't know anything about it, she either stole the stuff before they moved or she found it in the house. From my wish-I-were-professional viewpoint, I don't think she fits the criminal profile."

"So our hypothesis is she found them here."

"Yep. Is she sleeping?"

"Yes. I heard her mumbling in her sleep last night. Think I should try to get her to talk in her sleep?"

Ryan laughed. "I think it might be smarter to search her room. Is she a heavy sleeper?"

"I don't know, but I forgot to tell her to bring her dirty clothes downstairs so I've got a legitimate reason for rummaging around in there if she wakes up."

"Go. Do it. I'll hang on while you rummage around."

"Okay," she whispered.

He pictured her uncurling her legs and standing up. Where was she? In the living room? Kitchen? In the room that looked like a

Persian king's bedchamber? Like a room where the king's harem danced with jewels in their navels, fringe jiggling with gyrating hips. He smacked the cold glass onto his eyelid and tried to resist imagining a jewel in the navel he'd glimpsed on the beach.

"Okay. I'm going in." Her soft voice sent shivers along his arm.

He heard a door unlatch. Then another. The sound of hangers rubbing against a closet pole. Soft rustling. "Remember to check for hidden doors," he whispered. He stared at the clock above his kitchen sink. A minute passed. As he waited, he looked around his apartment—at the slanted lime green walls of his kitchen, the old white fridge, and the tiny two-person table with its cactus centerpiece.

Beyond the kitchen were two rooms—a bathroom with a single lightbulb on a pull string and a shower but no tub, and a bedroom with only enough room for a double bed and a dresser. And a Spider-Man poster. He stared down at the teal-and-green indoor-outdoor carpeting in the dinky living room. The room held four pieces of furniture—a cracked army-green vinyl couch, an orange velour recliner, a coffee table, and a bookshelf. Two years ago, the women in his life had tried to redecorate while he was on a ski trip in Colorado. It had taken him all of ten minutes to undo their girly touches—and take the trophies off the shelves. It wasn't hard to relive the rage he'd hidden from them at the sight of the gold idols to his foolishness lining the top of the bookshelf. The moment they'd left he'd pitched them into a box. A ricocheting gold football had left a scar on one of the coffee table legs.

He'd taken the trophies to a place that bought gold and gotten a miserly handful of money that he donated to the National Kidney Foundation.

"I'm out." Heather's whisper brought him back to the present. "I didn't find a thing. I'm going to check the other closets. I'm getting a crick in my neck. I don't have any hands left when I'm holding the phone and the flashlight. How about if I call you if I find something?"

"How about if you call me even if you don't?"

"Okay." Again, the soft, breathy tone. "How long will you be up?"

"As long as it takes."

CHAPTER 14

Feeling like an intruder in the house she was supposed to be house sitting, Heather opened Natalie's box-filled closet and stepped inside. The walls of the narrow room were papered in blue stripes. It was large enough that it could have been used as a nursery. She swept the room with light, looking for a box that wasn't marked with the moving company's logo.

On top of an open box she spotted a pale pink book. "My Baby Book." Were there pictures of Natalie and her ex-husband cuddling their baby? Happy times that had ended with divorce? Or had they never married? Natalie never talked about it except to say it was a subject she didn't talk about.

In the hallway, she ran her free hand along the walls. What other secrets was the house keeping from them? She checked the two empty rooms and then her own closet. Nothing. There had been plenty of times in the past week when Heather was busy in the kitchen and Izzy was in her room. She could have taken the secret stairs. Down. . .or up.

She pressed her hand against the wall at the end of the hall-way. It popped open and warm air tumbled down the stairs, rolling over her, mingling with cooler air rising from the basement—both breaking the normal laws of nature.

The skinny stairs creaked. Imagining herself a backstairs maid in lace-up shoes and long skirts with a candleholder in her hand, she felt along the walls, looking for any trace of another hidden door. She reached the top without finding anything. There was no landing at the top. The stairs simply stopped. She pushed on the wall and the door popped open.

Except for the two pieces of furniture, the little room was empty. *Izzy, where did you get that stuff?*

"Heather?"

Heather jumped and whirled around. In the dim light filtering up from the second floor, stood a mop-headed little girl.

"What are you doing up?"

"I heard something." Her cottony, sleep-thick voice held a tinge of fear. "What are you doing up here?"

"Just looking around." She walked down and picked her up. Did Natalie love that about her daughter? That even at seven she was still scoopable? Still cuddly. "Let's get you back to bed."

"I'm not tired." She yawned into Heather's shoulder.

Heather stopped. "Then let's explore." She turned and walked back up the steps.

Izzy slithered out of her arms. She walked over to the secretary desk and stood in front of it. Her hands slid behind her back and grabbed onto the sides of the desk.

Heather eyed the strange expression, the almost protective stance. She looked down at bare toes curling under and noticed something she hadn't seen before. There were casters on the desk legs. "That desk looks moveable."

Izzy's eyes widened. "I bet it's really, really *super* heavy."

"I'm sure it is. But we're really, really super strong if we work together."

Narrow shoulders drooped, then rose. "Why would we want to move it?"

"Because there might be something behind it." *Though I never would have thought so if you hadn't plastered yourself against it like a mini mama tiger.*

"But look"—Izzy motioned up and behind with her chin—"if a door was there you would see it. The desk isn't taller than a door."

Heather chewed on her bottom lip to keep from smiling. "You're right. It isn't."

Izzy breathed a not-so-quiet sigh. "Can we go back to my room and read?"

"In just a minute." Heather stepped to one side. Izzy mirrored her step. "But don't you think it's possible, in a house with so many secret doors, that there could be a door behind here that isn't very tall?"

"Why would anyone make a door that grown-ups couldn't walk through?"

"Why would anyone make doors without handles?" She stepped around Izzy and braced her hands against the sides of the secretary. "Let's just—"

"Fine. I'll tell you, but you're spoiling *every*thing."

Heather dropped her hands. "What do you mean?"

"It was my secret adventure and I wanted to show it to Skylar before anyone else so then it could be her secret adventure, too, and then I was going to show you, but now it won't be a secret anymore and Skylar won't want to come for a sleepover if there isn't an adventure." She let out a long, loud breath and hugged her arms to her belly.

Heather dropped to her knees and put her hands on Izzy's arms. "So you found something behind the desk?"

Izzy nodded, a pout slowly pooching out her bottom lip. "A treasure chest."

"Is that where you found the dresses and the watch?"

"Uh-huh." She looked at her toes, twisted her mouth to one side, then shrugged. "I guess you can see it." She braced against the side of the desk and, before Heather had even gotten into position, moved it several feet.

Enough to reveal a door about four feet high. This one had a handle. Izzy turned it and pulled the door open. Heather stepped in behind Izzy and kneeled in front of a barn-shaped chest. Izzy opened it. A plate on the inside of the cover proclaimed:

MANUFACTURED 1910
IF YOU WANT TO GET THE BEST MADE TRUNK
LOOK FOR TRUNKS MANUFACTURED BY
M. M. SECOR
MIDWESTERN TRUNK & TRAVELING BAG MANUFACTORY,
AT RACINE, WIS.

Heather ran her finger along the edge of the plate. "Your treasure chest is over a hundred years old." She sat back on her heels. "That little leather pouch that was in your backpack with the dresses—that came from this chest?"

"Uh-huh."

Heather rubbed her arm. "Have you ever heard of the *Titanic*?"

"I watched the movie a million times. It's my favorite."

Heather cringed. "Your mom lets you watch it?"

"Of course. I looooove Rose's dresses. They're just like the ones I found." Izzy's eyes brightened. "What if Rose lived right here in this house!"

"I think maybe Rose is just a made-up character for the movie, but I think a lady might have lived here who"—she didn't quite know how to finish—"I don't know."

Her phone buzzed with a text message. "Ryan! I told him I'd call him if I found anything. He's waiting to hear—" She corralled her tone. "Is it okay with you if I call him?"

A drawn-out sigh filled the closet. "I suppose. But he hasta promise not to tell Skylar 'cuz this is my adventure and I get to tell her. Promise?"

"I promise." *But it's my adventure, too, kid.*

⬥

Ryan was at the door at seven the next morning. Heather had made sticky buns and the three of them ate a hurried breakfast and headed to the attic room. They spread a sheet on the floor. Ryan had brought two LED lanterns and his camera. "Let's move it out of the closet. You take that end."

Heather stepped into the closet. As she bent to grab one of the handles, her backside bumped the wall. A familiar click echoed in the small space. She looked at Ryan. Izzy giggled.

"*Another* one?"

Izzy stood with her hand on the camouflaged door, inching it open as they hauled the trunk out. "It's a room. A *huge* room."

The room was empty. The walls were papered in the same stripes as Natalie's closet. Light fell in hazy shafts onto a distressed floor.

Ryan walked the length of the room then stopped. "Look closely at the floor. Look at the marks."

Heather bent and touched a round depression. The marks were repeated at regular intervals. "Beds. Doesn't it look like this was a dormitory?"

"Or a hospital maybe?"

Heather counted. "Twelve. Six on each side. What was this?" she whispered.

Izzy bounced. "Let's look at the stuff in the treasure chest."

Ryan took her hand and together they ducked through the low doorway. "Let's move slow and systematic. I want to take pictures and catalog each thing exactly where it is in the trunk before we take it out."

Heather lifted two flat books, one black, one silver. She turned them over. Yearbooks. The covers were imprinted with dates: 1975 and 1976. A picture fell out of one. Three boys, all in mid to late teens, sitting on the hood of what appeared to be a beat-up orange van. Izzy pointed to the boy in the middle. "He's the one in the picture we found in the desk."

"It's like a time capsule. There's a newspaper from 2011 and a couple from the nineties." She picked up a large brown envelope, thick with papers, and set it aside. "We'll look through these downstairs where the light's better."

Izzy picked up a black velvet bag with a braided cord cinching the top. "What's this?"

"It's a purse. I think they called them reticules back then."

"That's a funny name." She opened the bag. "Look." She pulled out a small round tin, dark blue with white lettering—NIVEA-CREME. Next she retrieved a wrapped bar of Sapolio Shampoo Soap and another of John H. Woodbury's Facial Soap. She dumped the purse upside down onto the contents of the trunk. A blue can fell out. On the front was a picture of a Geisha girl and the words *Mennen's Sen Yang Talc Powder.*

Heather opened the cover of the talc. A faint scent still lingered in the powder. She lifted two more dresses, one a pale ivory, the other a dusty rose. Several long skirts, blouses with high collars, silk stockings, and fabric-covered shoes. She wanted to linger over each thing. She picked up a pair of pink shoes. Ryan reached toward her and she handed him one.

"It looks new, doesn't it?"

She smiled up at him. "Actually, it looks about a hundred years old."

"Funny. I mean, the shoes aren't stretched at all and nothing looks worn or like it's been washed. Whoever packed this had one fun shopping marathon."

"Or they ordered it from Sears and Roebuck."

Ryan nodded, his expression distracted. "At first I was thinking maybe the person who owned this—"

"Rose. I'm pretending she's Rose." Izzy held a silver earring to her ear.

"Okay." Ryan's smile was slow and easy. "At first I was thinking Rose might have returned from a trip and just never unpacked her things. But now that I see it's all new—new *old*—I don't think she ever took the trip."

A shiver skittered up Heather's back. She rubbed her arms.

Izzy sat cross-legged on the corner of the sheet. "She packed her clothes to run away with the nice pirate, but the mean one kidnapped her first and she never, ever came back."

Ryan sat next to her. "Maybe," he said, his voice sounding far off.

Silence descended on the tiny room as they each imagined the woman who had packed for a journey she'd never taken.

Heather wiped all trace of sticky buns from the kitchen table then set the thick brown envelope down and took the empty chair next to Ryan and kitty-corner from Izzy. She turned the envelope over.

HAMILTON LOCK AND LATCH
INVOICES—JULY 10–15, 1911
She slid the fasteners out of the way and pulled out two thick sheaves of tri-folded white paper. She unfolded the first.

Izzy gasped.

"Mouse stories!"

"What?" Ryan scooted to Heather's side. "Did you look at this already?"

"No. My mom read them to me when I was little. We found them in the piano."

"Wait." Heather looked down at the flowing brownish-black script on the page, *The Adventures of Magdalena Mouse*, scrawled across the top. "You put this in here?"

"No. I never saw it."

Ryan tipped his head. His brow furrowed. "Not the envelope. The papers. You put the papers in the envelope and then in the trunk."

"Why would I do that?"

Heather rubbed her temple. "It's the Matrix, the Twilight Zone—I'm telling you, this house has an alternate universe or time continuum or some such sci-fi thing."

Ryan let out a short huff of a sigh. "Okay, Iz, let's start at the beginning. How do you know about this"—he leaned over Heather, who hadn't found it necessary to right herself yet—"Magdalena Mouse story?"

The girl sighed as if she'd explained it a thousand times and was losing patience with the slow adults. "When I was a baby my mom found the stories in a book in the bench of my dad's piano."

"Were they handwritten like this or was it printed like a storybook?"

"Just like this."

"The same handwriting?"

"Yep."

Heather shook her head. "One of them must be a copy. Maybe the author made copies and sold them."

Izzy tugged on the papers and Heather let her take them. She picked up the second bundle of pages, unfolded it, and stared at the title.

ESSAYS ON LIFE AND GOD'S PLAN FOR WOMEN

She read the first line. " 'In the beginning, God created the sun, the moon, and the stars in the heavens. He formed platypuses and emus and humpbacked whales. And then, from a handful of mud, He fashioned man and said, 'It is not good.' "

As she locked eyes with Ryan, a laugh burst from her lips. "*This* was written a hundred years ago?"

Ryan rolled his eyes. "No wonder men wouldn't let women vote back then."

After an elbow jab to his ribs, she turned back to the script that flowed in ruler-straight lines across the page. " 'So He took a rib from the man and whittled and carved until He had sculpted the most exquisite creature yet and He called her woman, because she was the best part of man.' "

Heather let out a short squeal. "I love this. I wish I'd writ—"

Izzy tugged at her sleeve. "This is the beginning." She tapped her finger on the "mouse stories." "This is like the 'Once upon a time' part. I can't read cursive really good, but the stories Mom read were like the middle of a story." She handed it back to Heather. "Read it."

In spite of the dizzying sensation of being at the center of the Matrix, she began to read.

" 'In a fanciful land just west of your fondest dreams and due east of the Isle of Imagination, Magdalena Mouse lived between the walls of a grand and beautiful mansion on the shore of a grand and beautiful sea. It was Magdalena's job to make everyone else who lived in the grand house happy. She fed them, she clothed them, she nursed them when they were sick, and let them throw things at her when they were mad. Because of all Magdalena did, the whole world thought the Tabbycats, who lived in the magnificent house, were a happy, grand, beautiful, and magnificent family.

" 'Magdalena's other job was to never, ever, ever tell the world the truth about the Tabbycats.

" 'On one particular morning, the sun was still snoring when Magdalena pulled back the covers on her tiny iron bed. She let out a squeak as her feet hit the cold floor. The house was still chilly because it was Magdalena's job to start the fires before anyone else, including the sun, awakened.

" 'As quick as a mouse, she slipped on her black stockings, pulled her black dress over her head and put on the starched white apron hanging on the back of the door. A moment on her knees in prayer, a splash of water from the pitcher, a little tooth powder, and a quick brushing of her tail, and she was ready to face the busy day.

" 'She scurried off between the walls, first to Mr. and Mrs. Tabbycat's bedroom, where, as quiet as a mouse, she struck a match and touched it to the kindling she had stacked in the fireplace the night before. The wood burst into flames and she scampered out. Down the narrow stairway she flew without a sound and walked into her favorite room in the whole house.

" 'It was so early in the morning, she had to light the gas lamps to find her way to the cookstove. It was an old stove, but Magdalena liked it and it liked her. Together they had made thousands of delicious meals, but all that was about to change.

" 'Everything in the big house was about to change.

" 'Christmas was coming—and so was Leo Tabbycat.' "

January 12, 1912

Be home, Charles. And think fast.

Maggie walked into the Caswells' kitchen without knocking. Hilde looked up from peeling potatoes. Her face turned rigid. Like the anise candy Maggie had made for Christmas, Hilde had reached the hard crack stage. From warm to brittle in a mere second.

"What do you need?"

"Charles. Is he here?"

"He's in the stable. He's *working*. Why do you need him?"

I need him because he *is my friend.* Maggie turned back to the door. "I'll tell you about it later." Though the way their friendship was going she'd probably never have the occasion to explain. She ran back to the stables.

One enormous red-painted door stood open. Warmth, the body heat generated by four magnificent animals, engulfed her as the smell repelled. She'd often watched in disbelief as Charles opened the massive door and inhaled deeply of "the sweet smell of manure and fermenting hay."

Straight in front of the door was an almost new, spit-polished Mitchell automobile.

"Charles?" Her eyes had yet to adjust to the darkness.

"Over here, Mags. By Lightning."

Hay rustling beneath her feet, she took quick long strides to the second stall from the end and skidded to a stop in front of him. Auburn corkscrews sprang out from under his cap. The buttons on the vest beneath his coat strained tight. One was missing. "I need you, Charles."

Pale, freckle-spattered skin pinked. Twinkling green eyes locked on hers then darted away.

"Is Mr. Caswell home?"

"He is. Is it really me you have need of, or him?"

"It is both of you. Mr. Hamilton is not going to Boston after all and Mrs. Hamilton's lunch guests will be here in three quarters of an hour and—"

"And she wants no men on the premises to hear the hens cackle about their roosters."

"Y–yes."

Charles brushed off his pants. A smile crept into his eyes as he tapped a finger on his chin. Maggie hid nervous hands in the folds of her apron. She would not give him the satisfaction of seeing how he tortured her. She studied a row of photographs and articles cut from newspapers and nailed to a post. Stepping closer, she looked at a drawing of a massive ship with four smokestacks billowing black smoke. Rows of small white circles dotted the black hull. As she imagined staring out from one of the miniscule windows, her starched collar seemed to tighten.

THE WORLD'S LARGEST VESSEL, THE TITANIC, NOW BEING BUILT

Here is an architectural picture of the steamship Titanic, which is being built for the White Star Line in Belfast. The White Star company is to have two of these leviathans and they will be in commission early in 1911. Their launching will signalize a most important era in maritime achievement, for—

"You could get on her, you know."

Maggie stared at Charles and then at Lightning. "I don't know how to ride."

"Not *her*." A scarred finger gestured toward the article she'd been reading. "*Her*. I happen to know how you could be on her maiden voyage." His eyes had a faraway look, filled with all the yearning of a young man in love.

With a boat.

He folded his arms across his broad chest. "Did I ever tell you about the voyage Grandma Hannah and Granda Liam took in 1883 when they went back to England and Ireland after my mother was married and—"

"Charles."

He grinned. "Sorry. We were talking about a different voyage. Yours."

Maggie stifled her exasperation. "Assuming I had an interest in being on a boat bigger than the public library, how is it I would go about getting on a boat in Belfast, Ireland?"

"She's not a boat, she's a steam*ship*. And her first voyage will start in Southampton in England and end in New York."

Time was slipping away. She dare not irritate Charles if she wanted his help, but once he started talking about his sailing dreams, he would lose all track of the world beyond his imagination. "And I, you may have noticed, live on Lake Michigan, not the English Channel."

"But you just happen to know someone who is sailing to Denmark in February and hoping to return on the *Titanic*. And. . ." He lingered on the word for torturing effect, though it had none on her. She did not share Charles's love of being on the water. "And they are about to lose their domestic help."

Now that news piqued her interest. "Who?"

"Mr. and Mrs. Hansen."

"I know three Hansen families."

Again he paused, clearly enjoying the suspense. "Peter and Jennie."

"Lydia is leaving?" The Hansens treated the peppy round-faced

Lydia almost as if she were their own daughter. Maggie had never heard her utter a single complaint.

Charles's face reddened. "It seems she has spent a bit too much time with the butcher's son."

"She is—" Feeling her own cheeks warm, Maggie looked away. "Has she given notice?"

"No. She told me she would tell me the day she does so I could tell you."

A flutter of hope stirred in Maggie's belly. She tried to squelch it.

Charles doffed his hat. "I will see what I can conspire to help Mrs. Hamilton, madam."

It took a moment for her thoughts to return from the white house four blocks down. A much smaller house. A much kinder employer. The shock and sadness of sweet Lydia being with child warred with the possibility of an answer to a long-standing prayer that had become, with Mr. Hamilton's pronouncement that his wife would learn to keep house, a fervent prayer. "My mistress will be forever in your debt, kind sir."

"And what of the girl who runs your mistress's life—I mean household. Is she also in my debt?"

"*She* is merely carrying out the duties of her employment. She has no reason to be indebted, but she might be inclined to repay your kindness with a batch of fudge." A piece of straw drifted from the rafters and landed on her shoulder. Charles reached it before she did and brushed it away.

How strange a thing, the imagination. Maggie was sure she could feel the heat of his touch through her coat.

"The thought of a morsel of your fudge would speed me on my mission, but there is something I would prefer."

"What is that, Mr. Gallagher?"

"Will you play for me?"

She waved away the question. "I haven't gotten near the piano in months." She looked away from pleading eyes.

"Will you wait for a note?"

"Would you deliver it?" She tried to hold back the smile. "If I promise to play for you?"

"I would deliver it even if you promised nothing, but, alas, now you are obligated." He touched the brim of his cap, winked, and raced toward the house.

Thirteen minutes after Maggie pushed the button and hung her coat out of sight there was a knock at the door. She opened it, took the folded paper, and smiled. "Come in. I will deliver this and bring your answer immediately."

"And *I* will come back to hear you play 'Let Me Call You Sweetheart.'"

Cheeks warming, she gave the briefest of curtseys—why she did not know—and walked in as unhurried a fashion as she could manage into the front parlor.

Mrs. Hamilton perched on the edge of a chair, hands folded in what appeared to be a demure pose. Maggie hoped Mr. Hamilton would not notice the whitening knuckles. She waited for him to take a break from complaining about the inadequacy of a railroad that could not clear its tracks in an "efficacious" manner.

"What is it, Maggie?"

"A note, sir. Delivered by Charles."

"Well, don't stand there like a fence post. Hand it to me."

She gave it to him, folded her hands behind her back, and waited.

He sighed. "If I did not know the measure of your integrity, Evangeline, I would be apt to believe you arranged this to get me out of the house."

"Maxwell!" The shock in Mrs. Hamilton's face was genuine. She had, of course, had nothing whatsoever to do with the convenient invitation. "What does it say?"

"Harvey wants me to come and help him and that stable boy with that ridiculous ark they're building in his cellar."

"It's a sailboat, Maxwell. A sailboat with Hamilton hinges and latches. Think what that could do for—"

"Enough, Evangeline. I don't need you feeding me the lines I regurgitated in a weak moment." He pushed heavily out of the chair, slipped back into the coat Maggie hadn't had time to hang, and stomped to the back door.

Just as Emma Rose Mitchell, the girl who would be perfect for the man sleeping upstairs, came to the front.

CHAPTER 15

Andrew minimized the spreadsheet responsible for his headache and looked again at the online bio of Natalie Brooks. Twenty-four hours had passed since his last communication with Jerry and still no information about Heather. They knew the house and car were in Natalie Brooks's name. They knew she'd been at the top of the Coventry Midwest ladder and they knew what had caused her to topple from her rung. How hard could it be to find out how Heather was related or associated? How hard could it be to find that one piece of information that would open the door to everything else?

All he needed was her last name.

He rubbed his temples and tried to visualize a new route out of the box. On more than one occasion, Parker had introduced him as "Andrew Rivera, VP of our Impossible Problems Division."

Think. This was what he got paid for. But the lightbulb in his head only dimmed. He'd checked for Heathers in Racine, Wisconsin, on every social networking site he could get his fingers on. He'd friended and linked with several possibles who all ended up either asking him out or not fitting what he knew about her.

Which was. . . ? That she had just gotten her master's degree, she was working on a business plan, had long dark hair, and a mole near the center of some very tight abs. That last, definitive little bit of information had made him sound like a predator and had quickly ended two online chats.

But Jerry had resources and connections that should have garnered him leads. Either he wasn't the expert Andrew had thought he was, or he was holding out on him.

All that meant only one avenue seemed likely to produce quick results.

He'd give Jerry one more chance to come up with something concrete.

And then he was heading back to Racine to get the information he needed.

Straight from the source.

"Do you want another drink?"

Stephannie held up the plastic cup and pointed the end of the bent straw at her father. He grinned and held up his hand. "You trying to drown me?" He lifted the hand with the clear tube trailing from it. "I'm being watered 24/7, you know."

"Just trying to be useful." She smiled at her own words. Had she ever said that phrase? Had she ever had that thought?

Her father reached out for her hand and she scooted her chair closer to the side of the bed. "You've changed, Steph. What's going on in that beautiful head?"

You've changed. The words swirled around her, lifting her like the music they'd once played together. "I can't exactly explain it. I think almost losing you was like. . .like they'd used those paddles on me. I feel kind of jolted, you know? Like I was only half awake or half alive and now all of a sudden I'm living in the here and now and I'm seeing myself and my life in a whole new way." She ran her thumb across the back of the hand that no longer matched the bedsheet. Her eyes suddenly stung. "I'm so sorry for everything I put you through."

"I put my parents through far more, honey. That's what adolescence is for—testing your wings."

His answering smile felt like cleansing rain. She smiled through the burn of tears. "I almost broke mine."

"Almost. But you didn't. God has a plan for you, Steph. I know it." He squeezed her hand. "Pastor Dave said the two of you had coffee the other day."

Stephannie nodded. "He doesn't act like a pastor. I mean, he does but he doesn't. Does that make sense?"

"Perfect sense. Exactly what I thought the first time I met him. He introduced himself as a life coach who encouraged people to recognize truth."

"And do you now?"

"Recognize truth? Some of it."

Stephannie looked toward the window. "Do you have a lot of regrets from when you were my age?"

He was silent for a long time. She turned back, wondering if he'd fallen asleep, but his eyes were open and clear. Deep ridges formed between his brows and he pressed his lips together. "I try not to focus on things that can't be changed, but of course I have regrets."

"Like what? What's the hardest one to look back at?"

"I wish I hadn't been so selfish. I had tunnel vision about my career for so many years and it hurt you and your mom."

"What about before I was born? Before you were married?"

His eyes darkened as if a shadow blocked the overhead light. "I think the answer is the same. I didn't allow anything"—his gaze rose to the ceiling—"to interfere with my plan. Anything that got in my path was"—he blinked hard—"pushed aside."

Pushed aside. *As in, given up for adoption?* She waited, but it was clear he wasn't going to offer more. "Can I ask a personal question?"

"Sure."

"Why did you and Mom only have me? Why didn't you have more children?"

The blinking increased. He shook his head. Slightly. Slowly. Then closed his eyes. "Selfishness," he whispered, and closed his eyes. "This medication makes me so sleepy."

Stephannie waited until his breathing became deep and regular. She scanned the bedside table for his phone, but didn't see it. She slipped off her sandals and padded in bare feet over to the narrow closet. The flat black phone sat on the shelf. Walking to the door, where she was out of sight if he woke, she turned it on and went to his text messages.

There were now two messages after the one with the picture of the girl with the long brown hair. One from her father: FEELING STRONGER. DOCTORS ARE OPTIMISTIC. DO YOU HAVE A NAME AND ADDRESS FOR THE GIRL? One in response: THANK GOD FOR GOOD NEWS. ONLY HAVE AN ADDRESS.

A shiver of fear combined with a sigh of hope as she committed the address to memory. She slipped the phone back onto the shelf, slipped her sandals back on her feet, and kissed the place where ridges still lingered on her father's forehead.

She was going to Wisconsin.

To meet her sister.

♔

SLS. The silver letters on the back of the car shimmered in the sunlight as Stephannie pulled out the gas nozzle.

Steph's Little Sportster. That's what her father said the letters stood for.

The car had been waiting for her on the afternoon of her twenty-first birthday—parked in her spot in the parking garage with a giant red bow that covered the roof of the sleek black machine. She'd screamed and cried when her father jumped out from behind another car. *Happy birthday, baby.*

And then she'd taken it for a joyride with her two best friends. She vaguely remembered her first legal drink—a Bond Girl at the Underground. And her second—Bacardi and Coke at the Transit. Then something bluish-green with a sprig of mint at Excalibur. All she remembered of the NV Penthouse Lounge—where they'd gone to "cool down"—was the bathroom. It was all she'd seen before passing out. It didn't matter that her memories of coming of age were fuzzy. The photographer who'd followed her the whole night had chronicled it nicely.

She took her receipt, crumpled it, and threw it in the octagon-shaped trash can. Until this car, her father had gotten gas for her. Once, twice, sometimes three times a week. Her friends had laughed, calling her "Daddy's girl." She hadn't minded. She was.

She still was.

It had hurt when he'd handed her the gas card and said a woman of twenty-one needed to pump her own gas, but she'd done it. Except when she could get Andrew to drive her car instead of the Jag.

She pulled away from the pump and headed north. She had two hours to figure out what to say to her half sister. Or full sister.

A girl who, thanks to the photographers, just might recognize her.

⚜

Gripping the curved wrought iron railing, Heather gazed down at the monolithic shadow of the Wind Point Lighthouse on the grass nearly a hundred feet below. She followed the ribbon-candy bands of color surrounding the point of land the lighthouse occupied—a strip of beige sandwiched between bright green grass and the deep blue of the water. The sky, a shade lighter than the water, was dotted with fanciful cloud shapes. They looked down on red-roofed outbuildings and a white fence. A flag flapped in a soft breeze, adding another splash of color. She ran her hand along the ninety-year-old white-painted bricks of the lighthouse. "What a beautiful place."

Ryan sidled a few inches closer and casually rested his arm across her shoulders. She tried not to smile at the endearing awkwardness of the moment. Heart fluttering like a giddy teen, she leaned into him. His hand conformed to her shoulder.

"That's the oil house." He pointed to a small white building with a red roof. "The light was originally powered by a kerosene lamp."

"Did they use mirrors to magnify it?"

"This one had a Fresnel lens—a series of prisms and magnifying lenses. The lens revolved around the lamp twelve times an hour. It intensified the light and formed it into twelve beams, so one of the beams would flash over the water every thirty seconds. It could be seen almost twenty miles away."

"I imagine our Rose would have taken a train if she'd gone East to sail to England."

"Probably, but there were passenger steamers on the Great Lakes. If she really liked the water and wasn't in a hurry, she could have taken the leisurely route."

"Izzy's rubbing off on me, I guess. I want to think of her standing

169

on deck on a starry night with her beau's arm around her and the lighthouse beam flashing on them every thirty seconds."

"What a romantic you are."

Heather tipped her head to one side and looked up at him. "I've never thought of myself that way."

"Why?"

"I don't know. I'm too practical or something. Jen's the hearts and flowers one."

Ryan's arm slid away. For a moment she wondered what she'd said. But then his fingertips lifted her face to his. "Do you always compare yourself to your sister? And come up short?"

"No." She stared into eyes that waited for an answer, basking in the almost palpable connection. "I always compare myself with my sister and come up too tall."

He smiled. "You need to stop that and start seeing who you really are. Maybe you're night and day different from your sister, but why does that have to be bad? She's blond and you're brunette. Who in the world ever told you blond is better?"

Without warning, her eyes stung. She didn't have to think about the answer to that question. A shrug would have sufficed, but for some reason she felt compelled to tell him. "My grandmother."

"You've got to be kidding."

She shook her head. "My father's mother. I was about five when I heard it the first time."

"What did she say?"

Her breath shuddered in her chest. "She said, 'You'd think they could at least have gotten one with our coloring. How hard is it to find a child with blond hair and blue eyes? It's going to be obvious in every family picture that she's a transplant.'"

Ryan braced her shoulders with warm hands. "Heather." His voice, low and hoarse, caressed her face.

"I didn't even know what a transplant was. I asked my mother and she blew up. I'd never seen her get so mad." She smiled as he brushed a tear from her cheek. "I hid in the laundry room and held the door open just a crack. My mother's just a tiny thing, about a head shorter than my grandmother, but she stood on her tiptoes and shook her finger in my grandmother's face and screamed, 'Heather is our daughter! She may not have formed inside me, but I birthed that little girl in my heart and she is as much a part of us as the one with blue eyes.'"

His hands loosened. "And after all that you can still doubt you are special?"

It was time for the shrug. "When my grandmother grabbed her purse and stomped out, it was the first time in my life I knew beyond the shadow of a doubt that I was loved unconditionally. I've never doubted my parents' love."

"But...?"

"When Jen got to be kindergarten age my dad caved in to his mother and let her take her 'real' granddaughter on a weeklong vacation every year."

"Just her?" His eyes widened. He shook his head.

"Just her. It was the only thing I ever heard my parents argue over—and they got into some doozies. My dad always won and my mother always compensated. I got some great presents out of it, and when I got old enough to understand how much it hurt my mother, I started acting like I was happier to be home. Like I never wanted to go to Disney or spend a week at my grandmother's house in Florida."

Ryan's hands lifted to the back of her head. She stopped breathing when his fingers slid into her hair. "That was so unfair."

Again, she shrugged. "Life is," she whispered.

"But things do even out."

"They do?" Her voice squeaked out just above a whisper.

"They do." He leaned closer. His skin smelled of sunshine and fresh air. "The blond got the jerk and look at you—free and beautiful and standing on top of the world with a really handsome guy."

She blinked hard, not wanting a second of this to blur in her memory. "You're right."

"Of course I'm right." His breath tickled her mouth. "I'm a superhero"—his lips touched hers, light and brief—"and superheroes are always right."

What now?

The kiss hadn't seemed to surprise Heather, but Ryan stared

down at her with a dazed, disoriented feeling—slightly tipsy, as if, instead of touching his lips to hers, he'd leaped to the top of the railing circling the lighthouse.

He wasn't the kind of guy who kissed a girl just because it was fun or expected. Or just because he could. It meant something.

It meant he liked her. A lot. But where was this headed? He stroked her cheek with his thumb. "Before I do that again—and I definitely want to do that again—I need to know something."

She tipped her head to the right, inviting his question. Or another kiss. He took a deep and heady breath, hoping the increase in oxygen would clear his brain. It only made the dizziness worse. Maybe he'd been hyperventilating. Maybe he should cover his nose and mouth and rebreathe his own air. Or move in closer and inhale hers.

"I know your future is kind of up in the air"—he grinned as she glanced over the railing and grimaced—"but I'm wondering just how far you'd go. . ." He paused to decide how to word it. Her eyes shot wide. She drew back.

"No!" He laughed. "I need to know how far you'd consider moving. Away. From me. I mean, if you're thinking you might end up in San Francisco or Cairo or something, I'd like a hint."

"So you can put on the brakes?" Her eyes glimmered with the tease.

"So I can put in applications for police academies in all those places."

She lifted her chin, inviting another kiss. "I think I'd like to stay right here."

⚜

Heather sipped a mocha drink that didn't come close to Racine Beans quality as she watched Izzy choking a colored pencil at its tip, designing a new business card for Heather on the back of an old one. Thanks to Natalie's indiscretion, Heather had over two hundred useless cards to spare.

"This place has a cool logo." Izzy pointed to the coffee cup outlined on the front window of the coffee shop. "It's not as cool as Racine Beans, though." Her forehead rippled. "What if you had

172

three *C*s all different sizes and the words stick out from the *C*s. Confab Coffee Connection."

"I like it. I just may hire you to be my graphic designer. You can be the one to draw all my posters and make ads for the newspaper."

"And TV and the Internet. You hafta have a website."

Heather tapped her fingertip to the end of Izzy's nose. "Absolutely."

"Okay. I'm starting over." She tore the card in half and slurped her strawberry-banana smoothie as she scanned the shop.

"Tell me what you do like about this place." Heather pulled out her notebook and pen along with several pages of *Magdalena Mouse* and *Essays on Life* Izzy had fed into the scanner and Heather had printed the night before.

"The flower pictures are nice." Izzy set down her glass, picked up her camera, and aimed it at a watercolor of an iris. "But they're not really my thing."

She sounded like a little throwback from the sixties. "Not your thing, huh? So if you were going to open a chain of coffee shops, like Starbucks—with lots of them all across the country, what would you put on the walls?"

Izzy's lips pursed. She scrunched her mouth to one side. "Hmm. I think I would put up picture frames—not real ones—the kind where you can play pictures you took yourself. You could show pictures of the city or a holiday. Like if you had a coffee shop in Chicago, you could show pictures of the silver jelly bean and the fountain with a face, and at Christmas you could change it to show Baby Jesus in the manger and shepherds and angels and stuff."

Heather scribbled—and not just to please Izzy. "I love that idea. It would make it so easy to change the décor."

"Is that like decorations?"

"Exactly. What else?"

"Real music, not the kind that comes out of the ceiling." She pointed at a small round speaker in the corner above her head. "You hafta have a piano and maybe a guitar or drums."

"But they'd have to play quietly enough that people could still talk."

"Sure. I can play piano really, really quiet."

"Do you know any songs?"

"Just pretend ones. Oh, and 'Twinkle, Twinkle' and 'Chopsticks.' One of my babysitters in Chicago taught me." She took a long swig of smoothie then cringed and rubbed her forehead. "Brain freeze."

"Here. Take a sip of my coffee. It's not too hot." Heather slid her cup across the table. Izzy wrapped her fingers around it and brought it to her lips. Before she even took a drink, her eyes widened and her face contorted in a grimace that made Heather laugh. "You're not a coffee fan, I take—"

"Don't turn around," Izzy whispered. "That man, the one from the beach, is here. He's looking around like he's looking for some-body. I bet he's looking for you."

"That's ridiculous." She swiveled in her chair and felt goose bumps rise on her arms. "He wouldn't know I'm here and I only met him that one—" Breath held, she watched him stride the last two yards toward them.

"Heather. Right?"

She made an attempt at swallowing. "Mike." She hoped what showed on her face was pleasant surprise and not fear. Her insides roiled. This was not a coincidence.

"So we meet again." He nodded at Izzy. "And you have one of your sand castle builders with you."

Izzy glared.

"Mind if I join you?" Full lips framed dazzling teeth.

I don't know. Do I?

Ryan's words echoed. *If he does show up again, you are free to call me.* "And you'll be my real live hero?" *she'd answered.*

I'll do everything in my power to be your hero.

Her hand slid toward her purse. She could say they had to leave. She could say Ryan was coming to meet them and this wasn't a good idea. But she agreed with Ryan—this was no coin-cidence. The guy had followed her. He had to be connected with the photographer.

Or he might have found her for other reasons. Ryan had tracked her down with a license plate number. Maybe Mike had, too. Maybe he was the good kind of stalker, the kind who simply liked what he saw. She hadn't exactly looked hideous in the blue two-piece.

If that was the case, she'd let him down gently and send him on his way.

"Please." She gestured toward an empty chair. Izzy's toes connected with her shin. "Have a seat."

But be warned. I'll *be the one asking the questions.*

CHAPTER 16

Ryan stood on the top rung of his stepladder aiming a silicone caulk gun at the wall plate on the last of five motion sensor lights he'd just finished installing on a Tudor house near Wind Point. He'd chosen one that sensed motion in a two-hundred-forty-degree arc up to one hundred feet away. He'd mounted them on all four corners of the house and one above the main garage door. This was just one layer of security he wished Izzy's mom had given the go-ahead to install on her house.

His phone buzzed in his back pocket. He climbed down two steps and jumped the last three feet to the ground as he fished it out. "Hello?"

"Ryan?"

For a second he thought the scared little voice was Skylar's. And then it registered. "Izzy?"

"I'm in the bathroom at a coffee shop." Her words came out fast and breathless. "That guy from the beach is here."

Ryan's blood seemed to congeal in his veins. "Has he seen you? Where's Heather?"

"He's sitting at our table. Heather is talking to him."

Lord, no. Don't let her say too much. "Are you at Racine Beans?"

"No. Another place."

"What's it called?"

176

"I don't know."

Frustration built like pressure cooker steam. He collapsed the ladder and sprinted toward the truck. "Tell me what it looks like on the outside."

"It has big windows and a big coffee cup painted on it with music notes coming out of it like steam."

He shoved the ladder in the back of the paneled truck and breathed a sigh. *Coffee Sounds.* "Okay." He ran back for his tools. "I know where you are." He kept talking to her—over the sound of the Spider-Man theme song playing in his head in his brothers' voices. The truck engine came to life and he slammed it in gear. Gravel from the side of the road spit at the mailbox behind him. "I'm on my way."

It sounded corny and superhero-ish. Maybe Heather wasn't in immediate danger.

But this guy was trouble.

⚜

Izzy twisted the strap of her camera as she walked slowly back to the table where Heather sat across from the creepy man.

Ryan had told her not to tell the man anything. Not her name or where she lived or anything. Ryan was like a policeman. Maybe he could put handcuffs on the man and take him to jail. In her head, she pretended Ryan was saying, "Put your hands in the air, mister." The man would look at Ryan's muscles and be scared.

The man's smile looked like the wax lips and teeth Mom bought her at Halloween. "Izzy," he said. "Is that short for something? Elizabeth maybe?"

She shook her head. She couldn't believe Heather had told him. But he didn't know her real name and he sure didn't know anything about names anyway. Girls named Elizabeth were called Liz. Or maybe Beth. "Just Izzy."

"How old—"

"So, Mike"—Heather put her hand on Izzy's arm and squeezed—"I think you were about to explain what you're doing here."

Good. Heather was smarter than she'd thought. The man's creepy smile got even bigger and creepier. He laughed. "I was. And

177

I will. But first I want to know how old 'just Izzy' is. I'm guessing eight."

"Not yet."

"Wow. You're very bright for your age."

"I'm precocious. I was reading by the time I turned three." She answered him like a teacher correcting a not-very-bright kid 'cuz that's what he acted like. He was trying to get her to say the kind of things Ryan told her not to say.

"So let me get this straight. The man I met at the beach—Ryan, right?—he's your uncle."

"He's—"

"Yes." She wasn't supposed to interrupt adults, but she was scared of what Heather was going to say. If the man thought Ryan was her uncle, that was okay.

"How long have you lived in Racine?"

She made a loud slurp on her smoothie. Heather gave her a squinty-eyed look. Maybe to tell her not to make noise. Or maybe to tell her not to say anything. Like she wasn't smart enough to know that. "A really long time," she answered. She was still pretty much telling the truth because sometimes it felt that way. Sometimes it felt like Mom had been gone for weeks and weeks and like Heather had always been there. Sometimes she wished it were true and then she felt bad for thinking it.

She stared at the man. He was looking at her funny, like maybe she'd been thinking about not missing Mom for too long. Mom yelled at her when she daydreamed, but daydreaming was a good thing. It kept her from being bored or, like now, from being mad or scared.

"Did you stay overnight with Heather last night?"

She shrugged.

"So what do you think about your uncle and Heather? Are you hap—"

"Now would be a good time to explain how you found us here." Heather's voice sounded mad and her eyes got more squinty.

Izzy looked back at the man to see if he could tell Heather was getting mad at all his dumb questions. The man's wax smile shrank. His laugh sounded like a doll she used to have that made a wheezy sound when its batteries were going dead. "Would you believe me if I said it was just a coincidence?"

"No."

"How about fate?"

Heather shook her head. "I don't believe in that either."

"Well then, I guess I have to confess that I followed you. I found out where you live and I drove up here today with every intention of just dropping in on you, but you were pulling out, so I followed you here."

"You found out where I live." Heather's eyes looked like they were on fire.

The man nodded and gave a goofy smile. "That license plate is rather memorable."

"The day at the beach. Did you—"

"Now *that* was coincidence. No. That was fate, whether you believe in it or not. It was a gorgeous day and I needed to clear my head from a rough week at work, so I headed north, ended up here, and decided to check out the beach."

"You just happened to have swim trunks in the car."

"I stopped and bought them." He wiped the side of his pointer finger under his nose then put his elbows on the table and folded his hands really close to Heather's. "That day"—his voice got deep and quiet, almost a whisper—"was destiny."

The man was lying. Izzy was sure.

Heather pulled her hands closer to her then grabbed her coffee cup.

"Okay, I'm just going to lay it all out. I'm not all that great with expressing my feelings, but here it is." He took a deep breath and it all rushed out again. "I live in a high-rise apartment. I take a cab to work because it's impossible to drive or park in that part of the city. I look out the window of the office building where I work and I see ant people rushing around, not looking at each other, not apologizing if they slam into someone. So one day I just had to get away from it all. I got in my car and I just drove with no destination in mind, and I ended up on the beach"—he smiled his wax-looking smile—"in need of ice. And there you were." He whooshed air out of his mouth. It made Izzy's napkin flutter around like an almost-dead butterfly.

Izzy looked at Heather and couldn't believe what she saw. Heather didn't look mad anymore. She looked like Snow White after the prince kissed her. Izzy stopped sucking her smoothie and watched the pink stuff slide back down the straw. She felt like she was going to be sick.

The man leaned a little closer to Heather. "If it were a movie, there would have been music."

Oh puhlease.

"Here was this gorgeous woman handing me a cup of ice. It was like stepping from the desert into an oasis. . .a spiritual moment. And I don't mean to make it sound like it was all your looks—though that was huge—it was the expression on your face, the fact that you didn't hesitate before helping me out. Big city people aren't like that. If I asked anyone back home for ice, I'd be lucky if I got it thrown in my face."

Duh. Izzy had lived in a huge city all her life and she knew tons of nice people. She once saw a lady take off her coat and give it to a homeless woman. And Martha read her stories about Jesus and gave Christmas presents to poor children. Those people would give ice to anyone who asked.

The smoothie goo rolled around in her belly like lava. It would be really embarrassing to throw up all over the table—or the man—but it would make him leave. She put her hand over her mouth. Not because she was really going to be sick, but because daydreaming about it made her want to laugh. She could just picture all that pink stuff splattered on the man's nice yellow shirt. Sticky and icky and smelly.

Her hand slipped away and she accidentally laughed.

♔

Heather had no explanation for the laugh that popped from Izzy, but it startled her as effectively as a bucket of ice on her head. Startled her out of Mike's low budget movie scene. *I ended up on the beach, in need of ice. And there you were.*

Gag. He'd snared her for a moment. For a split second she'd experienced what it must be like to be the cute, curvy girl pursued by incredibly hunky guys with expensive cars.

To be Jen.

Do you always compare yourself to your sister? And come up short?

With renewed focus, she turned on him and nodded toward the window. "Jaguar."

"Yes."

"And you work in HR."

"Yes. Well, that's part of my job description."

"Did you mention where you work?" She glanced at Izzy. The girl was getting antsy. She pointed to her phone, already in Izzy's hand. "Angry Birds," she whispered, hoping the game would occupy her for a few more minutes.

"I don't think I did. I'm in the hotel business."

Goose bumps rose on her arms. "Really. So was I."

Just as she realized what she'd said, Izzy's toe connected with the already sore spot on her shin.

Mike's eyes gleamed as if he'd discovered more than just a connecting point with an almost stranger.

Bile rose in Heather's throat along with a silent scream. Nothing about this made sense. What did he want with her? Why had she just played into his hands? But she hadn't given away anything he could use. She no longer worked for Coventry.

A point-blank flash from Izzy's camera blinded her. Another went off. Through the blue spots dancing before her eyes, she could tell it was pointed at Mike.

"I have a printer and a picture album. I'm taking pictures of all the coffee shops Heather and I go to every day." Izzy aimed an odd smile at Mike as she chattered, but her left hand, under the table, pointed toward the window.

Heather followed the line of Izzy's index finger. Her coffee slopped over the side of her mug.

Ryan.

♔

The Jag parked right in front had to be "Mike's."

Ryan stuffed his keys in his pocket where they wouldn't tempt him to engrave a nice little ten-grand stripe along the side.

He grabbed the handle of the coffee shop door with no idea

what he was going to say when he got inside. *Hi. Just happened to see your car, Heather. And yours, Lifeguard Man.* Should he just be honest and say Izzy called him? What was he walking into? Was Heather in there getting snared by the guy's lies? Was she trying to get away from him but couldn't?

His palms were sweaty, but imagining the relief on her face gave him the strength to walk in. He pulled his shoulders back and dried his hands on his pants, wishing for the weapon he carried at some events TKJ staffed. Not that he thought he needed it here. He just wouldn't mind the guy knowing he knew how.

Detect. Deter. Observe. Report. He knew the drill. He wasn't the kind to take on more than he could handle.

He opened the outside door, stepped into the miniscule entry-way, and was almost clobbered by the inside door flying open.

"Mike. What a coincide—"

"Ryan, right? Good to see you. Sorry—can't chat—emergency."

I just bet there is. He walked in, scanning the room, feeling fairly confident *he'd* been the emergency.

"Ryan!"

He didn't need to follow Izzy's voice. She tackled him, then grabbed his hand and dragged him to the table where Heather sat... without a hint of hero worship on her face.

"You followed me? Again? Is that a service your company offers? What does it cost to hire a stalker?" Her arms crossed her chest. Body armor. "Lucky me. I get it for free."

Izzy giggled. "That rhymes. Lucky *me*. I get it for *free*."

Heather shot a fiery glare at the poor kid then turned up the heat as she lasered him. "I was making the guy talk. I was learning things. And then you come in stalking like—"

"I'm not stalking. I—"

"You're following me. How else did you know I was here? Or he was here?" She snatched her purse from the chair beside her and motioned for Izzy to pick up her cup. "It was a little flattering before, but this is freaky. Did you attach some kind of device to me? Can you hear everything I say? Is that what drew you to your profession? Maybe your whole family is just a bunch of peeping..." Each word came faster and louder. She stood, then moved close enough that his lips wouldn't have far to stretch to touch hers.

What was wrong with a guy who could think of kissing, think she was adorably amusing, in the midst of being shredded in public?

". . .you hired people so you don't have to follow me yourself? Is there a camera in my purse or on my car or a GPS or—" With a huff, she grabbed Izzy's hand. "I can take care of myself. I don't need a security guard."

She swished past him and marched out the door.

♛

January 1912

"Apathy, ladies. Apathy is our greatest enemy." Mrs. Morton jabbed her fork at each woman in turn. "And not that of our men, or of public officials. *We* are our own greatest enemy! Look at the average woman browsing beside you at Porters or Rasmussen Jewelry or lunching at the next table at Hotel Racine. That woman will say she wants the vote, however. . ."

Maggie broke a biscuit in two as she tuned out Mrs. Morton's rant. Maggie had never set foot in Rasmussen Jewelry. The only time she'd "browsed" at Porters Furniture she'd been walking behind Mrs. Hamilton, jotting measurements and notes on color and pattern in a small black book. She had, however, spent hours and hours in the restaurant at the hotel. Peeling potatoes.

Magdalena coiled her tail in a tight swirl behind her as she stared at all the paw prints on all the glasses she had washed and polished and set on the snow-white tablecloth she had ironed. A smudge of gravy, a greasy lip print. Did any of them stop to think who would wash these dishes and dry these dishes and put them away while they were home soaking their bunions and patting their furry backs for all they had done for the world today?

Mrs. Morton's voice rose, making it impossible to ignore. "The women of Wisconsin must be roused into enthusiastic support for the referendum before we can expect our men to vote for it. And to do that, we must expand. Though I respect Mrs. Brown highly, I deeply disagree with two of her tenets. She is a proponent of the WWSA keeping a low profile, but if the Wisconsin Woman

183

Suffrage Association does not begin ruffling feathers the way the Political Equality League is, I cannot help but conclude that we are destined for extinction." She exhaled loud and long, her shoulders lowering dramatically. "Please take no offense, Evangeline, we all have different crosses to carry at home, but I believe the time has come to let the world know what we are about. We are a proud chapter of the WWSA and we must not cower nor deceive. If our men do not approve, there is a very large body of water not far from here in which they may all go soak their heads!"

The women burst into laughter. All but one. Evangeline Hamilton stared at her teacup in strained and stony silence.

"Also, I believe the time has long passed for the luxury of exclusivity. We, in this small group, have forged paths never imagined by the likes of our foremothers. We. . ."

Though Maggie tried to focus on every one of the increasingly animated words, her thoughts were as firmly divided as her buttermilk biscuit—between the little girl with reddened, work-roughened hands who had responded with an inordinately grateful smile when Maggie handed her two paper-wrapped biscuits stuffed with chicken to take with her, and the man who might, at any moment, descend the stairs. And then, in the midst of her scrambled thoughts, her gaze wandered to the piano and the notes of the song she'd promised to play for Charles.

"Look around this room, ladies. While Olympia Brown directed her message to those of her own social standing, we have reached out to our sisters of many professions and clas—roles." A graceful hand swept toward Maggie. "Those women know the fallacy of women being a protected class. They know what it means to work harder than a man for half the pay, to feel powerless to effect change in the workplace. To those women"—again, the hand singled out Maggie.

With a low, throaty growl fit for a lion instead of a mouse, Magdalena stared at the hand that swept toward her. We may be powerless to effect change, but you, in your big hats and your big houses, are not. Change could start with you not twitching your whiskers every time one of us walks in the room.

". . .must turn to these women for the enthusiasm and passion, for the drive needed to forge ahead to November. To those women we will owe homage, a debt of gratitude, when the referendum passes and Wisconsin women take a giant step into a future of equality."

A polite-but-not-passionate round of applause met her words. "Next week I will present a list of coming events at which we simply must have a presence and make ourselves heard. Last year saw successes, and now, in 1912, we must increase our efforts. At every fair, every picnic or parade in the county, the women of Racine will make noise. We will drive from town to town, we will speak to workers as they leave the factories, we will bombard the governor's office with mail. In short, ladies, we will do what it takes." She gave a single nod, a gesture that said her part of the meeting had come to a close. She picked up her fork and jabbed the last remaining piece of what must by now be very cold gravy-coated biscuit on her plate. "Evangeline, I just may steal Miss Parker away from you. Maggie, dear, this is the best creamed chicken I have ever tasted."

"Thank you, ma'am."

"None of that 'ma'am' business. We are all equal in this room, aren't we?"

Then why do you keep pointing out that I'm one of "those women," and why are you talking about hiring me to work in your kitchen? Why not simply invite me for tea and I'll share my recipe?

Mrs. Morton pushed her plate aside—where it would stay until after the meeting ended. There was no one to clear the table since the Hamiltons' only domestic sat at the table as an "equal."

Emma cleared her throat. "Maggie and I have some wonderful things to report about our visits to manufacturers in the city. We've been pleasantly surprised with the receptivity." She sat with a prim demeanor and spoke with an articulate properness that was missing, fortunately, when she was not in the company of such esteemed ladies. Maggie could not have abided hours working side-by-side with *this* Emma Rose.

"The response from the children has been mixed." Emma turned a shared-secret kind of smile on Maggie. "We have several who I believe will be gobbling books like candy, but others who seem to show no interest. That may be in part due to not enough sleep and poor nutrition, which brings me to the next—"

185

"Richard!" Mrs. Morton lifted her hand and nine heads swiveled in unison to stare at the man who stood at the bottom of the stairs wearing brown pants with suspenders and a shirt the color of an August sky. Maggie's hand flew to her bodice as if pressure would calm the galloping mustang set loose inside her chest.

Mrs. Hamilton held out her hand. "Come and say hello, Richard." She turned to the ladies. "Richard surprised us last night. He's here for the weekend and to attend a dinner hosted by our Emma." Her smile said she hadn't given up hopes for a Mitchell-Hamilton wedding in her future. "Richard, I don't believe you've met all of the members of the Ladies' Art Guild."

"Ladies' Art Guild?" Richard laughed and aimed a brazen wink at Maggie. "No need for euphemisms with me, Mother." He tucked his thumbs under his suspenders. "You're looking at a card-carrying member of the Men's League for Woman Suffrage."

"Hear, hear!" Mrs. Morton raised a fist in the air.

Mrs. Hamilton blinked twice. Her smile stiffened. Maggie couldn't decipher the emotions playing on the woman's face. Shock, yes. And most likely more than a little fear at what Richard's father would do if he found out. Oddly, there appeared to be not a smidgen of pride.

Emma clapped. "Good for you, Richard. They're promoting voting our way on the referendum at the university, aren't they?"

"Absolutely." He nodded at Emma. "There are groups like yours meeting on campus in Madison all the time. And not just for the right to vote. I heard just a bit last night about what some of you are doing for the children at some of the factories in town. I commend you." Again, the wink that scalded Maggie's already fiery skin. She would have a talk with him as soon as the women left.

"...for children whose parents are unable to adequately care for them. Similar to an orphanage, but. . ."

What was Richard talking about? In her irritation, she'd lost track of what he was saying. Maggie leaned forward.

"And it appears that's exactly what my mother has begun right here in our home."

Mrs. Hamilton gasped. Her napkin shot to her mouth.

"Evangeline? What's going on?" Mrs. Starbuck tsked. "What is he talking about?"

"He's just being silly. We did take in a poor little girl who had no place to go last night, but we're looking for a place—"

"Aren't you proud of my mother, ladies?" Richard put a hand on his mother's shoulder. "We don't use our third floor at all. There's room for maybe a dozen beds and—"

Evangeline Hamilton's head lolled toward her chest and she toppled against her son.

CHAPTER 17

Heather rubbed the steel-like muscles in her right shoulder and took a long pull of cocomocho. Racine Beans was beginning to feel more like home than the place she was living, and this was exactly how she'd envisioned spending her time—hopping from one coffee shop to another.

But not with a seven-year-old. And not because she was trying not to think about the scene at the last one.

She'd overreacted. *Again.* Ryan was only trying to protect her. And she probably needed it. But she didn't want to need it. What she wanted was to not be spineless, to know she could take care of herself. And to know that everyone else in her life knew that about her.

Slumping against the back of the chair, she stared at her charge over the top of several pages from *Essays on Life and the Role of Women.* Izzy's tongue stuck out the corner of her mouth as she struggled with a word search book written for fifth graders. *I'm precocious. I was reading by the time I turned three.*

Heather shut out the scene at the other coffee shop and went back to the *Essays.*

> God *"brought her unto the man" as a gift, as the part of him that would make him better. In that shining, breath-stilling moment, Woman realized her fullest potential. Taken from the side of*

*Man, she knew true equality and was cherished by Man, who
received her as a blessing from the hand of God.*

*Scripture tells us nothing of the space of time between
the end of the second chapter of Genesis and the beginning of
the third. Did they know days, weeks, possibly years of walking with God and each other in the cool of the day? Or was it
merely minutes before equality with Man and walks and talks
with God became not enough for Woman and she succumbed to
the seductive promises laid out by the serp—*

Another tug at her sleeve.

"*Now* can we read the mouse stories?"

"Yes. Now. Thank you for being so patient." Heather set down
the essays and picked up the mouse stories. "When your mom calls
tonight, we have to ask her about the mouse stories she found in
your dad's piano."

Izzy only nodded, crossing her eyes as the last of her drink slid
up her straw.

"Do you think there's any chance we could ask your dad about
the stories?"

"Um. I don't know. Maybe."

She was treading into unknown territory here. She lowered her
voice. "Do you ever see your father, Iz?"

"Mom says if anyone asks about him I'm supposed to say it's a
secret." She wrinkled her nose.

"Everyone has secrets."

"Do you?"

"I have one I've told some people, but a lot of people don't know."

"What's that?"

"My mom died when I was little. I don't remember her. And I
was adopted when I was four years old."

"Did your dad die, too?"

"No." She looked away from curious blue eyes and took a sip
from her cup. "He wasn't able"—*or willing*—"to take care of me, so
some very wonderful people adopted me and gave me a home. And
a sister." A twinge, a pinch of sadness, caused an almost physical
pain in her chest.

"Where is your daddy now?"

"I don't know."

"Do you sometimes imagine that he came to find you and he scooped you up in his arms and twirled you around and says he loves you and he's so, so sorry for not playing with you and reading you stories and taking you places like other daddies do?"

Heather slid her hand out of Izzy's. The question, she knew, had been pulled from her small, broken heart. "Do you wish that—"

"Excuse me."

The barista who always wore her hair in a single thick black braid tied back with a scarf that matched her uniform, approached their table.

"Sorry to interrupt. We're slow and bored, so I thought I'd offer you two free refills."

"Thank you"—she looked at the name on the name tag, spelled out in cockeyed lettering that matched the Racine Beans sign— "Jalissa. I'd love some more coffee, but I think we'd better switch the sugar fiend here to water."

A melodramatic groan came from the precocious one. "Not fair."

Jalissa had a musical laugh. "Neither is getting hyper from too much sugar and driving people crazy." She looked down and tapped a swirled pink and orange fingernail on the *Essays*. "Gorgeous writing."

Heather handed the papers to her. "This is a copy of some papers we just found in an attic. We think it was written in the early nineteen hundreds."

" 'Essays on Life and the Role of Women.' Sounds fascinating. Were they any smarter back then than we are now?"

"Whoever wrote this was. At least I think so. I just started reading it."

"There's a whole staff of women here wondering what their role in life is. And I'm right in there with 'em. Wish the father of my babies had figured it out, too. I'd love to hear what you learn from this." She held out her hand. "I'm Jalissa Myers. I've seen you here before."

"Heather Conrad. I'm new to the area."

"Wait a minute. You're the one Detective Tobin and the

Hawaiian shirt guy were asking about a couple weeks ago."

Heather felt suddenly chilled. The same kind of feeling she used to get as a kid when Zach shoved wet snow under the collar of her jacket. The cold slid from her neck to the small of her back. "He asked about me?"

"Yeah. This guy came in right after you left and asked if we knew who you were. And then Ryan asked about you and we know him and we'd seen you talking to him so we told him about the guy and then he flew out of here."

Ryan hadn't told her that part. But then she'd never asked why he thought she might be being followed.

"I'm sorry." Jalissa rested her hand on Heather's shoulder then picked up her empty cup. "Maybe I shouldn't have said anything."

"No. That's fine."

"I hope so. I'll shut my mouth now and go get those refills." She set the papers down, picked up the empty cups, and walked back to the counter.

Heather took a heavy breath. "Let's read."

"*Fi*nally."

Heather yanked a blond curl. " 'Magdalena loved Christmas. She was not so sure what she thought about Mr. and Mrs. Tabbycat's son.

" 'Within minutes, Magdalena had a fire roaring in the belly of the old stove. The water pump clanked as she filled the big white coffeepot. She set the pot on the stove. Mr. Tabbycat wanted to wake to the smell of coffee. And the smell of bacon and three-minute eggs. Magdalena was quite sure three-minute eggs still in their shell had no smell, but she would never, ever argue with Mr. Tabbycat.' "

Heather turned the page upside down on the table. At the top of the next was what appeared to be an address—*1203 Columbus Circle, Janesville*—written in thick lines like a marker. "Iz, when you put the papers in the scanner, did you see this?"

"Yeah. It was red. Why do you have that funny look on your face?"

"They didn't have felt-tip markers at the time that trunk was packed."

"So?"

191

"So it probably has something to do with the person who put the yearbooks and the newspapers in the trunk."

"Oh. Can we read now?"

"Sorry, ma'am. I'll try to stay focused." Heather bent over the page, resting her cheek on her fist. " 'When the oatmeal bubbled, Magdalena gently set three eggs into a saucepan and covered them with water and a very tight lid. As the bacon fried, she listened. As she squeezed the oranges, she listened. As she sliced the bread, she heard it. The third floorboard from Mr. Tabbycat's side of the bed. When it whined, she set the saucepan on the stove. When the water boiled, she flipped the egg timer on the windowsill. Grain by grain, white sand slid through the timer's tiny waist.' "

Heather looked up at the sound of a soft giggle. Jalissa stood several feet away, tray in hand. She set their drinks on the table. "Sorry. I was eavesdropping. Is that in the essays?"

"No. It's a story, written by the same person. You're welcome to listen. Are you allowed to sit with us?"

"I just might—"

A silver-haired couple walked through the front door. Jalissa shrugged. "Back to work."

"Thank you for these, and here"—Heather handed her the first page of the essay—"read this if you have time. We'll be here for a while."

"Thank you. I will."

Jalissa walked away and Heather took a sip from the cup. " 'As Magdalena turned the bacon, she watched the sand. As she toasted the bread, she watched the sand. At the very moment the toast turned the exact shade Mr. Tabbycat required, the last grain topped the sand mountain.' "

A muted sigh pulled her eyes off the page. Heather glanced at Izzy. "What do you think so far?"

"I don't know." Deep valleys dented Izzy's forehead.

"What are you thinking?"

"It's not mice."

"Tell me."

"Mr. Tabbycat sounds like Mom." Both of Izzy's hands slid over her mouth. After several seconds she lowered them and puffed out her cheeks. "I always say things I shouldn't. I think them and before I can stop the words they just *whoosh* out of my mouth."

Heather laughed. "I know exactly what you mean. I do the same thing."

"Like with Ryan, huh? When you yelled at him for following you."

"Just like that. It's okay to say what's on your mind, but we need to work on saying it nicely. If something bothers you about your mom, I think she would want you to talk to her about it. Nicely." She set the papers down. "The way I should have explained my feelings to Ryan."

Another sigh. "Mom is like Mr. Tabbycat because she always tells people how to do everything her way and she gets mad when they don't. I heard her get mad at you lotsa times at the office 'cuz you did things your way and not hers."

Heather cringed inwardly as she spread her hand over the pages of flowing script. "Don't you think everyone is like that at least a little bit? We all think we know best and we all get upset when people don't do things our way."

"I guess. But when I get to be an adult, Mom can't tell me what to do anymore and I will get a job where I'm the boss and I will be nice to people and no one can tell me—"

Izzy's eyes gravitated to a spot beyond Heather's shoulder. Heather turned. A strikingly attractive blond woman approached their table, holding a cup in one hand and a Racine Beans bag in the other. She stopped and stared, not saying a thing. Heather smiled. "Hello." It wasn't possible, but the blond could be a clone for a face that appeared in newspapers and tabloids on a very regular basis.

"Hi. I bought a chocolate chip cookie because they're kind of my weakness and they looked so good, but it's way bigger than I should eat, so I was wondering if you two—if you're not busy—if you'd want to share it with me."

"Aren't you"—*Stephannie Lansing?*—"generous." It *was* her. It had to be. She wore glasses, no makeup, and a slouchy hat slid low over her forehead, but nothing could hide cheekbones like that. "Thank you." Heather set the papers upside down on top of the ones she'd already turned over and gestured toward an empty chair.

The blond sat. "I hope I wasn't interrupting anything."

"We were just reading a story." She tapped the papers.

The woman picked up the entire stack. As if she was used to not asking before she did what she wanted. "Did you write this? The writing is cool. It looks old-fashioned."

"I wish I could write like that. We just copied these. We found them in an attic. We're guessing it was written a hundred years ago. Maybe more."

"Hmm." The woman who absolutely had to be Stephannie Lansing leafed through the pages. " 'The sun was still snoring when Magdalena pulled back the covers on her tiny iron bed.' What a fun story." She paged through several more. Her mouth opened. Her face blanched. "That address. I know that address."

♔

"You read the mouse stories, *too*?"

The little girl chattered on about a mouse as Stephannie back-pedaled. She ripped her gaze away from the black scrawl. She'd already given away way more than she'd intended. She'd strayed far from the script she'd rehearsed all the way from Chicago and in the twenty minutes she'd sat in the car half a block from the big house on Main Street, trying to work up the guts to walk up to the door. She was going to pretend she was studying the history of old houses. And then the garage door opened and a car backed out—with the person who might be her sister behind the wheel. So she'd followed, making up a new script as she drove.

Two pairs of eyes stared at her like she was crazy. *Act it out. You can do this.* She smiled at the brown ones, at the girl who could be her own flesh and blood. Her hair was shinier in person, her skin tanner and more flawless than the picture had shown. The kind of beauty that didn't rely on aestheticians and chemical peels to enhance what nature had provided. The muscles in her belly knotted. If they'd grown up together they probably wouldn't have gotten along. They would have fought over clothes and boys and who was the prettiest.

Stephannie wasn't sure she would have won.

She sat in the chair and set her purse on the floor. *Act it out.*

Squinching her eyes, she chewed on her bottom lip and looked back at the numbers, this time hiding the shock. "Oh. Wait. My bad. The one I'm thinking of is 1205 and I'm pretty sure it's *Columbia* Circle. My uncle in—oh, you don't care." She turned an heiress smile on the little girl. "I'm Annie."

She'd vowed before God that she would change. That promise probably needed to include lying. But giving only half your name wasn't exactly a lie.

"Hi." The little girl didn't offer her name.

"I'm Heather." The brunette held out her hand. "Nice to meet you. Do you live around here?"

"No." Dampness collected on her top lip. *Heather.* Her maybe-sister's name evoked scenes of green hills covered with acres of lavender blue. Her father had taken her to Scotland for her eighteenth birthday. She rubbed her lip as if she had an itch and wiped away the dampness. *Don't let it show.* "Just here on business. This looked like a good place to get a wake-up drink before getting back at it." She opened the bag and took out the cookie and the plastic knife she'd asked for. The barista had done a double take when she'd placed her order. There used to be a time when being recognized everywhere she went was a rush.

"What do you do?"

Remember your lines. "I've got a pretty cushy job." Definitely no bending the truth there. "I get to check out the accommodations at hotels and resorts for businesses who want to book conferences and events." A little distortion there, but her father had asked her to report on the competition wherever she traveled.

"Sounds fascinating. Do you travel far or just around here?" A thin edge of something—suspicion?—seemed to sharpen Heather's words.

"I've seen quite a bit of the world." *More than you will ever know.* Stephannie divided the cookie into three parts. "Thanks for keeping my calorie count down."

"Ditto." Heather's smile appeared genuine.

With the moment of possible suspicion seemingly gone, Stephannie relaxed against the back of the chair. "You don't look like the type who has to watch what you eat." Did the envy show?

She didn't want it to. This person might just end up a big part of her life. *God, You know I'm not all that good at being nice. Show me how.* She looked at the little girl. "Are you enjoying this story?"

The girl puckered her mouth and studied her then nodded. "Magdalena Mouse is a maid who lives in a great big house and takes care of a cat family. She works really hard cooking and making fires and three-minute eggs and nobody ever tells her she does a good job."

Heather laughed. "It sounds depressing, but it's actually entertaining. It gives a little window into the way women were treated a century ago. Izzy here has decided this isn't just a story, but someone's real life. Makes you grateful we have the career options we do today."

Stephannie glanced away, watching the barista slowly wiping down the next table as she thought of her conversation with her mother. *You can be anything you want to be. As long as it makes us look good.* "There are still too many things standing in our way."

"Like men." The barista straightened and turned to face them. "Here I am eavesdropping again." She nodded at Heather. "I read that page you gave me. Man, did that girl have it right. A hundred years ago and she knew wha's up more than me or my girlfriends." She pointed at the pages on the table. "I know I only read one page, but I'm thinkin' there's stuff in there the whole world needs to hear. You need to print up like a million copies."

Heather sucked in her bottom lip. "Jalissa, you just may be on to something." She pointed to Stephannie. "The same person who wrote the mouse stories also wrote some essays. The best I can figure so far, they're about how society messed up God's design for women and how we need to rediscover our rightful role."

"As God's gift to men," Jalissa added.

Stephannie laughed. She couldn't remember the last time she had. "I'll buy a copy."

Heather's eyes lit, as if tiny sparks suddenly fired in each pupil. "Maybe we should start a book club. An essay club."

"I'm in." Jalissa looked at Stephannie. "You in?" Her eyes narrowed. She wiped her hand on her apron and extended it. "I'm Jalissa, by the way."

Stephannie shook it. "Annie."

Jalissa's curls dipped toward her shoulder. Stephannie felt the heat of her stare.

"You look so familiar. Have you been here before?"

"No. This is my first time, but I've heard that before. Guess I have one of those faces." The girl who might be her sister smiled. Stephannie tried to read her eyes. If she thought she recognized her, wouldn't she ask? "So, do you want to join our essay club, Annie? We'll meet right here next"—Heather looked at the barista— "what's a good day and time for you?"

"Kylee and I both start at three on Wednesdays. What if we meet at one o'clock?"

"Sounds good. Annie, are you in?"

Logic screamed no, but she returned the smile. "Yes. I'd like that."

She'd come back next week. Calmer. And ready to act the part.

⚜

"Thanks for meeting me."

Heather kicked a stone. It skittered across the sand and hit the water. Up ahead, Izzy held up a wave-smoothed piece of green glass then stuck it in her pocket.

Ryan held out his hand. "I'm a sucker for a woman begging to apologize. Can't get enough of that 'You were right, I was wrong' stuff."

Heather stared at his hand, as if waiting for something. It took him a moment to figure it out. "You're thinking you're not the only one who needs to apologize for overreacting, right?"

"Right."

He kept walking. "I'm installing motion sensors at your house. I don't care if I don't get reimbursed."

"Now *that's* overreacting."

He narrowed his eyes at Heather. "Is it?"

"I agree there's something weird going on, but I don't think we're in actual *physical* danger."

"You don't, huh? You're sure the blond recognized that address?"

"She tried to cover it up, but I'm sure she did."

"And you're positive she's Stephannie Lansing?"

"I'm sure." Heather bent and picked up a tiny cone-shaped shell. "I found a picture of her online and showed it to Izzy. Without batting an eye she said, 'That's Annie.'"

"I'm starting to believe in this alternate dimension thing. First the cameraman, then the guy who probably isn't Mike, and now the richest girl in the entire Midwest all just show up in Racine. Her family's in the hotel business, Mike is in the hotel business, you were in the hotel business, Izzy's mom is in the hotel business. She lives in Chicago. You and Izzy's mom used to live in Chicago. Mike says he 'hails' from Indiana, but doesn't say he lives there now. We know he lives in a big city. It's all connected somehow, but none of it makes any sense."

He stopped, watching Izzy, about twenty yards ahead, wading up to her knees. Planting his bare feet in the sand, he swiveled until he could see the big white house then turned slowly back to Heather. "This will probably make you mad, but I have to ask. Are you sure there's nobody from your past—personal or business acquaintances—that might have a reason to be watching you?"

"No. Nothing."

"Not your ex?"

"No." Her hands clamped on her hips.

Ryan followed the placement of her hands. She wore denim capri pants and a yellow top with skinny straps. The bright yellow was the perfect contrast to her skin. The fabric flowed over her curves in—

"Ryan?"

"Oh. Sorry. Guess I was lost in that alternate world." *You. You're my alternate universe, girl.* "So. . ." *Where was I?* Oh yeah, she'd just answered his prying question with an annoyed no. He toyed with the ends of her hair, hoping a playful touch would lighten the moment. "It's not that I think you're hiding anything. It's just that we have to look at every possibility." He kicked a rock. "No stone unturned, so to speak."

"Cute." She took a ragged breath. "I know there are people who don't like me, but I have no known enemies." Her eyes closed for a fraction of a second. "Unless. . ."

Goose bumps galloped from his triceps to his fingertips. His hand shifted from her hair to her shoulder. Sun-warmed skin. Soft as satin. "Unless?" he whispered.

"Natalie lost her job at Coventry because she had an affair with a guy from another chain. There were a lot of ugly rumors going around. That was three months ago. I just found her termination papers. She agreed to not work for any of Coventry's competitors for a year. Which means what she's doing right now is in breach of contract. I guess it would make sense that someone in the business would try using me to get information about her." She rubbed her arms.

He stepped beside her, brain scrambling to find a way to return to the sunshiny, barefoot-in-the-sand feel the day had had up until his questions had darkened the mood. "Can I change the subject?"

"Please."

"I bought new cable and pulleys for your dumbwaiter. I figured you could use it for laundry and disappearing when the bad guys come."

"That's your idea of changing the subject? That is *sooo* overreact—"

He pressed two fingers to her lips. "*Shh.* The real question is, will you go out with me? Just you and me. Alone. No kids, no sightseeing, no talk about anyone's past, present, or future but yours and mine?"

She did a slo-mo turn, hair sliding in fat waves from her shoulder to her back. Her eyes glittered like the diamonds scattering the lake. "I'd love that."

CHAPTER 18

Andrew paced between his bed and the island in the kitchen as he listened to the *brrr* of his phone ringing Jerry. Bracing himself for Jerry's high, whiny voice-mail message, he went over the concise words he was going to leave. *If I don't get something concrete from you in—*

"Andrew. Sorry I haven't gotten back to you. Busy life, you know. Funny thing, when the economy tanks, the hotel PI business picks up. People get more paranoid when times are—"

"What have you found out?"

"You sitting down?"

Andrew ran a hand through his hair and strode to the window. He couldn't stand the guy's theatrics. "Yeah. Sure."

"Her last name is Conrad. She's no relation to Natalie Brooks, at least as far as I can tell, but. . .you ready for this? She was Brooks's girl Friday at Coventry Midwest."

"Whoa." Andrew walked to the couch and sank. "I don't get it. Draw me a diagram, Jer." It couldn't hurt to make the guy think they were best buds.

"I'm trying to fit all the puzzle pieces myself. Let's look at what we know. Somebody was looking for Lansing's daughter, probably hired by him. They found her in Racine at a house recently purchased by Natalie Brooks who recently lost her position as a VP for

Coventry Midwest. I can't find any trace of info on who she's working for now. My guess is she's not. She's an untouchable after what happened. Conrad lost her job or quit at the same time, so maybe she was involved in the scandal. The kid is Brooks's. I confirmed that. So best I can figure, Conrad's living with Brooks and taking care of the kid."

"Natalie Brooks is the kid's mother?"

"Yep."

Ryan had said Izzy was his sister's kid and Izzy had agreed he was her uncle. That meant Natalie Brooks was Ryan's sister. Which meant maybe Ryan and Heather were simply joining forces on the beach to watch her. Maybe there was nothing more than that between the two of them. And why did he care?

Because the more he learned about Heather, the more he knew something had to be done about her before Parker was well enough to connect with her. And if he was going to be a part of that something, liking her would make it all the more fun, and knowing she was free would make it all the more possible.

Andrew rubbed his temples. "So Parker must have had contact with Heather at some time in her life. Maybe all along and he just recently lost track of her."

"What makes you think that?"

What makes you not *think that? This is what I'm paying you for. I shouldn't have to think at all.* "It's a little too much coincidence that Parker Lansing's daughter just happens to have a master's degree in hotel management, don't yah think?" *Doofus.*

"Maybe it's in her blood."

"That's an expression, Jer. People don't inherit an interest in the hotel business. He had to have steered her, maybe paid for her education."

"Then why was she working for a competitor? A huge competitor, I might add."

As if you needed to. "Maybe they had a falling-out." Maybe that part *was* hereditary. Maybe Parker only spawned children who couldn't get along with him.

"Can I ask a question, Andy?"

Andrew's fingers curled under on his knee. Nobody called him

Andy. Not since the day he'd slammed Timmy Shimkus into his locker in seventh grade for shortening his name. "Ask."

"What're you going to do when you find out all there is to know about her? I mean, even if she ends up in line for half his fortune, Stephannie still gets enough for her—and you—to live high on the hog for the next century. What's the big deal?"

"It's not about money, Jer." He forced his hand to unclench. "It's about business." And a girl with a brain and a business plan.

The daughter Parker Lansing always wanted.

👑

The Mercedes seemed to be on autopilot. Stephannie felt like she'd just awakened from the kind of dream in which you know you're dreaming but can't do anything about it. When she finally became fully conscious of her surroundings she was in Lincolnshire, a block from her father's house.

What am I doing here?

She parked in front. Baxter's bark rattled the car windows. It made her strangely sad that he didn't recognize the sound of this car. "It's just me, Bax," she called as she neared the door and pulled out the house key. She didn't need a Great Dane glomming onto her leg to round out the day. "Settle down, baby, Stephy's home." She knocked, but no one answered. No "Who's there?" from the groundskeeper, no "Be there in a jiff" in her father's voice. She unlocked the door and pushed it open. Two massive paws made contact with her shoulders. A tongue the size of her face welcomed her home.

"Lonesome, baby?" She ruffled the pointy ears and nuzzled her face in Baxter's soft neck, on the fur that once absorbed the sting of every break-up, every snub from a girlfriend, every longing-for-Mom-time ignored. "Are you in on this, Bax? Do you know Heather? Has she been here?"

That's what she was doing here. Answering that question. Was Heather the daughter her father had never met, or had they had an ongoing relationship all these years? Had she simply, like Stephannie, disappeared for a while? Is that why someone had been looking for her? And that brought on another question. Had her father looked for her in those first few days after she'd left for

202

Belize? By the fourth day, the paparazzi had found her and he didn't have to wonder where she was or what she was doing.

Heather didn't look like the type to party for a week straight, to not care what she drank or smoked or swallowed, or where—or with whom—she spent the night. Heather was the good daughter.

Stephannie was the prodigal.

She walked through a hallway cluttered with family portraits and into the kitchen. She stood at her place at the kitchen table, imagining all four chairs filled.

Would she have grown up happier, more sure of herself, if she'd had someone to share life with? Would her father have stayed home more if he hadn't been running from the guilt of giving up a child? Would her mother have given up the corporate world if home was a place where all four chairs were filled?

Or was Heather only a product of her father's mistake and not her mother's? Would the smiling illusions she'd just passed in the hallway never have happened if her mother had known about the end result of his unfaithfulness?

She touched the polished tabletop then pulled away. It wasn't a place they'd spent a lot of time together, yet still she had good memories of laughter—over frozen pizza or her sad attempt at blueberry muffins. When had things started to go bad? Was there an event that triggered the landslide or had regret slowly eroded the love her parents must have felt at one time?

Suddenly exhausted, she pulled out a chair, the one that would have been Heather's, rested her head on her arms, and let the tears fall until they puddled on the table.

♔

By the time her tears stopped, finger-like shadows from the ornamental cherry trees outside the window splayed across the table. Stephannie stood, mopped the table with the bottom of her shirt, and walked into the hall.

Where her parents' wedding picture once hung, Dad had put a framed picture of Stephannie on her little pink bike. Her first day without training wheels. He stood behind her, one hand on the bike seat, the other on the handlebars. His smile said it all.

Pride. *Dear God, I want to see that smile again.*

She walked into her father's office. An old address book or a letter from her uncle would answer the nagging question. If the address she was looking for matched the one on the paper Heather had been reading at the coffee shop, she would know Heather and her father had met. Maybe years ago, maybe when Heather was a child and Uncle Stan still lived in Janesville, but it would mean they knew each other.

Knowing that would hurt so much more. And make everything so much harder.

She didn't remember seeing an address book when she'd gone through the file cabinet. Opening the double-fold doors of the closet, she scanned labels on a column of file drawers. A shelf ran the length of the closet. Golf trophies, one with a bronzed shoe with wings sprouting from the heel.

Her mother didn't live here. There was no longer any reason for them to be relegated to the closet. She took one down and set it on the mantel. When she reached for another one, her hand bumped something soft. It toppled with a soft thud. Standing on tiptoes, she grabbed it.

A stuffed mouse. About six inches high, it wore a red-striped apron and a tiny white cap. Miniscule wire-rimmed glasses perched on a pointy nose.

She'd never seen it before.

The mouse stories. What had Izzy said about them? Why hadn't she been listening?

Her eyes, still sore, smarted. She tossed the mouse far back onto the shelf and closed her eyes. Her brain spun. Like vertigo, but not physical. She began opening file drawers. In the top one, medical records were filed behind labeled dividers. Parker. Dianna. Stephannie. Only three. Not four. Not one for a child whose medical bills he'd paid for twenty-some years.

She flipped through the slim file behind her mother's name. The oldest only went back two years before the divorce. Blood test results and a prescription record. She opened the next drawer, shuffled through warranties and guarantees, then opened the third one down. An old black plastic Rolodex, its dog-eared cards fanning out from two black loops. Blue dividers with alphabet tabs jutting above the ivory cards with black lines. Addresses and phone numbers in her father's bold print filled the black lines on the cards. She turned to the *Ls*.

> *Stan and Carly Lansing*
> *1203 Columbus Circle*
> *Janesville, Wis.*

Why was her uncle's old address scrawled on a page of the story Heather had said they'd found in an attic?

You read the mouse stories, too?

Her aunt and uncle had left Janesville years ago. How many years? Eight? Ten? Dad had let her drive the last half of the trip to visit them shortly after she'd gotten her license. As far as she could remember, that was the last time. Had her father taken his other daughter to visit his brother?

Her head ached with unanswered questions, but she couldn't handle any more answers. She needed air. From a concealed hook behind the blinds on the foyer window she took Baxter's leash. The sound of the chain rattling in her hand called him.

As they walked down the half-circle drive, she imagined two little pink bikes leaning against the step.

Baxter held his head high as they walked the familiar street. His antics lifted Stephannie's spirits and brought her, once again, to the conclusion that all of this was just a massive, twisted misunderstanding. If she hadn't been warned more than once—by her mother, her father's doctor, and Pastor Dave—not to "upset your father," she'd simply ask him about Heather.

Ask him. She slowed Baxter as they passed a sea of multicolored mums and pulled her phone out of her pocket. She had to try again. If she asked the right questions, maybe he'd stay awake to answer. She dialed his hospital room. He answered on the third ring.

"Hi, Daddy." *It's me, Stephannie.* The foreign thought stabbed her. It hadn't occurred to her until now that maybe she wasn't the only one calling him Daddy.

"Hey, princess. How's my girl?"

The stab deepened. Did the words mean anything at all? "I'm good. I drove out to the house and Baxter and I are taking a walk."

"Good girl." Emotion roughened his already weak words. "Bet he's happy to see you."

"Yeah. Hey, I was looking in your office for some old pictures and I found this funny little stuffed mouse."

A weak laugh. "Don't you remember her?"

"No. Should I?" *Are you sure you're thinking of the right daughter?*

"I guess you were pretty young when I read the— Oh, Steph, I have to go. They want to stick me with needles again. I'll call you later, okay?"

"Sure."

"Love you, princess."

"Love you, too." She slid her phone back and turned Baxter around. "Enough for today, baby. Steph needs a break." *And a drink.*

In the house, she hung up the leash and wandered into the kitchen, to the cupboard above the stove. She opened it. Empty. She walked down the half flight of stairs to the bar in the den and opened the cupboard to the right of the sink. Empty. The fridge held soda cans and two near beers. As she headed back upstairs, she heard a muffled *beep* coming from her father's office. She walked toward the desk, waited, but didn't hear it again. A smoke alarm battery signaling it needed to be replaced? She scanned the ceiling, but the beep had sounded like an answering machine. She opened the drawer where she'd seen the machine she'd assumed was disconnected and gave a startled yelp. A bright red "2" glowed through a sheet of paper. "Weird." Why had he claimed to get rid of his landline if he hadn't? And why hide it? The real question was why, at this point, anything about her father should surprise her.

She pushed the button.

Message received Tuesday, July 10.

Stephannie shivered. That was the day her father ended up in the hospital.

"Hey, Parker. It's me. Where are you, buddy? I sent a picture to your cell. Can't wait to hear your reaction. Can I photograph your first meeting? How I'd love to see the shock and joy on that cute face. Sure hope you got the picture. If not I just wrecked the surprise." A warm laugh filled the room. "God bless. Guess I don't have to say that. He already has."

The voice wasn't familiar. Who was this person? She looped back through the important points. "First meeting," he'd said. *How I'd love to see the shock and joy on that cute face.* So Heather had never met her father.

And probably didn't even know who he was.

The next message began. It had been sent the day after his heart had stopped and they'd shocked him back to life.

"Heard about your setback. Praying for you. Got my men's group lifting you before the throne, too. I know you won't hear this for a while, but when you do you'll know that God heard the pleas of His people—and the heart cry of a girl who needs a relationship with her father."

Stephannie's hand slid over her mouth and she folded onto the floor. "*I* need a relationship with my father." But what if, before she could prove she was changing, the perfect daughter stepped into the picture and she never got the chance to reclaim what was rightfully hers?

Her father.

God, I don't care about the money. She can have my inheritance. If my dad feels guilty, he can give her my car and my apartment and anything else I have.

"I just want my daddy."

♔

January 12, 1912

The dampness from Maggie's hands had seeped through her gloves. Peering between two taper candles in silver holders, she studied Emma, chattering with the corpulent white-haired gentleman to her right with confident and animated poise. *Oh, to be at ease in a place like this.* Why couldn't she be the self-assured Woman she wrote about in her essays?

Maggie rested her left hand on her napkin. Richard's hand slid beneath the tablecloth and covered hers. She kept her palm against the linen folded on her lap. He mustn't know how nervous she felt. He leaned toward her. The sleeve of his black coat touched her bare arm. "You look dazzling. Have you noticed all the other men staring?"

"No. I have not. You imagination is very active tonight."

Richard gave a guttural laugh. "You have no idea, my dear."

Something about the words, combined with the suggestive laugh, chilled her. This was not the Richard she knew. But did she really know him? Her imaginings had made him into a fairy-tale knight on a white horse who waited for just the right moment to charge in and take her away from a life of drudgery. The real Richard had never voiced the desire to do any such thing. The real Richard had not even the courage to tell his parents they had gone to the party together.

Had he asked Emma Mitchell to accompany him to a dinner party he would not have added "Our secret."

She pulled her hand away and pierced the stuffed bird before her with the tines of the third fork she'd used so far, then sliced into it with a knife twice the weight of the Hamiltons' silver. Scrolls and curlicues pressed into her palm. She held the knife so tightly she wondered if she would walk away with an *M* emblazoned on her palm. "The capon is delicious, isn't it?" Taking a bite and chewing with exaggerated slowness, she waited for an answer. When none came, she tried again. "Do you like the asparagus stuffing? Would you like me to fix this for you sometime?"

Did she imagine the moment of tension? It disappeared in seconds and Richard's arm slid along the back of her chair. "Tonight, Maggie Parker, you are forbidden to think of cooking or cleaning or anything but enjoying the food, the music, and the company."

Maggie laughed, an awful tinny, tittering sound. She liked the feel of his arm around her. She did not, however, like his use of *forbidden*. Even though he said it in jest, it sounded far too much like the senior Mr. Hamilton. She took a bite of potato croquette and chewed slowly, buying time to sort her thoughts. When her lips parted, she suddenly realized she was about to ask him if he preferred chives or dill in his croquettes.

Think like these women. Speak of something scintillating. But the things that came to mind were controversial, non-party topics. Well, that was better than nothing. "You were a bit taxing on your mother this afternoon—all that nonsense about a home for children. I'm not sure she'd quite recovered by the time we left." She liked the sound of *we*, even though they hadn't become a couple for the evening until the moment she jumped into the passenger seat of the touring car and Richard whipped out of the drive and onto Main Street like the car had a demon for an engine.

After bringing food and a chamber pot to Angelica and telling her to stay in the room and not make a sound, Maggie had flown down the back stairs, across the kitchen, and out the back door like a scared little mouse in fear Mr. Hamilton would realize she was joining his son in the car.

The ride here had been dreamlike. Even though she had her own blanket over her knees and Richard had his, there was something intensely intimate about sitting in such proximity, under covers, in such a small, enclosed space. His warmth and scent had triggered thoughts she never even knew she was capable of.

Richard drummed his fingers on the tablecloth. "What part of that is nonsense?"

She stared at the sharp angles of his profile, the steely glint in his eyes. "You can't be serious."

"Why not?" He turned, his whole body facing her, leaning slightly so as not to be overheard. "I wish you could sit in on the rallies at school and see all that's happening. It's like being in the center of a volcano—everything that's changing in this state starts in that town. Labor reform, rights for women and children. Why shouldn't we be part of that? Look at what you've done for that poor little waif. You may have saved her life. Can't you imagine multiplying that many times over? Look at the room we have upstairs."

Magdalena stared at Leo Tabbycat in disbelief. And who will cook for these poor little waifs? And who will wash their clothes and sit with them while they're sick?

"That's the kind of thing people talk about all the time on campus—how we can take part in the solutions rather than propagate the problem. It's why I joined the Men's League. I've been looking for a way I could make a difference, and last night it just seemed to all fall into place."

Maggie formed her mouth into the most demure of smiles and added a pinch of admiration to the expression in her eyes. "That's beautiful, Richard. This is a compassionate side of you I have never seen before. To think you would give up your education to care for unfortunate children and support—"

His laugh interrupted her accolades. "That is not what I meant, Maggie dear. Can you imagine me. . ." He waved away whatever preposterous image had come to mind. "What I will do is clear everything with the city if there are any codes or anything we—"

"You're serious about this, aren't you?" Somehow, the *we* in this sentence hadn't warmed her the way the previous one had.

"Of course. You love children. This is the kind of thing you were destined to do."

Maggie felt her bottom lip dropping away from her top in a gape that must be most unbecoming. She blinked, but the intensity of his expression didn't change. Turning away, she stared at the coif of the woman two chairs down from Emma. A string of pearls wound through her chignon. A matching rope encircled her neck and another, her wrist. Maggie studied the intricate pattern painted in gold leaf on the china and the sparkle of tiny glass spoons in each cut-glass saltcellar. The wealth represented at this table alone could feed hundreds of Angelicas for a year.

She looked down at her plate. The dissected capon suddenly looked mangled and gruesome. Gravy had congealed on her potato croquette. She took a sip of water. "I can't quite see your father mirroring your enthusiasm."

Another laugh. "I have an answer for that."

"You must have lain awake for hours last night making plans."

"It didn't take hours. It just all fell into place in my mind. I thought of the expressions on my friends' faces at school when I told them of what my family was doing for unfortunate children and the second I did, it hit me that, while some folk will, of course, think we are insane for doing this, others will hold the Hamiltons in the highest esteem for our progressivism. And these are the people my father most desires to impress. If he thinks it is good for business, he will embrace the idea. And it's not like he has to have any direct contact with the children himself."

"Of course not. That will be all left to me."

"Is that what you're thinking?" He shook his head. "No wonder you're not showing more excitement over this. What an insensitive oaf you must think I am. I have no intention of leaving all the work to you. We'll get backers and we'll hire another domest—person to help. Maybe a laundress or a cook. You can decide. And Mother will help. She can put into practice all you're teaching her. And eventually we will build a separate building downtown."

"An institution."

"Well, yes. I mean, it doesn't have to *feel* like an institution. It will be like the YMCA maybe, but for children."

"But most of these children are not orphans. They have parents who want to care for them, but can't. Why not put effort into making employers pay a living wage so that children don't have to work and parents can. . ." Her words slowed then ceased altogether as Richard's attention drifted over the top of her head. Maggie turned to see several men at the end of the table rise from their chairs.

"There are several of our future backers right now. It appears we men are to have our dessert in the parlor. Will you be all right without me for a few minutes?"

Considering the fact that you didn't listen to any part of my last three sentences, I can't imagine your absence will make much difference. "Yes. I'll be fine." She looked at the door leading to the kitchen and watched two women in black uniforms and white aprons and caps pass each other carrying trays of lemon chiffon pie. She would be fine if she could tie on an apron and join them. The man on her right, with whom she'd exchanged a mere handful of words, rose and offered a polite adieu. Maggie smoothed the gold overlay on her dress with damp hands and searched in vain for someone to talk to.

"Miss Parker?"

She looked up at a dignified-looking, though somewhat round, gentleman with a florid face and hair graying at the temples. "Yes?"

"I'm Ralston Clark. Miss Mitchell is otherwise engaged and most likely will be all evening, but I wanted to commend both of you for what you are doing to promote an education for every child in our city. It is a despicable thing that we have children working at all, let alone in such deplorable conditions, but I do see Racine making strides far ahead of most cities and you, madam, are part of that change. Not only are you educating these young people, but you are drawing attention to the problem and putting fear into business owners. So I want to thank you and"—he pulled out the recently vacated chair and sat—"I want to give you a map that will aid in your future endeavors." He held his hand out to her. "Shake my hand, Miss Parker."

She did. A tightly folded paper slid from his hand to hers. She reached down, picked up her reticule, and slid the paper into it.

"I guarantee you will find this distasteful and it may challenge the strength of your convictions, but I believe you and Miss Mitchell are in a better place to tackle this than any of the rest of us."

"I will follow up on this."

"Thank you." He reached into his vest pocket and withdrew a small card. "Godspeed, Miss Parker. Here is my card. If anything, anything at all, causes difficulty for you, I want you to contact me immediately." He stood and touched his fingers to his forehead as if doffing a hat. "You are not alone in this, Miss Parker. Not alone at all."

"Maggie. What was it I said that you found so offensive?"

Richard leaned against the cupboard as he waited for her to finish the cocoa. Dark wet circles dotted his shoulders from the fat clumps of snow that had drifted down on them as they walked from the carriage house to the porch. It could have been a beautiful moment—holding hands, staring straight up as lazy snow clusters landed on their faces. It could have been a moment filled with laughter.

But it wasn't.

They both still wore their coats—Maggie, because she was chilled to the bone from more than the ride home. Richard, because he'd been too busy gesturing with his hands as he painted the vision for the Hamilton Home for Disadvantaged Youth. His vision might have stirred a deep excitement and a sense of being kindred spirits. . .if his talk all the way home from Emma's party had not centered on his run for student body president.

He'd asked for cocoa when they got home. If he were her suitor and not her employer's son, she would have said no. But she could not, so she'd poured sugar, cocoa, and a pinch of salt into a pan, added a bit of water, and brought it to boil. Richard had talked nonstop as she added the milk. She'd interrupted him once to run upstairs and check on Angelica. The girl was sound asleep on the floor rather than the bed where she should have been. The fire still crackled with newly added wood, and on the bed was a handmade card. *Thank you. You are the nisest person I no.*

Richard's hands finally stilled. And reached out to her.

Every muscle in her body tightened as a battle raged between her heart and her mind. She had never been held in the arms of a man other than her father. And that was becoming a dim memory. She had spent nights imagining the feel of Richard's strong arms around her, had burned more sauces and puddings than she would ever admit because of daydreaming about the very same. Yet here he stood, reaching out for her, whispering her name, and her brain said no. She shook her head.

A deep, shuddering breath escaped her lips. She turned to the new stove and added a splash of vanilla to the cocoa. "What you are talking about might be a wonderful thing, but I can't help but wonder at your motives." Resting the spoon on the side of the pan, she switched off the heating element then hugged her arms across her coat as she faced Richard.

He sighed and pulled out a chair. "None of us can do anything out of totally pure motives. If I choose to do a charitable thing and I also gain from it, is that so wrong?"

Yes. She pondered the Bible verse that came to mind. If she awakened his anger, she might well find herself outside looking in. This time she was not so assured of having a warm place to stay at the Caswells'. And this time it was not only herself she was responsible for. Still, there were times it was wrong to remain silent. " 'Though I speak with the tongues of men and of angels, and have not charity, I am become as sounding brass, or a tinkling cymbal.' "

His eyes blazed. Maggie's insides tumbled. She turned away and quickly ladled cocoa into two cups. Her hand shook as she turned back. Just as she set a cup and saucer in front of him, Richard laughed.

"Oh, Maggie, you are so good for me. How can I defend my actions when you spout scripture at me?"

Relief coursed through her, weakening her knees. She sat at the opposite end of the table. But what, exactly, did he mean? "What are you thinking?"

"That I need you in my life to keep me on the straight and narrow."

Cocoa-scented steam licked her chin as she lifted her cup. Her face flushed. How could she hold a grudge against a man who warmed her more thoroughly than any fire she had ever built?

"Will you work with me, Maggie?"

"Yes." Her answer floated on the steam. "But I cannot imagine your father agreeing—"

The door to the dining room swung open. "Agreeing to what?"

Mr. Hamilton walked in, wearing his burgundy silk robe over the blue pajamas Maggie had just laundered and pressed. Though she'd seen the man often in his robe and had served his breakfast in bed on countless occasions, seeing him like that in the kitchen made her uncomfortable. She averted her eyes. "Would you like some cocoa, Mr. Hamilton?"

He gave a curt nod. "And a sandwich, too."

She rose from her chair and her steaming cup as Richard took an audible breath. "Father, I've come up with an idea I believe will resound with your convictions and, as Maggie and I were just discussing, will show this town just how generous and socially conscious a man you are."

Mr. Hamilton's gaze went from his son to his maid. His eyes travelled down to the gold gown peeking from beneath her coat. "You were discussing my reputation in town with *her*?"

"Yes." Richard cleared his throat. "Maggie was also invited to Emma Mitchell's dinner party and we both just arrived home."

Maggie yanked the handle on the icebox door. Richard made it sound as though they'd travelled separately. What a coincidence that they'd both just happened to get home at the same time. Just in time for her to make him cocoa and light the fire in his room and turn down his covers before he headed to bed. The cold from the icebox felt good against her face. She sliced roast beef with an intensity the job didn't require, then applied the same force to the unfortunate loaf of bread she'd baked yesterday before fixing lunch for the meeting she was allowed to attend as an equal.

". . .unfortunate children whose parents want to care for them but can't, need a place to sleep. Really that's all they need, that and maybe two meals, but how much does a child really—"

"Get to the point, boy."

"Well, sir, I thought that, since we have all that unused space on the third floor, we—"

A coarse laugh boomed from Mr. Hamilton. "You thought we'd keep the little darlings *here?*" A meaty hand slapped the table. "Oh, Richard, that is priceless. You are a wonder, my boy. I cannot wait to see what happens when you leave that ivory tower and step into the real world." The laugh echoed again, bouncing off tall white cabinets. "Put it on a tray, Maggie, and bring it to my room. I can't wait to wake Mrs. Hamilton to tell her what her boy has thought of now." His laugh continued until the door swung shut on his amusement.

CHAPTER 19

Ryan tapped his fingers on Marissa's cluttered desk. For some reason, he'd thought he could think better in the TKJ office than upstairs in a too-quiet apartment.

He was wrong.

Rubbing his forehead, he stared cross-eyed at the fourth or fifth blog post his Internet search had uncovered about Natalie Brooks losing her position at Coventry Midwest. While he'd found several short blurbs on hotel industry sites about the change of command, blogs and social media were the go-to places for juicy, albeit maybe not accurate, details. He turned on the desk lamp and read one touting to be the place where the hottest scandals first hit the grapevine.

*I don't believe for a nanosecond that the Mrs. didn't know.
And no one's going to convince me the tart in question seduced
the Mr. "once and only once." I was at a New Year's Eve party
attended by the Enfields and the now infamous Natalie Brooks
and her personal assistant. If the electricity between the illus-
trious Mr. Enfield and said tart could have been harnessed it
could have lit Wrigley Field for the next decade. The feelings,
as they say, were mutual, and if this were nothing but your
garden-variety triangle, the buzz would have died five seconds
after it began. But this little tryst involved corporate secrets.*

I guarantee it. Pillow talk went beyond smoochy-smoochy and into "Tell me about the board meeting, sweetums?" Such a shame she got caught warming two pillows in the same night.

So, if this source was to be believed, Natalie Brooks was guilty of far more than an extramarital affair. The woman was a corporate spy.

And Heather was her assistant.

He shut off the computer. *What have I gotten myself into?*

⟡

"Just having another one of those I-want-my-mommy-and-daddy moments."

Heather gripped the phone as she peeked in on Izzy, soaking in a mountain of peppermint-scented bubbles in the upstairs bathroom. A suds-coated hand rose. The fingers wiggled. Heather continued her hall pacing.

"Anything wrong?" her father asked. "Izzy behaving?"

"She's wonderful."

"And the boy?"

Her mother had evidently relayed some information. "Ryan. He's fine."

"Just feeling homesick? Or is this about something deeper?" His tone left no doubt what he was referring to.

"Just homesick." *And confused. And a little scared.* She longed to pour it all out, to tell him about "Mike" and "Annie" and the guy with the camera, to hear her father say it was probably nothing. But she wouldn't do that to him when he was so far away and couldn't do anything to help. "This pretend-mommy thing is eating up my time and by the end of the day I don't have any brain cells left for working on my business plan and I haven't applied for a single job and I don't know what I'm doing after Natalie gets home."

A pregnant pause filled the miles between them. "You're always welcome here, you know. I know it would be hard for you, but—"

"I know. Of course I know that."

"So how are you doing with the Jen and Zach issue?"

She smiled at the directness she loved. "It still sneaks up and stabs me once in awhile, but the more time goes by, the more I

217

realize how much I was over Zach long before I knew he had feelings for Jen."

"Good. If you're sure about that, would you mind talking to Jen? She's been here all afternoon moping because you didn't answer her e-mail with the wedding picture and she's convinced she's destroyed her relationship with you forever."

With a laugh and a swipe at unexpected tears, she nodded. "I'll call her to—"

"I'm out, Heather!"

"My charge awaits. Time for a bedtime story and then maybe I can get some work done."

They exchanged good-byes and Heather picked up the remaining pages of the "mouse story" and followed damp footprints to Izzy's room.

✧

" 'Saucepan in hand, Magdalena scampered to the sink and doused the eggs in cold water.

" 'Overhead, the board in front of the bathroom sink groaned, and Magdalena became a blur of black and white and gray. She buttered the toast, dished the oatmeal, filled the cream pitcher, drained the bacon, poured the juice, set the three-minute egg in its cup, folded the napkin, poured the coffee, picked up the tray, flew through the swinging door, and stood at the foot of the stairs. Shoulders back, abdomen tight, chin up, tail neatly curled, she waited.

" 'Mr. Tabbycat descended. At the bottom step, he raised his spectacles, peered down at his tray, and nodded. Some days he said, "Jam." Some days he said, "Peaches." On cold days he said, "Fire." On warm days he said, "Porch." Today, because he carried a stack of papers under his arm, he said, "Table."

" 'Magdalena arranged Mr. Tabbycat's breakfast on the lace tablecloth and waited to be dismissed. Mr. Tabbycat cracked the egg, dipped the toast into its perfectly soft, orangey-yellow center, and nodded.

" 'Magdalena traipsed back to the kitchen, wondering what it would be like, someday, to hear a soft, kind voice say, "This is delicious, Magdalena. Thank you for all your hard work." ' "

Heather turned the page upside down on the bed. "Had enough?"

Izzy yawned and rested her head on Heather's shoulder. "No. Keep reading until you get to a happy part. I feel sad for Magdalena. I'm imagining that I'm her, scampering up and down the twisty stairs between the walls and running back and forth through the swinging door with food for the fat cat."

The pages dropped, along with Heather's hands, to her lap. "What if Magdalena isn't a made-up name for the story? What if that's the real name of the person who owned that trunk?" She sat up straight. "We have to check the passenger list of the *Titanic*."

Izzy gasped. "But you and Ryan said she never took a trip."

"Maybe she didn't. But maybe she did and she had a lot of trunks and just forgot this one."

"But that means she maybe died."

"Let's see if we can find out. There were survivors."

"Go get your computer. Quick!" Izzy commanded, as if Magdalena Mouse's life depended on it.

Heather ran down the hall in stocking feet and slid back into Izzy's room in seconds, laptop under her arm and feet losing traction on the polished floor. She tumbled onto the bed.

Izzy clapped. "This is scary and fun all mixed together."

"This'll only take a minute." She found the official *Titanic* passenger list on encyclopedia-titanica.com. "We know she had a first class ticket. Or someone did. And the name on it was Hamilton. That could be Magdalena's last name or the name of the person who purchased it for her. Maybe the family she worked for was going. It would make sense they'd take their maid." She ran her finger down the alphabetized list. "Look. There's someone listed as a personal maid."

The entry read: BARBER, Miss ELLEN "NELLIE." In a column labeled "Group," she was listed as "Servant," and in the "Job" column, amid "stockbroker," "shipbuilder," "property developer," "singer," and "Justice of the Peace," Miss Barber's occupation appeared as "personal maid."

"Looks like we can click on her name and get more information."

Heather moved the cursor and an entire page dedicated to Miss Nellie Barber popped up. Izzy leaned so close to the screen it was hard to see around her as she read. "Name: Miss Ellen 'Nellie' Barber. Age: 26 years. Occupation: Personal maid to Mrs. Julia Florence Cavendish. 1st Class passenger. First Embarked: Southampton on Wednesday 10th April 1912. Ticket number: 19877. She paid seventy-eight pounds and seventeen shillings—that's British money—for her ticket. Rescued on boat six. Disembarked *Carpathia*—that's the ship that rescued the survivors—in New York City on Thursday 18th April 1912."

"So some of the maids survived." Izzy's breath tickled Heather's cheek. "Look. There's a picture of her house. We have to find Magdalena and see if she lived and if there's a picture of this—*my* house."

Heather scrolled to the *H*s. "No Hamiltons in first class. Let's do a search for 'Magdalena.'" She typed it in. "Nothing. Okay, let's try the other classes." She repeated the search for second and third class with no results. "So maybe her name wasn't Magdalena or Hamilton. Wait." She raised one finger. "Let me try something." She typed in *Titanic passenger Racine, WI*.

"Whoa." Her pulse kicked into high gear. "Mrs. Jennie Louise Hansen." The listing brought her back to encyclopedia-titanica. com. "We struck gold, Izzy-girl," she whispered as she skimmed. "Maiden name was Howard. Married to Claus Peter Hansen. Born December 20, 1866. Third class passenger. She was forty-five when the *Titanic* sank. Destination Racine, Wisconsin. Rescued in Boat 11. Died December 15, 1952. That would have made her almost eighty-six. And she's buried right here in Racine."

The bed jiggled as Izzy bounced on her knees. "Is that her picture?" She pointed at a sepia-toned photograph of a woman in a high-collared lace dress and an elaborate flower-decked headpiece and veil. "Is she our Magdalena? Maybe she just made up the name for the story. I make up stories and I don't use my real name sometimes."

"Let's see what we can find out about her." Heather enlarged the font size on the page. "Before her marriage she lived at 2036 North Main Street, Racine. That's the other side of downtown, I think. 'Jennie was a frail woman who had been poor in health for years. She had lived through several catastrophic events in addition to the *Titanic*: She was a pastry cook in the Blake Opera House and Hotel which burned to the ground on 27 December 1884. She made the last trip in the elevator before flames gutted the shaft. Prior to the fire by several months, she was found lying unconscious in the kitchen overcome by gas fumes from the stove.'"

Izzy laughed. "I know it's not funny, but she's like a cat with nine lives, isn't she?"

"Guess maybe God wanted her to stick around for a reason."

"Yeah. I guess. Is that her wedding?"

The first photograph they'd seen was apparently cut from this group shot. Jennie, veil flowing to the floor, clutched a spray of flowers as she sat next to, but not quite touching, the man who must be her husband. Two couples stood behind them.

"I just love the dresses." Izzy sighed. "I'm letting my hair grow so I can wear it all puffy like that with a big bow on top."

"They married on July 25, 1900, so they'd been married for almost twelve years when they sailed on the *Titanic*. It says they never had children."

"That's sad. Did her husband die when the boat sank?"

"Let's read the whole thing. 'In 1912, Peter and Jennie were going to Denmark to visit his parents and three brothers, whom he had not seen for twenty-one years. Before leaving Racine, Jennie told her brother that she dreaded making the trip. She said she had a feeling she would never return alive.'"

"Can you say crrreepy?" Izzy rubbed her arms.

Heather laughed. " 'The Hansens left for Europe on board the Cunarder *Campania* on February 14, 1912.' "

"Valentine's Day." Izzy folded her hands. "That's so romantic. I really, really hope this is our Magdalena and her husband was okay and they lived happily ever after."

"*Shh.*" Heather nudged Izzy's shoulder and continued to read. " 'When the time came for Peter and Jennie to return to America, Peter's twenty-six-year-old brother, Henrik, decided to leave Denmark and accompany them to the new world. Peter bought their tickets at the White Star agent in Maribo, Lolland, and the three boarded the *Titanic* in Southampton as third class passengers. After the collision, Peter put his wife into a lifeboat with the words: "Jennie, you had better go so that there will be one of us to tell the story back home."'"

Izzy gasped and pressed her knuckles to her mouth. "He didn't live, did he?"

" 'Peter and Henrik both perished in the sinking.' "

"Ohhh. I knew it. That's so, so sad."

"It is." Heather scanned the rest of the article and decided not to share most of it with Izzy. It said that Jennie suffered such a shock to her nervous system that she was unable to shed a tear after the *Titanic* sank and that she suffered such severe nightmares that her brother and sister-in-law had to hold her down on the bed. "It says she remarried three years later, and she lived a long time after that. I think she must have ended up having a very happy life, don't you?"

"I don't know. Would you if your husband froze in the ocean like Jack? I don't think Rose on the movie had a happy life, else why did she throw the blue diamond into the ocean when she was an old lady?"

Heather didn't have an answer for that one. "You think too much. Enough history for now." She closed her laptop.

"But not enough mouse story. Will you read until I fall asleep?"

"If you close your eyes."

"I will."

Heather picked up the papers and began to read. " 'On the eve of Christmas, Magdalena worked very hard to make everything perfect. She cooked the oysters in butter until their edges curled like the lace hem of a lady's petticoat and then she added thick, rich cream, a dash of pepper, and just the right amount of salt. The little round crackers were homemade. The fruitcake sat on a pink glass plate, waiting to be sliced, and Magdalena sat on pins and needles, waiting for Leo Tabbycat to walk into the room.' "

Chapter 20

Why was it, when she'd determined to check out every coffee shop in Racine, that she always ended up at this one?

Izzy was already at Amanda's, giving Heather two hours before she needed to start getting ready for a date with "No kids, no sightseeing, no talk about anyone's past, present, or future but yours and mine."

She spread paint and fabric swatches across the table and started eliminating the ones that didn't say "Gather round."

Tawny day lily, yellow haze, copper mine, Huntington green, golden bounty. She could smell the exotic spices that would complement the colors.

"What's all this?" Jalissa waved red-and-white-striped nails across the table.

"Dreaming." Heather rubbed her right eyebrow. "I have this crazy idea about starting a chain of coffee shops."

Shock registered on Jalissa's face. "Seriously?"

"Seriously. All I need is a location for my prototype and a wad of money."

"Hmm. Tell me your ideas." Jalissa pulled out a chair and sat. "What's going to make your chain stand out from all the rest?"

Heather's pitch rolled off her tongue like she'd practiced it a hundred times in front of a mirror. Because she had.

"Coffee and Connection. I like that. I like all of it. Kind of like what church should be."

"You're not the first person to say that."

"It's the truth. Makes me mad sometimes. I remember being too scared to set foot in a church. I knew where those feet had taken me and I knew they wouldn't want anything to do with the likes of me. But when some people who knew Jesus invited me to their house for supper, that I could do." She nodded toward the door. "People aren't afraid to walk in here and, like you saw, I'm not afraid to eavesdrop and start conversations. Natural, the way it should be."

"Natural. I like that." A strange, almost audible buzz started deep in her soul. Natural, the way it should be. Like she'd told Ryan, it wasn't the Jesus part that scared her, it was the freak part.

Jalissa picked up the square labeled "copper mine." "These are delicious colors. Designed to make you hungry." She put it down and picked up a pale sage color and a deep purple. "And these are relaxing. You'd need both in a place like you're describing." Her neck craned to the left. Her eyes narrowed as she scanned the coffee shop as if seeing it for the first time. "Makes me want to redecorate this place."

"It's comfortable here. Makes me feel at home."

"It could use some sprucing." Jalissa leaned on her elbow and rested her chin in her hand then suddenly sat up and looked around. "Where's your shadow?"

"She's with a friend."

"Feels good to get out without those babies once in a while, doesn't it? I had two of my own. They're fourteen and sixteen now."

Heather reared her head back. "You do not look old enough for that."

"Just hit the big three-oh."

"So you were. . ."

"Yeah. A baby when I had my baby. And then turned around and did it all over again with the same guy two years later." She nodded toward the counter. "That's why I try my best to knock some fear of God and life into these girls. This place hires single moms and women who've hit bottom and helps 'em get on their feet, and I do what I can to keep them from making the mistakes I made or repeating their own." She looked back at Heather. "That's why what I read in that essay gave me goose bumps. Hey, I meant to ask you, are you open to some others joining the club?"

"Of course." Heather reached into her bag and pulled out a copy of the *Essays*. "Make as many copies of this as you want."

"You're sure?"

"I'm absolutely sure."

"Okay, then." With a smack of her lips, she slapped the table and walked back to the counter.

♔

"You're a surprising guy, Spidey."

Heather touched a petal on the single pink rose floating in a crystal bowl between them. They sat at Kurt and Amanda's picnic table. Pink Christmas lights looped over their heads and more than a dozen votive candles in glass holders flickered on the table, the grill, and the deck railing. Ryan wore a dark, purplish-blue T-shirt that fit like she shouldn't let herself stare at it too long.

"Not all girls like surprises."

"As long as they're good ones, I love them." She motioned toward her half-empty pitcher of what tasted exactly like cocomocho and then to their plates where not a trace of chicken enchilada casserole remained. "So far. . .the music, the food, the company. . .this has been a good one."

"Ready for the next one?"

"I think so."

"Okay. Close your eyes and keep them closed until I tell you to open. I'll just be a minute."

She did as she was told. Footsteps retreated into the house. She covered her face with her hands and listened to the music coming from overhead speakers—music from the *Titanic* songbook. Her comment about surprising wasn't just to make him feel good. The whole evening, from the moment he'd picked her up in his brother's 1958 Chevy to his hand over her eyes as he'd led her onto the deck, had been unexpected. She'd expected anything traditional and got anything but.

As long as they're good ones, I love them.

Ryan Tobin was proving to be one of the "good ones." She thought back, searching for the last time Zach had surprised her with something good, but all she could come up with was the last surprise.

"Keep 'em closed."

She tracked the sound of his steps across the deck. The table groaned as he sat down. Her nose detected something fruity. Lemon.

Poof! Heat flashed her face. Her eyes popped open. A square plate sat between them. A skewer of mango, pineapple, strawberries, and blue and yellow flames lay on the plate.

The fire reflected in his eyes. "Blow it out."

She did, and then sat back, hand to her chest, waiting for her pulse to return to something close to normal. "Like I said, you're a surprising guy, Spidey."

"You're worth surprising." His hand reached across the table. Hers slid into it as if it belonged there. He nodded toward the pergola above them. "Listen to this. It's 'In the Shadows.' Would you like to waltz while our dessert cools?"

"I haven't waltzed since phys ed in junior high."

"Then you can teach me."

Eyes still on his, hands still joined, she managed to get on the other side of the bench without making a fool of herself. She put her left hand high on his back and held out her right. He pulled her into his arms and tucked her hand close to his chest. Close enough to know that hers was not the only erratic pulse. "This is comfier."

Their feet barely moved. His lips grazed her forehead.

Her eyes closed. She imagined wearing one of the dresses Izzy had found in the trunk. Ryan's chin brushing the pearl-studded pins holding her Gibson girl hair. Her gloved hand resting in his. Blue satin skimming the floor. Cellos and violins setting the world to music as the White Star Orchestra played "In the Shadows."

"Are you relaxing?" he whispered.

"Mm-hm."

"You deserve it. Have you had any time to work on your business plan between watching the precocious one?"

"It hasn't been all Izzy. The mouse story and the treasure chest and the strange people who keep popping up"—she pulled back enough to look into his eyes—"and the not so strange people, are making it seem not so important."

"Maybe it isn't. Maybe you're supposed to head in a different direction."

"Maybe. Any suggestions?"

"TKJ Security could use another installer."

His shoulder muffled her laugh. She hadn't been aware of drifting back to such close proximity to hard muscle and soft cotton and the hint of citrus that could have come from his cologne or the lemon extract he'd ignited minutes ago. "You never did tell me what TKJ stood for."

"Can you keep a secret?"

Easier to keep one than be kept out of one. She blinked Zach and Jen out of her head. Her sister had no right to horn in on this moment. "Yes."

"It's the product of a family meeting when Paul was fifteen and dreaming of his first car and my dad was just thinking of starting his own company. It stands for Tobin Kid Job Security."

"You're kidding."

"I wish I were."

"I love it. I love your family."

"Hmm." His hand rested on the side of her head, muting night sounds, magnifying the now-rhythmic beat of his heart. "Seeing that I, by definition, am part of my family, that must mean you. . ." He left the thought unended. A fill-in-the-blank question that wasn't really a question.

"It's a little early for me to finish that sentence, but. . ." Two could play at that game.

"But later maybe?"

"Maybe."

"Later tonight?"

She laughed at the little-boy hope in his voice. "Do you realize how short a time we've known each other?"

"Yes. And your point is?"

That so many things in my life that have seemed too good to be true have been.

"Okay. Sorry. I'm told I can be a pushy guy."

"That's what makes you a good salesman."

"And a lousy date." In spite of the banter he kept perfect time to the music. "Change of subject. Will you spend the night with me?"

Heather's feet responded to the siren in her head. Her hand, the one not clamped in Ryan's, slid off his shoulder. And Ryan laughed.

"Would you and Izzy like to join Skylar and me at a Zoo Snooze?" He responded to her confusion with another laugh and lifted her hand back to its original position. "It's a campout at the zoo. Sit around a campfire, make crafts, talk to the animals. And while the kids have fun learning about animals"—he touched his forehead to hers—"the grown-ups can have fun learning about each other." His lips touched the tip of her nose. "And just so's you know, we will have two tents—a girl tent and a me tent."

Camping with Ryan. A sky full of stars, the air crisp with a tinge of wood smoke, snuggled under a blanket by the fire, sipping hot chocolate and whispering secrets. . .

"Heather?"

She blinked back to the reality that was as romantic as the fantasy. "Sorry. Daydreaming. Evening dreaming. Just imagining a campfire. . .with you." Her voice grew hoarse.

"Don't let me interrupt you. Just dream out loud, okay?"

She stared up into eyes that made her feel accepted and cherished and edgy and terrified all at the same time. "I didn't answer your question before. About what my point is."

"That's kind of a rhetorical thing."

"But I need to answer it." She looked away from the safe gaze that made her answer seem unnecessary. "My point is that I'm really, really scared."

"I know you are." His voice slid over her like a feather-soft quilt. "And that's why"—his feet moved with hers, slowly, in time to the orchestra music floating around them—"I'm following your lead."

Where once we walked beside Man as his helper, encourager, and confidant, we now fall into one of two extreme camps. Either we think of Man as the mortal Enemy, the one who

desires only to trap us, chain us, steal our freedom, and doom
us to a life of submission and servitude, or we become weak,
dependent, spineless—

Heather gasped and sat up straight on the couch. "That's *my* word." She looked up at the carved molding surrounding the fireplace, picturing Magdalena, the real person, scurrying around the room in a long white apron and ruffled cap, touching every surface with a feather duster as she dreamed of a different life. *Did you ever break free, Magdalena? Did you ever find a man you could walk beside?*

She glanced at the cover page of her business plan, glaring at her from the laptop occupying the other end of the leather couch. Pointing her toes, she brought them gently down on the cover of her computer, closing it, then looked down at the next page.

. . .spineless creatures doubting our ability to think on our own
without a man to tell us how to look at the world. Sisters! How
and why have we allowed ourselves to wander so far from God's
original plan? Yes, we can blame it all on Man. He is stronger,
more powerful, who are we to stand up to him? But one thing
we forget: "Greater is he that is in you, than he that is in the
world." We are not powerless if we know the Lord Jesus Christ.

Powerless. The word grabbed her. She knew the moment powerlessness had seeped into every pore of her being. As she'd kicked and screamed to no avail against the arms that pinned her. As the door had closed.

Why then do we act as if we did not have a Holy Champion,
the One who is the defender of widows, the Father to the
fatherless?

Something bristled inside. She tried to ignore it. It seemed wrong, irreverent, to give words to the feeling. But it pressed against her spirit, pushing for release.

"Where were You? If You are Father to the fatherless, where were You when I needed a defender?" Tears slid down her face and dropped onto the paper. "Where are You for Izzy, for Jalissa's children? God, You know I believe, but I don't *feel*. If You are who You say You are, I want to feel it. I want to know." Her pulse quickened with the last word. Did she?

Somewhere, in the dim shadows of her memory, a switch clicked, as if an unseen hand pushed PLAY.

"Have some of the cookies your other granddaughter made. Heather worked hard on these and they're wonderful."

She'd been ten when she'd eavesdropped through the laundry room door and overheard that exchange between her father and his mother.

"I only have one granddaughter and I wish you'd quit trying to force me to have feelings for that girl. Jenny is part of me, of us, and I never will understand why you thought she was not enough."

She could see herself, the skinny girl whose hair didn't match anyone in her family, sitting on the dryer and reaching toward the hook that held her backpack. She would leave. She would find her real grandmother and she would cry because she never wanted her granddaughter to be given up for adoption and she would say she had been searching and searching for her all these years. They would make cookies together and they would go to Disney.

She remembered looking into her backpack, wondering how long she could live on the apple and granola bar left over from her lunch. And then a crash pulled her eyes back to the crack in the door. Her father stood. His chair lay on its side on the floor. He pointed to the back door. "Heather is my daughter. She doesn't need to be flesh and blood to be part of me. If you can't accept that, leave. And don't even *think* about coming back."

And she hadn't. For five peaceful years.

Heather's love for her father had never been as huge as it was at the moment he knocked over that chair. But why was it that the words of the woman she'd come to refer to as "Jen's grandmother" were the ones that came to mind so often? Why hadn't she focused on the "part of me" part and not the rejection? Unlike Magdalena Mouse, she knew what it was like to hear someone say, "This is delicious. Thank you for all your hard work." She knew what it was like to be chosen and wanted, so why had she let herself believe she would never be as good as her sister, that she didn't deserve what Jen had?

When, in a moment of wine-induced honesty, Jen had confessed her lifelong crush on Zach, something had died in Heather. There was no point in trying. Jen would get Zach because Jen was supposed to win. That's the way the story went. That's the way every story went.

She wiped her bottom lashes with the back of her hand and went back to the essay. The bristling feeling was gone.

⊂⊃

"This is so spot-on."

Jalissa flipped her braid behind her shoulder as she plunked onto the chair across from Heather and set the *Essay* on the table. "Is it okay that I gave Izzy a chocolate chip whip?"

Heather looked over at Izzy, curled in a fuzzy brown chair, playing a game on Heather's phone with one hand, her drink in the other. "Thank you. She looks content." Jalissa's first comment suddenly registered. "You finished it?"

"Yeah. So did Kylee. I don't think she's all that stoked about it, though. She's not so sure about the God stuff."

As if on cue, Kylee's twig-like form spun around the corner of a table. "Sorry I'm late." With a wave at Izzy, she slipped into the booth next to Jalissa. "Is the blond coming?"

"Annie?" Heather's voice caught and the back of her neck prickled. "I hope so." She looked down at the first page of the *Essay*. "What were your overall impressions?"

Kylee tsked. "The sister who wrote this reminds me of the lady who lived next to us when I was growing up. She used to twist every conversation around to God. I could bring her a pie my mom just baked and she'd say, 'My, that looks good. Thank You, Lord, for little green apples and have you given your heart to *Jeee*sus yet?'"

Heather laughed, but it was Jalissa who spoke first. "Be thankful you had someone speaking truth into your life. The lady who lived next to me brought out her tarot cards every time I came over."

"Cool."

"Not." Jalissa picked up her essay. "Well, let's do this—" The shop door opened. Annie walked in.

231

January 13, 1912

The sun stuck its peach-tinged nose out of the water only to be splashed by an angry wave. Pink light coated the underbelly of dark clouds pregnant with snow.

Maggie shivered in the sweater she'd thrown over her uniform as she set a box of luncheon leftovers in the sleigh. The snow was too deep for the automobile. Her gaze followed the petite footprints, pressed into fresh snow, leading from the porch to the street, and she whispered a prayer for Angelica. So far, hiding her had been easy, but after last night she shuddered to think of the explosion that would greet Angelica if Mr. Hamilton were to discover her existence.

Shaking snow off the tips of her shoes, Maggie turned away from the prying eyes of the red-haired man sitting on the high seat of the sleigh. Charles didn't need to be clairvoyant to know something was not right.

"Is that it, then?" She spoke to Richard's stiff shoulders as he bounded up the steps to the house.

"I'll just go say good-bye to my par—to Mother." He turned pleading eyes on her. "Wait here for a moment?"

She nodded.

Charles laid the reins down and jumped down from his seat. "Mags? Can I talk to you?"

"Of course." Did her voice sound as melancholy to his ears at it did to hers?

He stepped within three feet of her and stopped. His eyes seemed to comb her face as if looking for something. He shook his head just slightly, giving the impression he hadn't found what he searched for. "Lydia is leaving the Hansens' in two weeks. She is going to give her notice in a few days and it would be so much easier for her if she could tell them you were interested."

Maggie swallowed hard. "I can't."

"Why not? Mags, it's clear you're miserable here. Look what they ask of you and for what? Are you making enough to stash away for that trip you dream of? The Hansens are not demanding, they pay a fair wage, and they're traveling to Denmark on the *Campania* and returning on the *Titanic*! You have the opportunity of a lifetime here. Sure, it won't be first class, but can you imagine the—"

"There's a child." She blurted it without thought.

Charles looked as if he'd been slapped. His face flamed crimson. His eyes darted to the porch door. "Richard." His voice hissed. "I'll kill—"

"No! Oh Charles, no!" Her hands flew to her burning cheeks, but no sooner had the shock and embarrassment hit than it was overtaken by the sheer absurdity of the situation. There was nothing she could do but laugh. And laugh. Until her side hurt and tears stung her eyes. All the while Charles stood in helpless confusion.

"Not m—my child," she finally stuttered. "A little girl. She works at the mill and she had no place to live so Emma Mitchell brought her here and we thought we'd go looking for a place for her, for someone to take her in, but she works all day and she's so quiet that—"

A flash of relief smoothed his brow, but the deep ridges quickly returned. "She's staying *here*?"

"Yes. For now."

"And Mr. Hamilton approves?"

Maggie stared down at Angelica's footprint. Large flakes began drifting down to fill it. "He doesn't know."

A pop of air burst through Charles's lips. "Oh, Mags, what have you gotten yourself into?" He closed the gap between them. His hand cupped her elbow. "That big heart of yours is going to cost you your job, *cailín álainn*."

She tipped her head. Charles only slipped into the Gaelic he'd learned from Granda Liam on rare occasions. Generally when he was upset. "What does that mean?"

He turned toward the lake. She followed his gaze. The sun now hung like a ripe peach from the bank of clouds, bathing the space between choppy water and black clouds with gold. "It means 'beautiful girl.'" He turned back to face her. "Mags, I have an answer for you and the girl if only you'd be open to it. I've a bit of money. I know I'm not the—"

"Ready, Charles?" Richard leaped over the bottom two steps. "Let's hop to it." He motioned to Charles with a flick of his fingers. "My train leaves in forty minutes." His Oxfords skidded in the snow and he came to a stop inches from Maggie. A grin spread across his face. "There is more to that woman than meets the eye." He nodded toward the house. "My mother is on our side."

Our *side? Do* we *have a side?* As of last night, they appeared to be moving in different directions—Richard toward caving under his father's ire and giving up his sudden desire to save the underprivileged children of the world, and Maggie toward protecting the life of one helpless child.

He gripped her arms. "Maggie, this is not at all how I envisioned this, but"—he suddenly dropped to one knee in the snow.

A violent shiver racked Maggie as she gaped down at him. Charles gasped.

"Will you do me the honor of becoming my wife?"

"I. . ." *Can't breathe.*

He stood and laughed. "I won't press you for an answer, but you will write tonight, won't you?" He pecked her on the cheek, squeezed her arms, and jumped into the sleigh.

Maggie spent the day in a numbed stupor. She completed all her chores and promptly did whatever she was asked, but she could not force herself to enthusiastically engage in the constant banal chatter coming from Mrs. Hamilton as Maggie attempted to teach the woman how to make riced potatoes. As usual, writing the story in her mind was all that kept her sane.

"What if I forget the salt? Can I just add it at the end? And if I do, how will I know how much to add?"

"It is best if you add it before cooking, ma'am, as the potatoes absorb the salt from the water, but if it were me and I forgot, I think I would change the menu to include *mashed* potatoes."

"Why is that? Do riced potatoes not absorb the salt you would sprinkle on after they are riced? Or would you add it after they are cooked and before you put them through the ricer?"

Magdalena Mouse thrust her hands into the air and let out a shrill squeak. Was there no brain at all in Mrs. Tabbycat's huge round head?

"You can't mix the salt in after the potatoes are riced because you need to treat them delicately or they will lose their. . .riceness."

"Riceness." Mrs. Hamilton giggled.

"So if I happened to forget to salt the water, I would mash the potatoes instead of ricing and then salt them to taste."

"To taste?"

It was as if she were teaching a parrot instead of a giant, paw-licking, thick-brained cat. Magdalena picked up the ricer.

"I would stir in a bit of salt and then taste it to see if I'd added enough."

"A bit?" Mrs. Hamilton framed her forehead with both hands, her thumbs anchored on her cheekbones. "*That* is why I will never be a cook. A pinch of this, a dab of that. It's a secret code all good cooks know and people like me can never. . ."

Maggie gripped the edge of the sink and stared out the window at the darkening world. For a moment, only her own reflection looked back at her, but within seconds she noticed movement. A lantern swung, low to the ground. Maggie squinted and leaned closer.

A man kneeled in the driveway, inches from the spot where Richard had proposed. Was her mind playing tricks on her by attempting to re-create the scene and give it a different ending?

In the flickering light she recognized the mannerisms. The man reached out, beckoning. She knew the arc of that arm as if it were her own.

Charles. "What is he doing?"

"What is who doing?"

"Charles." Maggie flew to the back porch. "He's out in the drive. I'm going to see what he needs."

"But the potatoes. Mr. Hamilton will be home soon and. . ."

Maggie slid into her coat as she set her foot on the top step. The lantern drew closer to Charles. "Charles? What are you—"

The lantern rose higher, illuminating another face. A child's face. "Charles?"

He turned toward her. "I came over to borrow a wood splitter and I found them hiding on the side of the garage."

"*Them?*"

"I'm sorry, Miss Maggie." Angelica stepped into the circle of light. "I didn't have nowhere else to go. My mother brought my brother to the mill because my grandma is sick and can't care for him and my mother didn't know I wasn't staying at the mill and she thought I could keep Woody, but—" Her hand rose to her face and she broke into sobs.

Maggie felt the numbness seep from her soul into her limbs. She barely felt the ground as she stepped toward the sobbing girl and opened wooden-like arms. "You did the right thing, Angelica." Her body jarred as the girl wrapped around her legs, followed by a second thud as the cherub-faced Woody copied his sister. Maggie looked up into smiling eyes. Charles shook his head.

"Your big heart may cost your job, Mags, but you may have saved a life today." He reached out and brushed her cheek with his gloved hand. "What can I do to help?"

"Can you get your hands on some extra blankets?"

"There's a trunk of them in the barn. Anything else?"

"Yes. Clean clothes. I'll have to burn these. Even if they're yours—I'll cut them down to fit."

"Consider it done. Anything else?"

"Yes. You can make room for the three of us in your barn and pray we won't need it. And you can tell the Hansens I want the job. I'm thinking I'll be needing a new one soon."

CHAPTER 21

Stephannie rubbed the cords at the back of her neck with one hand and picked up the cocomocho Heather had recommended with the other. Her head hurt like her legs did after dancing all night. Her brain was tired and her nerves were raw. She was sure Heather and Jalissa recognized her, but they weren't letting on. Maybe, like so many people, they knew they'd seen her face somewhere, but that was the extent of it.

They hadn't begun reading the essay yet. They were chatting about their relationships with men. Kylee had just described herself as a keep-your-distance-till-I-say-different-or-I'll-smack-you kind of woman. Heather rested her chin on the tucked-under fingers of one hand. "When did that start?"

"I stopped trusting men when I was three."

Heather leaned toward Kylee. "What happened?"

"My father chose watching basketball over watching my solo as the Spring Fairy in my preschool play."

Stephannie laughed along with the others. She couldn't believe the conversation had steered, without her help, to this topic.

Jalissa elbowed Kylee. "At least the guy was home. My dad wasn't around enough to know I *went* to preschool. He did, however, show up for my dance recital when I was nine to tell me I moved like a flatfooted camel."

237

Kylee laughed, but Heather's smile was sympathetic. "Lovely. And we let those labels stick in our heads, don't we?"

Stephannie let herself, for a moment, imagine she had no connection with Heather other than a chance meeting in a coffee shop. If her last name wasn't Lansing—and if Heather's wasn't supposed to be—they could have been friends. The game of pretend lasted only a second. "It seems to come down to our fathers, doesn't it?" she asked. "That's where our ideas of men—whether we can trust them or not—come from. How about you, Heather, what kind of relationship do you have with your father?"

A tight-lipped smile played on Heather's lips. The kind of smile you have when the subject's so close to your heart you're afraid you'll cry.

Stephannie's throat tightened with tears she couldn't show. She didn't want to hear the answer to the question she'd just asked.

"The best." The truth of it reflected in Heather's eyes. "I've spent most of my life in my sister's shadow, but my dad always made me feel like I was in the spotlight." She shook her head and slapped a hand over her face. Peeking between spread fingers, she laughed. "That was übercorny."

Stephannie gripped the papers rolled in her hand until her thumb whitened.

"Yes." Jalissa sighed. "But nice corny. You know you just made us all feel like trash, right?"

"If it helps any, I have a grandmother who used to introduce my sister and me as, 'This is my sweet granddaughter Jen, the singer, and that's Heather, the adopted one.'"

Adopted. Stephannie let her eyes close briefly. So the father who put her in the spotlight wasn't her birth father.

"Harsh." Jalissa crinkled her nose.

"Oh, that's just the beginning. More than once I overheard her say, 'You'd think they could have done a better job finding one that matched.'"

Kylee's large brown eyes grew wider. "That's nasty. I mean, that cuts deeper than getting slapped, doesn't it? I hurt for you, girl."

"Ditto that." Jalissa pointed a polka-dot fingertip at Stephannie. "Your turn. Please tell me your daddy disappeared or beat you or at least called you names."

My daddy calls me princess. Even when I don't deserve it. "When I was a kid, my father practically lived at his office. He didn't have time for me. To be honest, neither of my parents should have become parents."

"How does that affect you now?" Heather's body language reminded her of every one of the counselors who had paraded through her life because her parents shouldn't have been parents. But there was something different about the way she looked at her. Like she actually cared.

"I guess I was always one of those classic looking-for-love-in-all-the-wrong-places girls." *Except now. Andrew is not a wrong place.* "But my dad is changing. He says he's found God." *He doesn't say he's found his other daughter.* She couldn't help looking over at Heather. *Do you know who I am? Is this all a charade?*

"That's cool." Jalissa reached across the table. Her dark hand patted Stephannie's. "I bet he's praying for you and this essay is an answer to his prayers."

"Why do you say that?"

"I don't want to give a spoiler. You haven't read it yet, have you?"

Stephannie shook her head. "Please tell me it's not a God-will-fix-everything book."

Jalissa twisted her face in a comical frown. "It is, but at the same time it isn't. It's changed the way I look at every relationship I ever had."

"I'm still thinkin' it over." Kylee tipped her head to one side. "But I gotta say the God part didn't freak me out near as much as my neighbor did. I want to talk about it."

Heather spread her hand on the paper. "This is only a dozen pages. I think we should make a pact to stick it out until we've read it together and talked it through to the end. Deal?" She held up her hand.

"I will if you will." Kylee slapped her hand.

Jalissa followed then joined the other two in staring at Stephannie. "You in?"

Was she? Was it worth the drive? She suddenly realized her head didn't hurt and the knot at the base of her skull was half the size it had been. She liked these girls. She felt comfortable here.

And maybe, for the first time in longer than she could remember, she'd found a place she could be herself. "I think—" Her phone rang. She glanced down at the lit-up screen.

Mom.

Dianna Lansing did not make personal calls at any point during her fourteen-hour workday. A call from her mother meant something was wrong.

"Excuse me. I need to take this." She stood on legs that shook and walked toward the window. "Mom?"

"Your father's in another crisis. Arrhythmia again. They're going to try cardioversion. But they're not sure how he'll handle the shock, so I wanted you—"

"I'll be there. I'm out of town, but I'll get there as fast as I can."

A familiar gnawing spread through her body as she walked back to the table. "I need to go. My father"—she picked up her papers and her purse—"is in the hospital. His heart rate is irregular and—" A sob drowned her last word and the next thing she knew, she was weeping on Heather's shoulder.

"I'm so sorry, Annie." Heather held her tight. "I'll go with you. You shouldn't drive like—"

"No!" Stephannie jerked out of Heather's arms, her spine suddenly rigid. "I'll be fine. I would never—" *Never* screamed in her brain. She searched Heather's face for any reflection of her own emotions. *Why are you offering? Because you need to be there yourself?* But all she saw, once again, was compassion. "I'll be fine." She pulled out her keys.

"We'll be praying, Annie."

"Thank you." She was halfway to the door when a hand on her shoulder stopped her.

"Here." Heather held out a business card. "Nothing on this is current except my name and phone. Call me when you get there, or on the way if you want. Promise?"

Stephannie glanced down at the card. Heather Conrad. Coventry Midwest Hotels.

The numbness rose to her face. *Coventry.* A gasp pleaded for release, but she clamped her lips and nodded as she dropped the card into her purse and walked out the door without answering.

Coventry. Heather had worked for one of Lansing Corporation's stiffest competitors. It didn't make sense. Nothing made sense.

Dear God, what's happening? The headache returned in full force as she got in the car.

⟡

"What's wrong with Annie? Why was she crying?"

Izzy aimed her camera at the lake as Heather parallel parked a block from the zoo.

Heather shut off the car, got out, and opened the back door while trying to figure out how much of life a person was supposed to share with a second-grader. "Her daddy is very sick. He's in the hospital." But the sadness had started even before the phone call. Heather regretted coming off like the special one, the one with the perfect daddy. Why had she chosen to temper it with a story about Jen's grandmother when she could so easily have shared her memories of her birth father?

Because she didn't know any of them well enough to trust them with that kind of wound.

"That's sad. We should pray for him." Izzy walked around to the trunk and held her arms out as Heather loaded her down with her backpack, pillow, and sleeping bag.

"Yes. We should." She shut the trunk, slung her bag over her shoulder, fit the rest under her arms, and stepped onto the curb. She'd taken four steps before she realized she didn't hear the pitter-patter of Izzy's feet behind her. "Iz?" She turned around.

"Well?" The girl stood, loaded down like a miniature pack mule, right where she'd been when Heather closed the trunk.

"Well, what?"

"Let's do it then."

"Do what?"

"Pray for Annie's dad."

The temperature, already in the high eighties, seemed to rise. The humidity doubled. "I thought we could pray tonight. When you go to bed."

"But he's sick right now. What if you were sick right now and I said I would call the doctor tonight when you go to bed? God is like the doctor and if Annie's daddy is really, really sick then we need to call Him now."

"I guess you're right." Heather dropped her sleeping bag onto the sidewalk and sat on it. Izzy copied her, sitting on her sleeping bag with her legs folded close to her chest. A woman pushing a stroller and leading two toddlers gave them a strange look as she maneuvered around them. Izzy dropped her chin to her knees and closed her eyes. "God, Annie's daddy is really sick so please make him better and help Annie not be so sad. Oh, and also"—she paused and Heather opened her eyes to see Izzy, eyes still closed, playing with her pink shoestrings—"also please let Heather not be sad 'cuz she was adopted."

Heather's eyes popped open. She opened her mouth, but the closed-eye concentration on Izzy's face stopped her. She lowered her head. "Dear Lord, You know all things. You know exactly what Annie's father needs, so please send the right doctors and give them the knowledge they need to treat him. Be with Annie and give her peace." She waited several seconds. "And help me explain to Izzy that being adopted is a wonderful thing and I'm very, very happy I was chosen by my parents. Amen."

"Amen. Are you?"

"Am I?"

"Really happy you're adopted? I heard you talking about your dad with the club ladies and he sounds nice, but even if you like him it's not the same as your real dad, is it?"

It didn't take a psychoanalyst to figure out Izzy wasn't talking only about Heather. "How often do you see your father, Iz?"

"Oh, you know. . ." Izzy stared at her shoes. "We should probably go or else Skylar and Ryan might think we're not coming." She stood and reloaded her arms. "Heather?"

"What?"

"How do you get adopted? I mean, how do you get other parents?"

Heather walked to the shady side of the sidewalk. "There are adoption agencies, places where people who want to adopt a child can go and they fill out an application—"

"Like when you get a job."

"Right. They fill out a paper telling everything about themselves and then when something happens and a baby or a child is left without parents, the adoption agency matches the child up to just the right family waiting to adopt them."

Izzy's profile altered. Her mouth clenched. Her eyebrows lowered and drew together. They'd almost reached the ticket office when she stopped. "So what's the something that can happen so a child doesn't have parents? I know people can die, but what else?"

With no idea what was going on under the mop of blond curls, Heather hesitated to answer. She scanned the intersection for any sign of Ryan and Skylar. "Well, sometimes a mother knows she can't take good care of her baby and because she loves her baby so much she wants him or her to have a better life with a good family so she goes to the adoption agency and asks them to find the perfect parents for her child."

"Is that how you got a dad who made you feel like you were standing in a light?"

"An agency matched me up with just the right family."

Again, Izzy fell silent. Contemplative. *What's going on in that precocious brain?* After a minute she looked up. "But do moms sometimes give up their kids just. . .because?"

Heather felt the question in her gut. "Oh, Iz. Your mom would never—"

"Izzy!" Skylar ran toward them, decked out like a pack mule just an inch or so taller than Izzy.

Behind Skylar was a man who carried a duffel over one arm.

And pulled her in for a kiss with the other.

⚜

Time suspended under a navy and indigo sky peppered with stars. Heather breathed in the heavenly chocolate steam wafting from the Styrofoam cup she held between two hands. The sweetness mingled with the tang of Ryan's aftershave to produce a delectable ambience.

Another rush of air whooshed through her lips and she relaxed with it. With Izzy fully engrossed in s'more making and listening to a zoo volunteer's rendition of "How the Elephant Got His Trunk," she let go of a week's worth of stress. She leaned against Ryan's arm. "Can we just stay here?"

"That's the plan."

She started to nudge him and then remembered the hot chocolate. "I'm not talking about tonight. I'm talking about forever."

"I suppose that could be arranged." He dipped his chin and turned amused eyes on her. "They said they weren't getting another panda for a few months, so that leaves a nice little space for us. Private swimming pool, a year's supply of bamboo. Bet we could get them to throw in a few peanuts and some RyKrisp. Maybe even a bucket of—"

"Would you *stop*?" Even as she said it she knew stopping was exactly what she didn't want. "Actually. Don't. I haven't laughed like this in forever."

Dark eyebrows converged. "That's sad. The world was a lesser place when Heather Conrad wasn't laughing."

She shook her head. "You wax a bit poetic once in a while. Where does that come from?"

"Duh. I was raised on poetry. Think of that scene where Lois Lane is flying with Superman for the first time. The sky is black and the moon is huge and they're twirling in midair with their arms around each other and then she says it: 'Can you read my mind?'" His swallow was audible. He blinked as if to hold back tears. "And then she asks if he knows what he does to her. Like a kid in school she's a fool, all quivering and shivering because he can fly in the sky." A soft sigh and he closed his eyes. "Sheer poetry."

The chill left the night air. Her laugh made only the softest rustle. She'd never before been aware of the *feel* of stars in her eyes. "That was beautiful," she whispered.

His eyes opened. Mirth danced in gray-green pools. "Thank you. I was so afraid you wouldn't appreciate my sensitive side."

"Oh, but I do." She looped her arm under his. "How could I not appreciate the kind of man who asks me to spend the night with him under the stars with the sounds of crowing peacocks, honking camels, and laughing hyenas to lull us to sleep? And then, wonder of wonders, the man is a poet." She sighed for the hundredth time. "I appreciate. Don't ever forget that."

She felt her hair catch on the stubble of his beard. "Can you read my mind?" he whispered. The warmth of his breath tickled her ear.

"Do you know what you do to me?"

It was her turn to close her eyes. She'd know the answer if she'd asked the question. Quivering and shivering was the answer to that one.

⚜

Morning sunlight painted halos on the girls' bent heads. Skylar pinched Izzy's hair then put her fingers to her mouth. "Yum."

Izzy giggled and reciprocated then flashed a smile. "We're monkeys."

Heather felt the rumble of Ryan's laugh as she leaned against him. "You're telling me?" She laughed with him at the grooming rituals playing out on both sides of the metal fence. With a contented sigh, she let yet a bit more pent-up tension dissolve in the warmth of a cloudless day and the security of strong arms. "Remind me again why I thought I wanted a month of peace and quiet all to myself."

"Because you wanted to find a job and a place to live and start your career."

"Oh. That." She yawned, loud and fake. "Planning for one's future is way overrated."

He tightened his arms around her waist. "I so agree. Best just to let the future unfold as it will. And while it does, just enjoy the moments."

"So how would you like to spend some moments—" Her phone vibrated in her back pocket.

Ryan pulled his arms away and stepped back. "Better get that. It's your future calling."

Her eyes rolled toward the sky as she pulled it out.

"Mark my words. It's a job offer."

"Right." She pressed the green icon and brought it to her ear. "Hello."

"Did you read Hotel Buzz?" Natalie's voice was shrill and loud. Heather held the phone an inch from her ear.

"No." She hadn't read the online tabloid since she lost her job and hadn't once missed the steady stream of hotel gossip. "Why?"

"Malcolm posted something horrid."

Aren't you used to that by now? Had Natalie done something newly newsworthy? Like being seen with a mystery man at a Venice hotel pool in a skimpy red bikini? Heather tried to muster some empathy, but couldn't manage it. "About you?"

"No, Heather. About *you*." A terse breath shot through the phone. "I can't deal with this, Heather. Anything they say about you is going to come back on me."

Did you not just say it was about me? "Why would he write about me? I've been out of the industry for months and—" She had a sudden flash of a caption under a picture someone—a cameraman masquerading as a tourist—could have taken yesterday. *Heather Conrad shooting the breeze with Stephannie Lansing. More subterfuge afoot?* "Read it to me."

" 'Out of the shadows comes a name we've all heard, but probably can't place. Heather Conrad. Think back to last year's biggest and best hotel set scandal—Coventry's Natalie Brooks and Staffordshire's Collin Enfield and the affair that rocked the Midwest. From Chicago to Minneapolis, from St. Louie to Cincinnati, we were talking that one up, weren't we? And then, as if that weren't meaty enough, we found out there was a little more than fraterniza—' " Natalie sighed. "That part isn't about you. Here. 'At the time Conrad claimed innocence, but how do you handle the intricate details of someone's schedule without having some clue what she does with her time? The answer is, you don't. I always suspected Conrad was more than a bystander. Even figured there was a chance she was the instigator in. . .' "

Heather gasped. Natalie kept reading. " 'Now, thanks to an ongoing investigation, the results of which were leaked to me by. . .' "

She fought to absorb the words as they tumbled from the phone. *Accomplice. Possibly the instigator. Even if charges aren't filed, it's a cinch this girl won't ever again work in the hospitality business.* She didn't wait for Natalie to reach the end. "Who would do this? Who fed him that?"

"You tell me. Who's got it in for you? Your ex?"

"No. Absolutely not. Zach would never do that. He wouldn't even know how."

"Your sister?"

"*Natalie.* That's. . ." She couldn't find a word to match the bile rising in her throat. "Jen isn't that kind of person."

"She stole your fiancé."

"He wasn't my—" There was no point defending anything to Natalie. She sucked her lips in and waited it out.

When the barrage finally stopped, it was Natalie, not Heather, who let out a sob. "Get to the bottom of this, Heather, or it will ruin both of our futures."

"How could this—"

"I have to run." The connection ended, saving Heather from a remark that might end her nanny career, too.

Ryan caught the phone as it fell from her hand. And then he caught her. Not physically, but she had the distinct sense that his very presence was all that was holding her upright.

CHAPTER 22

Heather leaned against the Porsche's front grill and stared at an expression that matched the intensity of the sun he blocked.

Ryan stuck his hands in his pocket. His shoulders fell. "I'm installing those sensors."

"Whoever is behind this wants to ruin my future in the business, not murder me in cold blood."

He glanced at his watch. "I have to get to work. Thanks for taking Skylar home."

"My pleasure. I need the motormouth occupied for a bit."

Ryan leaned in for a kiss. "I'm not going to be able to keep my mind on my work tonight." He smiled. "Come to think of it, I haven't since the day we met. Of all the coffee joints in all the towns in all the world and she walks into mine." His lips rested on hers, but she couldn't manage to erase the smile to make them cooperate.

"How can you make me smile when my future is in ruins?"

"Because I'm a Jesus freak. I know who's really in charge of your future." He touched his fingers to his lips, waved, and walked away.

Even with Skylar in the backseat absorbing the seven-year-old jabber that would have been aimed at her, she couldn't think. Her mind whirred one moment and stalled the next.

Who would start a rumor like that? Who had something to gain? Natalie was the only one in the industry who knew about her business plan, and that wouldn't have been a threat to anyone anyway.

Logic led to only one possibility. Somehow or other Stephannie "Annie" Lansing figured into the equation.

But why? Why had she shown up in the first place? Why act so open and vulnerable if she was on a backstabbing mission? There was no reason under the sun why a nobody like Heather Conrad would ever bleep on Stephannie Lansing's radar.

The girls piled out the moment she put the car in PARK in Kurt and Amanda's driveway. Heather stared at the door handle. For a moment she couldn't remember what she was supposed to do with it.

Inside the house, she kept a facsimile of a smile in place while she chatted with Ryan's sister-in-law and waited for Izzy to say good-bye to Skylar and her little brother.

Amanda yelled to the kids that there were cookies in the kitchen then turned back to Heather. "Did you find out anything about the dresses?"

Dresses? It took her a moment to transition from libel and slander to vintage gowns. "Izzy's mom didn't know anything about them."

"So you think Izzy found them in the house somewhere?"

"Yeah. It looks that way." She wasn't in the mood to talk about secret stairways and treasure chests.

"You should get in contact with the previous owner."

"I hadn't thought of that. It's not my house so it feels kind of awkward to go around investigating its history."

"It's all public record. When I was in college I worked at City Hall. If you need any help I'd be happy to help you find info."

"Thank you. When I have a minute to myself"—she nodded at the two girls holding hands and spinning in a circle around a giggling Paxton in the living room—"I might start doing some research."

Amanda offered a sympathetic smile. "Seven is the age of silliness. Ryan told us how you ended up with this job. I can't imagine suddenly having that responsibility shoved at you. It's hard enough when you start with a planned pregnancy and have years to prepare for a seven. I hope her mom's paying you well."

"I love Izzy. You should have seen her big, sad eyes after she found out her vacation with her mom was cancelled. There was no way I could have said no. But, yes, I'm also being nicely compensated. Among other things, Izzy's mom may be able to pave the way to a backer for my business idea."

"A coffee shop chain, right?"

"Yes. I'm working on a different twist—coffee and connection. If you travel for business and you want to meet people, you go to a bar, but what about people who want a different kind of atmosphere? There should be places in every town where you feel welcome even if *not* 'everyone knows your name.'"

Amanda's mouth twisted into a high-on-the-right smile. "Used to be that churches were places where strangers felt welcome."

"That's what your brother-in-law said." *Among others.*

"Great Tobin minds think alike."

Heather laughed. "I guess." She stared beyond the dizzying dance at a living room and kitchen that seemed to reach out, like welcoming arms. "Did you do your own decorating?"

Amanda laughed. "If you can call it decorating, yes. I call it hodgepodge."

"Eclectic."

"Same thing, isn't it?"

"Not at all. I've been researching this stuff, so I know. I read a definition of *eclectic*: a mix of styles that creates a whole that is free-flowing, artsy, and unrestrained."

"Hmm. I definitely fit into the unrestrained category."

"It's welcoming. Homey. Makes me want to kick off my shoes and put my feet on the coffee table."

"Wow. Thank you. I don't know if I could have put it into words, but that's what I hoped to achieve. We host a couple of small groups—sorry, that's church talk—Bible studies and gatherings here, and I want people to feel comfy, to know they've got refrigerator rights, you know?"

"I love that." Heather chewed on her bottom lip. Talking about decorating made her world seem momentarily back in the right orbit. But had Hotel Buzz shredded her plan before she finished it? "You wouldn't by any chance want to help put some concepts together for my business plan, would you?"

Deep blue eyes lit like a hundred-watt bulb. "Are you serious?"

"Absolutely. And if this idea ever takes off, I'll even pay you."

Amanda waved away the idea. "I don't need money, I need an outlet for all this 'unrestrained' creativity. I started on the garage last month. I could just picture barn-red walls with black-and-white photos of Kurt overhauling the Chevy or teaching Skylar to ride her bike."

"I can picture it."

"Yeah, well, that's because you have estrogen. Kurt put a quick stop to that. Somehow thought he'd be the laughingstock of the neighborhood." Her eyes twinkled. "Men. So anyway, yes, I'd love to help you. Tomorrow?"

"Perfect." *If I'm not in the loony bin or on my way to Chicago to lynch an heiress.* "Do you mind if Izzy and I come here? I'd invite you over, but other than cool architecture, there's nothing inspiring about where I'm living."

"Come at eleven. I'll fix lunch and we can talk about decorating and seven-year-olds, and maybe throw my little brother-in-law into the mix."

"Deal. I think." Heather bent and picked up Izzy's backpack. "Just so this isn't a trick to get me into the infamous inquisition I've been warned about."

"Oh no. Believe me, when that happens, you'll *know* it."

♔

"You can read the mouse story to me while I mix the dough or you can help. I don't care."

Izzy hadn't done anything to make Heather mad, but something was wrong. She said "I don't care" the way Mom did. Mad-like.

Heather set the bag of flour next to her mixing bowl and turned around with her hands on her hips like Mom when Izzy asked too many questions. Her face was red and blotchy and her words came out of her mouth sounding hard, not soft like usual.

"Did you and Ryan have another fight?"

"No." Heather opened her eyes like a Chihuahua. "Why?"

"Because you're acting weird like you're mad." She bit down on

251

her tongue. She shouldn't have said *weird*. "I heard him say at the zoo yesterday he couldn't keep his mind on his work because of you. That's what Mom says when I bug her."

"Ryan and I did not have a fight. Now, cookie dough or reading?"

"I'll read, but you should talk. If something is bothering you it's good to talk about it, and don't think just 'cuz I've never had a boyfriend that I don't understand stuff because I do."

Finally, Heather smiled. Almost a smile, anyway. "Thank you for offering." She opened her hand and moved it toward the mixing bowl.

"I think"—she rumpled her nose and pursed her lips—"I'll read until it's time to dunk 'em in cinnamon and sugar."

"The story is in your room."

"I'll get it." She ran upstairs. She had the story in her hand when she noticed something on the carpet under the window. At first she thought it was a mouse. That was just because she had mice in her brain. The thought of mice in her brain made her laugh. She walked closer. The thing on the floor was a clump of dry mud. She hadn't gotten it there, so she didn't pick it up. There was dirt on the windowsill, too, and a shoe print on the rug. "Somebody's gonna get yelled at," she sang as she ran down the stairs.

She settled in a chair and picked up a paper then set it down again. "Ryan left a mess in my room," she yelled over the sound of the mixer.

Heather shut off the mixer and whirled around, only one hand on her hip this time. "*Ryan?* Ryan hasn't been in your room."

"Yuh-huh. I think when he was here before he went out on the roof to think about that motion thingy."

"Sensor."

"Yeah. That. He left mud on the floor and I think we hafta make him clean it up."

Heather smiled an almost real smile. "I think you're right. He's coming over tomorrow night."

"We'll give him a bucket and a rag when he walks in the door."

"Good idea."

"If we're going to Skylar's house tomorrow and then to the coffee shop and then Ryan is coming here, can Skylar go to the coffee shop with us and keep me company while you do club and then come here to keep me company while you and Ryan kiss or fight or whatever you're going to do and then Ryan can take her home?"

Heather laughed. She looked not at all mad when she did that. "Yes, she can come over."

"Good. 'Cuz then she'll be here to help me get you two back together if you fight just like in *The Parent Trap*."

Heather shook her head. "You watch too much TV, Isabel Brooks."

"You'll be happy I do when you get in that fight."

Izzy ducked as a gob of snickerdoodle dough flew from Heather's finger.

Only eight o'clock and Izzy was already asleep.

Heather flopped onto the couch and surveyed her options. There were still boxes to be unpacked.

Or not. The thought didn't sound like her own. *Who says you have to finish? You're not the mouse maid.*

She smiled. Her face muscles thanked her. "You're right. I'm not the mouse maid." She looked over at the dining room chandelier and once again imagined how the house had looked a hundred years earlier. A gaudily carved straight-backed settee might have sat in the place of the squishy black leather couch she sat on. On the opposite side of the room, she could see two chairs with tufted backs in pale not-for-children ivories and pinks. In the corner where the giant speakers flanked the entertainment center, scratchy music flowed out of the huge brass trumpet of a gramophone. The personified Mr. and Mrs. Tabbycat sat in the rigid chairs, sipping tea.

More cream, Magdalena. And cookies and sugar and jam. Polish the silver, Magdalena. Hurry, Magdalena. Scrub the floor, wash the windows, sweep the porch, bake a cake, cook the eggs, not too soft, not too hard, draw my bath, light the fire, chop the wood. . .

"You didn't have choices, did you, Magdalena?"

Suddenly she pictured Natalie Brooks with Gibson-girl hair. The wealthy mistress barking orders as she sipped her Earl Grey.

File this, Heather. Call them, Heather. Get it done yesterday, Heather. Unpack my boxes, Heather. Watch my daughter, Heather. Cover up my affair, Heather.

A gasp echoed off the walls. "I didn't do that. I didn't know you were—" She couldn't finish her reply to the specter in the high-collared blouse with leg-of-mutton sleeves. True, she hadn't *known* until the day it all came out and Natalie got fired. She hadn't known it in her head. But her gut was another story altogether.

She hadn't actually been surprised when "the wife" stormed into the office demanding to speak to Natalie. She hadn't been appropriately shocked when people insinuated that Natalie had shared a bit more than long lunches and occasional weekends with Collin Enfield. But Natalie had denied the trading of secrets. Though no one believed her, something had transpired behind the scenes and Natalie had simply walked away from Coventry, head held high, dragging the tatters of her once-skyrocketing career—and her personal assistant—behind her.

"Why did I leave?" There had been an in-house investigation, and no one had pointed fingers at Heather. Coworkers surrounded her, murmured all the appropriate condolences. So why hadn't she stayed and asked for another job?

Because Natalie had asked her to leave, to follow her to her next position. *You'll never find another job like this one, Heather. You'll start out on the bottom, Heather. I can open doors for you, help you move up. You need me to get you where you want to be, Heather.*

You need me, Heather. The voice morphed. Rough and deep. *You belong here with me. On the farm.*

"*I* have choices!" She jumped off the couch, shouting at imaginary people in imaginary chairs. "I am not the mouse maid. I don't have to unpack boxes. I don't have to be the good little wife. I don't have to envy my sister. I can make my own way. My own life. I have choices. I have a brain. I can make decisions. I can find a job. I can live on my own. Do you hear me? *I will not be pitiful! I am not the mouse ma*—"

A scream halted her declaration. She loped toward the stairs and the terrified little girl she did not choose.

But would if she could.

❧

January 26, 1912

"I had no idea what I was getting you involved in, Maggie." Emma chewed on her bottom lip as she stared across the front seat of the touring car. "We'll find a place for them both, I promise."

"Thank you. They're fine for right now. We have a system. The Caswells are letting Woody help Charles during the day and every night I tiptoe upstairs and listen for Mr. Hamilton's snoring. As soon as I know he's asleep, I put a candle in the porch window and Charles brings Woody home."

"Charles sounds like a man with a big heart."

"He is." Her voice roughened. "Where are we?" She angled the paper until sunlight hit the cramped lettering on the hand-drawn map.

"I've never been out this way. My uncle would have my head on a platter if he knew I'd taken a car instead of the buggy."

"Because you may run out of gas?"

Emma shook her head. "Because it may not start again in this cold if I shut it off."

Maggie looked down at Emma's shoes peeking out beneath a thick fur robe. They were not walking shoes.

"We can't be more than five miles from Union Grove."

"Turn right at the next corner. Does it make sense to build a factory this far out of town?"

"It certainly doesn't make sense to me. And if Ralston Clark was implying that these people employ children, where do they come from? There's nothing but farms out here and farm children work on farms, not in factories."

A horn honked and a truck rumbled around them on the left. The back of the truck was covered with a tarp. Emma shook her head. "What can be all that important out here that anyone needs to drive at breakneck speed?"

The truck turned into a long drive leading to a farm.

"Slow down." Maggie tapped the map. "That's it. That's where we're going."

"That's a farm." Emma pulled to the side of the road.

"Look at the map and see what you think." She handed the creased paper to Emma.

"You're right. It has to be."

"The barn is huge." Maggie rubbed her right temple. "What are we getting ourselves into? We've walked some very frightening streets in the past few weeks, but this feels more dangerous somehow."

"If we screamed, no one—" Emma slid a suede-gloved hand to her mouth. "I'm sorry." She took an audible breath. "If God is with us who can be against us, right?"

"Right. I hope. Why didn't we bring someone?"

"Because we are brave, strong women." Emma gave a weak laugh.

"Maybe we should go back and return with—"

"Richard."

Maggie blinked. "Yes. Richard." That had not been the name on the tip of her tongue. Hard as she tried, she could not picture his shiny brown Oxfords setting foot in that barn. She stared through the dust kicked up by the truck. As it settled, she saw movement at the end of the long drive. "Emma. Look. There are. . ."

"Children."

The tarp had been raised from the back of the truck and people hopped out of the truck bed. Several adults and maybe ten boys and girls. She couldn't be sure of ages from this distance, but there was one boy who couldn't have been more than eight. "Let's go."

"Back to town?"

"No." She pulled her shoulders back and straightened her hat. "We are teachers. That's all." She picked up the stack of books leaning against the fur robe covering her feet. "Just here to offer the employer an opportunity to provide an education for their workers of all ages. Here to offer them a service."

Silence settled in the interior of the car and then Emma filled it with a loud inhale. "Lord, grant us courage." She put the car back in gear.

"And protection. 'He shall give his angels charge over thee, to keep thee in all thy ways.' " Maggie repeated the verse three times as they bounced over the frozen ruts toward the barn.

The last child, a girl in a dress that ended inches above her ankles, its hem tattered and frayed, trudged through the barn door. The door closed behind her.

Emma turned the car off. "Teachers," she whispered. "We are teachers—naive, powerless do-gooder women who know nothing about child labor laws, just here to offer you a service."

A giggle began to bubble, vibrating Maggie's diaphragm, chest, and then spouting out of her like a miniature geyser. "Emma, only you can turn this into a laughable situation."

"Might as well laugh. Wouldn't you rather go to your doom with a smile on your face?"

"I've never actually thought about it before, but I believe you're right." Maggie gripped the books in one hand and the door handle in the other. "Here we go."

A thick stench assaulted her senses. Not a barn smell. The overpowering stench came from the outhouse within six feet of the barn door. The next odor was one she was all too familiar with. "Brass," she whispered.

The barn door opened. A little girl, seven years old at best, ran out. A stream of angry cursing followed her as she yanked open the wooden door of the outhouse. "No breaks for you today. How many times—"

Maggie's toe contacted a pebble, sending it flying toward the door. The voice stopped. A man stepped into view. Wrinkled, hunched over, wearing a patched gray coat over baggy brown trousers, and a scowl that appeared permanent, the man glared at them. "What do you want?"

"We're teachers, sir. We'd like to speak to the owner or manager about an opportun—"

"I'm the manager. Speak your piece."

Emma cleared her voice. "For no cost to you, sir, we can provide classes in reading and arithmetic to your employees who haven't had the opportunity to attend—"

"Not interested."

"Well, sir, our offer has been accepted by many. . ."

While Emma talked, Maggie inched to her right, eyes straining in the sunlight to see anything at all in the darkness of the barn.

She didn't need to. She had seen the little girl's black hands. She knew the sounds of punch presses and grinders.

Over the noise, footsteps reverberated on wood planks. The sound came from behind the hunched over little man. "What the devil is going—"

The door flew open.

Maxwell Hamilton stood in the opening.

CHAPTER 23

I d–dreamed there was a man at the window and he had a mask on his face and I screamed and he disappeared."

Heather pulled the trembling girl onto her lap and pressed her against her chest, as if the closer she could hold her, the more fear she could absorb. "It's okay, baby, I'm here now."

"It's my fault."

"What's your fault? You can't control nightmares."

"I snuck a cookie when you were in the bathroom. And milk. I know it's bad for me, but they smelled so good and—"

"*Shh*. It's over now. I think you dreamed that because of finding mud on the floor. Let's blame Ryan for it, okay?"

Izzy giggled and pulled out of her arms. "Now he has to clean the rug and buy me a treat to make up for giving me a nightmare."

"Not a sugar treat."

"Or a dairy one."

Heather ruffled wild curls. "Somehow I don't think he'd mind being forced to take you out for a treat."

"I like him. And I like that you like him. But. . ." The word trailed into the darkness.

"But what?"

"Everything's going to change. Will you still live here when Mom comes home?" The night-light silhouetted a reprise of the skillful pout. Eyes with an agenda turned on Heather. "Pleeeease?"

No. I will not. I will move out and find my own apartment and my own job. I will not be dependent. I will not be under your mother's thumb. I will not be pitiful. I will live on my own. Make decisions on my own. I am not the mouse ma—

"Heather?"

"Sorry. I'm tired. Let's just take one day at a time, okay? Even if I live in a different house, I'll still come to get you and we'll do things. Who else would go with me to Racine Beans?"

"Ryan."

"Oh. Him. Well, then he'll bring Skylar and it'll be a party."

"But I'll be in school and Skylar will be in a different school and I'll be in day care after school and you'll get a job and Ryan will go to school and it will never, ever be the same." Crocodile tears hovered on her bottom lashes then plunged over the side. Izzy flopped back into Heather's arms and mashed her face into her shoulder. "Will you r–read to me?"

"Of course." She took the papers from the table beside the bed and snapped on the lamp.

" 'Leo Tabbycat had changed. His fur was sleeker, his eyes a brighter yellow, his whiskers pointier. And Leo Tabbycat had a cause to fight for.

" ' "Mice should not be slaves," he said. "Mice should have the right to go to school and learn to read and mice should vote just like cats.' " But that was not the only thing Leo said he would fight for. " 'I will fight for you, Magdalena," he said one night when he had cornered her in the kitchen. "I will fight for the chance to court you." ' " Heather looked up. "Courting is kind of like dating. It's when people spent time together to see if they liked each other enough to get married."

Izzy gasped. "A mouse can't marry a cat."

Heather blinked. For some reason, Zach's face flashed before her eyes. "Let's wait and see. 'Magdalena was so very happy. She liked being with Leo because sometimes when she was with him she could pretend she wasn't a mouse.' "

"But"—Izzy twisted up her mouth—"she should be proud to be a mouse. She works hard and the Tabbycats just sit around and make her do all the work and eat the food she makes and get fat. I don't think I like Leo."

" 'Chippy, the mouse that cleaned the neighbor's stables, didn't like Leo Tabbycat. Magdalena could tell by the way Chippy said Leo's name. That made her sad, because Chippy was her friend. He was the one who stuck a flower in her hair at a picnic and brought her lemonade when she hung clothes on the line. Chippy had laughing eyes and always knew what to say to make her laugh.' "

"Duh!" Izzy slapped the blanket. "Chippy the Mouse is the one she should love."

"Maybe she figures that out at the end."

"She better or I'll be really, really mad. That's as dumb as you talking mushy with that Mike guy."

Heather's jaw unhinged. "I *never* talked mushy with him."

"Yuh-huh. I heard you. When I said I was going to the bathroom but I stayed in the hall and I listened and I heard him say you were beautiful and you giggled and said thank you and so I called Ry—" Her hand slapped over her mouth.

"Ryan didn't just show up? He came because you called and told him I was with Mike?"

"I didn't like him and somebody had to watch out for you and—"

"Go to sleep." Heather stood, tossed the papers on the floor, and shut off the light. "We'll talk about this in the morning. Right now, I need to call Ryan."

She ran down the hall and straight to her phone.

Which was ringing when she got to it.

⚜

"Why didn't you tell me Izzy called you to come to Coffee Sounds?"

"I didn't want you being upset with her."

"So instead you just let me go all crazy on you? Of course you had to come when a little kid called you. I would have understood that." She sat on the couch and pulled her knees to her chest. "Ryan?"

"Yes?"

"I'm a mess."

His laugh was whisper-soft. "How do you mean that?"

"I feel like a pendulum. Or a metronome. Or something that

goes back and forth and back and forth. I love that you want to protect me, I really do. But I have to learn to take care of myself and I don't know if you're going to want to hang around while I get things figured out. All my life I've let people make decisions for me. I've given in to everybody else's needs before my own and I don't know how to—"

"Heather?"

"...depend on my own common sense and—"

"Heather."

"...I just need—"

"Heather!"

"What?"

"You're adorable."

"Don't laugh at me."

He did. "I'm serious. You make me smile. For all the right reasons. Here you are working on a business plan while you take care of a kid who was dumped on you and then strange people show up in your life and instead of running scared you walk headlong into it and try to figure out what's going on. You may feel like a pendulum or a metronome or something that goes back and forth and back and forth, but you do not—I repeat—you do not look that way to me. I am in awe of you, adorable girl."

She leaned back, rested her arm across her face, and allowed a smile. "Why did you call?"

"To tell you I'm bringing dinner tomorrow night and Skylar wants Izzy to go roller-skating with her."

"Izzy will be thrilled, but it's my turn to make dinner for you."

"I can deal with that."

"Ryan?"

"Hmm?"

"I'm sorry. You weren't expecting a banshee on the other end when you called."

"Banshees are fine. As long as they don't fight my super banshee-taming powers."

"I'm finding out I'm pretty powerless against your powers, Spidey."

"Good. Let's just keep it that way. Sleep well, Banshee."

"You, too."

Heather curled in the corner of the leather couch, feet tucked under her, Ryan's whispered "Sleep well" covering her like a down comforter. She took a sip of chamomile tea and picked up the essay.

How many of us have not experienced the heartthrob, quickening of our pulse when Man looks our way? Our world turns upside down. We cannot eat or sleep. We burn the pudding, scorch the shirt, walk out in the rain without thought of an umbrella. And if, perchance, Man asks for a stroll in the park or a ride in his new automobile, we can scarcely breathe. The inner turmoil continues throughout the courtship and then, tragedy of tragedies, The Problem steps onto his stage. It may be his career. It may be his family. It may be Other Woman. Suddenly we are kicked aside like so much soiled laundry. We are finished. Surely the earth has stopped spinning and we will fly into oblivion. We are nothing without Man.

And then we rally. We shake our fist in the air. "I do not need you, Man! I will not need you! Never again will I stretch out my hand to one of your kind."

"Ouch." Heather took another sip of tea. "Are we all this dumb?" She pictured Natalie, a competent and successful woman in her forties, giggling on the phone like a schoolgirl. She thought of every friend she'd had through high school and college and the women she'd worked with since then. How many versions of "I'll never trust another man as long as I live" had she heard? Her monologue on the flight from Manhattan to Chicago had been just another verse of the same sad song.

Then along comes Another Man. He is tall. He is dashing. He is the one who will lift us from the drudgery of our mundane lives. We bask in his light. We are complete once again.
And then The Problem steps onto his stage.

"Magdalena, girl, you sooo get it. You're telling my story." For now, this moment, there was no Problem with a capital *P* standing between her and Ryan. But how long could it last? "So what's the answer? We can't live without them. God said, 'Go forth and multiply,' not, 'Go forth and be nuns.'"

> *So I ask, sisters, how do we stop this destructive cycle? We stop it by knowing who we are.*
>
> *Not all of us are blessed with an earthly father. Many of us spent childhood under the thumb of a man who believed his children were his property, or maybe the man who should have represented a loving heavenly Father was absent. It is hard, then, to imagine that we are loved. Since we were children we have sung "Jesus loves me, this I know," but do we know? If we did, we would know that we do not belong to anyone but Him. We would know that we are not someone's property, that we have a brain and a voice and that we need not live a life of subservience. If we did, we would know that God, in His tender mercy, rejoices over us with singing and if there is not a Man in our lives, we can still be whole and strong because we are complete in Christ.*

Heather set the papers down and lay back on the couch. "It's not that simple. Not that easy." But as she closed her eyes, tears rolled onto the black leather and a song she'd sung in church as little girl—a little girl with a brand-new daddy—echoed in her memory.

Stephannie gripped the *Essay* in both hands.

"*But my God shall supply all your need according to his riches in glory by Christ Jesus.*" As she leaned against a mountain of white pillows, she couldn't explain the tears that made a steady *plop plop* on the sheet. Her father was fine. Shock therapy had returned his heart rhythm to normal and a new medication was keeping him stable. Andrew had left an "I love you" text just minutes ago. Why, at a time when there was no logical reason for her to feel needy, did this verse grab her and hold her? Breathless. As if she were afraid the promise would vanish from the page if she exhaled.

Scripture abounds with verses about God supplying our needs. Jesus told us not to worry about what we'll eat or what we'll wear. "Behold the fowls of the air: for they sow not, neither do they reap, nor gather into barns; yet your heavenly Father feedeth them. Are ye not much better than they? Which of you by taking thought can add one cubit unto his stature?

"And why take ye thought for raiment? Consider the lilies of the field, how they grow; they toil not, neither do they spin: And yet I say unto you, That even Solomon in all his glory was not arrayed like one of these. Wherefore, if God so clothe the grass of the field, which to day is, and to morrow is cast into the oven, shall he not much more clothe you, O ye of little faith?"

She glanced at the open door of her closet. At tiers of clothes, some still with tags. Her gaze moved to a wall of shoes and floor-to-ceiling shelves crammed with bags. Coach, Prada, Vuitton, Chanel, Gadini.

Vision blurred by an increase in the tears she couldn't explain, she continued to read until she got to

But did you know He longs to supply not just your needs, but the secret things you long for in your heart of hearts?

Do you know how deeply He knows you? He is the architect, the designer, and builder of you. He knows your thoughts even before you do. He knew your response to these very words before you read them. He knew whether they would anger or frighten you or feel like sweet rain to your parched soul.

Do you know how much He loves you? It doesn't matter how old you are, you are still His little girl. He cherishes you and longs to give you the desires of your heart.

Stephannie covered her face with both hands and gave in to sobs.

"Am I still Your little girl?"

CHAPTER 24

Heather attempted a smile as Jalissa set a whipped cream-topped cocomocho in front of her. "On the house. You're good for business."

"*I* am?"

"You'll see. Where's the munchkin?"

"Hanging out with Detective Ryan's niece."

An artfully shaped brow rose. "Uh-huh. I got the picture."

"What's that supposed to mean?"

"It means you're in with the man's family, that's what it means." One shoulder lifted as she repeated, "Uh-huh."

"The girls like to play together."

"And so do the grown-ups, from what I hear."

Ice clinked as Heather pressed the glass to her cheek. The hiss of released steam was imaginary, wasn't it? "What do you hear?"

"That he fixed you a dinner that was over-the-top romantic." She glanced toward the door for the third time. Was she hoping for a midafternoon rush?

"He told you that?"

"Who do you think made the pitcher of cocomocho? And maybe gave him a few little tips on how to treat a lady." Her generous mouth spread into a smile wider than Heather had ever seen. "Not that the man needed much instruction, mind you, he had the details all worked out. Got to see a side to him I wouldn't have known existed in all the years he's been coming in here. Way, way more to that boy than police books and detective novels. Way more." The eyebrow wiggled. "But don't you worry, his lips were sealed after the date. I don't know a thing about what happened."

"Nothing happened."

"Oh, I didn't mean it that way. Boy's got scruples and you do, too, I know that. But you don't have to cross any lines to have a niiiiice time." The left eyebrow joined the right.

Cold plastic warmed quickly as Heather held the drink to her other cheek. "Is your A/C on the fritz?"

"No, honey. Your furnace is just working overtime." She laughed and turned toward the door.

"You okay? You seem fidgety."

"Sure, turn the focus on me. I am a little antsy today, but it's a good antsy. Coffee buzz. Occupational hazard."

The front door opened. Two women walked in. One dark-skinned and long-legged in a verging-on-illegal short skirt, the other appeared to be Hispanic. She wore a flounced and ruffled gold blouse, unbreathably skinny jeans, and heels higher than the step stool Heather used to reach the top cupboards. They both waved to Jalissa.

"In the back room, ladies."

"Do they work here?"

"No." Jalissa patted the table. "Well, better go get my papers. Kylee's coming. On time, she says."

"Good. I have a feeling we won't be seeing St—Annie."

"No. But cool how our prayers worked, huh?"

"What do you mean?"

White valleys formed between ridges on Jalissa's brow. "She didn't call you?"

"No."

"Oh. I just figured she had. She called here a couple of days ago and talked to Kylee. Her dad's okay. Looks like he'll be coming home. . .must be today. He's going to have private nurses at home. I'm guessing the guy's loaded."

"Yeah." Heather fought a mix of hurt and something ugly. "I'm guessing, too."

Jalissa waved at three women in pale blue baseball jerseys. "She said she'll be here next week."

"Oh. That's nice."

"You okay? You got kind of pale all of a sudden."

"I'm fine. Just tired. Go get your stuff." *I'll just sit here and think bad things about Stephannie Lansing.*

Instead, she folded her arms on the table, put her head down, and called up every verse she'd ever learned on not hating. *Bless those who persecute you. Love your enemies. Do good to those who hate you.* "*It is mine to avenge. I will repay," says the* LORD. *Do not repay evil with evil, but with blessing, because to this you were called so that—*

"Heather?"

She opened her eyes to Stephannie Lansing standing over her.

♛

"Jalissa told me to come and get you."

Heather stared into lusterless eyes underlined by dark shadows. She'd heard rumors about the rapid-fire changes of Stephannie's mercurial personality, even suggestions she might have borderline personality disorder. This was neither the heartbroken Stephannie who'd gotten the call about her father nor the defensive one who shunned Heather's offer to drive her home. This was a contrite face.

Did that mean a confession and apology were soon to follow or was it just some kind of cover-up? An emotional disguise to go with the glasses and slouchy hat. *Love your enemies love your enemies love your enemies. Even if they give false information to Hotel Buzz.* "What do you mean *get* me, *Annie?*" "Get" as in stab a part of my back not already bleeding?

Enough with the theatrics.

"Come with me." She picked up Heather's papers. "Can we, maybe, talk after the meeting?"

"Sure." It came out without thought. Maybe this was the confession. Or maybe she'd been wrong to think Stephannie had anything to do with the blog post. Maybe it was coincidence. Maybe somebody else was out to trash her. The look on Stephannie's face could have been rehearsed and be nothing but a reflection of skill or an unstable mind, but Heather made the decision to believe it. She stood and followed "Annie" around tables and toward a door she'd never noticed before. That was beginning to be the story of her life. Unseen doors that opened onto unknown problems.

Scratch that. Unknown adventures.

She walked through the doorway and gasped. The walls were bare. Tan with splotches of white where holes had been filled. The floor was wood. Scarred and scuffed and beautifully old. But it wasn't the lack of décor that made her gasp. It was the chairs in the center of an otherwise empty room. She scanned them. And counted.

Nine chairs. Each one filled.

With women of varying ages, shapes, and sizes.

Each holding a sheaf of papers.

"Wow." Heather blew her nose as she looked around the room, formulating a conclusion to the book club session. She smiled at ten pairs of reddened eyes. "Anyone else?"

The woman with the short skirt raised her hand then laced long, tapered fingers and propped her hands on her knees. "I can't tell you how I needed to be here. Jalissa gave me this on Monday and on Tuesday my boss"—shimmering eyes darted around the room—"who was more than my boss. . .fired me." She took a shuddering breath. "I thought I was literally going to go insane. I went completely nuts, screaming and throwing things. I reached for my phone to call him and tell him I was going to kill myself and"—she gave a weak smile—"my phone was sitting on these papers." She wiped her face with both hands. "I read the whole thing straight through and when I finished I just fell on my face and cried out to Jesus and then I got up and I took a shower and I went out for breakfast. All by myself. And I knew, for the first time ever in my life, that it was okay to be alone because I really wasn't."

Someone to Heather's right began to clap. She turned. Tears streaming down her face, the woman who still claimed to be Annie applauded and the rest of the room joined in.

In the silence that followed, Annie raised her hand. "I just decided something and I guess I need you guys to say a prayer for me." Her shoulders rose. "I have to break up with my boyfriend."

Jalissa walked behind her, put a hand on her shoulder, and began to pray.

When she finished, Heather leaned forward, rolling the papers in her hands. "We're all in different places as far as what we know or believe about God. I've called myself a follower of Christ since I was a little girl. I've sung 'Jesus Loves Me' hundreds of times. I've told other people how much He loves them. But never, until this week, did I really, truly *get* that He loves *me*." She pressed her hand to her chest. "That's a game changer. Because that's enough. If I'm alone, I have Him. If I'm blessed with a man in my life and he disappoints me, I have the One who knows my every thought, and supplies all my needs.

"No matter what, we're still His little girls." She set the papers down. "Thank you, ladies. I'm looking forward to next time. Put your name and e-mail on the list by the door if you want to stay in touch between meetings. Let's hold each other up."

"Amen, sister." Kylee shot a thumb in the air.

Annie nodded. "Thank you," she whispered. Then darted out of the room.

Heather felt a tap on her shoulder. She turned and wrapped her arms around Ryan's sister. "Marissa. I'm so glad you came."

"Me, too." She nodded toward the door. "My big brother's picking me up. Poor boy will use any excuse he can to see you."

They walked out into the coffee shop. Annie was gone.

Jalissa walked toward her, tying her apron, and engulfed Heather in a hug. "Wow. That's all I can say, girl, just wow. Oh, and one more thing. How'd you like to work with me?"

"Work? For you?"

"Yeah. No. Work *with* me. Did I happen to mention I own this place? And I sure could use a business partner with vision."

"P-partner?"

"Just until you become world famous." She swept her arm in a wide arc. "You help me transform this place and I'll foot the bill for your prototype."

"I don't know what to say."

A deep laugh sounded behind her. She turned and almost bumped into Ryan.

"Seems like 'thank you' would be a good place to start."

👑

Stephannie blinked hard to clear her vision as she sped onto I-94. She'd practically run out of the room when the meeting ended. Not because she didn't want to talk to Heather. But because she *did*.

In the state she was in, she knew she'd say too much. She would have spilled everything about her father, *their* father, about her relationship with Andrew, about walking into her closet and feeling suddenly sick at the thousands of dollars lining shelves and dangling from hangers. Money she'd spent to make herself feel exactly the way she did at two o'clock this morning for the first time in her life.

Loved. Accepted. Complete.

That feeling hadn't left, but the tears had started all over again during the meeting. Because, like she'd told her new friends, she needed to break up with the man who told her all she needed to do was look inside herself to find the strength she needed.

"You were wrong, Andrew." She fumbled for her phone. "So very wrong."

👑

Andrew hung up the phone and with an elongated sigh, slumped onto his desk chair.

His stomach cramped. His head thundered with voices all shouting "What now?"

He'd tried the soft approach. *Slow down, baby, let's talk about this. You're upset. You've had so much stress with your dad being sick.* He'd tried the firm *You're confused right now. Lean on me and we'll get through this together* tack. Nothing had worked. "Andrew," she'd said, "for your sake as well as mine I need to end this. It's nothing you've done. I just need to do the right thing for a change." And that's when he lowered himself to begging. *How can I live without you, Steph? You're my life. You're the very air I breathe.*

He could swear she'd laughed at that point. A quiet kind of laugh, as if she'd seen right through his words. "I'll pray for you, Andrew. Someday maybe you'll find out it's not me you can't live without."

And she'd hung up. Just like that.

He pushed a button on his phone. The screen lit. Icons in neat rows over the Chicago skyline.

After what he'd fed to Hotel Buzz, he'd had no intention of making another move. Until now.

All he'd wanted to do was taint Heather Conrad's reputation. To make sure Parker would see her as too great a risk to the company and, when they did finally connect, it would be strictly a father-daughter relationship.

But things were different now. He wasn't sure he'd even have a place in the company come morning. Parker wasn't shallow enough to let him go because of the awkwardness, but Parker still listened to his ex-wife and he still had no clue if this would help or hurt his relationship with Dianna.

What wouldn't hurt would be having an in with the other Lansing daughter.

The logic fell together like an automated Rubik's cube. *Chink. Chink. Chink.* All the pieces slid into place. Right along with the story he'd use to cover his tracks. . .

He'd checked Parker's personal phone while the poor man was unconscious. It was his responsibility, after all, to make sure no appointments were broken or communications missed. He'd seen the text about Parker's daughter and took it upon himself to check out the situation. To protect Parker and Stephannie. To make sure it wasn't a scam, that the woman wasn't the type who would cozy up to the family just for the money or prestige.

He did it for the corporation.

And if, in the process, he happened to develop some feelings for the dark-haired daughter, who could blame him?

Especially considering the other one dumped him.

Who could blame him?

He pressed an icon that opened his contacts list. And scrolled to the *H*s.

꧁

January 26, 1912

"Maggie, I'm so sorry."

Supple leather stretched tight across Emma's knuckles as she gripped the steering wheel. She stared straight ahead, her face a rigid mask of shock mixed with fear.

Maggie turned and looked behind them. "I keep thinking someone's going to come after us."

"I do, too." Emma pressed the gas pedal. "What should we do?"

Maggie's breath rattled in her throat. "Report him." The words crystallized, hovering in front of her before it vanished as quickly as her job. And her home. "We have no choice. He is breaking the law employing children that young."

"He'll let you go."

"If I'm lucky."

"You don't think he's capable of. . ." The unfinished thought hung between them.

Maggie shrugged. "He's not a kind man, but I would never have thought him capable of what we just saw." A sudden thought flashed. "The day we went to the trunk factory and Holleb told us he'd been fired for having a book, he said he worked at the schloss-fabrik. I've seen 'schloss' written on papers on Mr. Hamilton's desk. Did you know what it means?"

"It's German. *Schloss* means"—her eyes opened wide—"lock. Oh, Maggie. The lock factory."

Maggie nodded, her thoughts tumbling back to Emma's unfinished question. Mr. Hamilton had not said a single word to her. Raging eyes, wilder than she'd witnessed even in his worst arguments with his wife, had burned into her as he stepped out of the barn and ordered his lackeys to "escort the ladies to their vehicle." She'd only gotten a glimpse of long assembly line tables with children, some no more than six or seven, standing shoulder-to-shoulder under the blazing glare of two muscled men with shirt sleeves rolled above their elbows. It was all she needed to see.

She rubbed the ridge forming along the right side of her neck. "Hamilton Lock and Latch almost folded three years ago. Mr. Hamilton let the rest of the house staff go and I overheard many late-night talks about selling the house. And then things seemed to take a dramatic turn. He spoke with such pride about the smartest business decision he'd ever made." She shivered. "He even gave me a raise." Her eyes closed. "I don't know what he's capable of."

It didn't really matter. Maxwell Hamilton's actions had already sealed her fate, stolen any possible future she might have had with his son. The truth of it jarred her as if she'd run face-first into a brick wall.

"Are you afraid to go home?"

Maggie struggled for a breath. "I'll stay the night at the Caswells." If Hilde wouldn't let her bunk on the floor in her room, she'd hide in the barn and just let people talk if they wanted. "I have a chance at another job." She felt her mouth lift at the corners. "Remember how you said you hoped I'd have the opportunity to travel?"

"Yes?" Emma answered breathlessly. "You have a chance at a job that will allow you to travel?"

Possibly. Third class. "If you could give me a day or two before we report this. . ."

"Oh Maggie, of course. As much as I want to see justice carried out, I won't do a thing until I know you're not in danger."

"Thank you. For now, if you could take me to Charl—the Caswells, I would appreciate it."

"You'll be safe there?"

"Yes." For the first time she rested against the back of the seat. Her eyes closed and she pictured Charles's muscled arm reaching for the gun hanging in his "office" on a rack made of deer antlers. "I'll be safe there."

⚜

Maggie stood at the Caswells' back door, watching Hilde's peaceful expression through the window. Hilde sang as she held a bowl on her hip and stirred something thick and brown with a wooden spoon. Her famous chocolate cake. Probably Charles's favorite food in all the world. A pinch, a painful twinge beneath her breastbone, accompanied the thought of saying good-bye to her two best friends.

Even the one who'd barely spoken to her since Christmas.

It would have to be good-bye. If the Hansens hired her, she would go to Denmark with them and then sail back to New York. From there, she did not know. She could not return to Racine.

She raised her fist, wrapped her knuckles on the glass, and turned the handle. Maybe the way to keep the serene expression from fading was to tell the hardest part first.

Hilde jumped. The spoon froze in midstroke.

"I have something to tell you." She didn't bother with the customary greeting. "I'm leaving. I'm quitting the Hamiltons and leaving town. For good."

Cool eyes appraised her from across the room. "So you're in the family way, too."

"What? Hilde! How could you say such a thing?"

"Why else would you be leaving?"

"I can't explain right now. You'll hear soon enough." She gave a shaky smile. "The only good part is that since I won't be seeing Richard again you don't have to be jealous that I have something with him that you wish you had with Ch—"

Hilde smacked the bowl down. "What does Richard have to do with anything?" Her eyes narrowed. "Quite a coincidence this." Lusterless eyes looked toward the window. "I gave my notice two days ago. Because of you."

"Me? Why? Hilde, what is it you think I've done? I haven't understood your coldness to me these past weeks. If Richard saying he wanted to court me is not the reason, I surely don't see—"

"It is not because of *Richard's* feelings for you that I am angry. How blind can you be? It is because of *his* feelings for you that I'm leaving." She jabbed a finger toward the window. Maggie spun on her heel just as Charles burst through the back door.

"Mags! What a surprise. To what do we owe the pleasure of this vis—"

"She's leaving, Charles. Up and quitting the Hamiltons and leaving town for good." Hilde stood for a moment, hands on hips. "What did I tell you?" she hissed at Maggie. . .as the color drained from Charles's face and he slumped against the door.

His mouth opened, then closed, then opened again. "For *good?*"

CHAPTER 25

Boneless Pork Chops with Mushroom and Thyme
Twice-Baked Potatoes
Grilled Asparagus
Butternut Squash Rolls
Mocha Pots de Crème
House Selection of Flavored Coffees

This is soooo romantic!" Izzy giggled as she set the hot-off-the-printer menus on china plates. "Can Skylar come here instead of us going roller-skating?"

Heather set down the napkin she was folding, made a fist, and bopped her gently on the nose. "What about *that* would be romantic?"

"We wouldn't be in your way, I promise. We could put on aprons and serve you." She squealed. "We could be mouse maids."

"No mouse maids in this house, sweetie. No women being subservient to other women."

"Sub-*what?*"

"It means doing what someone else tells you."

"I already do that. I do everything you tell me. Except 'Don't eat cookies and milk before bed.'"

Heather picked up a crystal goblet and stared at her convex

reflection. Straightened hair, dangly amber earrings, dark brown scoop-necked tee with a turquoise tank peeking out beneath it. "Go get your stuff. Marissa will be here in five min—" Her phone rang.

"It's Skylar saying she's sick and she can't go skating and I have to stay here and be sub-whatever like a mouse maid and. . ."

Heather answered the phone as the giggly voice wound up the stairs. "Hello."

"Heather."

The voice, smooth as the cheese sauce waiting to grace her twice-baked potatoes, was familiar, but she couldn't place it. "Yes?"

"This is Mike."

"H-hello." Her pulse skipped, then pounded. She walked through the swinging door and into a kitchen swirling with the aromas of the supper she would serve Ryan in approximately ten minutes.

"Is this a bad time? Are you in the middle of something?"

"I'm expecting company any minute." *What do you want with me?* "Can I help you?" She made no attempt to disguise the ice in her voice.

"You can, as a matter of fact. I'm wondering if you'd be willing to do me a favor. I need to check out the Corner House in Racine to see if it would be the right location for a business meeting. Unfortunately, I suddenly find myself a very single man, and it's a little awkward going to a four-and-a-half-star joint alone. I'd really like to treat you to a meal. If Ryan wants to come along that's fine. It's the least I can do for the person who saved my life with the gift of ice." He laughed, soft and rippling. It made the hair on the back of her neck stand up.

Heather swallowed hard, picturing dumping the cooler full of ice on the man who called himself Mike. "I'm afraid I have to decline."

"Nothing I can do to change your mind?"

"Nothing."

She said good-bye as the motion sensor lights Ryan had installed yesterday flooded the front of the house and a knock sounded at the back door.

"This is, hands down, the best meal I have eaten in my entire life."

Ryan lifted his glass and touched it to Heather's. Her eyes reflected flames from the candles floating in glass bowls in the center of the table. His compliment heightened the color in her cheeks.

"I recognize hyperbole when I hear it, but thank you."

"I'm serious. You're a fabulous cook and the best company a guy could ask for." He dipped his spoon through a whipped cream cloud and into the richest chocolate pudding he'd ever tasted. Heather had claimed she was too full, but she'd eaten every bite he'd offered. There were three more dishes in the kitchen. He wouldn't mind sitting here and feeding her dessert for the rest of the night. He didn't ask this time, just lifted his spoon to her mouth. The whole process of lips parting and closing on the silver spoon fascinated him.

"Thank you. Again." She wiped her mouth on her napkin. "I've said that a lot tonight."

"So have I."

"Finish this and let's take the candles into the living room." She glanced at her watch. "We have an hour and a half until the skaters return." Once again, her cheeks pinked. "I..."

He laughed, uncannily sure he knew where she thought he thought her thoughts were heading. He pushed the dish aside. "Let's go sit where it's more comfy and talk by candlelight."

She copied his laugh. "Do you know what I like about you?"

"Is there just one thing?"

"Do you know *one* of the things I like about you?"

"No. What?"

"You get me even when I don't say what I mean to say."

He wiped a smudge of chocolate from the corner of her mouth with the edge of his thumb. "And I like that you give me a second chance even when I say what I mean to say."

He carried the candles and Heather brought their drinks into the dark living room where Tony Bennett sang "The Shadow of Your Smile." Ryan set the candles on the coffee table and took his glass—and hers—from Heather, and set them both on the table. He held out his hands and she slid into them. "I'll follow you," he whispered, as they swayed in front of the couch. When the song ended, he tilted her head and pressed his lips to hers. "Chocolate." He breathed the word against her mouth. "Delicious."

"I th–think we came out here to talk."

"Mm-hmm. I think you're right." He pulled away. Her hand, trailing along his arm, said he was not alone in his reluctance. Maybe they should have let the girls stay and be "mouse maids" like Izzy had suggested. Little ears and eyes in the corners might not be a bad thing. He pulled her onto the couch beside him. "So tell me about *Essays on Life and the Role of Women.*"

She picked up her glass then tucked her legs beneath her, facing him, knees just brushing his. "It taught me something so astonishing I'll never be the same after reading it." Her eyes shone as if she'd just discovered a diamond floating in the bottom of her glass. An idea to tuck away for some later date.

"What's that?"

"Jesus loves me."

He blinked hard and tried to keep his smile in check. "That's quite a revelation."

A soft fist pressed into his arm. "For me, it is. I finally believe it. In my gut. And I finally understand that that's what's been missing ever since. . ." Her lips pressed together and her gaze drifted to the window.

He took her glass, set it next to his on the table, and rubbed a slow circle on the back of her hand as he waited.

"My mother died when I was two. My birth father—I could never call him my *real* father—left me with my grandmother. From what I've been told, he had a demanding job and I only saw him on weekends. I have three memories of him. In the first, he carried me to bed on his shoulders. I remember giggling as I had to duck to get through the door. In the second, I was clinging to his leg and crying as he peeled me off and handed me to someone. It may have happened the same time as my final memory. Someone was holding me. A woman. I was kicking and screaming and doing everything I could to get away from her so I could run to my father. It was like one of those nightmares where you're trying to run or yell, but no one seems to hear you. The woman didn't budge and my father just smiled and waved and walked out the door. I never saw him again."

Her eyes glistened. His arms slid around her and he pulled her into his chest. Her shoulders shook and a sob sounded as if it ripped from somewhere deep inside. He held her until her tears finally stopped. Her breath came in quivering spasms. "I haven't cried about that in so many years and now I can't seem to quit. It's that moment that made me the pathetic mess I am today. I mean, the mess I *was*. It was that moment that made me a doormat—too weak to ever say no to Izzy's mom or walk away from Zach. I was so scared of what I'd be without him."

Ryan pulled damp strands off her cheek and tucked them behind her ear. "And then you were scared of needing someone like that again."

"Mm-hm. But when the lightbulb turned on the other night, it's like it took the fear with it."

" 'Perfect love drives out fear.' "

"Yes."

"And without fear, it's easier to accept an imperfect person who can only love you imperfectly no matter how much he wants to do it right."

He traced the curve of her cheek with his fingers as her eyes found his and the meaning of his words found their mark.

Even in the dim light, she could tell something had changed. She'd made a silly comment and suddenly his eyes looked shadowed. "Ryan? What is it?"

She spread her hand over his. "Talk to me."

"Sometimes the superhero thing makes me. . ." He took a ragged breath. "Eight years ago Kurt was diagnosed with kidney disease." He turned his hand over. His fingers curved around hers. "I was away at school. The doctors suggested that the family get tested for possible donors. Everyone back here got tested. No one was a match. I was in the middle of football season and coming up on finals. My parents told me to stay the course and not think about getting tested until I came home for Christmas. But I was hearing things from Marissa they weren't telling me. Time was ticking for

Kurt. He was on dialysis and getting weaker and weaker.

"I went to the hospital in Eau Claire. I didn't tell anyone I was doing it. I was the same blood type. I was young and tough and cocky and sure I'd be a match. I had it all planned. I was going to cut out a picture of a kidney and put it in a box with a bow and stick it under the tree."

"But you weren't a match."

He didn't nod. Or shake his head. Again, she waited for an answer. Again, his chest shook with a savage breath. "I was. The only match in the family. But I'd been taking steroids since I started playing football in high school. I'd damaged my own kidneys and they couldn't consider me." His gaze fixed on something beyond the room. "I came home for a month and watched my brother slipping away while my family thought I was too selfish to get tested. They still think that."

She bent her head to his shoulder and squeezed his hand.

"They'd given him less than a month to live when they finally found a donor. Because of my stupidity, my brother had to wait for somebody to die so he could live."

As she pressed into him, trying, like she had with Izzy, to wick some of the pain away, he turned his face to hers. "You're the only person I've ever told."

CHAPTER 26

Ryan ignored his sister's eyebrow gymnastics as she leaned against Heather's counter, savoring the last of the *Mocha Pots de Crème*. "She made this for you? From scratch?" She nodded toward the dining room as she referred to Heather who was upstairs helping the girls get ready for their sleepover. "This is love. This is love in a ramekin smothered in whipped cream."

"Love in a what?"

"Ramekin. The dish, dummy." She licked the spoon. "Nobody goes through this much trouble unless they're ready to give up their freedom for-*ev*-er."

"That explains a lot. If that's how you view relationships, you just might be dealing with a bit of self-fulfilling prophecy."

Nose in the air, she set the whatever-it-was-called down and strode to the oven to check the girls' before-bed soy cheese pizza. She'd just slid it out of the oven when the giggles descended the stairs and burst through the door. Marissa tipped her head. "Time to go, bro."

Heather locked eyes with him and the most attractive pout he'd ever seen pooched her bottom lip.

Izzy gave her own signature version. "Aren't you staying for pizza?"

"No. Marissa needs her beauty sleep. You don't want to see her in the morning if she's missed it. Uuuuugly." He held out his hand to

Heather. She took it and, while Marissa cut the pizza, they stepped out onto the porch.

He slid his arms around her. "I still don't like the thought of you being here alone. The windows don't lock, the door locks aren't up to—"

"I have motion sensor lights bright enough to light a runway. And I'm not alone. I have the world's loudest screamer to protect me. She's better than any super-duper quadruple alarm system in your arsenal, Security Man."

"Funny. I'll admit I may have overreacted a bit with all the seeming coincidences. The more time that goes by without any more of those incidences hap—" The quick shift in her eyes stopped his words. "What? Is there something you haven't told me? Something that maybe-Stephannie-Lansing said? What?"

She rocked back on her heels and stared at her toes as if she'd never seen them before. "I got a call tonight just before you got here. From 'Mike.'"

"And you were going to tell me when?"

"It wasn't a big deal. He wondered if I—if you and I—would go out to dinner with him. He needed to check out a restaurant for business and he didn't want to go alone."

"I just bet he wanted me there. A nice little threesome."

"Stop it. I told him no."

"It didn't cross my mind that you wouldn't. But now that we know beyond the shadow of a doubt there's no coincidence involve—"

The door from the kitchen popped open. "Did you make him clean up the mud?" Izzy's teasing yet accusing eyes lasered him.

"Mud?"

Heather turned Izzy around by the shoulders. "Don't interrupt grown-up conversations. Go eat your pizza."

"Did you tell him it's his fault I had that dream about the guy in the mask who. . ." Her voice muffled as Heather guided her into the kitchen and shut the door behind her.

"What was that all about?"

Heather sighed. "You left a chunk of mud on her windowsill and a footprint on her rug when you were figuring out where to put the lights."

"On her rug? What do you mean?"

"In her room. It's no big deal. It looked like you just stepped off the roof and that first step left a print. I used some carpet cleaner and it came right up, but thinking about it triggered a nightmare about a guy in a mask trying to get into her room. She had another night terror and woke up screaming and talking about—"

"Heather." He gripped her arm as a chill snaked through his body. "I didn't open that window. I didn't set foot in Izzy's room."

꙳

Heather woke to the smell of frying bacon. She opened one eye and squinted at the clock. 10:04. In the *morning*?

She patted the rumpled covers on the other side of the king-size bed as she pieced together the events of the night before. The events that ended with a man sleeping on the couch in the living room.

And apparently now fixing breakfast.

Flopping back on the pillows, she rubbed her face. She wasn't going downstairs until she'd showered, dressed, and figured out how she felt about Ryan Tobin sleeping on her couch.

10:04. That meant she'd actually fallen asleep. Sometime after three in the morning she must have shut down her brain. By then, Ryan's snores had been drifting up from the first floor for over two hours.

He'd told her to call the police. When she'd said it was crazy to call the cops over a chunk of dirt, he'd said she and Izzy should get a room at a hotel. She'd told him he was overreacting again. So he'd said he was spending the night.

She hadn't fought that. And it made sense when he moved the girls into Natalie's room rather than Izzy's that had access to the window from the roof. Things didn't start going bad until Natalie called and Ryan grabbed the phone and informed her he had installed motion sensor lights and he was coming back in the morning to put in an alarm system whether she was paying for it or not. But even that wasn't the tipping point. He'd handed the phone back to Heather, leaving her to deal with a near-hysterical long-distance mother while he went to his truck.

To get his gun.

Maybe she would have been cool with that, too. If he hadn't said it in front of the girls. Who ended up sleeping in her room.

In her bed. With her.

That was the point of one of her less-than-shining moments. The moment she'd snapped, "You're not really Spider-Man, you know. Deal with it."

They'd gone off to their separate floors without saying good night.

She rolled her eyes at the blue and orange border. In the light of day the whole thing seemed almost funny.

Almost.

She stumbled into the bathroom. Adjusting the shower head to the setting that felt like acupuncture, she let her mind empty of all but the sting of the water.

Shampoo slid through the drain holes between her toes. There were worse things than a guy who was overprotective because he cared. Sure, he'd gone a little Rambo on her, but that was who he was.

She got out, threw on shorts and a T-shirt, and ran down the stairs. New day. New start.

Izzy sat at the kitchen table. Alone. A platter of perfect-looking pancakes sat in front of her.

"Sorry I slept so late. Where are Ryan and Skylar?"

"They left." Izzy looked up, eyes shimmering with unshed tears. "He asked me a bunch of questions about the man I dreamed about. I made up some things. I said he only had one arm like in *The Fugitive* and he smelled like cough drops." Her gaze dropped to the clean plate in front of her. "He got mad when I said I was joking. I don't think they're coming back. Ever."

February 2, 1912

Maggie stared down at the trunk. She had no idea who it belonged to or how it had gotten to her room. Had Mr. Hamilton snuck home, dragged it out of the attic, and then decided it was too heavy to tote as he fled public opinion. . .and quite possibly the law?

The last time she'd seen him was a week ago. Standing in the door of the barn, commanding her to leave. But he was coming home today. For what, or how long, she did not know. All she knew was that she had to leave before he arrived.

Maybe he would just come home to pack his bags and then he would leave for good. And she could just stay.

And live in fear every day of her life.

No. Whether he returned or not, she would sail to Denmark with the Hansens. That was as far ahead as she could think.

She rubbed her hand over her eyes and kicked at the trunk. Solid. It didn't even vibrate. It appeared brand new. She dropped to her knees, lifted the lid, and stared down at the contents. Two gowns were folded on top. A gold-handled brush lay between them. An envelope sat on top.

With her name on it.

Heart knocking like a frantic woodpecker, she tore open the envelope. Two pages fell out.

Two telegrams. Both from Richard.

PLEASE BELIEVE I KNEW NOTHING. MUST STAY TO SORT THINGS OUT. THANK E. MICHELL FOR SHOPPING. TRAVEL IN STYLE. ENJOY DENMARK. WILL MEET YOU. WILL WED IN LONDON. RETURN TOGETHER. RICHARD.

The second telegram fluttered to the floor, faceup. A receipt for two first-class tickets on the *R.M.S Titanic*.

Two floors below, a door slammed. Mrs. Hamilton wailed, "How could you? I'm ruined. *We* are ruined. Your son—could you not have thought of his future? And those children. . ."

"Is she gone?"

"Who?"

"Franklin Parker's double-crossing daughter. I knew we shouldn't have taken her in. She's no different from her father. *She* is the one who ruined our lives. Keep her out of my sight, Evangeline. I cannot be responsible for what I might do to her."

CHAPTER 27

Heather's hand shook as she fastened the clasp of her necklace.

This was either a massive mistake, or a very *not* spineless way to put an end to the craziness.

She'd made two calls after finding out Ryan had left. One to ask Jalissa if Izzy could spend a couple of hours at the coffee shop this evening. The second to tell Mike she'd changed her mind.

She'd borrowed a dress from Natalie's closet. Its rightful owner would fill it out better than she did, but the dress gave the illusion of curves where none existed. She didn't want to guess what it had cost.

She glanced at the time on her phone. She'd told him she had two hours and that was all. She needed to be home by nine to get Izzy to bed. In Heather's bed. She wasn't letting the girl sleep in her own room until her mother came home and she was no longer responsible for her safety.

But tonight Izzy could have the bed to herself because she had no intention of sleeping. She'd leave the lights on and sit in the living room with a fireplace poker in her hand.

That was something that, if Ryan were still speaking to her, she would never tell him. He didn't need to know she wasn't sure which of Izzy's stories was the truth or that finding out the footprint wasn't his had shot ice through her veins. Or that she'd felt safe with him sleeping on the couch.

As she picked up an earring in a clumsy finger, she spotted the old watch peeking out from behind a scarf on her dresser. *Did it bring you luck, Magdalena?* She made a face in the mirror. She was talking to a woman who might have perished on the *Titanic*. She turned away, then stopped and picked up the watch. Something about it represented safety. It had survived for at least a century. Maybe it would make it through one more night. It and her.

She pinned it on the dress then walked down the stairs on legs that wobbled. Her breath came in shallow gasps and at times she realized she'd simply forgotten to breathe and had to put her head down as she inhaled and regained her equilibrium.

In the kitchen, she opened a bottle and took something for the headache hovering just above her right eye. "Calm down. It's only two hours."

Two hours to find out who he was and what he was up to. Two hours to watch her back and her front and everything in between. "Lord God, I know this is crazy, but I have to find out what's going on and put a stop to this. Help me be smart. And strong. And take care of myself."

As she opened her eyes, the doorbell rang.

Ryan's knuckles whitened as they gripped the steering wheel of Marissa's car. There was no mistaking the car parked in Heather's driveway.

His heart pummeled his ribs. "What are you doing, Heather?" He couldn't believe he'd been that wrong about her. "Be smart. Please."

He waited. Just because the guy walked into her house didn't mean she'd ask him to stay. The clock marked a full minute. Two. Ryan grabbed the door handle. And the front door opened. He breathed a sigh. "Thata girl. Send him packing and—"

Heather walked out. Dressed in something blue and flowing with no straps or a pitiful excuse for them.

The guy's hand adhered to her back as if he owned her.

His pride told him to go home and forget about her. But he was no longer in the habit of listening to his pride. The other voice told him not to let her out of his sight. "Keep her safe, Lord."

The Jag backed out. Ryan put the car in gear, imagining the rage on Heather's face if she found out he'd borrowed his sister's car so she wouldn't recognize it. *You're not Spider-Man, you know. Deal with it.*

He followed several car lengths behind. They turned on to Fourteenth Street then angled on to Washington Avenue. A minute later the Jaguar pulled into the parking lot behind the Corner House. Ryan parallel parked on Owen Avenue, put the seat back, and prepared to wait.

As long as it took.

⚜

"You look stunning tonight."

He leaned toward her. Candlelight danced on his tanned face and flickered on a deep red tie and white shirt. He reached across the table, and touched her arm, diamonds in a thick gold ring catching the light as he moved. "Dare I ask why you changed your mind?"

Heather tried to ignore the crawling sensation beneath her skin. "My evening freed up and I've never been to the Corner House."

"And your boyfriend? Does he know?" The last question floated on a conspiratorial whisper.

"He had other plans tonight." *But, oh, how I wish he were here.* Second thoughts churned in her belly.

He gave a smug smile.

What are you after? Like some sleuth in a bad movie, she'd checked his shoes for mud as they walked to the car. She couldn't quite imagine him donning a mask and crawling through a window to. . . What? Attack her in her sleep? Steal something?

Sweat rolled down her sides. The filmy fabric of Natalie's dress clung to her skin. She fingered the watch, finding comfort in the feel of the carved flowers on the cover.

"That's lovely. It looks old."

She shrugged. "It's just something I picked up." *In a treasure chest in a hidden room.* Her breath caught. Was that it? Did he know about the chest? Was there something valuable in there? Something like the thing pinned to the front of her dress?

"You have good taste."

Andrew Michael Rivera. Now that he'd told her his full name the feeling she'd seen him before came back with full force. Where had she heard that name? Where had she seen that face?

He smiled. "You're an intriguing woman, Heather. Tell me about yourself."

Be vague. Don't give him anything.

"What would you like to know?" *Other than what I learned from my ex-boss or what's in the treasure chest?*

"Where are you from?"

"I've lived in a few places, but I'm a Midwest girl all the way."

"You mentioned you were working on a business plan. What's that all about?"

She pulled off a casual laugh. "That was really just a pipe dream. I'm actually going to start working for a friend next week."

Andrew nodded, closed his menu, and rested his chin on his hand. The posture, the eye contact, what every woman wanted from a man, made her feel suddenly chilled.

His head dipped to one side. "In what kind of business?"

Heather took a sip of water, but it did nothing to relieve the dryness in her mouth. Her tongue felt thick and her lips parched. "Just a little local shop. Let's talk about you for a change. Tell me about *your* business."

Their server stepped to the table and asked for their order. She ordered a petite cut of prime rib. While he gave his order, she looked around for the first time. The ambience was serene. Warm colors, soft lighting. The kind of place she'd love to come to with someone she felt comfortable with. She tried to shut out the image of sitting here enjoying easy banter with the man Izzy thought was never coming back.

He handed their menus to the server and thanked her by name. Well-defined lips spread over the whitest teeth she'd ever seen outside the pages of a magazine. "Have I mentioned you look amazing?"

She managed a tittering laugh. "I think we were talking about your business."

"I'm the executive vice president of Lansing Corporation. I'm sure you're familiar with. . ."

Her heart slammed her chest then stopped, started again at a rate that wouldn't let her catch her breath. She coughed, reached for her glass, but her hand shook too wildly to pick it up.

"Are you all right?"

She waved her hand in front of her face as spots danced before her eyes. "Just swallowed wrong." She stood, searching frantically for the restroom. "Excuse me." Her voice rasped. She wheezed a thin breath and almost ran in what she hoped was the right direction.

Closing the stall door and locking it, she leaned against the wall. *Dear God.* Ryan was right. They were in cahoots. That had to be why he'd looked familiar. She must have seen pictures of him with Stephannie. *I suddenly find myself a very single man.* Was Andrew Rivera the person Stephannie said she had to break up with? So maybe she wasn't involved. Maybe she'd found out what he was trying to do and that's why she broke up. Or maybe she didn't know but she'd followed him to Racine to find out what he was doing. Maybe Stephannie had been ready to warn her at the coffee shop when she'd asked if they could talk. Heather couldn't force herself to believe that the tears and openness and vulnerability were all a ruse. She would believe the best about Stephannie Lansing until she learned the worst.

She should have brought her phone in here. But who would she call? Ryan? *Guess what, you were right. Can you just forget what I said about you not being a superhero and come and be one?* Stephannie? *I'm at a restaurant with the guy you just broke up with. . .*

She walked out of the stall, smoothed her hair in front of the mirror, took a deep inhale, and exhaled a prayer. *I can do this. I am not pathetic. I am not alone. With God all things are possible.* She would be calm and act naive, like she had no clue. She'd give nothing away, but find out whatever she could from a man who appeared intent on doing exactly the same thing to her.

⟡

Ryan's fingers tapped a staccato beat on the steering wheel as he watched them walk up to the house. An ugly mix of anger, hurt, and disbelief roiled in his gut.

His motion sensor lights had blazed on the moment the Jag

turned in to the driveway. Heather was right. They were bright enough to light a runway. They gave him a clear view of the guy's hand on Heather's back, of her head shaking when they reached the door. Of the smooth lean that brought his face to hers, and the last second turn of her head that landed the kiss on her cheek.

Again, she shook her head. Mike's hands went out in a pleading gesture.

"You're pitiful, man. The girl said no. Deal with it."

Finally, the guy turned and walked back to his sleek little car. Ryan hissed at the smirky smile on the guy's face. As the Jaguar backed out and headed north on Main, he allowed a long, slow sigh.

But two seconds later the garage door opened and Heather walked out the back door and into the garage. Ryan leaned forward then flopped back on the seat. She was just going to get Izzy. Wherever she was. That had to be it, but he was going to follow her anyway. He was going to make sure they got home safe, or, if she'd been smart enough to believe just one thing he'd said, to a hotel.

And then he'd park in front of wherever she was. And watch. He set his phone on the passenger seat.

And laid his pistol beside it.

CHAPTER 28

Izzy's favorite movie. *Titanic.*

Enough drama, romance, and suspense to keep her awake. After that she'd put in her own favorite. *Maid in Manhattan.*

Heather stacked the DVDs and searched for another one. She needed enough to last until daylight.

She should have gone to a hotel. But she hadn't wanted to scare Izzy. And who was to say Andrew Rivera wouldn't have followed her there? And if he knew she was gone, and what he was after was in the house, he'd have free rein of the place.

With fingers that wouldn't cooperate, she put a DVD on the tray and pushed the button then settled on the couch with her phone a handbreadth from her thigh. She had a perfect view of the street and the front door. She'd taken the fireplace poker idea to another level. The smashed cardboard boxes she'd piled on the porch were now rolled into logs and tied with string. The contents of every wastebasket in the house served as excellent kindling and she had a respectable cardboard-fueled fire crackling in the living room fireplace. The end of a brand-new, never-used poker glowed red as it rested on the wrought iron grate. She'd branded many a calf in her day. She could wield a hot poker.

Fingering the watch brought a moment of calm. The borrowed dress was airy and comfortable in the room that had felt too warm even before she lit the fire. She'd take it to the cleaners tomorrow. No point in taking it off now. Maybe it would send a dressed-for-a-movie-not-sleep signal to her brain. She took a sip of strong coffee. It would take a lot to convince her exhausted body to not succumb to the lull of a quiet house.

As the screen came to life she tried to relax—enough, but not too much—and tried not to dwell on the near kiss that had ended the night, or the lack of information she'd ended up with. She'd Googled the guy as soon as she'd gotten Izzy to bed. Everything he'd said was true. She'd tried to get him to come right out and say he'd been dating the Lansing heiress, but she'd wanted to play it as dumb as she could, so she hadn't managed it. But the evidence was all over the Internet. Pictures of Stephannie hanging on his arm abounded. But what was her part in whatever he was after? She still had no clue.

The *Titanic* soundtrack filled the room, blotting out Andrew Rivera's final comment. *Thank you for a wonderful night, Heather. May this be the first of many.*

👑

Heather gasped and groped for her phone. Her heart slammed her ribs. Her stomach knotted. The *Titanic* credits rolled on the television. She'd fallen asleep and awakened from a horrible dream where Izzy was screaming and—

Was it a dream?

She took the stairs two at a time. Her steps echoed as she ran past the room with the closed door and the chair wedged under the handle. Another thing she'd never tell Ryan if he ever spoke to her again.

She flew into her room.

The bed was empty.

"Isabel! Where are you? Izzy?" She threw back the covers as if somehow she could have missed a child in her bed. Dropping to her knees, she looked under the bed then ran to the closet. "Izzy!" Her call became a yell. "Tell me where you are."

She darted into the bathroom, then across the hall to Natalie's room. Under the bed, in the closet. . . She repeated it with the empty guest room.

At the end of the hall, she slammed her hands against the camouflaged door. It popped open. She ran up, into the little room, opened the closet. "Izzy!"

She ran back down the stairs, into the second floor hall. She needed her phone. Her foot stumbled on the landing. She caught herself and jumped over the last two steps. She grabbed her phone and punched Ryan's number. *Answer-answer-answer. Please.* Voice mail. A calm voice that made her eyes sting. Waiting for the beep, she grabbed the hot poker and ran to the kitchen. "Ryan. I can't find Izzy. She screamed and I ran to check on her and she's gone. I need you."

The basement. She hadn't checked the basement. She flattened her hands against the wall and rushed through the door. "Izzy? Are you down here? Say something. This isn't funny. It's not a game, Iz. You're scaring me. Answer me!"

Silence. The basement was empty. She set the poker against the wall and punched 911. As she rattled the details, a sliver of light caught her eye. An opening, a slit between the two sides of the bulkhead door. She ran toward it and stepped on something hard. She pointed her phone at the floor.

It was the padlock Ryan had put on the night they'd met. The rounded end was sheared off.

♔

Ryan steadied his pistol with a hand on his right wrist. He kept to the shadows just beyond the reach of the motion sensor light. His ears strained for the sound of a siren. But maybe they'd come in silent.

A black figure slid behind the next house. Holding his breath, he slid the safety off the gun, ran across the grass, and pressed against the siding. The figure darted into the yard.

"Stop! Security! Hands in the air!"

With his back to Ryan, the man stopped, raised his hands. The outline of a gun was barely discernable in the filtered glow of a tree-shaded porch light.

"Drop the gun."

The man's right hand lowered.

295

"That's good. Easy. Toss—"

The figure spun. The gun arm straightened. Ryan aimed. Pressed the trigger. The man swore. The gun dropped. The man grabbed at his right shoulder, slumped, then straightened and turned around.

"Don't move. This time I'll—"

"Hands in the air. Both of you. Drop the gun."

Footsteps pounded the ground on both sides. He clicked the safety and dropped the gun.

⚜

A gunshot. That had to mean the police were here already. Heather could barely keep her hand closed around the phone as she ran back up the winding stairs. "Answer. Answer."

"Hello?" Stephannie's sleep-thick voice mumbled.

"Stephannie, this is Heather. I know who you are and I need you to listen. I don't know what your part is in this, but Andrew has Izzy and—"

"Andrew? What do you mean Andrew has Izzy? I just saw him and he—"

"When? When did you see him?"

"An hour ago. Maybe a little more. I met some friends at our hotel and he showed up in the bar so I left, but he was alone. Why would you think. . . How do you know Andrew?"

"He's been up here in Racine. Several times. I saw him again tonight and now Izzy's gone. It's not a coincidence. What was he doing here? What were you doing here?"

"Oh, Heather, it's a long story, but I swear it has nothing to do with Izzy. Hold on. I'm putting you on speaker. I'm going to get dressed." Her voice echoed. She sounded breathless. "I have a key to Andrew's apartment. He's only a couple miles away. If I call he won't let me in. I'll go over there. Did you call the police? Did you report it?"

"Yes. I think they're here. Outside." She wouldn't tell her about the gunshot. Maybe she'd been mistaken. Would Andrew have had time to drive back here after Stephannie had seen him? Had he made sure he was seen at the hotel for a reason?

"Okay. I'm dressed. I'm out the door." Her words came in short breaths. "I can explain what I was doing in Racine that day. I was there to meet you."

"Me? Why me?"

A car door opened. The engine roared.

"I'm on my way. No traffic. I can be there in five minutes. I can't believe he'd have her. He's not like that, Heather. He's not capable of kidnapping. He's—"

"Why *me?*"

"Because. . .Heather, I think—I think you're my sister."

"Your *what?*"

"You were adopted, right?"

"Yes." The answer was barely above a whisper.

"I found a picture of you on my dad's phone. A text. I don't know who sent it, but it said, 'I found your daughter.'"

Heather grabbed the railing and dropped onto the step below the first-floor landing.

"Heather? I know, it's hard to process, but—" A sharp inhale was followed with a screech of brakes and a chilling, wrenching sound. Glass shattered.

The connection ended.

⚜

Ryan knocked on the back door. Three seconds later, Heather slammed into his arms.

"It's okay. They got him. He's in handcuffs."

"They got who? What's going on? And it's not okay. Izzy's gone and I th–think Stephannie was in an accident."

Heather clung to him, shaking. He held her close with one arm and lifted her chin with the other. "Have you searched the house?"

"Everything but the attic." Her eyes searched his. "Is it him?"

"Mike? No. Some thug-looking guy with tattoos on his neck. Stay here. I'll tell them she's missing." Before he touched the door handle, an officer opened the door.

"We got two calls from here. One about a little girl."

Heather grabbed the man's arm. "I can't find her. I was asleep. I think she screamed and when I got there she wasn't in bed."

He spoke into the radio clipped to his shirt. "Get some backup here, Rob." He turned to Heather. "Give me a description I can put out to our squads in the area."

"She's seven. Slight build. Blond. Wearing a striped nightgown."

He repeated Izzy's description into the radio. "I'll do a sweep of the house first in case the guy wasn't working alone." He stepped into the kitchen, already sweeping the room with his gaze. "Any clue what he was after? Do you think he scared the girl or would anyone have reason to take her?"

Heather slouched against him. "I don't know what he was after."

Ryan nodded toward the open door to the curved stairway. "There are some secret doors and hiding places. She's hidden from us before."

The officer nodded and pulled Ryan's gun from the back of his pants. He nodded toward Ryan's cap. "My first job was with TKJ. Good company." He handed over his gun. "You obviously know how to use this. Show me around."

"Through there." Ryan nodded at Heather. "She checked everything but the attic."

He guided Heather to a chair. "Stay here."

Knowing full well she wouldn't.

⚜

Izzy cowered in the dark, knees pulled up to her chin. She shivered even though it was way too warm and getting hotter with the heat from her body.

Please, God, don't let him get me. This time she was sure it wasn't a dream. The same black mask. The same smell. But this time he didn't see her. He snuck into the guest room and she snuck up the stairs. *Please don't let him find me and don't let him get Heather. Make him go away. Make him not see Heather. Please God, send Ryan here and let him find me just like before.* She put her hands over her ears and scrunched her eyes shut even though it was pitch-black.

She felt like she couldn't breathe. Like she was locked in and couldn't get out. But she could. She'd tried it and the cover wasn't locked. It wouldn't lock without the key.

What if the man had a key? What if he locked her in and she couldn't get out and she screamed and—

The cover of the treasure chest popped open and she screamed and covered her ears tighter. "Don't get me. Don't shoot me. Don't—"

"Izzy."

Her eyes shot open. "Ryan!"

Strong hands grabbed her and lifted her. Strong arms wrapped around her and swung her back and forth and she started to cry and cry and she couldn't stop and then she felt his chest vibrating and Ryan was crying, too.

A second later, she heard another sob. Heather smashed her face against hers. "You're okay. You're okay. Thank God. Thank God."

"Better thank this guy, too."

Izzy looked up. A real policeman stood in the little room. He pointed at Ryan. "He stopped your intruder in his tracks. He's the real hero here."

Heather leaned her head on Ryan's shoulder and stuttered "Thank you" over and over while she wept.

⚜

April 10, 1912

The morning sun struggled through a gray haze of smoke and fog that rose off the Southampton Harbor. It had climbed halfway up its arc of the eastern sky by the time Maggie stepped onto the wharf behind the Hansens. Peter and Henrik talked nonstop about the hulking ship while Jennie gripped the handle of her reticule as if it were a poisonous snake that would strike if she eased up.

Eight weeks had passed since they'd walked up the gangplank on the Cunarder *Campania* on Valentine's Day...the perfect day for Richard to surprise her, to show up with the trunk she'd left behind when she fled, ahead of the Hansens, to New York City.

But instead of showing up, he'd sent a telegram. WILL MEET YOU SOON. ENJOY YOUR DREAM TRIP. RICHARD.

Dream trip. The voyage that was supposed to end with a wedding was feeling like a nightmare.

Almost ten weeks had passed since she'd stood at the train station, staring up through the blur of tears into the reddened eyes of her closest friend. "I never played that song for you," she'd whispered

299

before kissing him on the cheek. *Good-bye, Charles.* He'd responded with a kiss of his own. On her lips.

Yet in spite of the weight of sadness that crossed the ocean with her, she had enjoyed much about the past two months. She'd come to see that her role in the Hansens' lives reached beyond washing, pressing, and serving tea or meals on trays when Jennie wasn't feeling well. She was also there to calm fears, to talk and pray her mistress through moments, and days, of unexplainable anxiety.

Denmark was a beautiful country and Peter and Henrik's parents had been gracious and delightful. She was heading home with a journal full of impressions and experiences—written in her own voice. She no longer needed to hide behind the guise of Magdalena Mouse.

Heading home, wherever that might be. For now, she planned to stay in New York and look for a job. A new town, a new start.

A whistle blew. The people at the head of the line began to move. One last time she turned and scanned the crowd of hat-waving onlookers. One last time she let out a long-held breath.

Richard was not coming.

Peter put his arm across Jennie's shoulders. "Say good-bye to jolly old England, my dear."

With a weak smile, Jennie turned. And staggered. Her hand flew to her mouth then dropped to Maggie's arm.

"Maggie!"

The voice, deeper, stronger than the last time she'd heard it.

Maggie whirled. "Charles!"

In seconds she was in his arms. Engulfed in the familiar smell of his coat.

"Mags." His chest heaved.

"How—? What are you doing here?" she rasped against his coat.

"Ralston Clark paid for my passage. He said you would understand why. I came. . .to deliver two messages. One is from Richard Hamilton."

The pull of gravity seemed to double. Maggie felt herself being sucked down by emotions she couldn't sort. Fear. Anticipation. Disappointment.

Charles closed his eyes. She counted the seconds. *Two. . .three. . .*

four. His eyes opened, holding her as firmly as his arms had. "He's not coming, Mags."

The pull released its hold. Of all the swirling emotions making her dizzy, relief topped the list. She nodded, then wrinkled her brow. "You said you have two messages."

A smile she'd desperately missed formed lines that splayed like rays of sunshine from the corners of his eyes. "The message is"—he suddenly dropped to one knee—"I won't ever mind being second best if you'll agree to marry me."

Around the sob that shook her, she squeezed out, "Yes. Yes. Yes." As he rose to his feet, she caressed his face. "There is nothing second best about you." She stood on tiptoes and brought her lips to his ear. "Nothing in the world would make me happier than marrying my best friend."

"Does that mean you'll play 'Let Me Call You Sweetheart'?"

A tear dropped onto his collar. "Yes. Over and over and over."

CHAPTER 29

Heather woke with a kink in her neck. For a moment she didn't remember where she was.

In the car. Ryan was driving.

Eyes still closed, her hand rose to the watch pinned to the dress she still wore. She pried her eyes open. Buildings rose on both sides of the street, almost blocking the sun, now halfway up the sky. She'd fallen asleep long before they reached Chicago. "Where are we?"

"West Ohio Street. Just a few more blocks."

"Have you heard anything?"

"No."

Ryan had used his connections to find out what hospital Stephannie was in, but couldn't get details about her condition. Heather turned and smiled at the little blond snoring softly in the backseat then aimed her smile at Ryan. "Have I told you lately how amazing you are?"

"Not for the last hour."

"You are by far the smartest, bravest man I know. And I am by far the dumbest woman I know."

The sound of his laugh rolled over her like a warm breeze. "Not dumb. Just stubborn. Too stubborn to see the difference between controlling and caring."

"Not anymore."

"No?"

"No. You can care for me any time you want, Security Man."

He grinned. "I hope you're serious, because I intend to take you up on that." He turned into a parking garage and they rode the ramps in silence until he parked on the third level. "Do you know what you're going to say if she's in any condition to talk?"

"No idea. What do you say to someone who suddenly tells you she might be your sister?"

"Your very, very rich sister."

"We are not going there. But now that you brought it up, how ironic is it that I've spent my whole life in my beautiful sister's shadow and now I just might be doing it on a bigger, brighter scale?"

"But you can handle it now."

"I can?"

"Yeah. Because you have the confidence and security of knowing who loves you." He pulled the keys out and swiveled in the seat to face her.

"Jesus loves me."

"Yes, He does." He leaned across the seats until his breath tickled her cheek. "And so do I."

✧

"I'm sorry. Miss Lansing has asked that no visitors be allowed." The woman behind the desk peered over half glasses. A silver chain hung from the bows.

"Would you please call her room and ask? Tell her that her sister is here."

"She didn't say anything about family other than—"

"Please."

The woman nodded and picked up her phone. She spoke in a tone so low Heather couldn't make out the words. After a moment she looked up. "She's in room 4328. Take the elevators on your right to the fourth floor and follow the signs."

"Thank you." Heather swallowed around the lump in her throat and nodded to Ryan, who shifted a half-awake Izzy higher onto his shoulder and followed her.

"Are you sure you don't want to do this alone?"

303

"I'm sure. You're my *security*."

"Cute."

Izzy raised her head when they got on the elevator. "I'm thirsty."

Heather patted her leg. "Help us look for a drinking fountain."

The elevator dinged on the fourth floor and the door opened. They turned right, following arrows on a sign on the wall, and walked down a long corridor, the soles of their shoes echoing off the walls. Heather rubbed her hands on the dress that didn't absorb perspiration.

"Looking a little nervous there, beautiful."

"That doesn't come close." She slowed her steps, reading the numbers next to each door, then stopped. "4328."

"There's a fountain." Izzy pointed down the hall.

"You go in. You two need a moment alone." He lowered Izzy to her feet. "We'll join you in a sec."

She watched them walk away, anxiety growing with each foot that separated them. With a deep breath, she walked through the half-open door.

Stephannie sat up in bed. Her foot, wrapped in thick elastic bandages, was propped on a pile of pillows. To her left sat a white-haired man in a wheelchair. "Heather! Come in." She held out her hand. "I just got my phone back and got your message. I was so scared. I'm so glad you found her. I— Wait." A huge grin spread across her face. "First things first." She turned to her left. "Daddy, I'd like you to meet your daughter."

The man's jaw unhinged.

Heather groped for something to steady her. Taking a step forward, she grabbed the end of the bed with both hands. She stared at the man. Parker Lansing. She'd seen his picture many times, but she would never have recognized him. Hunched over, his face thin and lined, his skin pale. She tried blinking away the years. Tried to remember. His face looked kind. He was nothing like the image in her mind.

Stephannie reached out and nudged the stunned man's arm. "Daddy?"

"Th–that's not my daughter." He shook his head. His gaze shifted to the left then suddenly brightened. His chin lifted. A startled smile transformed his face. "*That's* my daughter."

Heather swung around as Izzy walked into the room.

Parker Lansing's eyes filled with tears. His hand stretched out to Izzy. "That's my little girl."

👑

Heather slid her phone back in her purse and looked around the hospital corridor as she steadied her emotions. She hadn't felt ready to face the man who had deserted her, no matter who he was, yet the disappointment had still been sharp. But this moment was about Izzy, not her. With a deep breath, she walked back into the room.

She looked at the man who was not her father. He sat quietly chatting with the little girl who stood in front of him holding the string of a Get Well balloon. His hands were folded on his lap as if to keep himself from wrapping his arms around Izzy. He looked up when Heather entered, a pensive look on his face. "What did she say?"

"Natalie was on her way to a meeting. She asked that you call her at noon, our time."

The man's face fell.

"She also said it was fine for you to tell Izzy."

Eyebrows rose. His eyes filled again with tears.

Heather studied Stephannie. Her tears matched her father's. She looked up at Heather. "I have two sisters," she whispered. "A half sister and a Jesus sister."

Parker cleared his throat. "Isabel, I have a secret to tell you."

"I love secrets."

"This is one everyone in this room can hear."

"Can I tell my mom?"

"Your mom already knows this one. She's known this secret since before you were born."

"What is it?"

"The secret is that I'm your daddy."

Izzy's lips parted. She turned to Heather and then Ryan.

They nodded in unison.

"For real? I don't need a pretend daddy anymore?"

"Nope. You've got the real deal. A real daddy who should have

305

met you a long, long time ago."

Her bottom lip pushed out and began to quiver. Heather stepped closer. "Iz? Are you okay?"

An exaggerated nod made her curls quiver. "I'm okay. I'm just so—" With a sob, she wrapped her arms around her daddy.

Izzy curled on the bed next to Stephannie.

Heather fought the old familiar twist in her gut. She'd spend most of her life with her insides roiling with envy. *No more. Lord, show me how to let it go.*

A warm arm wrapped around her shoulders. Ryan pulled her close. "You okay?"

"I'm fine," she whispered. "Now." She leaned in, extracting strength. "Have I told you lately you're unbelievable?"

"Nope. That's a new one."

"How 'bout this one"—she lifted her chin so her lips touched his ear—"I love you."

His arm tightened. "Another new one. I think, so far, that's my all-time fav—"

"Heather." Parker gestured toward her. "Excuse me, I hate to interrupt what you've got going there, but that watch you're wearing. . .may I see it?"

"Of course." She unpinned it and set it in his hand.

He pushed the stem. The cover popped open. Along with Parker Lansing's mouth. "Where did you get this?"

Izzy scrambled off the bed. "We found it in a treasure chest with dresses and more mouse stories and shoes—"

"And hats and cosmetic bottles and old yearbooks?"

It was Heather's turn to gape. "How. . . ?"

"Where did you find it?"

"In the house Natalie just bought."

A second stunned smile crossed his lined face. "She bought the house?" He shook his head. "That shouldn't surprise me. She said she would someday."

Stephannie raised the head of her bed. Her brow was as furrowed as Heather was sure her own was. "I think you better start at the beginning, Dad. Like how you knew about the house and the treasure chest and where you met Izzy's mother."

"That's a topic I don't want to discuss with little ears present."

Ryan stood. "Iz, let's go get another drink."

"Okay." With a nod, Izzy hopped off the chair. "Here you go, sis." She grinned at Stephannie and handed the phone back.

Parker's gaze followed them out the door. "I hope I have energy for this." He took a deep breath. "I knew about the house because I grew up there."

"You grew up in Wisconsin? How come I never knew that?" Stephannie wrinkled her brow at her father.

"You didn't know because I didn't want you to know. I had a horrible falling-out with my parents when I was in college. That's just one thing in a long list of regrets I'll tell you about sometime. They both died before you were born. The house was left to me, so I rented it out. I loved that house. The maid's stairway, the secret doors. . .and the steamer trunk full of history. I'd locked it away while renters were there. I thought about giving it to a museum when I sold the house eight years ago, but it seemed to belong there. Years earlier I'd put some of my own things in it—like a time capsule—and I suggested the new owners add their own treasures. I can't believe they didn't just sell all that stuff." He paused. "Maybe. . .maybe they felt what I felt. That the trunk and everything in it belonged to the house."

He nodded toward the door. "Isabel is another regret. Not fathering her, but the fact that that's all I did. My relationship with her mother was a contractual one. I was newly divorced when I began spending time with Natalie Brooks. She wanted to have a child." Frail fingertips swept across his eyes. "I couldn't add that complication to my life. She knew that and she was fine with it." He shook his head. "I can't believe that just eight years ago I was that shallow a man, but it seemed somehow noble at the time, a way of redeeming a mistake I made before I was married." He turned to Stephannie. "There is so much I need to tell you."

"You and Mom had an abortion, didn't you?" Nothing but compassion filled her voice.

Parker nodded, staring beyond his daughter, then blinked back to the present. "Natalie wanted nothing more from me. It wasn't all my decision. She didn't want to live with the fear of people knowing I was the father of her child. She was afraid of the very thing that just happened. And now it's a threat we'll all have to live with."

His shoulders shook with each breath. "I had just sold the Racine house when Natalie found out she was pregnant. I took her up there on the day of the estate sale. She loved the house. I gave her the piano I'd learned on—for the child I thought I'd never meet. That was the last time I saw Natalie. I heard through mutual acquaintances that she'd had a little girl. I spent seven years trying not to think about the child I'd fathered. But God, and my heart problems, have been working on me the past few months, so I asked a friend of mine to find her." He reached out and took Stephannie's hand. "I wanted to meet my other daughter and I wanted her to meet her amazing sister." He ran the side of his hand across his eyes. "And now we have."

They sat in silence until he regained control. He turned to Heather. "Would you like to hear what I know about the woman who owned the trunk?"

She let out a sigh. "I was afraid to ask. Are you sure you're not getting too tired?"

"I'm sure. This is actually energizing."

"Let me get Ryan and Izzy for this part." She ran out in the hall and waved them back.

Parker waited for them all to settle in their chairs. "My great-grandmother, Maggie Parker, worked in the hou—"

"Maggie?" Izzy clapped her hands together. "Is that short for Magdalena like Izzy is short for Isabel? Is she the mouse?"

Parker laughed. "Her name was just Maggie, but she wrote the Magdalena Mouse stories."

"I knew it!"

"The stories were an allegory of her real life while she lived in the house."

Izzy bit her bottom lip and grimaced. "Did she get on a lifeboat? On the *Titanic*?"

Parker shook his head. A tiny cry slipped from Izzy's lips.

"She didn't get on a lifeboat because she never got on the ship. Maggie was standing in line, ready to board the ship, when Charles

Gallagher, the man she really loved but didn't know she loved, found her and got down on his knee and asked her to marry him. They decided to get married right there in Southampton and honeymoon in England and Ireland. Their plan was to return to New York when the *Titanic* made its second voyage from England to New York."

"All those people died." Izzy sighed. "It's good there were some happy endings."

Parker took her hand in his. "There's a lot of sadness in the world, Isabel, but there are lots and lots of happy endings—and beginnings—too. Do you want to hear about the good things that began that day?"

Izzy nodded.

"Then pull your chair very close and I'll tell you the rest of Maggie's story."

"...and instead of marrying Maggie, Leo Tabbycat, who was really Richard Hamilton, married Maggie's good friend Emma."

Izzy gasped. "That's sad."

"Apparently all was forgiven because the four of them eventually worked together to open the Hamilton Home. The house you live in, Izzy, used to be a home for orphans, and mothers with little children who didn't have a good place to live."

Izzy's eyes opened wide. "The bed marks! On the floor in the attic!"

Parker nodded. "They turned the attic into a dormitory and Maggie and her friend Emma taught them to read and write and helped the mothers find jobs and they worked hard to make sure there were fair laws so young children didn't have to work in factories. Years later, Maggie's son, Parker, married Emma's daughter, Esther, and they lived in your house and they had a daughter and she had a son and he had a daughter...and that daughter was *you*, Isabel Brooks."

EPILOGUE

Ryan got out of the car and slung his book bag over his shoulder. He waved through the window, pointed at the sign above the door, and grinned.

CONFAB RACINE
COFFEE AND CONNECTION

He didn't need to read the small print below it: A CONRAD-LANSING ENTERPRISE.

He thought back to Stephannie's statement in her hospital room. *I have two sisters. A half sister and a Jesus sister.* Though they still lived more than an hour and a half apart, the Jesus sisters had become almost inseparable. And the half sister shadowed them whenever she could, which was fairly often now that her mother worked late hours at a department store. Izzy was also spending every other weekend with her dad.

Ryan opened the door and almost toppled Izzy, who stood smack in front of him, holding out a wrapped package. "Surprise!"

A chorus of voices echoed her.

"What in the world is going on here?" He scanned the room, past tables full of customers, some he recognized and some he didn't, to Stephannie, Jalissa, Kylee, and the two latest single moms they'd hired—both wearing shoes donated by, and sporting hair-styles created by, the oldest Lansing heiress. The person who stood out, even though she was beginning to fit in, was Izzy's mom. Since she'd lost her job and a chunk of money because she'd broken her noncompete agreement, Natalie Brooks had been attending the book club. As Heather and Jalissa were constantly saying, *no one* is impossible for God.

He finally found Heather, grinning behind a coffeepot. She sidled over to him, eyes locked on his. "It's a happy-first-day-of-the-semester party."

He opened his arms and she slid into them, as natural as if she belonged there. Which she did. He touched his lips to hers for a too-short kiss then released her. "You guys will use any excuse for a party."

Stephannie laughed. "That would be the concept."

Izzy slid her hand into his. "Come to the Connection Room. Quick. I have to get to my book club." She gestured toward a table of girls about her age. "Today we're going to read about Magdalena and the new stove."

Heather raised one finger. "Just a minute, Iz. There's something else. Natalie just got some news. This is also a 'Conviction Lands Would-Be Kidnapping Orchestrator in Prison' celebration."

Ryan closed his eyes. Finally. They'd waited a long time for closure on this one. The thug he'd caught behind the house had been sentenced months ago. Andrew Rivera had been acquitted within weeks, though he'd lost his job even before Stephannie had been released from the hospital. The PI he'd hired had figured out that Izzy and not Heather was the Lansing heiress and had arranged the kidnapping. No one doubted it, but there hadn't been enough evidence until the thug finally accepted a plea bargain and talked.

"This is one happy day, huh?" Stephannie wiggled her eyebrows and elbowed Jalissa.

Izzy tugged his arm. "Come on."

"Yes, ma'am." He winked at Jalissa and Stephannie as he walked past the counter.

Heather took his other hand. "Close your eyes."

"I'll trip over my feet."

"No, you won't." She squeezed his hand. "Just follow my lead."

He laughed. "Always and forever, my sweet." He let them drag him into the back room.

"Now open."

He did. The blackboard wall at the back of the room had been shaded in red. Superimposed on top of the red was a spider on a white web. "Wow. Who did that?"

Ruby, a girl they'd hired only days ago, raised her hand. Stephannie put an arm across her shoulders. "Our new artist in residence. She's going to do murals for every event."

"That's perfect. Nice touch."

"Open this." Izzy shoved the gift at him. Metallic blue paper tied up with a wide red bow.

"In front of everyone?"

"Yep."

With a premonition of the heat soon to creep up the back of his neck, he untied the bow then snapped the tape. The paper fell away from a white box. Looking at Heather, then Izzy, he grimaced and opened it. Red. Bright red. Exactly the color his face was soon to be. "I have an awful feeling I know what this is." He pulled it out. "A cape. It's. . ." He gave up trying to find a fitting word and simply laughed.

Heather planted a kiss on his cheek. Over her shoulder he shot another wink at the women whispering in the corner. They nodded and left the room.

"Put it on."

Feeling the expected heat climb toward his face, he complied then caught Heather in a bear hug and glued his lips to hers as he dipped her. By the time he righted her, Stephannie and Jalissa had returned with two trays. A tall glass on each. Jalissa held hers out to Ryan. "Maple latte for you, sir." He took the glass.

Stephannie swung her tray in front of Heather. "One coco-mocho for you, ma'am."

"You don't have to wait on—"

"Just take it." Ryan handed his glass back to Stephannie at the same moment Heather picked up hers. And screamed.

In the center of the damp circle left by the glass was the diamond he had entrusted to Stephannie's care before leaving for school. He picked it up. Jalissa grabbed the cocomocho just as it was about to slip out of Heather's hand. In the next few seconds they quietly evacuated the room and Ryan dropped to one knee, cape rippling around him. "Heather Conrad, I love you with all of my heart and I want to follow you for the rest of my life. Will you marry me?"

With an adorable sound—half sob, half hiccup—she stuttered a yes and pulled him to his feet. And into her arms.

BECKY MELBY has been married to Bill, her high school sweetheart, for forty years. They have four married sons and eleven grandchildren. Becky has co-authored nine books for Heartsong Presents and is working on her third novella for Barbour Publishing. Becky's favorite pastimes are spoiling grandkids and taking trips with Bill in their RV or on their Honda Gold Wing. To find out more about Becky or her books, or to let her know your thoughts on *Today's Shadows*, visit www.beckymelby.com.

Discussion Questions for *Today's Shadows*

1. Heather's thirty-day-vacay plan takes a shocking right turn before it begins. How would you have handled that major life interruption? Have you experienced a time when you thought Point A led in a straight line to Point B and then life veered off at a sharp angle, dragging you with it?

2. In the face of unrelenting demands, Maggie uses her story world to keep sane. What techniques do you use to feel like you're on solid ground when life is swirling around you?

3. At the beach, Heather mentions that guys need the "hero thing." Do you think that's an outdated notion, or do most men still hope to rescue a damsel in distress?

4. If twenty-first-century men want to feel like heroes, are there still women who long to be rescued by a knight-in-shining-armor type? How do you see Jesus filling that role in a Christian woman's life?

5. When Ryan blurts, "I'm a Jesus freak," Heather's response is "I have no problem with the Jesus part. It's the freak part that scares me. I'm of the opinion that faith ought to be lived, not shoved." Have you met shovers? What was your reaction? Do you think there are situations that call for us to shove our beliefs at others?

6. How do you think Stephannie might have reacted to the possibility of a sister if she had lived her life differently? Put yourself in her shoes. Even if she'd been the model daughter, what might her emotions have been if she'd suddenly found out she might have to share her father, her "title," and her inheritance with the "svelte, tanned woman with long dark hair"?

7. Maggie is looked down upon because of her position. Heather is taunted by her grandmother's words and by not measuring up to her sister. Stephannie knows she doesn't measure up to either of her parents' standards. Feelings of inadequacy are a part of the human condition. What is the solution? Have you come to a time in your life when accepting that God knows you intimately and loves you radically has made a difference in your sense of self?

8. Have you ever uncovered an old family heirloom, letters, or a hidden room or secret passageway? What were your favorite secret hideaways when you were a child?

9. One of the common life issues shared by Maggie, Heather, Stephannie, Izzy, and several other characters in *Today's Shadows* is the father-daughter connection. How has your father's influence or absence affected your view of God and your ability to trust and connect in other relationships? Psalm 68:5 says that God is "a father to the fatherless." Do you find that verse comforting or hard to believe?

10. What were your thoughts when Charles showed up on the Southampton dock? Were you disappointed it wasn't Richard? What was your prediction for Charles and Maggie's future before Parker revealed it?

11. Stephannie seems thrilled to have a little sister. If the story had continued, do you think she would have wrestled with the same kind of insecurities she'd experienced when she thought Heather was her sister? Why or why not? How could having Izzy in her life change her for the better?

12. Heather's dream of opening a chain of coffeehouses appears to be coming true, though in a way she never could have guessed. All of the "interruptions" in her thirty-day vacay worked together—not only to bring about her "coffee and

connection" vision, but also to turn it into a business that helps single moms and young women learn job skills. What are your dreams? Even if they seem impossibly big, pray about them, write them down, and voice them to trusted friends. God is in the "impossible" business!

13. What do you think the future holds for Ryan and Heather?